P9-DCV-992

ANY MINUTE NOW

BY ERIC VAN LUSTBADER

ANY MINUTE NOW

ERIC VAN LUSTBADER

A TOM DOHERTY ASSOCIATES BOOK
NEW YORK

This is a work of fiction. All of the characters, organizations, and events portrayed in this novel are either products of the author's imagination or are used fictitiously.

ANY MINUTE NOW

Copyright © 2016 by Eric Van Lustbader

All rights reserved.

A Forge Book
Published by Tom Doherty Associates, LLC
175 Fifth Avenue
New York, NY 10010

www.tor-forge.com

Forge® is a registered trademark of Tom Doherty Associates, LLC.

The Library of Congress Cataloging-in-Publication Data is available upon request.

ISBN 978-0-7653-8551-2 (hardcover)
ISBN 978-0-7653-8552-9 (e-book)

Our books may be purchased in bulk for promotional, educational, or business use. Please contact your local bookseller or the Macmillan Corporate and Premium Sales Department at 1-800-221-7945, extension 5442, or by e-mail at MacmillanSpecialMarkets@macmillan.com.

First Edition: August 2016

Printed in the United States of America

0 9 8 7 6 5 4 3 2 1

For Victoria, as always, with deepest love

ANY MINUTE NOW

PROLOGUE

The wind came shrieking through the interior of the helo, demonic and vicious, like a cop hell-bent on pursuit.

Greg Whitman, eyes closed, listening to Artie Shaw's version of "Begin the Beguine" on his iPod, didn't hear it. Cole Porter, he thought. A giant among men. So was Hoagy Carmichael. His "Star Dust" would be coming on next, but Whitman knew he'd skip the song. He should have deleted it, but he couldn't bear to do it. The pilot tapped him on the shoulder, saving him. He opened his eyes, stowed away his iPod, and substituted the helo's comm unit for his earbuds.

"Rain," the pilot said in Whitman's earpiece. "Here it comes."

He wasn't kidding. The first burst was like flak hitting the side of the helo. The aircraft banked, and dipped sharply, swinging like a pendulum between the peaks of two mountains, keeping time—the slow, drawn-out minutes before the boots on the ground moment when time accelerated like an arrow shot from a bow. Inside the helo it was like an orchestra warming up, or Hoagy Carmichael at his piano picking out a melody that was not yet quite there.

Before the pilot was able to right the craft, Felix Orteño had taken up his position at the rear of the helo, vomiting into a plastic bag.

Jonas Sandofur smiled as he checked the trio's weaponry for the sixth and last time, making certain the ammo was as he'd requested it from Armaments: .500 S&W Magnum. He checked every single bullet; there would be no misfires on his watch. Sandofur was smiling because Orteño's distress was a sign of good fortune. The communications and electronics expert always threw up just before insertion. It was a guarantee of the mission's success. Not that this trio needed it. In the five years since Whitman had put the team together, when he had been hired by King Cutler, the head of Universal Security Associates, the team had never failed in their ultra-black missions of insertion and termination. Each plastic bag was saved, like a notch in a belt or a scalp on a length of rawhide.

"Seven minutes," the pilot said in Whitman's ear as they shot past another obsidian mountainside—he didn't have to add "to insertion"; they all knew.

Whitman, a slim, leathery cowboy of a man, had been born and raised in Montana, but that life seemed part of someone else's past, not his. All his adult years, and some before, had been spent overseas, in places marked out in bright red on Pentagon maps. He was in charge of planning and tactics; the trio was on the path he devised and designated. With a small flashlight held between his teeth, he bent over the plastic-coated topographical map, though he had previously memorized each and every formation. He had the ability to instantly translate two dimensions into three. In so doing, he had already been to their target area many times in his mind's eye. When they landed he would be on familiar ground.

Another gust of wind sent the rain rattling against the helo's skin like buckshot. Orteño staggered as he made his way forward, the flat of his hand against the gunship's metal bulkhead.

"Hey, Flix," Jonas said into his swing mike, "how's the gut?"

"Nothing a couple of tacos with a squirt of hot sauce wouldn't cure."

The helo creaked and groaned like a seventeenth-century ship of the line in a storm far out to sea.

"I'll stake you to 'em after we get home."

Orteño grinned, cocked his forefinger like a gun barrel at Sandofur. "I'll hold you to that."

"Settle down, ladies," Whitman said without looking up from his map.

"Two minutes to the drop point, Sandy. Make sure our protection's kosher."

Sandofur handed over the small-arms weapons he had so lovingly prepared. "Into the valley of heathens dropped the three sombreros," he intoned. This, too, was a ritual performed before each drop.

"*Ai de mi!*" Orteño yelled, getting into it as he settled the parachute more comfortably between his shoulders.

The gunner slid open the helo's side door.

"Valley dead ahead! Get the hell off my ship!" the pilot shouted over his shoulder. The trio had ditched their comm sets for Flix's wireless earwigs. "See you girls at oh-five-hundred sharp, before the sun rises. And, for fuck's sake, don't any of you break a leg!"

Out the open doorway, into the stinging blackness, one after the other, an unholy shrieking in their ears, a rush of adrenaline, a hollowness in the pit of their stomachs as they fell between leaning black walls, the ground, invisible in the rain-swept night, rushing up to meet them with hellacious velocity.

As usual, it was Sandofur who landed first. Shrugging off his parachute rigging like a sailboat in dry dock, he raced to the metal case that had landed a hundred yards away, one corner buried in the soft, loose earth. Righting it, he set about releasing the clamps.

By the time the others had come up beside him, he had the case open. He distributed the AR-15s and other large-bore weapons with a sure hand. He had done this so many times he could have parceled out the armaments one-handed and wounded, a point of pride with him.

The rain beat relentlessly down, but there was almost no wind. Whitman, glancing up at the roiling clouds, hoped that the poor weather would continue as the forecast predicted. It was the time of the full moon, and he had argued for waiting until the waning crescent, but King Cutler had insisted they move at once.

"For the first time we have positive intel concerning Seiran el-Habib's whereabouts," Cutler had told Whitman. "He's too big a catch. We can't wait."

But the weather had turned in their favor, the night black and impenetrable as pitch. Whitman fired up the GPS, plugged in the coordinates of the private villa where el-Habib was currently holed up, and, silently signaling to his team, took point as they headed out.

Their landing site was approximately a mile from their target. The villa was in the center of an armed compound, walled and wired. This much they knew for certain; the rest they would have to find out when they arrived.

It was a long, hard slog, along muddy lowlands, then over rising, rocky hillocks, tufted plateaus, and narrow overlooks. Not that they could have seen much of anything without their next-generation night vision goggles, provided by DARPA, the Defense Advanced Research Projects Agency, to which Cutler had inside access, but using them for long periods of time was fatiguing on the eyes, inducing dizziness and, often, headaches. Cutler was forever shoving the newest weaponry—"toys," as he called them—at the team.

"Red Rover is my blackest of black ops unit, so far off the radar that no one on Capitol Hill knows of your existence. No one even knows NSA is hiring people like us," he'd tell them. "You deserve the fruits of the best and brightest sparks our government has to offer."

Despite the utter darkness and the filthy weather, the team had no difficulty negotiating the terrain. After all, they had spent hours traversing it in a three-dimensional simulation built up with photos and videos from numerous drone overflights. As a consequence, the ground was as familiar to them as their own backyards.

This was just as well, because Whitman's mind was firmly set on Seiran el-Habib, the Saudi-born terrorist mastermind who was their current target. According to the intel Cutler had shared with him that came direct from Omar Hemingway, their contact at NSA, el-Habib was highly connected—to what or whom was a mystery they had been sent to unlock.

If it had simply been a matter of taking el-Habib out, a drone could have done the deed almost as well. But their brief was to extract el-Habib from his compound, then rendezvous with the helo.

"El-Habib isn't like your other targets," Cutler had told Whitman. "He's a very special case that needs to be handled with kid gloves. You get me?"

"As always, boss," Whitman had replied.

Cutler's green eyes had bored into Whitman. "I hope to Christ you do, Gregory." He was the only person since Whitman's father to call him that. "We're getting triple our fee for the extraction, but we will get a shitload of money—even for us—once you unlock this sonuvabitch's mind."

"You mean we're not bringing him back for interrogation at the Fortress of Solitude?" He was referring to the USA safe house facility, as it was known internally, deep in the forests of rural Virginia.

"I mean you're not to take him anywhere near the Fortress and its inquisitors. You'll take him to the Well."

"The Well?" Whitman had echoed, his voice tinged with a special anxiety. "No one's been to the Well in years."

"All the better. And you know the Well better than anyone, don't you, Gregory? I mean, that's what Luther St. Vincent told me."

"St. Vincent should keep his trap shut."

"He and I have a . . . special business relationship, but that's not relevant to this conversation."

"The hell it isn't."

Cutler, intuiting the storm clouds gathering in Whitman, said, "Listen, he's the one who recommended I hire you."

"So you could keep an eye on me."

"Don't be paranoid."

"You pay me to be paranoid."

"Do you think I hired you simply on St. Vincent's say-so? You're special, Gregory. You know it; I know it. So go and do that voodoo that you do so well. This is one case where nothing short of your magic will work." Cutler's shark-like smile put Whitman's teeth on edge. "You're going to pry open el-Habib's mind yourself. That's how completely off the grid this op is."

Whatever magic Whitman possessed was dark magic. He didn't like to dwell on it; in fact, he resented Cutler every time his boss brought it up, as if it was a terrible secret he chose to hang over Whitman's head. Which was precisely what it was. On the other hand, Whitman knew he had no business blaming anyone but himself for the mistakes he had made in the Well. But were they really mistakes? The members of the Alchemists, his former cadre, had believed fervently in what they were doing, so St. Vincent had said. His Rubicon moment had arrived in nightmarish fashion in the Well, when he was faced with the truth about the Alchemists. In that moment of revelation, what he had done at their bidding came rushing back to haunt him like the undead. How could he have been so naïve as to think their aims were really altruistic? How could he have believed St. Vincent's honeyed lies. It would be far too easy to blame St. Vincent, Monroe, and the others, so instead he blamed only himself. The blood was on his hands, not theirs. He had refused to cross the Rubicon, to enter the Alchemists' Rome, but, considering what had transpired in the preceding days, hadn't stopped himself in time. This was what haunted him in those cobwebbed moments before, at the end of his rope, an exhausted sleep toppled into his grasp.

"Outlaws at your ten o'clock," Sandofur said in his ear.

Whitman froze, and the others with him. Whitman turned his head, as an owl will, without moving his body. "I got trees. You have eyes on, Sandy?"

"A deuce," Sandofur replied. He was on Whitman's left flank, with a far better angle on the outlaws, their name for enemies. "AK-47s, for sure, and bandoliers."

Slowly, carefully, Whitman crept to his left.

"Engage?" Sandofur asked.

"Negative. They're on a course away from us." Whitman made a futile gesture to wipe rain off his forehead. "We detour west, then continue on." He glanced at his GPS, whose history could be erased at a moment's notice. "We're almost to the ranch. We're here for a snatch, not a slaughter."

"Roger that."

Whitman could hear the disappointment in Sandofur's voice. He was a good man, an excellent armorer, and there was no one Whitman would rather have at his back in a firefight, but Sandy had a bit too much of a taste for blood for Whitman's liking. In another era, he would have made a first-class berserker.

No point in reiterating what his men already knew: if the outlaws were outliers from the compound, as seemed likely, they'd be in periodic touch with their home base. It was far too risky taking them out. Better to leave it all quiet on the western front.

Heading southwest, they came over a hillock so rocky it looked like an old man's rotten mouth. Lights glimmered through the rain in the swale below. They had reached the compound at last.

"No electronics on the perimeter," Flix informed them as they crouched behind a line of rocks that snaked along the swale. They had made three complete sweeps around the periphery of the compound, which was defined by a six-foot stone-and-mortar wall, crumbling in three places.

"No sign of the outlaw outriders," Sandofur said as they made their sweeps.

"Let's roll then," Whitman said, and the raid commenced.

It was Whitman who chose the spot to breach the wall, but it was Sandofur who went in first. He had scented the dogs on the humid night air, their musk rank and bitter. Whitman had chosen the break in the wall that was the least damaged. Through their night vision goggles they had seen movement behind the part of the wall that had crumbled to almost half its height. The section they chose was perhaps three hundred yards from where two guards stood smoking, talking in whispers.

The dogs—Pakistani bulls, white as ghosts and bred for fighting— charged Sandofur as he entered the compound. He raised his gun, shot them both with tranquilizer darts. They went down as if poleaxed, which was a pity because Sandofur loved dogs—dogs of all kinds, even Pakistani bulls, though he'd seen only one before this. It was a puppy, just twelve days old. How cute was that!

A high-pitched yelp from the second bull before it succumbed brought Sandofur's attention back to the present. To his right, the pair of guards swiveled in his direction, their AK-47s leveled. He shot them both with the same tranquilizer and they fell to their knees before toppling over, mouths open in surprise.

Sandofur pressed a remote and the incendiary charge he had planted at the other end of the compound exploded in a blinding green-white fireball. Whitman and Orteño followed him in. Flix was already at work jamming any communications from inside the compound.

The three raced across the sparse grass to the central villa that protected Seiran el-Habib. By this time, men should have been pouring out of the structure's two doors, and now Sandofur had another scent in his nose, so sensitive to the tremors of intention.

"It's a trap!" he shouted, moments too late. A bullet slammed into his chest, embedding itself in his body armor. He staggered, firing at the men who had melted out of the shadows along the periphery of the wall. They had been waiting in the darkness, waiting as if they knew precisely—

A second shot caught Sandofur in the throat. Blood and air poured out of him. His head lifted and the rain fell upon his face as softly as snowfall out of the Canadian Rockies. He smelled the blood of the felled elk and in his mind he ran to it, elated at his first kill. Soon, he and his father would slaughter the beast, then butcher it, making mouthwatering steaks three inches thick. In the here and now, he continued to fire, but now, on his knees, he could see nothing of the others. Then a third shot took apart his skull, rendering him oblivious to their fate.

"We've got to fall back!" Flix shouted, giving Whitman cover fire as he raced toward Sandofur. "Whit, get back here! We've no chance to nab the target! Whit! Let's haul ass!"

"I'm not leaving him behind!" Whitman shouted. "Keep me covered!"

Flix heaved a grenade at the nexus of enemy fire, ducked down at the resulting burst of stone, cement, and body parts. By this time, Whitman had grabbed Sandofur, hoisted him over one shoulder, and turned back toward the compound's wall.

Flix led them directly into the smoke and pink dust at the center of the blast, which had created a kind of sickening corridor for them, strewn not with rocks, but with bodies and bloodied limbs and, at one point, a head ripped clear off its neck.

Enemy fire continued, but it was lighter and more sporadic. Flix launched another grenade behind them, and they were over the wall by the time it went off. They raced through the rain, which seemed heavier now, coming in bursts like machine-gun fire. The sky seemed lower, the clouds roiling, as if being stirred by a giant's hand. Neither Flix nor Whitman had time to worry about whether the helo could make it through the low ceiling; they were too busy running for their lives.

Over the rocky terrain they fled, following their GPS path home. Behind them they heard what might have been another explosion. Or it could have been the throaty roar of an armored vehicle starting its pursuit of them. If that was the case, their chances of reaching their exit position would be severely lowered.

As they ran, Flix attempted to raise the helo on his emergency comm band. He tripped and fell into a shallow puddle. His left knee struck something sharp, and when he rose and carried on, it was with a distinct limp. He felt a hot trickle run down his shin, pool inside his left boot, but he did his best to ignore his loss of blood. They would be at the exit point soon; he'd worry about the wound then. At last, he raised the helo, gave the pilot their current SITREP.

"Hang tight," the pilot said in his earwig. "Coming to getcha."

An eighth of a mile to go, by Whitman's GPS reckoning. They were making good time, despite the worsening weather and his burden, which seemed to become heavier with each step.

He thought he could hear the helo's rotors chopping through the rain, and he glanced up. At that moment, shots were fired, and Flix went down.

The two outriders they had bypassed on their inward trek. Whitman cursed himself; in the flurry of the snafu he had forgotten all about them.

Taking shelter behind a boulder, he lay down Sandofur's corpse and crawled out to where Flix half-lay, one hand clutching his right shoulder. The enemy fire started up again. Grabbing the back of Flix's collar, he dragged him backward toward the protection of the boulder. The ground around them burst apart, sending a buckshot of dirt into their chests and faces. Turning his head away, Whitman redoubled his efforts and, with Flix helping him, scrambled back to the boulder.

"How bad is it?" he asked his comms man.

"Never mind me. How's Jonas?"

"He's not." Whitman took up his AR-15. "Stay here."

"You can't do this on your own, Whit."

"Hear that?" He pointed upward. "The helo's almost on top of us."

"Then let the gunner handle the motherfuckers."

"Do you know what they're armed with besides the AKs, Flix? 'Cause I don't. I'm not gonna give them the chance to bring down our ride home."

Without another word, he raced out from behind the boulder. No fire ensued. They couldn't see him, but he could see one of them, and he prepared to hunt both down.

The air began to dance, then turn into a whirlwind as the helo descended. Rain was flung into his face like shrapnel. He caught the first jihadist in the side. He'd aimed for the kidney, to cause maximum pain, and his aim was true. The jihadist screamed, as Whitman had wanted him to. The second one, drawn out of hiding, began to fire wildly, spraying bullets every which way. Whitman, flat on his stomach, took aim, squeezed the trigger, and a line of bullets flayed the target to shreds.

Then he was up and running in a semi-crouch back to the boulder. The helo appeared like an apparition from the underside of the clouds. A rope ladder was unfurled.

"Come on!" Whitman called.

He hoisted Sandofur onto his shoulder, pulled Flix to his feet with his free hand, then sprinted for the ladder, which rippled and spun in the helo's draft like a spectacular child's toy. Around and around its end circled. The gunner was halfway down its length, staring at them. He leaned down, his right arm extended as if in friendship.

"Get a move on!" he shouted. "Bogie vehicle approaching at speed!"

Whitman handed Sandofur up to him, and he began to climb back up into the helo. Flix winced as he dragged himself onto the ladder. Whitman launched him upward, then followed. A livid glow in the darkness of the night began to grow in both size and clarity. The armored vehicle was almost upon them.

Whitman pushed Flix, but his wounded shoulder had stalled his ascent. Clambering over him, Whitman reached back, clasped his left hand, and hauled him upward.

Below them, the armored car appeared out of the gloom, hulking and huge. Its machine guns swiveled around. A burst cut through the bottom of the rope ladder, pieces of it flying everywhere. Then return fire started up from the helo. Whitman at last gained the aircraft. The instant he hauled Flix inside, the helo shot upward like an arrow piercing the blackness of the heavens as it vanished from view.

PART ONE

FULL ASSEMBLY REQUIRED

Modern science is an incredibly demonic enterprise.

—Terence McKenna
on alchemy and Renaissance magic

1

"A mess," King Cutler was saying.

"A mess?" Whitman echoed. "It's a goddamned clusterfuck, is what it is."

Cutler watched Whitman with the eyes of a tiger, green and glittering. His torso, tense and leaning slightly forward, gave him the aspect of someone about to rend anyone who opposed him limb from limb. "Seiran el-Habib was an extremely high-risk target, even for you guys."

"And that's another thing," Whitman said, heatedly. "There *are* no 'you guys,' not anymore. Sandy is dead and Flix just got out of surgery. Red Rover is dead, gone, finished, kaput."

"Flix will be fine." Cutler struggled to maintain an even tone in the face of Whitman's rage and pessimism. "They got the bullet without any difficulty. No bones involved. With our accelerated PT program he'll be as good as new in a week, ten days at the outside."

"And what about Sandy? Will he be good as new? Are you going to resurrect him?"

Cutler made a disgusted noise in the back of his throat. They were seated opposite each other in Cutler's office, which had the look of a room in a gentleman's club rather than an office. Paneled in gleaming mahogany, its myriad shelves were filled with books on military history and biographies of great generals and admirals going all the way back to Alexander the Great. Only one anomaly appeared in the room, and it was a doozy: an enormous flat-screen TV set into the wall opposite a massive tiger-oak desk, on which played an endless rotation of scenes of battle zones from across the globe, images from closed-circuit and drone cameras, exclusive to Universal Security Associates.

"I know you've got your team to consider, Gregory, but I have to take in the big picture."

"Which is what? What's more important than one of your men being shot dead?"

"The president." Cutler stared at his flat-panel computer screen. "This fucking president is going to be the death of us all. He's just not that into war. On every front he's dragging his feet. This crap with the Islamic State in Iraq and Syria had breathed some new life into our business, but for how long? That's the question that keeps me up at night. We need wars, no matter the size. No American military presence, no business for us." He shook his head in consternation. "It's a new day, Gregory. Our world is becoming smaller and smaller. I'm lucky I have my contacts in NSA, otherwise the company's bottom line would be bottoming out."

Outside the bullet- and soundproof windows, the expanse of the Washington Mall flowed away like a stream on which ten thousand pleasure boats drifted back and forth.

Whit appeared entirely unmoved. He'd heard this lament before from the members of the Alchemists. "Like you say, my focus is on my team, and because of this snafu one of them is dead and another is injured. It's unacceptable."

Cutler was wrenched away from his contemplation of USA's future. "Are you really going to make me say that we all know the risks?" he said, clearly annoyed. "In our business, it's such a fucking cliché." He was a big man in all directions, tall and wide as a Mack truck. He was an ex-Marine, had seen combat three times that Whitman knew of. Divorced twice, two kids, one from each marriage. They stayed in touch, even if his exes didn't. "Worse than a cliché." He had a head like a football, his hair still shorn in a Marine high-and-tight, and there was not a gray strand to be found on him. His knife slash of a mouth was always grim, his nose constantly questing for danger. "Honestly, Gregory, this talk will go better when you simmer down to a rolling boil."

"You weren't there, boss. You didn't see . . ." Whitman gritted his teeth, stopping of his own accord. "We were betrayed. There was a leak, a breach of security, call it what you want. The upshot is that someone from inside—*one of us*, boss—didn't want us to get to Seiran el-Habib."

"We were warned that el-Habib had connections."

"No fucking kidding."

Cutler's green eyes seemed to flare. "What did I just tell you? Nothing's going to get settled when you're too hot to handle."

"Why shouldn't I be hot? It's a fucking miracle we weren't all killed. Not only did Seiran el-Habib's people ambush us inside the compound, but his patrol outside the perimeter knew our exact escape route, and were lying in wait for us. That meant they not only knew the day and time of the raid, but the details of the brief as well. But how could they have known? This is the question that's been eating at me ever since I watched the hellish landscape drop away as the helo took us out of there. There's only one answer. We need to go mole hunting."

Cutler held up a fistful of black-jacketed files. "Here is everyone who had knowledge of the Seiran el-Habib brief. I've already started vetting them—movements, travel, mobile phone records, bank accounts, family, friends, acquaintances, the whole nine yards."

"Yeah, well, everyone's already been vetted up and down the yin-yang, so don't forget to look in all the dusty, unremarked corners of their lives."

Cutler cut across his words. "That includes Orteño and you, hotshot."

"Maybe it was Sandy." Whitman's tone hung heavy with sarcasm. "Maybe he was shot on purpose to keep him from blabbing."

"That's enough." Cutler put down the files. "We need to move slowly and carefully. NSA and DARPA personnel are involved."

"Fuck them." Whitman jumped up, held out his hand, fingers wiggling. "Let me see those files."

"Were you suddenly elevated to CEO?"

Whitman, looming over the desk, appeared not to hear him. "It's my right. My team—my freaking right."

"Sit. The. Fuck. Down."

The two men, engaged in a staring contest, were immobile. The atmosphere in the room turned gelid, as if the clash of their respective wills had sealed them in amber.

Whitman, possibly coming to terms with the futility of his position, finally fell back. "Okay, okay." Slowly, deliberately, he sat back down.

Cutler, seeming to relax a couple of notches, shook his head. "This is typical of you, Gregory, you know that? I've got very powerful people perched on my shoulder like owls, their claws digging into my flesh. I've got the politics to consider, you don't. It's imperative to think things through clearly and completely."

"What's to think?" Whitman inched forward until he was on the edge of his chair. "Like other security contractors, we're hired by the NSA. Like other security contractors, we hose the government, but also give them access to services their own people cannot provide. We do the real overseas dirty work for the United States government. But unlike other contractors you have us—or at least you did. We did the real down and dirty work no one would trust even normal contractors to do. But there's nothing normal about what we do; it's the kind of crap that if it ever saw the light of day would surely topple the current administration, no matter how much plausible deniability they believe insulates them from the sewer Red Rover works in on every brief."

"What is this?" Cutler spread his hands. "A pitch for a raise?"

"Yeah," Whitman said sourly. "I want Sandy's salary as well as mine."

The edge of Cutler's hand sliced through the air, cutting through Whitman's sarcasm. "Your job, in case you forgot, is to return Red Rover to operational level. Assemble your team, Gregory. Leave the mole hunting to me."

The staring contest resumed as if it had never been broken off, while the tension in the room ratcheted up another couple of notches to strangulation level. Cutler's phone rang, but he ignored it. His assistant, Valerie, could be heard briefly outside his door, as she told someone in her not-to-be-brooked tone that the boss could not be disturbed. While inside, the staring match continued unabated.

"Listen, listen," Cutler said at length, apparently feeling it was his turn to back off. "It's not just Red Rover that's gone to hell in a handbasket, it's the entire world." His tone had lost its hard edge, was even a touch conciliatory, unusual for Cutler. But then Whitman was his most prized operative. The Red Rover team would have been inconceivable without him. "Do you think you can settle yourself enough to hear what I have to say?"

Whitman didn't reply, but neither did he get up and walk out. Cutler took this as a positive sign, because he continued. "Iraq, Syria, Lebanon—a Devil's triangle. After a decade of fighting overseas, battling Taliban, Hezbollah, al-Qaeda cadres of all stripes and nationalities, after losing men left, right, and center, we are back where we started. Al-Qaeda has retaken Fallujah, where our boys fought them back tooth and nail. For what? Post-American Middle East is worse than ever. A power vacuum has arisen, as all the major players have left the field. In their place a whole host of Islamic jihadists have rushed in, fire-bombing, massacring, destroying whoever does not conform to their particular brand of cruel sectarianism. In both Iraq and Syria, extremists of all stripes have parlayed their foothold into majority stakes.

"And now we have Islamic State to contend with, a terrorist organization so extreme al-Qaeda has distanced itself from them. Does the president give a shit? Doesn't appear so."

Cutler's hands were restless, roaming over the tops of the files, as if eager to get to work digging deep. "So who are the big fish in this wretched pond? The two who have always stood as the major antagonists: Shiite Iran and Sunni Saudi Arabia. Both countries are fanatical in their own way; the rational concept of coexistence is anathema, let alone an accord. The falling apart is a renewed call to the ancient enmities of clan and sect. It echoes loud and clear across the rubble and the corpses, calling forth battalions of teenagers eager to martyr themselves for the cause of jihad."

Throughout this speech, which sounded like a history lesson he had already absorbed countless times, Whitman moved from one buttock to another, restless in his barely stifled rage. "Is there a point to all this?"

Now Cutler did glare at him, and Whitman was smart enough to stifle whatever else was about to come out of his mouth.

"The point," Cutler said, leaning even more forward and interlacing his fingers in a gesture that seemed vaguely ominous, "is this: while you were away at the party the Saudis announced an aid package of French weaponry to the Lebanese, in order to counter the alarming inroads the Shiite Hezbollah has made in that country in recent months."

"How much was the package?"

Something flickered in Cutler's eyes. "That's the first intelligent thing out of your mouth since you stalked in here." He sighed. "The answer to your question is three billion dollars."

"Almost twice the annual Lebanese military budget." Whitman's eyes narrowed. "But still, that's not gonna get it done for Lebanon. The effect, if any, will take years. Meanwhile, Hezbollah is making mincemeat of the Lebanese army." He spread his hands. "So, I mean, why bother?"

"It's a shot across our administration's bow," Cutler said. "The Saudis don't like our new nonintervention policy in Syria, and they're furious over our reaching out to elements inside Iran. If, in fact, the Saudis push the Lebanese army to confront Hezbollah it will blow up the army along sectarian and political lines. The result will plunge the country into utter chaos."

"And that affects us how?"

"The NSA isn't sure. Last night I was at a briefing with Hemingway, where I was updated. Though the administration is in a muddle over this development, the NSA isn't. Hemingway is extremely concerned. He wants eyes on the ground in Lebanon. Eyes he can trust. He believes the threat posed to America's interests abroad is imminent, and he wants Red Rover in-country ASAP."

"I told you, boss, there is no Red Rover."

"Okay, come off the Captain America kick, Gregory. You had a loss. It isn't the first time, it won't be the last."

"It will, if I have to say anything about it."

"Be that as it may," Cutler broke in, clearly enunciating each word, "you will immediately determine Orteño's condition. You will find a new armorer and, if need be, a replacement for Flix. Is that clear?"

Whitman rose. "Any clearer and I could see my reflection in it."

2

Felix Orteño's fear of hospitals dated back to the death of his mother. She had been admitted for an emergency appendectomy, and had been wheeled out by people from the chief medical examiner's office. There ensued three years of trials, appeals, retrials until Orteño's father at last prevailed against both the hospital and the surgeon, thus gaining his pound of flesh. It was not a bargain he relished, though Orteño figured his father must have felt at least the same measure of satisfaction he did. But maybe not: soon after, his father turned to drink. Drunken rages became the norm, and because Flix reminded him of his dead wife, and thus kept his misery burning like a bonfire in his gut, he did whatever he could to drive his son out of the house. Finally, Orteño packed up and took his sister Marilena with him to San Luis Potosí, where his grandmother, Mama Novia, had been born and raised until, at fifteen, she had come across the border, pregnant with their mother. Upon returning to the states eighteen months later, brother and sister discovered their father had shot himself in the head. The suicide drove the siblings even closer together.

The U.S. military was happy to take in the orphan, who enlisted when he was sixteen. He looked older and he altered his birth certificate to make his ruse complete. He took to training and war like a duck to water. For the first time, he felt alive, as if he were making a difference he could see and feel each day. All the money he received he gave to Marilena, who was pregnant. The father, who should have provided for them, was something of a deadbeat.

Orteño never felt more alive than when he was in-country, in the thick of it in Iraq and, later, Afghanistan, where he came into contact with one of Cutler's people, who recommended him to his boss. If Flix liked being part of the military, he loved working for Universal Security Associates. Snafus were kept to a minimum and red tape was virtually nonexistent. Best of all, he never again had to deal with idiot officers impeding his way like so many clowns exiting a Volkswagen Beetle.

He had joined Red Rover five years ago, handpicked, as Sandofur had been, by Whitman. From the first, he fit right in. He was fearless rather than reckless, his skills were splendid, and, best of all, he lived to stick it to America's enemies. Though he was Mexican by heritage, he bled red, white, and blue. Born and raised in the San Antonio area, he spoke like a Texan, but thought like a Mexican. Neither Whitman nor Sandofur had thought less of him for it.

He was sitting up in bed, watching a football game on TV when Whitman entered his room. An IV was stuck in the crook of his left elbow. His heart rate, oxygen intake, and blood pressure were being electronically monitored.

"Well, aren't you a sight for sore eyes."

"How you feeling, señor?" Whitman dragged a chair to the side of the bed. Personally, he hated when people loomed over you while you were flat on your back and in pain. Bad enough the doctors and nurses did it.

"Good news! The doc says I'll be able to play the piano," Flix said.

"Yeah? You couldn't play it for shit before."

The two men laughed as only comrades who have shared real danger can.

"But seriously," Whitman said when they'd had their fun.

"What can I tell you? It only hurts when I shrug."

"Not so bad, right?"

Instead of answering, Flix pointed to the shallow wardrobe against one wall. "My wallet's in the back right pocket."

Whitman crossed to the wardrobe, fetched Flix's wallet, brought it back to him. Opening it, Flix took out a photo, showed it to Whitman.

"Beautiful girl," Whitman said. "Who is she?"

"Lucy. My niece."

"I didn't know you had a niece."

"I don't," Flix said. "At least not now I don't." He took the photo back, stared down at it, his eyes growing dark with painful memory. Being shot, lying here immobile had made him contemplate his own mortality. He had needed something to combat that. Showing what had been hidden to Whit now somehow helped dispel his morbid thoughts. "She left home, ran away when she was fifteen. Before I knew you. This was taken a week before she disappeared. It was the one we showed around, the one I took with me when I searched for her."

"You never found her?"

"Far, far away, *compadre*, you get me?"

Whitman nodded. "She didn't want to be found."

"You'd have liked her. She was smart, feisty, lawless . . . Shit."

"Don't talk about her as if she's dead, Flix."

"Why the fuck not? She's been dead to me and my sister for years." He glanced up briefly, but it was clear that taking his gaze from her photo for even a moment caused him pain. "Why'd she do it? I wish I knew. I wish she were here now. I wish she weren't dead. Family, you know?"

Whitman nodded again, touched his friend's hand. "Family's a bear."

Flix, smiling faintly, finally put Lucy's photo back in his wallet, lay the wallet in his lap.

Whitman, figuring it was time to change the subject, held up a metal-jacketed file. "I took the opportunity of liberating your chart from the nurses' station."

"Fuck you." Nevertheless, he leaned forward in anticipation.

Whitman flicked it open, scanned the pages. "Blah, blah, blah. Yadda, yadda, yadda." He slammed the chart closed. "Another couple of days here, then they'll ship you down to PT. You'll be good to go in a week."

"A week is a year in this place. Listen, be a pal. Get me the fuck outta here now."

"I wish I could, Flix, *emmis*. But I'm gonna do the next best thing. I'm gonna find us a new armorer."

"Good luck with that," Orteño said morosely. "Sandy was the best I've ever seen."

"Maybe," Whitman replied, "but I think I've got a line on someone even better."

Orteño stared at him. "You're freakin' kidding me." He shook his head. "I tell you, don't screw with a Latino in pain."

"Hand to God."

"There is no God."

"And this coming from a Catholic."

"Lapsed, baby, lapsed." Orteño made a face. "If God had witnessed what we've seen on the field of battle and done nothing, he'd be one sonuvabitch."

"Sixteen angels just lost their wings."

Orteño guffawed. "Like I care," he said. "So who's the candidate?"

"Party by the name of Charlie Daou."

"Never heard of him. He ex-military?"

"Not a bit of it," Whitman said. "Charlie wouldn't be caught dead in the military."

Orteño's expression darkened. "What? He's not patriotic?"

"Not enough money in it."

"So that's why you think he'll come and work for us."

Universal Securities Associates paid very well, indeed, even for a field consultant, as they were euphemistically known, and especially for the Red Rover team.

"That and other reasons," Whitman said vaguely.

Orteño wriggled himself into a more upright position. "Care to share?"

"Charlie and I go way back. I can be pretty persuasive when I want to be. I think it'll work out."

Orteño nodded. "Have at it then, my man. Make us whole again. The best medicine for both of us is to get back to work."

Whitman rose, bent over the bed, until his forehead touched Flix's.

"True dat."

The night was clear and almost balmy. Whitman ate at his favorite Thai joint, where they knew to serve him food they themselves ate, one dish more incendiary than the next. Afterward, he repaired to The Doll House, where, amid wretched shadows, he watched Sydny pole dance while she fucked him with her doe eyes. He paid more for aged, sipping tequila and still more for double-shots that weren't watered down. When Sydny's routine ended, she took him for a private lap dance that unaccountably did nothing for him.

"What's the matter, honey?" she said in her husky, honey-drip voice. "Bad day at the office?" He had told her he was a skip tracer because with his physique accountant just wouldn't cut it.

He lifted her bodily off him, handed her a wad of bills, and set her aside. Outside the club he took a deep gulp of air, wondered what the hell he was doing. By that time, it was hard on midnight. Time to take the bull by its very dangerous horns.

The last time Whitman had seen Charlie Daou was three years ago, and it wasn't an evening he often cared to remember. Every once in a while, his third right rib still pained him; Charlie was left-handed.

Charlie lived in a top-floor apartment on Massachusetts Ave, NW, in Cathedral Heights. The building looked like something out of a horror story, part-Gothic, part–Ottoman Empire, with fancy cement work and faux-medieval flourishes like a bell tower straight out of *Vertigo*. Charlie's apartment, to the left of the tower, came complete with a terrace sporting a Moorish-style arch.

Whitman hadn't exaggerated: Charlie loved money above almost anything else. He'd never been able to figure that one out. Whitman rang Charlie's buzzer, but there was no answer. Typical. He followed a tenant in, being as charming and unassuming as he could to allay any latent fears of a mugging. In fact, he asked about Charlie, but the tenant just shrugged.

Whitman took the elevator up. The tenant exited at the third floor; Whitman continued to ascend to the top. In front of Charlie's front door, he heard the bell ring hollowly inside. He knocked, just to make sure. Then he retraced his steps to the hallway window, an old-fashioned affair with grimy, wire-laced panes and a frame that had been painted over so many times it had lost its original shape. The half-moon metal lock, however, was easy enough to open. There was a good reason for that. He lifted the window up, reached around beneath the concrete abutment below, ripped the key and its bit of duct tape off the underside.

Inside, he locked the door behind him. A lamp illuminated a soft oval of the living room—a triangle of a marble-topped side table and a splotch of an expensive handmade Isfahan rug. The apartment seemed virtually unchanged since he had last been here: a dinner of take-out Thai that he had criticized, sparking the fight that ended in his bruised rib and the three-year breach. Now he had returned to try and persuade Charlie to join his team. Surely a fool's errand, despite how he had made it sound to Flix. That fight had had nothing to do with Thai food or his criticism of it. Its origins lay in a different direction entirely, and, for the most part, were hidden far below the surface. Until that night.

With no reason to snoop around, he took a seat on the sofa in a spot furthest away from the oval of light. Then he settled down to wait. Any interest he might have had in snooping was mitigated by the fact that Charlie would know, no matter how careful he might be. Charlie's tradecraft bordered on sorcery.

The soft sigh of traffic drifted in through the closed windows. He could hear a clock ticking in the kitchen, the slurry of a toilet flushing in the apartment downstairs and then, briefly, water rushing. He tried not to think of what was to come, but his rib started to ache, anyway. Think of something else—anything else, he admonished himself. His breathing slowed, became deeper. He emptied himself of thought, emotion, and intent.

Silence.

Until a key ground in the lock and the door opened. A figure came through the doorway, reached around, switched on the overhead light, and stopped dead.

Whitman rose from the sofa, saw a clean-cut, handsome male in his mid-thirties. He was in a designer business suit, but his tie was gone and his collar was unbuttoned. As were the first two pearl buttons of his shirt.

"Who the hell are you?" Whitman said.

And then Charlie came through the door. "Whit," she said. "What are you doing here?"

3

When Charlize Daou stepped through the door to her apartment, the man she was with faded to obscurity, at least as far as Whitman was concerned. Three years might have been three hundred for all the resemblance Charlie bore to the woman he had lived with for five incredible, fitful, combative years.

In the seconds that seemed to pour into minutes while the three principals were frozen in a tableau, Whitman breathed her into the dead place inside him that had opened up when she had thrown him out, this woman whose existence he had so successfully denied for three years. Except for that damn third rib on his right side which simply wouldn't let him alone, as if she had broken it off and wrenched it out of him before he had left. All this while he had told himself that he had frozen in her fire. Now, in a single instant, he understood how he had fed himself that fairy tale in order to keep himself from falling apart, something he would never again allow himself to do—not after his time at the Well.

She looked entirely different—and also precisely the same. How could that be? he asked himself. But as his reawakened knowledge informed him, when it came to Charlie, anything was possible. She seemed bigger, tawnier, though her hair was shorter, pulled back from her high-cheekboned face. Her eyes, so deep a brown they often seemed black, were the same—as large and wide apart as ever, curved up slightly at their outer edges. The shape of her ample lips was also the same, but she had quit wearing the violent reds and was now using nude-colored lipstick, which had the effect of making her mouth even more sensual than he remembered.

She was not a big-boned woman, nor was she particularly tall. Perhaps the change in her size was due to her shoulders, which were definitely more developed. She must have gone back to working out regularly. Whitman knew she could put most Marines down within ten seconds. Hence the rib that had never forgotten her, or the left-handed blow and the power behind it.

"What the fuck, Whit?" Charlie said now. She was wearing a mind-blowing red and oxblood Valentino with a bodice cut down to her waist that must have set her back somewhere north of seven thousand dollars, but she had a mouth like a sailor. "I mean *what the fuck!*"

"What?" he said, hands spread. "Am I intruding?"

"Duh."

The man who had preceded her into the apartment now turned to her. "Who the hell is this, Charlize?"

Charlize? Whitman thought. Jesus Christ. Now tell me he works for IBM.

"No one, Bill."

"Clearly he's not 'no one.' He's in your apartment. He has a key."

"He stole it," Charlie said dismissively.

"Even worse," Bill Whoever said.

"This doesn't concern you."

"The hell it doesn't."

She glared at him. "Let me handle this, okay?"

Whitman walked toward Bill Whoever. "Hey, Bill," he said, "d'you work for IBM?"

Bill turned to him. He wasn't belligerent, as Whitman himself would have been if their places had been reversed. His expression was pure bewilderment. Poor thing.

"No," he said automatically. "AT&T."

"Christ, it's even worse than I thought," Whitman said.

"What does that mean?"

Charlie, intuiting where their conversation was headed, quickly stepped in front of Bill and, before Whitman could antagonize him further, said, "Bill, it's time for you to go."

"What? Just because this sonuvabitch is here uninvited I have to—"

"Just go," Charlie said in a low voice that conveyed in emotion what it lacked in volume.

Whitman knew from experience that when her voice got low it was time to cover your genitals, and quickly.

She began to push Bill gently but firmly back over the threshold. "I'll call you."

"When?" Bill AT&T said. "When will you call me?"

"When I'm good and goddamned ready."

She never did like anyone closing in on her. Bill was in the hallway now, though not liking any of this. Too bad for him.

In a carefully manufactured softer tone, she persisted. "Bill, please just go home. I'll take care of this. I promise." Then she closed the door, locked it, and turned, pressing her back against it. This did wonders for the halves of her breasts revealed so artfully by the Valentino. She was the most un-selfconscious person he had ever come across. She could as easily use her body as a lure or as a weapon, as she saw fit.

Glaring at him, she said, "Your brass balls have grown."

"So have yours."

Without another word, she crossed to an Italian sideboard, poured a generous dollop of Pappy Van Winkle whiskey into one of her man-sized cut-crystal glasses. How in the world did her breasts stay inside that dress? Whitman wondered. Those Valentino tailors were goddamned wizards.

"I don't see any *añejo* tequila," he said.

"No need. You were gone." She approached him on little cat feet, gave him a nudge with her elbow in the precise spot where she had hit him three years ago. "Just Pappy."

She unlatched the sliding door and went out onto the terrace. Whitman followed. There was no use fighting it, or even pausing, to give himself a modicum of satisfaction. He knew it would be fleeting; worse, it would be petty, and petty was one thing he never was with her.

He stepped out. Beyond the ornamental cement balustrade a light mist was falling, turning the night into a pointillist painting by Seurat. Droplets had silvered her hair, the tip of her nose, where the spray of freckles lay most delectably, and her lips, which were half parted, shiny with liquor. She was like a candy cane. He felt like eating her up.

"So," she said. Her drink was already half finished. "Now that you've got what you want, why are you here?"

"A guy can't simply stop in and—"

"Cut the cute stuff." She swung on him. "I'm not in the mood." She took a smaller sip, and her eyes met his. "Frankly, I haven't been in the mood for three years."

"That can change," he said. "Everything changes."

"Not this, it can't."

She finished off her drink and made to pass by him to return inside. He caught her arm, stayed her. She glanced down at where he had hold of her, not hard, but certainly firmly enough to keep her in place. He took his hand away, and she moved on inside, refilled her glass.

"So how's life with Bill AT&T?" he said as he strolled back inside.

"Calm."

"Nice." He did not approach her; her signals were perfectly clear. "Calm is nice. If you're dead." She did not rise to the bait, and this made him uneasy. Maybe he had misjudged the situation, misjudged her, misjudged everything, in fact. He could hear Cutler saying, "That's just like you, Gregory." And maybe it was, which would be too bad for him. Possibly for Charlie, too. At least, the Charlie of three years ago. But he had yet to figure out how much of that person still existed.

He knew one thing though: to show any sign of weakness around her was a death warrant. So he didn't sit, but continued to stand, arms crossed over his chest, watching her drink her beloved Pappy. In their time together he had seen her put four men under the table at once without ever getting visibly high, let alone drunk. Another of her uncanny abilities.

Those were bets—high-stakes bets—not one of which she ever lost, as she moved from bar to bar, fleecing novices and know-it-alls alike. He had asked her once where she came by her drinking, to which she had replied, "What can I say? I'm a fucking fluke of nature."

"You mean freak of nature."

"No, baby, that's you."

He was annoyed with himself for remembering the conversation verbatim. He hated being humiliated.

Draining the last of her whiskey, she set the glass on the sideboard and, without a word, disappeared down the hallway into her bedroom. Whitman stood and waited. He had a sense of what was coming, or he would have had it been three years ago. But this was now. Did he still know?

Four minutes and thirty-two seconds later—he was timing her—she returned clad in a pair of skin-tight jeans and a man-tailored checked sports shirt. The jeans showed off her butt, long legs, and powerful thighs, the shirt opened low enough to reveal enough of her cleavage to be distracting. Having exchanged her Louboutin pumps for a pair of powder-puff blue Nike Air Jordans, she crossed to the vestibule closet, took out an oblong case made of hand-stitched stingray skin, which glimmered like liquid in the light.

"Going out?" he said.

"Bravo."

"To do what?"

She snapped open her case, displayed a custom pool cue in two parts that screwed together, drowsing in a bed of midnight-blue velvet.

He had got it right. His mind relaxed in a mental sigh.

She reached for the front doorknob. "Come or stay here, makes no difference to me."

In this sense, at least, it was like the old days. How many times had he accompanied her on her nocturnal forays into the lower dens of the city, looking for marks whose money she cheerfully would take? But unlike her drinking bouts, she lost her pool bets as often as she won. Clearly, she was learning the form, feeling her way toward a better ratio. It never came, at least not when Whitman had been with her, and he had at last come to the conclusion that time and again the game rejected her attempts at mastery. This was initially a mystery to Whitman. He knew her sense of geometry and vectors was impeccable. It was some time before he realized her weakness: she would not figure the odds correctly. He sensed she could do it if she wanted, but she clearly did not. She was reckless; she wanted to defy the odds, to rise above them into a kind of goddess-like plane. She never made it. She never crashed and burned, either, which, he supposed, said something just as important about her psyche.

It was very late when they entered The Right Cue, a divey pool hall and bar in the none-too-savory southeast quadrant of D.C.

"Who are you hoping to take money from tonight?" he asked. "The indigent and the homeless?"

He was beginning to think she would ignore him, when she abruptly said, "This is where the best players in town congregate."

She went not to the double rows of twelve green-topped tables, but to the bar, where she ordered a double Jim Beam. The bartender, a beefy man with a red face and wiry tufts of hair over his ears, complied without comment or interest. He had been watching ESPN when they had walked in, and seemed in no mood to be disturbed. There were two other people at the bar, both men, staring into their drinks as if trying to divine where their lives had made a wrong turn.

Whitman asked for an aged tequila, of which, the bartender said, there was none. He ordered a tonic water instead.

Behind them, the soft click of cues against balls was a slow-motion reminder to Whitman of the *clack-clack-clack* of mah-jongg tiles in Hong Kong dens he had frequented years ago. Being reminded of those days, when he was no more than a green-behind-the-ears field man, was good for him, especially at this moment in time when it seemed his plan for Charlie was teetering on the edge of oblivion and could so easily tip over into a horror show. Of course, what came after the golden days and crimson nights of Hong Kong was the FBI. And then St. Vincent had shown up. And then came the Well, a horror show of an altogether higher magnitude.

By this point in his musings, Charlie had knocked off her double Beam and had turned to face the tables. Most of them were taken and, from Whitman's admittedly amateur view, it looked like almost all of the players were involved in serious matches with serious money riding on them. Looking more closely, he could see that the play was almost pro-level stuff.

How on earth, he wondered, was Charlie going to make money off these guys?

As if divining his thoughts, she said, "You think I can't do it."

"I think you can do anything you want when you set your mind to it."

"That's what you tell a child before she starts reading her first book."

He wanted to tell her how full of shit she was, but he figured this wasn't the time, even though it might have been the place. Instead, he said, "I'm looking forward to the show."

She smiled dreamily, but not at him. She hadn't taken her eyes off the action at the tables. "And a show it will be," she said softly.

The opponent she found was a rotund man in his early fifties. He wore his trousers very high, supported by a pair of English braces. He had a head like an onion, nearly hairless, with the small ears of a simian, but his eyes were bright sparks, curious and cautious as a bird's. His name was Milt, he had just won a hard-fought match, and he was very, very good.

Whitman thought Charlie could have chosen someone with a bit less experience and skill to start in on, but obviously she had other ideas. The hubris of her goddess syndrome still appeared to be in effect.

They settled on the stakes—ten thousand. Whitman was frankly astonished. He stood against one wall and watched Charlie as she took out her cue, spiraled the two parts together. They broke for who would go first. Charlie pocketed one ball, but missed the second. Milt, following her, pocketed two. Smirking, he challenged her to double the bet. To Whitman's amazement, she agreed. Milt looked as pleased as a pig in a wallow.

He stuck a half-chewed cigar between his liverish lips and, bending over the table, got to work. He broke, then pocketed the next seven balls in a row. He missed on an elegant but difficult triple-bank shot, but only by a millimeter or so. Whitman wondered whether he had been caught showing off for his opponent. Either way, he appeared unconcerned as he stood up and backed away from the table opposite where Charlie was bending over. From there, he got quite an eyeful, which was mostly what he was interested in at this point. It seemed apparent to Whitman, as well as everyone else watching, that he could already feel Charlie's twenty grand in his pocket.

That was before Charlie finished up what he had left her without missing a shot, then ran the table twice. She would have done it a third time, Whitman guessed, but by that time Milt had had enough humiliation for the night. He slapped down his twenty thousand, took his cue, and went home in a huff.

After that display, no one in the place was willing to play her, at least not for money, and Charlie wasn't interested in playing pool unless it was to make money.

On the car ride back to her apartment, he said, "So many things have changed since I last saw you."

Charlie, driving in her typically controlled, intense manner, stared through the windshield at the passing city. "I wouldn't know where to begin."

Whitman sighed, but silently. He said, "Can we kill the foolishness?"

Abruptly, she pulled over to the curb. "Get out," she ordered.

"What? Here?"

She leaned across him, opened the door on his side. "Out!"

"But this neighborhood is—"

"You're a big bad boy. You can take care of yourself."

"Charlie—"

Her voice got low, and he slid out of the car, stood on the street as the door slammed shut and she took off. A block away the car came to a screeching halt. It stayed there idling, in the middle of the street. Not that there was any traffic this time of the morning. But still.

Whitman loped after her, feeling as foolish and giddy as a high school kid with his first crush.

When he reached the car, the doors were locked. He bent down and peered in. She was staring straight ahead. He wanted to tap on the glass, but instinct warned him otherwise. In a moment, her head turned and she stared directly at him. He tried like hell to read her expression, without success.

Keeping her eyes on him, her left hand moved and the electronic locks disengaged. He opened the door, but did not get in. He bent down, peered at her. He could see a pulse beating a tattoo in her right temple.

"Is it all right, Charlie?"

"No, it's not all right." She had not blinked once since turning to look at him, another one of her mysterious tricks.

"Well, then." He honestly did not know what she wanted, what he should do. This, he recognized, was a weakness in himself. The knowledge was an acrid taste in his mouth.

"You want to know how I did it?" she asked, after what seemed a lifetime.

Whitman blinked, as if coming out of a daze. "Did what?"

"Beat Milt."

"You were better than he was."

"No," she said slowly, "I wasn't."

Surprise arose in him like a flock of startled birds. "Yeah, I do want to know."

He slid into the bucket seat, closed the door quietly without looking away from her. She put the car in gear, stepped on the accelerator, and they sped off into the quickening night. To Whitman's chagrin he was sporting a raging hard-on.

4

When King Cutler and Julie Regan weren't making love at night, they watched DVDs of *The Tonight Show* with Johnny Carson. They shared a love of nostalgia, especially when it came to TV shows, as well as a penchant for insomnia. At three a.m., while Whitman and Charlie were on their way back to her apartment, Cutler and Julie were in bed, naked, amid rumpled bedclothes. While Cutler watched Carson doing one of his Carnac the Magnificent bits, Julie was in the shower, soaping off the smells of healthy sweat and sex. Cutler wished she wouldn't do that; he liked the way she smelled after they had made love, but cleanliness was a kind of obsession with her. While he waited for her to return, he ate handfuls of mixed nuts, washed down with a bottle of Mexican Coca Cola, made with sugar, not high-fructose corn syrup, which Cutler could not abide. He had a closely held private opinion that America's addiction to high-fructose corn syrup was draining its males of precious bodily fluids. He possessed a balanced enough mind to see how that idea might strike an outsider as nuts. Therefore, he had never mentioned it to anyone, certainly not to Julie Regan.

Julie worked for the NSA. More specifically, and importantly, she was the assistant to Omar Hemingway. No one knew of her liaison with Cutler, which was about as illicit as it could get, being that Julie was married and, by all accounts Cutler had sifted through, quite happily. That was the fiction Julie spread around cheerfully and adeptly. In fact, her husband was gay and in the military; theirs was a marriage of convenience.

She had her own key and key card, arrived via the underground parking garage, never at the same time as Cutler, and always in some form of light disguise: a wide-brimmed hat, one of several wigs, a scarf tied around her head Audrey Hepburn–style. She liked the wigs best—even while they were making love. She had always aspired to long hair, she said, but found the care and feeding of it too time-consuming.

Cutler laughed at Carson in his outlandish turban, holding answer cards to the side of his head as he matched them "psychically" with hilarious questions, then welcomed Julie, wrapped in a Turkish bathrobe and smelling of lavender and violets, back into bed.

The DVD came to an end.

"Stream something from Netflix?" Julie asked.

"Not tonight." He was sated in every way a man can be, and clicked off the smart-TV with the remote. "I've been watching screens all day." He passed a hand across his eyes. "I've had enough."

Julie, compliant, nestled down in the crook of his shoulder. She was a petite redhead with a foxy face, an enviable figure, and a mighty attitude that could stand up to her boss's bluster. It often seemed that Hemingway did his best to make her cry. Maybe it was a test of some kind. In any event, he had never succeeded.

"How's Hemingway's frame of mind? Since the Seiran el-Habib op blew up, I mean."

"How d'you think?" Julie said. "He's pissed at everyone and everything. Especially Luther St. Vincent. He thinks chain of the Lebanon brief came directly from POTUS to St. Vincent, who tossed it over to him, and believe me when I tell you that my boss does not like taking orders from him."

"Has he threatened to pull our contract?"

"Not that I've heard." Julie lifted her head to peer at him. "You do great work for him. Why would you even ask that?"

"I met with him this afternoon. He certainly is a cagey fuck."

Julie laughed. "I'll be happy to deliver the compliment."

Cutler poked her affectionately. "Don't you dare!" He shook his head. "But this Lebanon brief—I asked him why Red Rover was being given a different brief instead of taking another shot at Seiran el-Habib."

"And?"

"He told me Seiran el-Habib has vanished. He's in the wind again, lost without a trace or a whisper."

"You don't believe him?"

"Maybe he's lost faith in us. Maybe he's given the el-Habib brief to another firm. Right now, I honestly don't know what to believe. If you get even a whiff of what his thoughts are, I'd appreciate a heads-up."

She stirred against him. "I love giving you a heads-up." She slid down, her hands gripped his naked hips. Her head bent and she took him into her mouth. His head arched back and his eyes closed. She began to hum. Then, all at once, she let him slip out. His eyes opened and he looked down. There was a curiously sly smile on her face that caught his attention. His eyes narrowed. "What do you know that I don't?"

She held him in the palm of her hand. "Hemingway lied to you. NSA knows precisely where Seiran el-Habib is; he's still in his heavily protected villa."

"Then why—?"

"The rapidly morphing crises in the Middle East has turned them into children with ADHD; their collective eye has moved on from Seiran el-Habib. The situation in Lebanon has become too volatile. It's too compelling to ignore. Worst of all, it's affecting POTUS's numbers. The president is in trouble at home, he's given them an action directive: 'Look for high percentage situations and bring me major successes I can sell to the American people.'"

His hand on her head directed her back to work.

Afterward, wiping her lips on the sheet, she languidly rose up. "You're Omar's lethal right arm." The caterpillar curl of a smile inched across her lips. "Red Rover's being sent into the briar patch to come out with Br'er Rabbit."

"A show trial."

"A major triumph."

In truth, Julie was tired of talking business, but she suspected King would drop her if she stopped feeding him intel on NSA policy as it pertained to Universal Security. The thought of spending nights alone was more than she could bear. Even these embers were better than an empty hearth.

Though she could feel him against her, his gaze was far away. A dull ache started up around her heart. She placed his hand on her breast, but it might have been a plastic cast for all the life and warmth it provided.

"I have not gotten better," Charlie said. "I've gotten wiser."

"So that's what's different about you," Whitman replied.

She was curled up on her living room sofa, bare feet tucked under the Japanese robe she had changed into as soon as they had gotten home. Fierce-looking green and gold embroidered dragons chased one another over a frothy sea of blue silk. She held a glass of Pappy in one hand, the other lay flat against her thigh. She watched him out of the corners of her eyes, which, so far as Whitman was concerned, was a step in the right direction.

"I wonder," she said in a voice scarcely above a murmur, "whether you've changed."

"Everyone changes," he said.

"Not everyone," she said with a razor's edge to her voice.

"You promised to tell me," he said, to take his mind off her mercurial shift in tone, "how you beat Milt."

She stared down into her glass like the bar flies at The Right Cue. "You shouldn't have come back, Whit."

"Why not?"

She glanced at him. "Because I'm not going to give you what you want."

"You don't even know what it is."

"Payback for the shot in the ribs I gave you when I kicked you out."

He was astonished by her answer, and more than a little saddened. She still had the ability to break his heart, it seemed, even more than it was already broken. He decided to move on. "I'll settle for you telling me the secret of your pool win."

"It's all in the pool cue," she said matter-of-factly. He supposed that now she had plunged the knife in she felt free to speak openly. "I hand-turned it myself from African ebony and Hawaiian koa. This makes it beautiful and perfectly balanced, but that isn't the half of it. The core is made of a thin rod of tantalum." She took another sip of her drink. "Do you know anything about tantalum, Whit?"

"Why would I?"

"Right, why would you. It's an exotic metal with some very interesting properties. The one relevant to this discussion is how readily and rapidly it conducts heat and an electric charge."

Whitman considered the implications for a moment, before he said, "Where is it?"

As if watching a flower unfurl in slow motion, he saw her left hand open to reveal the tiny circular object stuck to the center of her palm.

"When it curls around the butt of my cue it comes in contact with a plate hidden just beneath the skin of wood."

"The charge launches the ball."

"And more. It guides the ball into the pocket."

"Now that's just impossible."

She smiled, as if to herself. "Pool balls are made of phenolic resin. There is something in the tantalum—a certain pentoxide, so I'm told by a chemist friend—that reacts with the resin." She raised her left hand. "*Et voilà!*"

"Why do you insist on inserting French phrases?"

"One of these days you should learn French," she said in a perfectly neutral tone.

"One of these days you should learn to drink *añejo.*"

"French comes in handy in Southeast Asia," she said, as if she had not heard him.

"It's arrogant and pretentious," he said, "and it makes me feel . . ."

She sat up so abruptly the last of her whiskey almost slopped over the rim of her glass. "What, Whit? What does it make you feel?"

He looked away, then directly at her because this was the only way to do it without losing face. "I am tired of being in the subservient position."

"Now you know how I felt." Setting her glass down, she rose, strode quickly out of the room, down the hall. A moment later, he heard the bathroom door slam and lock.

He sat back on the sofa and sighed audibly. This wasn't how he imagined the reunion going, but then what did go the way you expected? He closed his eyes, but every time he did so, he saw Sandy's dead eyes staring up into the Pakistani night, felt the weight of him on his shoulder. Owls were nothing compared to Sandy's corpse.

Not that he hadn't dealt with his share of corpses, first along the border north of Hong Kong, in the New Territories, and then, more significantly, at the Well. But that was different; everything was different at the Well.

Whitman stirred, opening his eyes. He reached for her glass, took a sip of her whiskey, relinquishing his hold. It wasn't half bad; in fact, he thought with time he could grow to like it almost as much as she did. He glanced at his watch. How had twenty minutes flown by so fast? When he thought about the Well, it seemed to him that he stepped outside of time. An hour could easily go by without him noticing.

He rose and padded down the hall, stood in front of the bathroom door. He listened, thought he heard something, but couldn't be certain. He was about to rap on the door with his knuckles, then hesitated. "Charlie," he called instead.

No reply, not even the sound of a body moving about.

"Charlie, come on out of there." He leaned his forehead against the door. "Charlie, don't do this. Don't hide away. Don't—"

Without either warning or sound, the door opened inward, putting him momentarily off balance in every way possible. She had been crying, and was crying still, silent tears rolling down her cheeks.

"Charlie, for the love of—"

"Why?" she cried. "Why did you do that to me?"

He was appalled; he'd never seen her like this, emotionally naked and vulnerable. He felt the pieces of his broken heart start to stir. "I didn't mean—"

"Of course you meant it, Whit! You mean everything you do!"

Then she slapped him hard across the face. He took a step toward her, and she fell against him.

5

Squeak, squeal, slap-slap. A female patient calling pitifully for an enema, followed by sniggers erupting from the nurses' station. Slap-slap, squeal, squeak.

How in the world anyone slept in a hospital was anyone's guess, Flix Orteño thought as he lay flat on his back, listening to the workings of the floor. They were somehow magnified at night, when the acrid odor of disinfectant could not quite hold down the faintly nauseous-sweet stench of sickness. The sounds caromed around in his brain like pinballs, seeming, at length, surreal. He was on the verge of shouting out for a pair of earplugs, but could not bear the thought of the nurses laughing at him as well.

He stared up at the ceiling so fixedly that a certain crack began to metamorphose into a spider. He was about to close his eyes when he became aware of someone standing in the doorway. He turned his head, but the figure was in shadow, the hall light falling on its back.

"Hello, Felix."

A male voice, one on the far edge of Orteño's recognition.

The man came into the room as silently as he had appeared in Flix's doorway. Orteño strained his ears but could no longer hear any sound emanating from the nurses' station; they all seemed to be elsewhere.

The man came up to the side of the bed, held out his right hand, then withdrew it. "Ah, I forgot. Sorry."

Orteño pressed a button and the upper half of the bed rose until he was in a more or less sitting position. He could see the man now: a narrow, angular face with salt-and-pepper hair, a long, Roman nose, leading to lips that were as full as a woman's. He had long, bony-fingered hands. He seemed ill at ease. Flix wondered whether he also had an aversion to hospitals.

"St. Vincent," the man said. His voice was oddly high, almost as squeaky as the trolley the candy stripers pushed back and forth down the hall during meal times. "Luther St. Vincent."

"Never heard of you," Orteño said.

"I'm gratified." St. Vincent cleared his throat. "I didn't come in until I was certain you weren't sleeping. May I have a minute of your time?"

Orteño laughed shortly. "Where am I going?"

"Thank you." St. Vincent pulled over a chair, turned it around, and sat on it backward, his arms folded casually over the back. "How are you feeling?"

"Who are you and why do you want to know?"

"To answer the second question first, you interest me." He had a megawatt smile. His cheeks were pink, clean-shaven, and a bit shiny, as if whoever had given him the shave had applied moisturizer afterward. "As to who I am, I'm NSA."

"Universal Security has no business with the NSA. How d'you know about me?"

"We both know that to be a lie. In any event, I'm in the business of knowing everything there is to know about persons of interest."

"Huh! Well, I'll be as good as new in a couple of weeks' time."

"Yes, but how about *now*, this very moment?"

Orteño had trained himself not to shrug. "I want to get out of here."

"Of course you do. But I wonder if that's all you're feeling. Are you sure?" St. Vincent sucked in his cheeks as if drawing on an ice cream bar. "No anger, resentment, anything like that?"

"I don't follow."

"Sure you do. I imagine you're pissed Sandy bought it. I imagine you're pissed the brief failed."

Orteño's heart lurched in his chest. What the hell? he thought. His eyes narrowed. "What are you driving at?"

"Well, Felix—may I call you Felix?"

Flix nodded. It was not lost on Orteño that an NSA bigwig was treating him with courtesy extreme enough to be almost comical. He had never even met Omar Hemingway; that was Cutler's department. He was strictly a field op.

"Okay, then. You're from Texas, right? Is it true they grow 'em bigger and better in Texas?"

"I think you'd know that better than me."

"Why would that be, Felix?"

Orteño regarded him for a moment as if he had grown another head. "That would be," he said slowly and distinctly, "because you're Anglo and I'm Latino."

"I'm sorry you feel that way, Felix."

"I'm sorry the world works that way. It does in Texas, anyway."

A minor quake must have erupted deep inside St. Vincent because his lips curled, producing a thin smile. "But we're not in Texas anymore, Toto."

"Meaning?"

"Meaning," St. Vincent said, "I'd like you to work for me."

"I already have a job, thanks."

"Oh, no. Nothing like that. Nothing about what I'm proposing would impact your current position in the least."

"All due respect, that's fucking difficult to believe."

St. Vincent chuckled. He lifted an arm briefly, waggled a forefinger. "I knew I had chosen the right person."

"For what?"

"Oh, nothing much." St. Vincent's voice was as nonchalant as a vacationer ordering a frozen daiquiri from a passing waiter.

He rose now, sauntered about the room, which was illuminated by the oblong of light spilling in from the area around the nurses' station, which was, Orteño noted, still as quiet as the grave. He paused in front of one of those meaningless prints seen in every mid-level hotel room in the Third World.

With hands clasped behind his back, he said, as if to himself, "I wonder who picks out these things? Some anonymous drone sitting in some dusty back office somewhere, paging through catalogs of this crap." He grunted.

"But he must have an eye for it, don't you think? I mean, not a single one of these prints ever looks out of place."

He turned abruptly and addressed Orteño. "This is what I want you to do for me, Felix. Be this print on the wall—the print that blends in so completely that no one gives him a second thought or look. Think you can do that for me?"

The cold and squirmy thing in Orteño's stomach that had announced itself at St. Vincent's appearance began to move, and it wasn't from the crummy hospital food. "Eyes and ears, is that it?"

The sun seemed to shine on St. Vincent's face. "Precisely."

"Report to you."

"Me and me alone," he nodded.

"What are you looking for?"

"Anything," St. Vincent said. "Anything out of the ordinary." He approached the bed again, but this time did not bother to sit. "Your last brief had a breach, Felix. A rather serious one, I'm afraid. Was it NSA or Universal Security Associates?" He bent forward slightly in order to emphasize what he said next. "We need to get this thing under control, pronto. Get me?"

"I do. But there's not enough money in the world."

"I appreciate that, Felix, more than you know," St. Vincent said mildly, "but there's a very bad apple hidden somewhere. You and I are going to make applesauce of it, get me?" He smiled. "In any event, money doesn't enter into this equation."

"You're asking me to spy on my own people."

"I'm asking you to help me ferret out a traitor."

Flix's eyes narrowed. "Work for the NSA?"

"Does that matter? Since you already do, albeit indirectly."

Flix laughed. "Are you fucking kidding me?"

St. Vincent nodded. "Point taken. I'm head of Directorate N. You can look me up."

"And Directorate N is . . . ?"

"Counterintelligence," St. Vincent said a bit too quickly. "What d'you say? Are you prepared to come to the defense of your country?"

"I do that on every brief my team undertakes."

"Of course. I didn't mean to underplay your current role in America's foreign policy. I'm merely asking you to take one more step."

Flix chewed this over for a while. "What you're proposing . . . if along the way my friends get hurt . . . ?" He let his words fade out. Then he shook his head. "No."

"Yes, I understand. USA is rather a closed shop, to say the least. A man like you, loyal to the bone, I imagined you'd turn me down. That, in itself, is good to know. A man venal enough to betray his fellows will easily betray his new master."

Orteño bristled visibly. "I don't have masters."

St. Vincent said nothing, seeming lost in contemplation. Then, appearing to start out of it, he said, "But you do have a sister."

Orteño stiffened.

"Her name is Marilena, yes."

It wasn't a question. Orteño didn't say a word; he was scarcely able to draw a breath.

"And Marilena has a son, Leo. He was nineteen two days ago. I know how close-knit Latino families tend to be. Yours is no different." St. Vincent sucked in his cheeks again. "I must remember to send him a present."

"You're not—" Orteño fairly choked on his words. "Are you threatening my nephew?"

"Good god, man, no. What do you take me for?" St. Vincent tapped his lips with a forefinger as if just now struck by a thought. "It's only that . . . well, Marilena had another child, didn't she?"

Orteño swallowed. His mouth was suddenly dry. With his good arm, he reached for the plastic pitcher of iced water, but St. Vincent beat him to it.

"Here, allow me." St. Vincent filled a plastic cup, handed it to Orteño, watched him circumspectly while he drained it. When he was finished, he continued. "No disparagement meant, but this child—her name is Lucy— she was two years Leo's elder, is that right?" He waited for a response, but when none was forthcoming, he went on. "According to the records I've seen, Lucy ran away from home when she was fifteen."

Just like my grandmother, Flix thought.

"That was, what? six, seven years ago."

"Six years, nine months, seventeen days," Orteño said dully. The sick feeling in the pit of his stomach was expanding. Almost a year of trying to find her had left him eager to join up with Whitman, get the hell out of the country, work off his frustration.

"Naturally Marilena tried to find her. So did you, as a matter of fact."

"Lucy's gone, lost to us," Orteño said. "We've all but forgotten her."

"Oh, I doubt that." St. Vincent stood as he had when contemplating the print, with his hands clasped loosely behind his back. "I doubt that very much. After all, family is family, am I right?"

Again, Flix refused to answer what was obviously a rhetorical question.

St. Vincent cleared his throat. "In any event, the good news is that Lucy has been found."

Orteño's heart began to pound. This was not at all what he had expected. "She has? Where? Where is she? When can she be brought back to us?"

"Not so fast, Felix. There are, um, complications. She's been charged with possession of narcotics with intent to sell. In the state where she was picked up, that's a mandatory twenty-five-year sentence if she's convicted, and believe me when I tell you that she will be."

"What?" As fast as elation had come upon him, it was plowed under by dread. He felt as if he were choking. "They can't—"

"I'm afraid they can, Felix." An artfully arranged expression of sorrow and pity arrived on St. Vincent's face dead on schedule. "And they surely will."

"Don't tell me. You know both the state police chief and the chief prosecutor well."

"True enough." St. Vincent studied his nails, which were as perfect and shiny as a runway model's. "But I'm also very well connected in the FBI. I can send in the feds and, well, you're a smart guy, you know the rest."

There was nothing more to say, so St. Vincent simply checked out the monitors Orteño was attached to. He had made his pitch. The rest was up to the patient.

Orteño put his head back on the pillow. He became aware that he was sweating. He hated sweating; he almost never did, unless he was sufficiently ill to warrant it. He closed his eyes, as if to blot out the man standing beside his bed. He remembered with vivid clarity his sister's almost unimaginable loss. How she had been inconsolable, how, had it not been for him, she would have slipped into a deep depression, a downward spiral from which there might very well have been no returning. He had gotten her into counseling, then to a meds psychiatrist, and slowly but surely she had righted the ship. But always in the back of her mind was the loss of her beloved Lucy. He imagined now how the news would hit Marilena. The joy that would suffuse her face, her entire being. Then he imagined keeping the news from her, keeping Lucy from her, Lucy in jail, and he knew that he couldn't allow any of that to happen.

He opened his eyes. St. Vincent was still there, but now his gaze had fallen upon Orteño. "The reunion," he said in a thick voice. "When?"

"As soon as you agree to my proposal."

"How will I contact you?"

St. Vincent produced a mobile phone. "This is only for us. It has no GPS, so it cannot be tracked. It also possesses the latest DARPA encryption, whether we speak or text each other. It's absolutely secure. My private number is built in."

St. Vincent held out his left hand—the hand of the devil, it was thought, in medieval times, and still today in areas of rural Mexico, Arizona, New Mexico, and Texas. Flix had no choice; he took it.

6

Whitman felt Charlie's heart beating wildly in her breast. Her breath was hot on the side of his neck. His arms came around her and he kissed her wet cheek.

"Don't," she said, almost choking on her emotions. "It's too soon, too soon."

He just held her then, feeling the involuntary trembling slowly subside, feeling, too, the gathering of her formidable inner strength as she fought to pull herself together.

Her arms fell away from him. "Step away, Whit," she whispered. "Step away from me." There was no edge to her voice now.

He retreated over the threshold, out into the hall, and, for a split instant, was uncomfortably reminded of Bill AT&T's short journey from Charlie's apartment into the hallway of, he believed, oblivion. Had Bill been simply a time-stamp, a coping mechanism, the latest in a line of males Charlie had been seeing over the last three years? He'd never know, and he'd never ask. The answer might easily be too painful for both of them.

Now that there was a respectful distance between them, now that she had recovered from her small equilibrium break, she said, "If you were considering saying you're sorry, don't. There is no excuse for what you did. It was unconscionable."

"What do you want me to say?"

Something behind her eyes flared, something dark, dangerous, feral. "You should never have come back."

He spread his hands wide in a gesture of peace, or at least compromise. "But here I am. There's been a death in the family, and now I need you, Charlie."

"I don't give a crap what you need. I only—"

Her voice faded out as her eyes rolled up in their sockets. She began to collapse, and Whitman was there to keep her from cracking the back of her skull on the bathroom's tile floor.

Her hands were as white and bloodless as a corpse's. No, he thought, no, no, no. Laying her down gently, he put two fingers against her carotid artery. No pulse; none at all.

Time was of the essence, he knew. Quickly now, he stepped over her, opened the cabinet beneath the sink, hauled out the old-fashioned physician's bag. From inside, he took out a disposable syringe, two small vials filled with clear fluid, and a larger bottle of alcohol. He swabbed the rubber tops of the vials. Ripping open the syringe packaging, he plunged the needle into the vial of prednisone, filled the syringe halfway. He did the same with the vial of Imuran, until the syringe was full. Flicking his finger against its side, he got rid of any remaining air, then he plunged the needle into Charlie's arm, injecting her with the serum cocktail. Throwing the empty syringe aside, he gathered her in his arms, rocking her gently, murmuring to her.

"Come on, Charlie, come on, snap out of it, Charlie, Charlie, Charlie," until it became a kind of chant or invocation, if not a prayer. He remembered taking her to the hospital for the coronary arteriogram and magnetic resonance angiography that, days later, confirmed that she had Takayasu's disease, an autoimmune inflammation of the arteries that caused terrible headaches, chest pain, high blood pressure, no pulse, and, in extreme cases, burst blood vessels, stroke, retinal damage, and paralysis, all from the impaired blood supply to various organs. Takayasu's could be controlled with the medications he had injected into her, but since its cause was unknown, it could not be cured.

He remembered standing in the rain with her after the tests. She'd appeared unperturbed, and he'd wondered how that could possibly be. And yet she had taken the diagnosis with the same frosty equanimity. So much so that, as they had left the medical building, he'd asked her if she had heard what the doctor said.

"Every word," she had said. "Let's get something to eat. I'm starving."

Now in the bathroom, in his arms, Charlie awoke. Her chest heaved once, twice, three times, as if he had just pulled her out of a rip current in which she had almost drowned. Her eyes stared up at him, a deep umber in the light.

"My hands," she said in a reedy whisper.

"Pink as the sands of Bermuda. How is your vision?"

"I'm looking at you, kid." The ghost of a smile infused her face, flickering on and off like a faulty fluorescent tube.

"So all clear."

"I guess there was a good reason for you coming back after all." She closed her eyes for a moment, then, as if shaking off the last coils of a bad dream, opened them and said, "Get me to my feet. I dislike this position; it reminds me of how things used to be."

Her arrow struck his armor and ricocheted harmlessly away. Almost. He unfolded his legs. Grasping one hand, he helped her up. She stood, one hand in his, the other on the edge of the porcelain sink. She looked at his left arm, grasped the curled dragon holding something in its mouth, tattooed on the inside of his elbow. Once upon a time, she had named it Violet, for the color of its furled wings. Now, she let it go, turned away, as if she found it repellent.

In the mirror, she could see that her cheeks were pink again. The blood had, indeed, rushed back to her extremities; the attack had been a mild one.

"Let's get something to eat." Her voice almost back to normal. "I'm starving."

Across the street from the DARPA facility in Arlington, Virginia, was a baseball field. It was part of a public park that included a pond, which was home to a family of ducks, a couple of swans, and, on occasion, served as a stopover for geese, who seemed to love the air more than they did the ground.

It was Dr. Paulus Lindstrom's habit to play ball with his team members in the very early mornings before reporting for work. The field—indeed, the entire park—was empty of human life then, which was just the way Lindstrom wanted it. Animals were another matter. He loved to watch the ducks swimming in circles and the swans paddling along without a care in the world. In some ways, he envied them. Then it would be his turn at bat. He approached the plate with an accelerated pulse and a firm belief something would happen. Sometimes he was right, and he hit the ball over Murphy's head. Other times, his mighty swing produced nothing more than a dribble. He never whiffed, though.

So far as Lindstrom could see, the pickup innings served as a mirror for his work on SUBNETS at DARPA. Sometimes there were breakthroughs, at other times false leads, or even paths that led to dead ends, but every breakthrough, no matter how small, led him closer to his ultimate goal.

Lindstrom had long ago reconciled himself to working on advance-stage weaponry. It didn't take much for him. He was on the milder side of the Asperger's spectrum. On the whole, he had no use for mankind, which, in his opinion, was using up natural resources in the most wanton, ignorant manner. It was mankind's fate, he firmly believed, to die off and be replaced by . . . what exactly? Lindstrom didn't know, but he strongly suspected it would be robots. The Singularity was almost upon mankind—the latest estimation as early as 2045—the moment when robots equaled and then surpassed humans in intelligence.

What would happen then? Renaissance or Armageddon?

He was brought out of his reverie; someone was calling his name. He looked toward the street and saw Valerie Revere, King Cutler's assistant. She was watching him from the sidewalk, her fingers curled through the cyclone fence that demarked the ball field.

His thin lips curled into a semblance of a smile. He adored secrets; especially the one he shared with Valerie.

Calling a halt to the game, he waited until his people had collected their gear, crossed the street, and entered the secure DARPA building before he approached her.

"Morning," he said. "You're up early." That was for anyone who might be listening, though he saw no one in the vicinity, no suspicious-looking vans that might house surveillance, both human and electronic. Still, you never knew; it paid to take every precaution.

"Do you have time for a walk?" she asked.

He made a show of checking his watch. "Sure," he nodded. He gathered up his glove and ball, stuffed them into a nylon backpack, which he slung over his shoulder. As he emerged from the park, he pulled the bill of his Nationals cap lower on his forehead. They crossed two streets to the parking lot catty-corner to the ball field.

Valerie had driven over in a dark-blue ten-year-old BMW. Though they met fairly regularly, she never arrived in the same car twice. They were not rentals, she had assured him early on in the relationship; all of them were completely secure.

She unlocked the car and they got in—she behind the wheel, him sitting in the shotgun seat. Now he had a moment to look at her naturally, rather than keeping her in the corner of his vision. She was a pleasant-looking woman, he supposed, though he was far from the one to ask about those things, rather full-figured, but all in the right places, so far as he knew. She was a redhead—natural, he surmised, from her pale coloring. Were he any other kind of male he would have liked her—perhaps he even did—though, again, he was hardly the person to ask about such things.

"How's tricks?" he asked.

She laughed, leaned forward, stuck the key in the ignition, and turned it halfway. She flicked on the radio. Country music filled the interior to the brim and then some. Lindstrom didn't much care for Toby Keith—Bach was more his speed, the mathematical notes falling on his ears like the parts of a physics equation—but he understood that the raucous noise was more beneficial for blocking their conversation from any electronic surveillance that might be in the area.

"I require your help," Valerie said.

"Whatever I can do," Lindstrom replied, "within reason."

Valerie peered through the windshield and at her side and rearview mirrors before continuing. "The NSA doesn't have its house in order."

Lindstrom appeared to roll this around in his brain for a time before he said. "That's not good."

"Nosiree, not for anyone."

"Should I worry? I mean, Mobius is an NSA initiative. It's completely shielded from the clowns on Capitol Hill. It's also shielded from DOD, CIA, and the rest of the alphabet soup agencies inside the Beltway."

"It should be shielded from us, as well," Valerie said, "but you're paid a small fortune into an anonymous overseas account to make sure Mobius runs smoothly, despite any government interference you might encounter. If NSA is compromised, then so might be Mobius."

Lindstrom frowned. "You mean it might be shut down?"

"Or worse. If one or more pieces of your . . . project were to find their way into hostile hands—"

Lindstrom shuddered. "Please. I can't even go there!"

"Precisely." Valerie's voice was cool and soothing. "And not only for the country. Your little side deal would possibly be exposed. Your money would be frozen, then impounded."

Lindstrom cleared his throat. "Is there a plan afoot?"

Valerie was constantly amused by Lindstrom's turns of phrase. "That," she said, meeting his gaze, "is more or less up to you."

The line between Lindstrom's eyes deepened. "Frankly, I don't see what I can do."

"You're in a unique position, Paulus. You understand that, don't you?"

Again the pause while Lindstrom processed what she had said. "I'm afraid I don't," he said at length.

"Then let me enlighten you." Valerie had the patience of a praying mantis, which was why Cutler had assigned her to Lindstrom. Irony was beyond him; so was sarcasm. She was used to spelling things out so he could see the angle. "DARPA is a nexus for all U.S. clandestine agencies, and your work, Paulus, is ground zero of that nexus. What you produce is of incalculable importance. Plus, you're a scientist. You're supposed to be dead neutral, to have no interest in either politics or the inner workings of the clandestine agencies' hierarchies."

"I don't," Lindstrom said.

This caused Valerie to laugh out loud.

"Have I said something amusing?"

"Yes, Paulus." Impulsively, she leaned over and pecked him chastely on the cheek. She knew he had an aversion to being touched, but this one time she couldn't help herself. "See, you've just answered your own question. Your very indifference to political maneuvering makes you the perfect candidate to listen and report."

He shook his head. "Listen and report what?"

"Anything," Valerie said. "Everything."

Whitman sat across from Charlie at a night-owl truck stop diner on the hem of the city. It was open from midnight till eleven a.m., which made it a perfect place to have a clandestine meet. The rumbling outside from rigs arriving and departing was constant. With mounting pleasure, he watched Charlie devour first a plate of eggs, bacon, hash browns, and whole wheat toast, then a second course of flapjacks and link sausage. He himself drank tea, very dark, and ate a bowl of oatmeal with walnuts.

Charlie ate with the full-out gusto of an animal, but with the manners of a doyen of society. This dichotomy caused a dissonance whose energy he could feel. He bathed in it as if it were silver blue light from a star.

"I think we should get you to the ER," he said, after a time.

"No," she said, around a mouthful of syrup-drenched flapjack, "we shouldn't."

He knew what that meant. "You went off your meds."

"I couldn't take it anymore. The prednisone was nauseating me and the Imuran was making me anemic. After twenty minutes at the gym I'd have to go home and take a nap."

"Takayasu's is nothing to fool around with."

"You're not the one to tell me that."

"If not me, who?"

She finished her last bite of sausage, put her knife and fork down, and pushed her plate away. Then she looked up at him. "Why do you think it's your job to take care of me?"

"Why do you think?"

"Then you never should have left."

"You threw me out!" He said this loud enough that the waitress paused in the act of pouring coffee and the patrons around them turned to stare.

"Nice going," Charlie said under her breath.

"You are so infuriating sometimes."

"That makes two of us."

He leaned across the table. "Do you always have to have the last word?"

Staring at him, she remained silent. After a time, things returned to normal in the diner. Drivers paid their checks, got up, went out. Others came in, sat down, and ordered. A smattering of locals arrived, yawning and calling for coffee. The waitress moved into a higher gear. Whitman and Charlie were anonymous again.

"I appreciate you being so quick on the draw," she said.

Whitman knew that was as close to a thank you as she was going to give him, so he accepted it graciously. "You're welcome."

Could that exchange have been more stilted? he asked himself. They sat like that for a time, watching each other warily, as adversaries will. Neither of them spoke. The homey odors of sizzling bacon and brewing coffee perfumed the air. They both seemed to have settled down into a kind of détente, which, Whitman supposed, was all that he could expect.

Charlie cocked her head. "I think you said something about a death in the family. Do I remember that right?"

He nodded. "One of my team bought it on our last trip."

She peered into his eyes, saw he was telling the truth. "I'm so sorry, Whit."

He nodded. "To the point, there's a position to fill. Sandy was our armorer."

"No," she said at once.

"I haven't even asked you."

"You didn't have to." A bit of her even white teeth showed between her partly open lips. "I know you inside and out."

If that were true, he thought, you'd never have gone out with me in the first place.

He sighed. "I need you, Charlie. Sandy was the best. He wasn't good enough. That only leaves you."

"I don't do your kind of work."

"You don't know—"

"Stop right there. Recall I once worked for the NSA."

"The NSA is all electronic surveillance. It doesn't do a goddamned thing on the ground."

"Nevertheless, I can guess well enough."

It was like trying to chip away at granite with a spoon, he thought. "You owe me, Charlie."

"What? I don't owe you a fucking thing."

"We're now bound to each other."

"Like hell we are," she flared.

And then he let her have it, all that was left in his arsenal. "I saved your life."

7

"Gregory, is this a joke?"

"You know me better than that, boss."

King Cutler jammed his hands deeper in his raincoat. His collar was up, his shoulders hunched against the rain. No one had ever seen him deploy an umbrella no matter how filthy the weather. The two men were walking the Mall. The Reflecting Pool, a stippled mass, reflected nothing today, not even the low, gunmetal sky against which slate gray clouds ran as if being chased by the devil himself. Near to six p.m., the light was failing, colors suppressed to muddied tones of gray and black.

"You know the rules. I will not countenance a female on any of my field teams, let alone Red Rover."

"Red Rover is *my* team, boss. You gave me that leeway when you hired me."

"Everything has its limits," Cutler said sourly. "Women are bad luck in the field."

"You mean like Mata Hari?"

"Don't cut cute with me, Gregory. I'm like a sailor plying the high seas in the eighteen hundreds. Women are bad juju."

"Bad juju is what we had on Red Rover's last brief," Whitman pointed out. "No women there."

Cutler stopped under the portico of the Smithsonian Castle. He ignored the water coursing down his face. "Listen, Gregory, I've afforded you immense independence—far more than any other team leader. I felt you needed it—and also, frankly, you deserved it. The places you go, the things you do are not for the faint of heart or the unsure of purpose. Let's call it a bonus, above and beyond the more than generous hazard pay USA deposits in your bank account every month."

"Then let me make Charlie Daou a part of the reassembled team."

Cutler shook his head. "Did you not hear a word I've been saying?"

"I'm particularly good at that." Whitman didn't bother smiling, taking his cue from Cutler's expression. "What if she could prove to you that she's a better armorer than Sandy was?"

"I hardly think—"

"That she's the best armorer you've ever seen."

Cutler laughed. "Boyo, if she can do that, I'll hire her on the spot." He shook his head. "But she won't, and I won't."

"Care to make a wager on it?"

"Yeah? How much? I'm not into puny bets."

"Ten thousand meet your threshold?"

Cutler seemed taken aback. "Well, let's not go overboard."

"Don't want to take my money all of a sudden?"

"No, I simply assumed you were bluffing." He waited a moment to see if Whitman would confirm his assumption, then he shrugged. "Always happy to make a tax-free ten grand." He rubbed his hands together. "Now where is this so-called marvel of yours?"

"She's busy right now." Whitman gestured with his head. "While we're waiting, let's take a peek inside."

Cutler, checking his wristwatch, said, "I don't have the time."

"Make the time, boss. There's something here you need to see."

One of the unsung perks of being hooked so deeply into the U.S. government was ID that gave you access to places like the Smithsonian after hours. The staff actually stayed late to accommodate you. Outstanding.

They passed through the strict security measures and were ushered inside. An attendant asked if they needed a guide, to which Whitman said no. He led Cutler past the rotunda, and the high-ceilinged rooms used for the presidential balls, following inaugurations. He was reminded of Versailles, of powdered wigs and buckled shoes. Not to mention the stink of high-level government. The West Wing contained many of the Institute's exhibits, including its impressive precious stone collection.

Cutler snorted. "I've seen the Hope diamond, thank you very much." Then, sensing movement to his left, he turned, watched a female maintenance worker paying more attention to her mobile phone call than to buffing the floor. "Another reason why this county's going to the dogs," he sneered. "No one takes pride in their work anymore."

As if she heard him, the woman left her electric buffer, strode toward him. By the time she was two strides away, her mobile phone had somehow been transformed into a knife with a four-inch blade, serrated along its cutting edge and with a wicked-looking gut-hook at the tip.

Cutler was so shocked that he failed to mount a defense as she rushed at him. All he had time for was a step back, which did him no good at all. An instant later, the serrated blade was at his throat. Far too late, he tried to counter, lifting a knee to bury in her groin, but somehow she had pulled what looked like a push-dagger from the buckle of her belt. As his knee rose, she slammed the crescent-shaped butt of the push-dagger onto his kneecap.

"Christ!" Dropping all pretense at defense, he grabbed his knee with both hands, hopping a bit to keep his balance.

Whitman was laughing.

"Gregory, what the fuck!"

"Boss, meet Charlie Daou, my new armorer."

Orteño was in rehab when Luther St. Vincent strode into the room and said to the PT nurse, "I am in need of your patient." At almost the same time, he beckoned to Flix. "Let's go up to your room and get you dressed. I have promises to keep and miles to go before I sleep."

Ten minutes later, he had bundled Orteño into a black Cadillac Escalade with smoked windows and enough room inside to erect a barn. The two men sat side by side while a driver in sunglasses, overcoat, and black leather gloves drove them very fast out to Rockville Pike, taking it north to Cedar Lane, then making a right. It wasn't long before the Escalade turned right again. Flix figured they couldn't have come more than five miles from the Walter Reed complex. Up ahead, he saw a sign for the Bethesda Institute of Mary Immaculate. Passing the sign, the driver immediately cut the Escalade's speed, like a motorboat in a no-wake zone. The two men had uttered not one word.

Flowering cherry trees, their buds just beginning to peek out, lined the gravel driveway on either side. Then the house loomed up, looking very large, very ornate, and very British. Inside, they were greeted by a woman who called herself Sister Margaret, a dour woman going on sixty, whose wiry, gray hair was tied back in a severe bun.

She walked them silently out of the entry, down a series of maze-like corridors, all of which had closed doors on either side. Behind one, Orteño heard laughter, behind another, sobbing. Eventually, they came to the conservatory—a large room filled with light streaming in through a pitched ceiling made of panes of glass. It faced the rear of the building. Flix could see a wide lawn sloping down to a set of four tennis courts.

"We used to have a pond there," Sister Margaret said, "until one of the girls drowned herself. Then we filled it in."

She reported this with the matter-of-fact tone of a talking head on TV. Orteño glanced at her, wondering whether she might be a sociopath. But his experience was with priests, not nuns.

Just then, Sister Margaret stopped and pointed to a figure in a chair near the left-hand corner. "Lucinda is just there," she said.

Flix looked around. "No cops?"

"No FBI, either." St. Vincent was studying his nails with the concentration of a manicurist.

If St. Vincent had meant to impress Orteño, then mission accomplished. Only someone very high up in the clandestine services could have pulled Lucy from the clutches of the FBI.

Sister Margaret cleared her throat. It was clear she had more pressing business elsewhere. "Take as much time as you need."

"You have thirty minutes," St. Vincent broke in.

Sister Margaret gave him the flicker of a humorless smile before she turned back to Orteño. "If there's trouble . . ."

"Why should there be trouble?" Flix asked. He could not take his eyes off his niece.

"If it comes to that, I'll handle it," St. Vincent said. To Orteño, he said, "Go on now," in a voice that was almost gentle. "Clock's running."

Flix felt oddly light-headed as he approached Lucy, as if he had wandered off the Yellow Brick Road into the field of poppies in Oz. The last he had seen of her she was just an adolescent, now she was an adult. She was playing old-school solitaire with cards, rather than on a tablet.

When his shadow passed over her hand she looked up. He was startled to see no recognition in her face. She was shockingly thin, almost frail-looking. Her eyes were sunken deep in their sockets, the skin of her face stretched tight over her mother's pronounced cheekbones.

"Lucy, it's good to see you."

Her head swung back and she returned to her game.

"Lucy?"

"I suppose I should know you." Her voice was reedy, as thin as the rest of her. Her thick hair was lank, greasy-looking. A sickly sweet smell wafted off her every time she exhaled. "The truth is I don't."

His heart plummeted. He sat down beside her. "It's Felix. Your uncle Felix."

"So I have an uncle?" She spoke entirely without inflection, as if she had died and been reanimated by the power of the Institute of Mary Immaculate and the power of Christ.

"You must remember." He leaned toward her and spoke low and urgently. "*Eres la hija de mi hermana.*" You're my sister's daughter. "Marilena's *niña.*" He felt perplexed, at sea. "*Seguramente te acuerdas de ella, tu madre.*" Surely you remember her, your mother.

"What makes you think I speak Spanish?"

Dios mío, Flix thought. "Because, *guapa*, you're Mexican."

She looked at him with those haunted eyes. "I'm the opposite of lovely. I'm a fucking mess."

"But you *do* speak Spanish."

They stared at each other for a moment, Flix desperately searching for even the smallest spark of recognition. Abruptly, he rose, crossed back to where St. Vincent stood like a sentinel beside the doorway.

"What kind of drugs is she on?"

"A cocktail of antipsychotics and tranqs."

"Take her off them."

"She had a break while she was being taken into custody," St. Vincent said as if he hadn't heard. "She almost tore an arm off one of the cops."

"She doesn't know who I am. Take her off all medication—"

"Felix—"

"—so I can talk to her. Otherwise . . ." There was no need to finish the sentence.

St. Vincent gave him a hard stare, then sighed. "To show my sincerity, okay?"

Orteño nodded, wishing he knew a Mayan curse he could put on this sonuvabitch. He should have paid more attention to his grandmother while she was alive.

St. Vincent gave the briefest of nods. "I'll talk to Sister Margaret."

"Now."

"Watch yourself."

"*Por favor.*"

Orteño watched St. Vincent stride down the hall, then returned to his niece. "Lucy, I'm going to get you out of here," he said as he sat down.

She stopped playing at once and stared at him with those dead-fish eyes. "When you get me out," she whispered, "will I still be able to play solitaire?"

Charlie smiled agreeably.

Cutler, still clutching his aching knee, said, "How did you—"

"Oh, and by the way, boss," Whitman cut in, "I'll expect ten grand to be deposited in my account by end of business today."

"That was just a love tap," Charlie said in that equable, almost bland, voice that belied what seethed like a volcano beneath her shiny surface. "I could just as easily have shattered your kneecap."

Cutler eyed her as if he had just discovered a coral snake under a rock.

She went back to the buffer, drew out a small plastic bag, which she brought and handed to Cutler. It held two chilled gel packs.

Cutler waved it away. "I don't need anything."

"Unless you want your knee to swell up to twice its size you do." She led them to a wooden bench, where Cutler sat and reluctantly put the gel packs on his knee. Whitman sat beside him, while Charlie stood between them.

Cutler pointed to the floor.

Charlie sat down, cross-legged, as if she might always be this obedient. Whitman had to laugh silently at that, also at Cutler's need to regain a measure of control over the situation.

"How in the world did you get those weapons through the metal detector?" Cutler asked now.

Charlie glanced at Whitman, who dipped his head. "Go on. Show him."

She handed him the knife and the push-dagger. Cutler studied them, turning them over and over in his hands. "They're too light to be metal." He peered down at her. "What are they made of?"

"A ceramic composite that's three times as hard and a third as brittle as ceramic alone."

He frowned. "I know all the cutting-edge manufacturers worldwide and I've never seen anything like these. Where did you buy them?"

"She didn't," Whitman said.

Cutler grunted his frustration. "Explain, please, and not both at once."

"I made them myself," Charlie said. "I make all the weapons I use myself. Those items I do buy, I modify until they're no longer recognizable."

"You modify them. Why?"

"So they can do what I want them to do," Charlie said. "Which is a lot more than what the manufacturers had envisioned."

He snapped his fingers. Having recovered from his shock, he was all business again. "Example."

"You're holding part of one," she said. "My mobile."

"You mean it functions as a phone, as well?" He recited a nine-digit number with an area code that, so far as the public was concerned, did not exist. He watched her like a hawk as she rose, stepped back four paces, and punched in the numbers one by one. A moment later, his mobile rang.

"Put the mobile down, face up," Charlie said.

"What?"

Whitman rose. "Do what she says, boss."

Cutler set the mobile down on the bench.

"Now place the gel packs on top of it," Charlie said.

Cutler looked from one to the other. "What the hell is this?"

"Please," Charlie said, her tone more insistent. "I only have a twenty-second window."

"For what?"

Whitman stepped in, took the gel packs off Cutler's knee, dropped them onto his mobile, and, taking him firmly by the elbow, moved him back to where Charlie stood, cool and relaxed as Sinatra had been onstage.

The instant they were far enough away, Charlie pressed her mobile's touchscreen, and something terrifying happened. The gel packs shivered, then burst into flame. Cutler looked so astonished Whitman thought he was about to have a heart attack.

Charlie went over and stamped out the fire before any alarms could go off, then she turned to Cutler. "Imagine what would have happened if your mobile had been against your ear."

"Assuming she passes the vetting process, you have your ten thousand," Cutler said to Whitman. "She's worth every penny."

"The bet was Charlie's. The ten large goes to her." Whitman grinned. "Call it a signing bonus."

8

What Dr. Paulus Lindstrom lacked in the tradecraft of spies he more than made up for by a finely honed sense of self-preservation. In this, in particular, his Asperger's was a help rather than a hindrance. Part of that was because his vigilance was entirely internal. He was required to neither ask other people for assistance nor to wonder how his actions or words might affect those around him.

Freed from these restraints, which he found painful, he was able to revel completely in his element. His talk with Valerie had made him feel like a spider to which flies were, sooner or later, going to approach.

For the first several days after he came under discipline, nothing out of the ordinary happened. In fact, he was so immersed in the latest fruit of the Mobius Project that when something interrupted his daily schedule it tended to throw off his intricately timed day. Which was why he tensed up whenever Omar Hemingway showed up for his chatty version of an update. Today, however, someone other than Hemingway entered his lab. He introduced himself as Luther St. Vincent. Lindstrom read something dark and distasteful in his eyes, and quailed inside. He did not like this man at all. In fact, something about St. Vincent frightened him.

"I'm here for an update, Doctor," St. Vincent said without even a pretense at politeness.

"Where is Mr. Hemingway? He's my liaison with NSA."

"Not anymore, Doctor. As of this moment I have taken over the Mobius Project."

A ball of ice formed in the pit of Lindstrom's stomach. "I'll have to call Mr. Hemingway's office."

"Do that, Doctor."

But as Lindstrom reached for the phone, St. Vincent leaned in, looming over him. "However, I wonder whether that's the best course of action."

Lindstrom froze, the receiver halfway to his face. "What do you mean?"

"Loyalty. Service. Obedience." St. Vincent smiled an icy smile. "These are the qualities NSA looks for in its stringers."

"Yes?" Lindstrom was completely terrified now. Hemingway had never spoken to him in this manner.

"What largesse has been given you, Doctor, can be taken away." He snapped his fingers, causing Lindstrom to start. "As quickly as that."

Lindstrom blinked heavily, his version of a spit-take, and then the LED bulb went off in his head and he remembered every word, every intonation, facial expression, and bit of body language in reference to his recent conversation with Valerie Revere.

With these matters foremost in his mind, he arranged his face in what he could only hope was a smile, though he had no real way of knowing, and said, "What you want and what I can provide may be two very different animals, Mr. St. Vincent."

St. Vincent regarded him for a moment before he burst into laughter. "You really are an odd duck, Doctor."

"There is nothing odd about a duck," Lindstrom said, a slight quaver in his voice ruining his facsimile of a smile. "Unless, of course, you are referring to the Madagascar pochard, the world's rarest duck."

"A Madagascar pochard," St. Vincent repeated, as if he had just fallen down the White Rabbit's hole.

"Indeed. By 1991, the pochard was considered extinct, until a flock of them was discovered in Lake Matsaborimena in northern Madagascar fifteen years later."

"All very interesting," St. Vincent said, "were I a conservationist." His smile was all steel teeth. "Shall we press on, Doctor?"

"Ah, yes, you wish to know how the SUBNETS initiative is progressing." SUBNETS was an acronym for System-Based Neurotechnology for Emerging Therapies. It had been begun in another section of DARPA as a way to help veterans overcome the stresses of combat: implanting electrodes in certain areas of the subject's brain, it was hoped, would alleviate chronic pain and depression, as well as PTSD. But, according to Lindstrom, that was dark ages stuff. Going forward, his idea was to devise "an implantable platform technology for precise therapy in humans living with neuropsychiatric and neurological disease, including veterans and active duty soldiers suffering from mental health issues," according to the abstract he had submitted to the powers that be at NSA, and for which he received funding.

He waved a pale hand. "It's all in my weekly report. Or you can consult Mr. Hemingway's files."

"My files now, Doctor. In any event, I'm not interested in what's in your weekly reports, nor am I interested in what you gab about with Omar Hemingway." He stepped in closer, lowered his voice. "I want you to move forward on the Mobius Project."

"What?" Lindstrom took a step back, as if he had been struck across the cheek. "My god, not here." He looked around wildly.

St. Vincent came after him. "Listen, Doctor, my time is too precious to waste, am I making myself clear enough?"

Lindstrom swallowed hard, then said in a strained voice, loud enough for the scientists closest to him to hear. "Why, yes, I could do with a cup of coffee, thanks very much." He stretched out an arm. "This way."

Out in the corridor, Lindstrom turned right, hurried along until he reached a door with a pebbled glass panel. The panel was dark gray, indicating the room beyond was unoccupied. Lindstrom unlocked the door and they went inside.

St. Vincent took out a long gray metal box, walked around the periphery of the room.

"What are you doing?" Lindstrom asked.

St. Vincent put a warning forefinger across his lips. When he had completed his circuit, pointing the box at all the light fixtures and switches, the telephone, in particular, he pocketed the box and returned to stand in front of Lindstrom.

"Okay," he said, "the only ones who can overhear us are the mice, and unless you've done something extraordinary to them they won't pay us any mind." He opened his hands wide. "To Mobius, Doctor. Hemingway may find your obfuscating charming but let me assure you that I do not. Cut the crap."

The Mobius Project took Lindstrom's SUBNETS hypothesis several steps further. Lindstrom had—almost by accident—stumbled on an alkaloid extracted from *Papaver laciniatum* called 'Przemko,' a virtually unknown cultivar of the opium poppy. It was lost in the shadows because of its very low concentration of morphine content—less than 1 percent, as opposed to 10 percent in the *Papaver somniferum* variety that was grown in profusion in parts of Southeast Asia. Przemko contained so little morphine because other, more complex and unstudied alkaloids crowded it out.

SUBNETS had started out extracting alkaloids from *Papaver somniferum* in an attempt to use them in the project, but to no avail, and that avenue of scientific inquiry was soon abandoned for others. However, the last batch of poppies Lindstrom received was adulterated with a half-dozen Przemko specimens. In an idle moment, he began extracting alkaloids from them, and discovered that one, tripentylheliorphine, contained all the qualities he'd been looking for, and more—far more. He experimented, tweaking its atomic structure again and again until he was satisfied. He anointed the alkaloid triptyne as soon as his experiments with mice gave every indication it was going to work.

He reported to Omar Hemingway at NSA, and the Mobius Project was born. It quickly became a totally dark project, whose funding was piggybacked onto Lindstrom's advanced SUBNETS initiative.

St. Vincent clapped his hands impatiently. "Snap out of it, Doc. I'm about to get pissed, and believe me you don't want to see that."

A sense of purpose slowly overlaid his fear of this terrifying man. "Yes, well, I have good news and bad news."

"I'm not interested in bad news, Doctor, so please refrain from including same."

"But you need—"

"I know what I need, Doctor, not you, not anyone else. You have progressed onto the monkeys, yes?"

"I have. But—"

"No buts, Doctor. You are to move on to human trials."

"What? But we haven't finished with—"

"No matter," St. Vincent pressed. "Your subjects will be arriving tomorrow. You will begin then."

"But, you must understand, this is against all scientific procedure."

St. Vincent leaned in again, his face close to Lindstrom's. "Are you telling me you refuse to move on with the trials?"

There ensued a deathly silence during which Lindstrom was aware only of his rapid heartbeat and the breath sawing in and out of his half-open mouth.

"No I . . . No, of course not," he said at length. "It's just that I think you ought to know something."

"And what might that be?" He raised a forefinger. "If it's bad news . . ." There was no need to complete the sentence.

"No, no," Lindstrom said hastily. "About the monkeys. I lost only one out of a hundred."

"What happened to that one?" St. Vincent asked in the same tone he used to ask his manicurist to buff his nails.

Lindstrom's face paled.

"Go on, Doctor, have at it. But you do know whatever you tell me won't change my mind."

"Of course." Lindstrom ducked his head submissively, thinking, If I could kill anyone, it would be this man. Then he said, without any sense of melodrama, "The monkey ripped its own face off."

Julie Regan listened for Omar Hemingway to return from lunch down in the bowels of NSA HQ, where all the bigwigs congregated like geese honking their arguments on what route to travel flying south. No one ever won or lost that argument; it was endless.

Julie herself had just finished her yogurt and fresh fruit, which she ate every working day, sitting at her desk. She did this so she could answer phones. Any call at any time might be important enough for her to alert her boss, drag him upstairs away from the constant honking.

Three days had gone by without her finding a proper opening to speak with Hemingway without arousing his suspicion. As her boss liked to joke: "Only the paranoid survive." Only with him it wasn't a joke. Anyone who worked for him who didn't get that was out on their ear in no time.

Julie had been with him for six years, coming to him when she was still wet behind the ears. She got him instantly, and he got her. Soon after, she became his strong left hand. "I'll keep my right, thank you very much," he said, when he had summoned her to his office to anoint her. He raised her three pay grades, which was almost unheard of, sent her off on a week's vacation, which, he said, was the last one she'd have for a long time. He hadn't been kidding. Julie got Christmas and New Year's off. Having no family to speak of, and her closeted husband out of town with his family in Missouri, she spent Thanksgivings with Hemingway, which was not nearly as bad as it sounded. Though he entertained few people, he was a tremendous host and, to her astonishment, an accomplished cook. She always stayed over, in the guest bedroom at the opposite end of the house from the master suite. He never once made a pass at her or said anything suggestive. There had been times when she'd wished he would. He had missed his chance, however, and now she had King Cutler to snuggle with. She was far safer with Cutler, anyway.

As usual, she heard Hemingway's booming basso before she saw him. Quickly tossing the remnants of her Spartan lunch in the wastepaper basket, she was already standing when he entered the outer office, which was, in a way, her territory.

He eyed her judiciously. "Calls?"

"Six," she said. "None urgent."

He took the clutch of pink notes out of her outstretched hand without breaking stride and vanished into his sanctum. He left his door open, however, and several moments after she heard the desk chair squeak beneath his weight, he called her in.

"Close the door," he said, as she crossed the threshold.

She did as he asked, thinking, Now, this is unusual. He has never had me in here while the door is closed, not even when he was anointing me.

Hemingway gestured. "Take a pew."

Not waiting to see if she complied, he swiveled around, stared out his slit-like window, elbows on the arms of his chair, fingers steepled, seeming in deep contemplation. Julie sat in a state of mild anticipation. What in the world could have provoked this behavior? she wondered. Did the honking downstairs finally come to an end? Had something been decided? Or—and here she felt a sudden dread chill her insides—had he somehow found out about her sexual liaison with King Cutler? Impossible, she reminded herself. Their security had been impeccable. But still . . . she knew, because she had heard Hemingway preach many times, that no security was ever absolute. Someone, somewhere was always devising a better mousetrap.

"I want to tell you about my best friend, Frankie. He wasn't my high school basketball buddy, and he wasn't my college roommate. We didn't go through officer training together. It was the meat-grinder where we met: in-country. 'Nam. At the very edge of the map, where there are no rules, laws, or second chances. We met on the firing lines. In the ten days we were together, we killed more than two dozen North Vietnamese. He saved my life. And when he got shot in the hip I carried him to safety."

Abruptly Hemingway swung back again to impale her with his eyes. "That's the meaning of friendship, Julie. The meaning of loyalty. The compressed time of war makes for trust, makes for friends for life."

Her head bobbed in silent assent.

"I trust you, Julie. I want you to know that."

"Thank you, sir." Her heart flipped over, thinking of her time screwing King Cutler. Why am I even doing it? she asked herself, although she already knew the answer. Self-esteem had always been a problem for her, no more so than in her sham of a marriage. But had her thought been correct? Did Hemingway know about her betrayal? All at once, she felt dirty, unworthy, humiliated, reactions all too familiar. "I appreciate your candor."

"Luther St. Vincent. You know him?"

"I wouldn't say know," Julie said. "But he's the head of Directorate N."

"And a fucking pain in my ass, excuse my French." Hemingway sighed. "Unfortunately, he not only outranks me, but he's protected by the mandarins on high." His hands curled into fists. "He's taken a project away from me. A very important project. I've prepared for this contingency with King Cutler. But now I've been thinking that isn't enough. St. Vincent has one weak spot—his bête noire, you could say. I need your help in this matter."

"Anything, sir. You can count on me."

He let his fists subside, so that his hands lay flat on either side of a slim file folder. "Whatever you have planned for tonight, cancel it."

"I was just going to have dinner, then see a movie." Actually, Julie had planned to spend the night with Cutler, but that wasn't going to happen now. She knew it shouldn't happen ever again, but she felt trapped, too weak to break it off or even walk away.

"Good." He opened the file, but didn't glance at it.

Hemingway's eyes shifted away from her, looking at nothing, so far as Julie could tell.

He licked his lips. His face held an expression that made her even more anxious.

"You ever hear of a place called The Doll House?"

"No," she said truthfully. "But I can guess it's not filled with Barbies and Kens."

"Quite right." Hemingway licked his lips again, then cleared his throat. "There's a person of interest who works there. Pole dancer, occasional lap dancer. She goes by the name of Sydny." He spelled it out for her. "Real name"—now he did consult the file—"Louise Kapok." He closed the folder, looked up. "She's working tonight. Starts at ten, but I want you to be there earlier to get the lay of the land, as it were." He chuckled as if just now getting the inadvertent double entendre.

Julie was have difficulty getting over her surprise. "Let me get this straight. You want me to stake out The Doll House?"

"That's right."

"But I'm not a trained field agent. Surely you have any number of—"

"I do," he said, "but I don't want a field man. I want you to talk to Sydny woman to woman."

"About what?"

"I'll tell you in a moment," he said. "I chose you because you report directly to me and this has to stay between the two of us. It's not an official inquiry, which, as you know, we are forbidden by law to conduct on U.S. soil." He turned, put the entire file through the shredder beside his desk. "Also I don't want her spooked."

"Why in the world would she be spooked?"

"Because," Hemingway said, "one of her best clients is Greg Whitman."

Universal Security Associates' vetting process was even more exacting than the government's, if that were possible. Whitman had warned Charlie of this, but he needn't have bothered. Charlie was all over it.

She passed the so-called box—the lie detector—with flying colors. That was the least of it; any well-trained agent could beat the box as successfully as any psychopath, which maybe said something pretty nasty about agents.

As far as her background was concerned, there had been some significant deep diving to do before Cutler and his team of earthworms began their digging through her past. This was not particularly difficult, though she was not herself computer-savvy enough to make that kind of magic. For that she needed the Elf Lord. Her real name was Lorraine Few, but only two people who knew her used it.

Charlie had met the Elf Lord at the H2K2 hackers' conference twelve years ago. They had hit it off right away, drank small-batch whiskey all night long, and talked nonstop for three straight days, after which Charlie collapsed in her hotel room and slept for a solid fourteen hours.

The Elf Lord lived in a section of a Georgetown residence that used to be a stable. Her landlords were a couple who worked for the CIA, which was a hoot, since they were under the impression that the Elf Lord made her living solely as a handbag and accessories designer by the name of Helene Riche, as did most of the world. Occasionally one or the other would visit her wholly legit website to order a present for Christmas, Valentine's Day, or the occasional wedding. They hadn't a clue who she really was or what she really did.

Physically, the Elf Lord looked like a Valkyrie: big, blond, blowsy, with an expansive sense of humor that had allowed her to make her den in the heart of enemy territory, as it were. The Elf Lord was always happy to see

Charlie, never charged her for work, no matter how complex or time-consuming. Every year, whether she had done work for her or not, Charlie sent the Elf Lord a case of carefully curated whiskeys, all beautifully aged and from the world's best distillers. In short, theirs was a perfect relationship, not the least because each knew all the other's darkest secrets. Charlie trusted the Elf Lord like no one else in her life.

"They can't know about my time in prison," Charlie said when she and the Elf Lord had finished their first whiskeys and got down to business. "Or anything else, for that matter."

"Goes without saying."

The Elf Lord spoke in a controlled soprano so rich Charlie often imagined her on the stage of the Metropolitan Opera, singing arias in *Manon* or *Eugene Onegin.*

"My darling, you have had a life that should never be made public." She gave a wry smile. "You would be so misunderstood!"

"I'm not ashamed of my stint in juvie, brief though it was."

"Good god, after what you've been through why would you be!" The Elf Lord, sitting in her handcrafted task chair in front of quadruple tiers of monitors, often spoke with an emphasis that demanded exclamation points. "As far as I'm concerned it's a badge of honor. You did what you needed to do, you went through the system, and came out the other side."

"Right. They shit me out." Charlie laughed. "Thank you very much."

As they spoke, the Elf Lord's fingers danced over her keyboards and touch screens. Monitors and peripherals were all she lived with; her powerful server banks, protected by complex algorithms that changed hourly, resided in Gibraltar, where no one could find them, let alone pry open their secrets. What Charlie wouldn't have given to spend even five minutes delving through their troves of what must be invaluable data on the Elf Lord's clients.

"So what are they going to see?" she asked.

"Whatever I want them to see—nothing more, nothing less." The Elf Lord was grinning. "An orphan, well, that's true in its way . . . a street urchin . . . *but* you were a child prodigy."

"In what?"

"Your choice."

"Piano." Charlie sang a few bars of "Stardust." "Hoagy Carmichael played the piano."

At once, the Elf Lord stopped inputting data and swung around. "Don't fucking tell me!"

"He came to see me a week ago."

"The rotten sonuvabitch!"

An uncertain smile flickered across Charlie's lips like a lightbulb about to go. "Not so rotten. Maybe."

The Elf Lord clutched her head with both hands. "*Oy vey!*" She only used Yiddish when she was genuinely upset.

"You're judging me again," Charlie said.

The Elf Lord's head came up, her broad face flushed. "I am not! How can you so easily forget what Whitman did to you?"

"That's in the past."

"Please!"

"Listen, holding on to the anger hasn't done me a lick of good. Anger's a poison, EL. You should know that better than most."

From the age of five onward, Lorraine Few had been abused by her uncle, becoming his de facto mistress by the time she was fifteen. This was the main reason she had chosen a profession where she could hide away, use another name, and never be found by any member of her family.

"Okay, but I just, you know, don't want you to get hurt again."

"I can take care of myself."

"Now."

"Yes," Charlie said firmly. "Now."

Sighing, the Elf Lord returned to her task. "I'd better give you different parents, no siblings, aunts, or uncles. The simpler the better, yes?"

Charlie closed her eyes, her past glimmering darkly in her mind's eye like an old-time movie. Except in this case there was no freeing revelation, no clinch between long-lost lovers, no happy ending.

9

"This is bullshit," Whitman said. "In what universe is Seiran el-Habib no longer a special person of interest?"

"In the NSA's," Cutler said, "which means in our world, as well."

"And I call bullshit on that."

"Say whatever you want, Gregory, but it is what it is."

The two men were sitting across from each other at the Louis XIV oak table in Cutler's party-sized dining room. The remains of a noble dinner lay before them, bones and skin, flecks of meat, interrupted swirls of mashed potatoes looking like week-old snow. Rain beat against the window-panes.

So far as Whitman could tell this feast appeared to have been conceived with someone other than him in mind, but what the hell did he know?

"I don't care what Hemingway has decided. Once Flix is operational we're going after Seiran el-Habib."

"The hell you are."

Cutler went into the kitchen, returned with a triple chocolate cake, which he cut into quarters. Now Whitman was certain his boss had been expecting someone else—someone, he was sure, of the female persuasion. Good for him. In Whitman's estimation, a bit of relaxation would do him a world of good.

"Instead, we're going to Lebanon, is that it?"

Cutler helped himself to one huge slice of the cake, licked icing off his fingers. "You'll go where I send you, when I send you."

Whitman brought out several sheets of paper, which he unfolded. "I haven't been sitting on my hands these last few days. I've worked up an alternate approach that I know will work."

Cutler snatched a mouthful of cake off his fork, regarded Whitman placidly while he took his time savoring the dessert. When he had cleared his mouth with a swallow of coffee, he said, "This plan of yours, was it vetted or approved by Hemingway?"

"You know damn well it wasn't, boss."

Cutler set his cup down, cut into his cake again. "Well, then."

"But that's the point. No NSA involvement; no leaks."

"Unless you've forgotten, we take our orders from our clients."

"Fuck the clients," Whitman said. "This is the right thing to do. I mean, what happened to the NSA's near-hysterical directive to find him? Has he suddenly become a friend of the United States government? Come on, boss." He pushed the papers toward Cutler. "At least take a look."

Cutler paid no attention to the plan. "Seiran el-Habib is no longer at the villa. He's off the grid. NSA has no idea where he is."

"Red Rover will find him."

Cutler put his fork down, pushed his chair back from the table. "Gregory, I'm only going to say this once. NSA is our largest client. It pays through the nose—the bulk of your salary and mine. Now let me spin out the scenario you're suggesting. Let's say I give you the go sign. Let's say by some miracle you manage to find Seiran el-Habib. Let's say, further, that the op is a success and you bring the sonuvabitch back. Then what?"

"You tell Hemingway that we've done the impossible."

"The op wasn't sanctioned; in fact, Hemingway told me in no uncertain terms to turn our attention to Lebanon. So what d'you think happens when I tell him we have Seiran el-Habib? He has a shit-fit—"

"He won't."

"—he fires us; we are no longer the recipient of the government's largesse. Ain't gonna happen, my friend. End of story."

———

Rain fell out of the sky as if it had nowhere in particular to go. It pattered on the sidewalk, the roofs of parked cars, got thrown off windshields in metronomic fashion by wiper blades. Charlie, walking home from the Elf Lord's apartment, had three whiskeys in her stomach and a sense that she was being followed.

She'd had no shadows since right after she was released from juvie, when she was still too green to know how to lose a tail—local muscle and then the odd detective, in those days. But she was clever and a fast learner. Subsequently, a tail could never hold her for more than three minutes, tops.

Now she had the feeling again—the crawling of the skin on her back, the itch at the nape of her neck. She saw no one suspicious, but they might be mobile—in a vehicle or a series of vehicles that switched off every couple of blocks. Whatever the setup, she was in someone's crosshairs. Years had gone by, and now just forty-eight hours after she had agreed to join Whit's team at Universal Security Associates, she was being monitored. For what? No clear idea, just a couple of nebulous thoughts she needed to let marinate before they would come into focus.

It was after eleven; the night was very dark, and the rain had shut down visibility almost completely. She stepped into the entrance of an all-night pharmacy. If she smoked, she would have lit a cigarette. Instead, she popped a square of teeth-whitening gum into her mouth and crunched down on it.

Several moments went by when nothing happened. The only thing moving seemed to be the rain. Then a man materialized out of the gloom. He wore a tan suit, rain-darkened at the shoulders and cuffs. She felt her muscles readying themselves as he approached her. Passing very close, he went into the pharmacy. Ten minutes later, he reappeared, paused in the entryway, stared out at the night. He did not look at her. No one entered or exited the pharmacy.

"Filthy weather," he said in a neutral tone. He might have been talking to himself. Charlie made no reply.

"I know a place that's warmer and drier." His tone was the one men used when they were trying to pick up girls in bars or clubs.

"Are you looking to dance with me or fuck me?" Charlie said in her least affable voice.

His head turned so quickly she could hear his vertebrae crack. He wasn't a bad-looking dude, she thought. She had half a mind to take him up on his offer, but at the moment she had more important matters to settle. Another time, another place.

"Did you really—"

"Get out of here," she said, and he did, hurrying out into the wet and the dark. Part of her actually felt sorry for him. Then she got back to work.

All the while their little encounter was unfolding her eyes had been moving, as she scoured the immediate environment for an anomaly. Now, having found it, she smiled to herself, and stepped out into the rain.

Julie Regan had prepared herself for the blare of music and the colored strobe lights, but she was startled by the prevailing smell inside The Doll House, especially up close to the circular stages. The stench of nearly naked human bodies was palpable. Perfume, hairspray, theatrical makeup was more or less completely overwhelmed by it. Julie's experience with strip clubs began and ended with *The Sopranos*. The world itself, in the flesh, reminded her of nothing less than Dante's *Inferno*. How men could get turned on by gyrating women who clearly had no interest in being there, let alone in them, was a mystery to her. She was far from a prude, but there were things in life she simply could not fathom. She liked sex well enough, she thought, though the missionary position was just fine by her, and she had never enjoyed the taste of a man in her mouth, though with King, through sheer force of will, she managed it without gagging.

However, sitting in the third row, watching the dancer named Sydny slide up and down the polished metal pole using just her strong, well-formed legs was a revelation to her. Sydny could have been an acrobat in the circus, but, she supposed, no circus could ever pay as well as the tips she made here at The Doll House.

And then something mysterious and terrible happened: watching

Sydny's perfect body, lubed and shining, writhing in the motions of simu-
lated sex, she found herself unaccountably depressed. All at once, she couldn't
breathe. She rose so abruptly she spilled her drink, which she hadn't
touched, and rushed out of the joint.

For what seemed an eternity, she stood outside watching the rain falling, silver and gold in The Doll House's garish lights. She huddled in her
leather jacket and wished she had worn jeans and a sweater instead of the
silk shirt and short summer-weight wool skirt she had chosen. Tears spilled
onto her cheeks. Who was she kidding about liking sex? Before King, she'd
been with exactly three men, two whose bumbling attempts at intercourse
had scarcely included her, and a third who had cut her to the quick. He'd
accused her of being frigid—"lying there like a corpse" were his precise
words. Christ, she had hated that guy, and after he left her, she had tried
harder with King. She thought King liked what they did together, but who
could really be sure? She sure as hell wasn't going to ask him.

But now, having watched Sydny and the others, she wondered what she
was doing when it came to sex. One thing was for sure: she could never let
herself dance like that; no way could she be so uninhibited.

And then she thought . . . A shiver ran down her spine. No, she couldn't
allow herself to go down that path. She stared up into the sky, wanting
nothing more than to be far away from here, tucked into her own bed with
the covers pulled up to her chin.

But Hemingway, damn him, had given her an assignment. She had to
see it through. Screwing up her courage, she turned and went back inside.
Sydny had already left the stage.

She found herself thinking about the stripper. As she picked her way
toward the backstage area, she felt as if she were in a plummeting elevator.
She could not feel her feet as step by step they led her toward the place
where a burly security guard was standing. He stared at her as she came up
to him.

"I'm looking for Sydny," she said over the din.

"Get lost, honey," the guard said with a sneer.

Hemingway had anticipated such a response. She held up the very real
DCPD badge he'd given her. "You don't want any trouble here," she said,
with her heart in her mouth.

The guard gave her a hard stare, which was about as far as he was willing to go, then stepped aside.

"Third door on the left," he said, his gaze fixed over her head. "Knock yourself out."

Julie bared her teeth and brushed by him. The backstage corridor was long, narrow, and cramped. It stank far worse than the club itself; she'd need a shower when she got home, and her outfit would have to be dry-cleaned.

The third door on the left was closed. She could hear female voices, raised and frantic, as the thumping music of the club receded to a deep, dull backbeat. Pushing the door open, she found herself in a windowless room, cluttered with the stage outfits, such as they were, of the pole dancers. A lighted mirror ran along one of the long walls, with a dozen canvas directors' chairs lined up in a row for the girls to use as they put on their makeup and sprayed their hair, or whatever pole dancers did before they went on stage. There were three girls in various stages of undress. None of them paid her any attention.

Julie found Sydny down near the far end of the room. She was sitting in one of the chairs, staring at herself in the mirror. Her gaze shifted when Julie entered her line of vision.

"I hope Derek didn't send you to me for training." She spoke directly to Julie's reflection. "You look like you've got too much class for this line of work."

"It's lucrative, isn't it?"

"Exceptionally." Sydny sighed, began to take off her makeup. "Assuming you know how to work it, assuming you've got big spenders who take you into Heaven."

"Heaven?"

"That's what we call the back room. You know, lap dances, blow jobs, quickies. Whatever." She laughed. "No, you can't be a newbie, though, god knows, you have the face and body for it. You're blushing." She put down the cotton ball she had been using. "So who the hell are you?"

"I'm doing a story for—"

"Say what?" Sydny frowned. "Reporters aren't allowed back here. How'd you manage it, kitten?"

Julie smiled in what she hoped was a sly fashion. "There are ways around everything and everyone."

Sydny laughed, a deep, rich sound that came from her lower belly. "So you're a wicked girl, after all."

Julie, who thought of herself as the antithesis of a wicked girl, pulled up a chair from the next station. "I'd like to ask you some questions."

"Not here, you won't." Sydny reapplied lipstick, a less lurid shade than the one she had used when dancing. She pointed. "Go through that door and wait for me. I won't be a minute."

"How do I know you won't run out on me?"

Sydny gave her an arched eyebrow look. "Kitten, why bother? I've got fuck-all to hide."

10

So it was a mobile operation. Charlie identified a single car—a black Ford sedan with smoked windows. Why did the feds and law enforcement use smoked glass in their unmarked vehicles, she wondered, when it was a dead giveaway to anyone with even a modicum of street tradecraft?

Having identified her watchers, she went home, walking at a brisk pace. As she neared her building, the rain subsided. The mist felt good on her face. She entered her apartment building, noting before she did so that the black sedan positioned itself with a clear line of sight to the entrance.

Upstairs in her apartment she went to her toolbox, selected an ice hammer and, stuffing it head first into the back pocket of her jeans, took the stairs back down to the basement. She walked past the rodent traps and the garbage cans to the rear service door, used her key to unlock it, and went through. A short flight of pockmarked concrete steps brought her up into the alley behind her building. She went down the alley, came out onto the street by the side of the building adjacent to hers. The Ford was still parked in its advantageous spot. Crossing the street, she walked at a normal pace until she was just behind the car. Then she pulled out the ice hammer and, leaning over, smashed the rear window. A shadow of spastic movement indicated there was only one man inside.

Quickly now, she strode to the driver's side window and smashed it in two powerful blows. The first one crazed the safety glass, the second caused it to disintegrate into tiny pieces.

The man behind the wheel was still turned around, staring over his right shoulder at the broken rear window. As he turned back, she spit her wad of gum into his right eye. While he was dealing with that, she grabbed him by the lapels of his coat and hauled him out through the window, until his hips got stuck. He was on his back, staring up at her.

"Who the fuck are you?" she said. With her face so close to his she was enveloped in the sour smell of the pizza and beer he'd had for dinner. "Why are you following me?"

"You're breaking my back," the man cried.

She shook him hard. "Do I look like I care?"

"Listen, listen, I work for Universal Security, same as you."

"Then why are you following me?"

"Orders," the man said. "From King Cutler himself." He gestured with his head. "My name is Mac. Go on. Call him, if you want."

"You bet I want." She took out her mobile and punched in Cutler's number.

"In the meantime, can you please just let me sit back down?"

"Fuck you."

Cutler's voice came on the other end of the line. "You're inconveniencing me, Charlie."

"Not as much as your little surveillance op has inconvenienced me."

Silence on the other end. Then, "I have no surveillance op running on you."

"Okay," Charlie said. "Then I'll find out who's running this jamoke and then I'll dump his body into the Potomac."

"What?!" Mac cried. "Are you insane?"

"What was that?" Cutler asked.

Charlie hit the mute button, said to Mac. "Shut the fuck up or I really will dump you." Then she unmuted and said to Cutler, "You heard me. I don't like being followed. I have a history—"

"I've read your history."

The Elf Lord at work, Charlie thought. "Then this guy's toast."

"Stop," Cutler said, after a short hesitation. "Mac is mine."

Which was precisely what Charlie suspected. "If you ever lie to me again, you'll live to regret it."

She heard Cutler suck in his breath. "Is that a threat?"

"Take it any way you want."

"Calm down."

"Don't tell me to calm down."

"Surveillance is part of the vetting process we run on all new hires. The shadow was put there for your protection as well as for our information."

"Are you seriously trying to feed me that line?"

Another short pause, as if Cutler was trying to regroup. She could feel that she had put him back on his heels. Clearly, he didn't like it. Who would?

"To be honest, I didn't expect you to pick up the tag. Mac is one of our best men."

"He's not good enough," she said.

Cutler did not respond.

"Listen, when I'm in the field—"

"You're in D.C., for Christ's sake!"

"This town can be as dangerous as any other," Charlie said flatly. "Just ask Mac."

"That was our new hire," Cutler said when he put down his mobile.

"Charlie?"

"She made Mac. She threatened to dump him into the Potomac."

A wry smile crossed Whitman's face. "She was never gonna do that, boss."

"Maybe not, but I think she might have hurt him." His hand cut through the air. "And cut the smirk, you look like a chimpanzee about to spit."

The two men had repaired to the living room, where Cutler had been presenting the Lebanon brief for Red Rover, which was to terminate an al-Qaeda leader ID'd by NSA as Ibrahim Mansour. There were several fuzzy surveillance photos of Mansour, clearly shot through a telephoto lens while he was on the move. According to the brief, Mansour was in Beirut, recruiting locals to al-Qaeda's world jihad. Again, according to NSA intel, ridding the world of Mansour would go a long way toward smoothing the Saudi's ruffled feathers. Whitman did not have to be told that placating the Saudis was a major administration initiative, as it had been for past administrations, never mind that the 9/11 terrorists were Saudis.

The brief included the usual material: local leaders friendly to American interests, rendezvous and fallback points, recognition codes, lines of communication, exceedingly difficult in Lebanon—all the tedious but necessary information crucial to red-zone ops. There were no agents in place anywhere in Lebanon, which Whitman found particularly dispiriting.

"He'll live," Whitman said, "I'm sure."

Cutler regarded him with a jaundiced eye. "You seem particularly sanguine about her reckless behavior."

"It wasn't reckless, boss. She was protecting herself."

"She went way overboard."

Whitman put down a map of Beirut he had been studying. "You're just pissed that she made Mac and fucked him up. Stupid."

Cutler blinked. "I beg your pardon?"

"You should be elated, boss. Charlie's ours now. I told you she was better than anyone I'd ever met. Clearly, you didn't believe me. Now you have the empirical evidence."

"Sure, Adam's a client of mine. A skip-tracer," Sydney said. "He's one of the really good ones."

"Meaning?" Julie took back the photo of Whitman she had showed Sydney.

"He's nice to me. He's a nice guy." She lifted an eyebrow. "Why is a reporter interested in this guy? Unless you're not a reporter at all."

Julie drank some of her coffee. "Okay, I'm not a reporter."

Sydney stirred, as if she were about to take flight. "Who are you then?"

They were in a café not far from The Doll House, a low-lit, low-slung place with a hipster bartender and a pair of female baristas who looked like they were scarcely out of high school, if that. A burbling old-school juke was playing "Moon River." Odd place.

You'd better get this right, Julie told herself, or the night will be a washout. "I'm a private detective, working for a client of Adam's—a potential client, I should say. My client just wants to make sure she's hiring the right person."

Sydny sipped a brandy. "Okay. Like I said, Adam's one of the good guys." In this light and with her harsh makeup off, she looked more alluring than she had wrapped around the shining pole. "Some of 'em can get a little, you know, out of control." She grimaced. "I've got the bruises to prove it."

Julie was appalled. "They beat you?"

"God, no. If they did the bouncers would take care of 'em. But slapping? Hell, yeah, sometimes."

"I didn't see any marks on you."

"Never my face—my thighs, butt, and tits, in the heat of it all." She made a wry face. "Makeup, kitten. Makeup hides a multitude of sins."

Julie sipped at her cup. The coffee was delicious—dark and strong. "So tell me about Adam."

Sydny shrugged. "What's to tell?"

"Adam ever talk to you about his job?"

"Just that he always gets the bad guys he goes after."

"I'm curious, why do you think Adam comes to see you? Is he in an unhappy marriage?"

Sydny sat back, thought about this for a minute. "Well, most of the guys, they're married, for sure. For them it's simple. They're looking for something their wives can't—or maybe won't—give them."

"Sex, right?"

Sydny regarded her for a moment before bursting into laughter. "Wow, what you don't know about my business could fill the Library of Congress."

Managing to brush aside the jibe, Julie said, "Enlighten me, then."

"Sex, sure. But sex is just part of it," Sydny said. "Scratch the surface and here's what you get: what these guys really need is someone to pay attention to them, someone who while they're with them makes them feel like a million bucks, like they're the most important person in the world."

"But it's all fake!"

Sydny laughed. "Jesus, what isn't in life?"

Julie thought that sounded insane. Everything she knew was right and true and real. Wasn't it? Or was it? How about the blow jobs she gave King. She faked liking them. She also faked other things in bed. The thought that Sydny might be on to something gave her the willies.

"And what about Adam?" she said to get her brain onto a less frightening track.

"Adam?" Sydny finished off her brandy, raised her arm for the waitress to see, pointed to her empty snifter, calling for another. "That man isn't married—nowhere near it."

"He tell you that?"

"Hell, no," Sydny said. "A good part of my business is reading people—especially men. I'm aces at it. Shit, you can't make money here if you can't. No, Adam's on his own."

"So he's just lonely—or horny—or both."

"I might've said that, until the last time he came in."

"When was that?"

"Couple nights ago."

"What happened?"

"To begin with, nothing. He came in and, like always, sat and watched my show. We made eye contact, like we always do. Then, like always, he took me into Heaven and I started out giving him a lap dance." Her eyes squinted up and the tip of her tongue appeared between her teeth as she concentrated, making her look like a little girl. "That's where things went south."

"Meaning?"

Sydny took possession of her second brandy. "This guy, he gets as hard as a rock the minute I spread my legs, but this time, *nada*. Not a wriggle outta his snake. I asked him what the matter was."

"What did he say?"

"Nothing. He had this weird look in his eyes, like he was far away, like I wasn't even there." Sydny shrugged. "Then he pays me, like always, and beats it outta there."

"He say anything before he left?"

Sydny stuck her nose in the snifter, inhaled deeply. "Nope."

"What d'you make of it?"

Sydny picked her head up. "What d'you think? He's got a new girl. As long as he has her you can bet he's never coming back to me."

II

Whitman sat in a plush chair on the far side of Charlie's bedroom, watching her sleep. The moon had arrived as if by invitation, its pale, silvery light etching the bold and beautiful lines of Charlie's face. She had the aspect of a lioness, he thought, recalling one winter in Kenya tracking a Chechen terrorist.

Once again returned to the magical atmosphere that surrounded her like an aura, he breathed her in. It had been a long time since he had been in here, a long time since he had sat in this chair, sleepless, watching her at rest.

"How long are you going to sit there without saying a word?" Charlie said without opening her eyes or stirring even a muscle.

"I don't know," he answered. "I have nothing to say."

"I hauled a man halfway through a window tonight."

"So I heard."

"News travels fast in your neck of the woods."

"The jungle drums were going to beat the band."

Her eyes opened, and at the same instant she gave him a curious smile, one he'd never seen before except maybe, once, on a dolphin.

"It's been a long time since you sat there." Her voice was barely above a whisper.

"I was thinking the same thing."

"We're not starting again, Whit." It wasn't a question.

"I know."

"I can't do it." Her eyes never left his. "I won't."

"I know that, too."

"Then why are you here?"

He stretched out his legs, crossed one ankle over the other. "Safe harbor."

For a long time, Charlie watched him, then she closed her eyes. Soon enough she was fast asleep, the curious smile still on her lips. Whitman had just closed his eyes when his mobile vibrated. It was time to go. For an instant, he considered staying. The truth was he didn't want to leave Charlie, did not want to leave this haven, damaged though it was, the past that enclosed them both.

Then he rose, silent as an owl. The company car was waiting downstairs.

"So, kitten, you're not a reporter, and if you're a PI, I'm Beyoncé," Sydney said. "So, come on now, who are you really and why are you so interested in Adam?"

Julie sighed. "The girl Adam was dreaming of that night? That's me." She paused, keeping her gaze steady. It was crucial now that Sydney believe this final lie, which was why she was going to leaven the falsehood with grains of the truth. And in so doing, she thought, maybe I'll get something out of this, too. "His name isn't Adam, by the way. It's Greg, but most people call him Whit."

"Makes no difference to me what his name is." Sydney had stopped drinking. "But go on."

Julie sighed again. "The truth is . . . well . . ." Her faltering was entirely real. "I'm not so good in bed, and when I learned about you, I thought, Okay, maybe she'll be able to help me."

"Help you with him."

"Yes."

"In bed."

"Right."

Sydney shook her head. "I don't know whether to laugh or cry."

Julie gave her a shy smile. "I guess either would be appropriate."

"Poor kitten."

Sydny looked like she meant it, which helped Julie pluck up her courage for her next question. "About orgasms . . ."

Sydny cocked her head. "What about 'em?" Then she held up a hand. "No, for Christ's sake, don't tell me. You've never had one."

"I don't think so, no."

"You don't *think* so? Kitten, if you'd had one I one thousand percent guarantee you'd know it. Plus which, you wouldn't want anything else when you fucked Adam or Greg or Whit, or whatever his name is."

Julie felt flushed with shame. "Then I guess I haven't."

"Poor kitten."

"What do I do? About Greg, I mean."

"It's you you have to work on, kitten, not Greg." Sydny stood up. "Now I have to get back to work."

Julie, heart thundering in her breast, stood up, too. "I just need a little more info—"

"About Greg, uh uh." Sydny gave her an arched eyebrow. "Pay the man, kitten."

Julie did as requested, then followed the pole dancer out the door. The street was cold and dark, inhospitable after the café and the club. Julie gave an involuntary shiver.

Sydny smiled a foxlike smile as she stood in front of her. "Okay, you're not a reporter, you're not a PI, and if you've never had an orgasm you sure aren't Greg's new squeeze, so now what's the deal?"

"I walked out, you know. I stood on the street outside the club for five or ten minutes before I went back inside."

As if she were a mesmerist, Sydny's eyes locked with hers. "You really are a poor kitten. We'll have to cure you of that."

"How d'you mean?"

The two women, face to face, were standing close enough to inhale each other's breath. Julie, terrified, had an urge to turn and run. At the same time, she felt magnetized to this spot, unable either to retreat or to advance. What on earth is happening to me? she asked herself. Her heart was fluttering in her chest like a frightened bird.

"I mean," Sydny said now, "I see more in you than you see in yourself." Her eyes seemed as big as lanterns, and as bright. "Someone told you to come here, to ask questions about Adam or Greg or Whit. Someone's interested in him."

Julie seemed to be in a kind of trance. "Wha—" She had to clear her throat of an unknown emotion. "What?"

"Who sent you here, Julie?"

"A man."

"Of course, a man. And you obeyed."

"He's . . . he's my boss."

"Yes, but you're under his thumb."

"Of course! I—"

"Stop. There are ways, Julie. If you stop being afraid. If you're brave enough to free the strength inside you."

"I don't understand."

"That's why you went back inside." Sydny leaned forward suddenly, and her lips brushed Julie's. The kiss, soft and knowing, lasted only an instant, but Julie's lips tingled for hours after. She stood, transfixed, the night seemingly on fire. With Sydny watching her, a gentle smile curving her lips, her heart expanded. It was as if she finally recognized the true nature of the person living inside her own skin.

12

At three a.m. precisely, Paulus Lindstrom contacted Valerie in the agreed upon manner. That is, he used a burner phone she had given him, punching in a specific number. He made the call out in the street. He did not much care for being on the streets at three in the morning, not because he was afraid of who might leap out of the shadows, but because it reminded him of his hellish teenage years.

In those days, his parents had no clue as to his condition. Unable to sleep, he would roam the streets at night, looking for what he could not say. But one cold, snowy winter's night as he stood huddled on a street corner unable to decide which way to turn, a limousine pulled up, one smoked glass window rolled down. Thinking the person inside was going to ask for directions, he stepped off the curb and bent to the window. A man handed him a five-dollar bill and said, "Go get yourself something hot to eat." He had stood in the gutter, paralyzed by a shocked humiliation as the window closed and the limo drove off.

"Yes?" Valerie said in his ear, startling him.

"Something's happened."

"I assume it's significant." Her voice was still sloughing off the fur of sleep.

"I was made uncomfortable by it." Lindstrom was still thinking of that five-dollar bill and all it implied. He'd thrown it in a trash can as he'd hurried home through the thickening snow, tears overspilling his eyes.

"Then you'd better tell me." But before he had a chance to utter another word, she said, "Are you walking? Keep walking. And tell me immediately if you see anyone around."

Lindstrom craned his neck. He imagined snowflakes caking his eyelashes. "There's no one."

"Okay, now step into a doorway and don't move. Do you see a vehicle slowing or stopping?"

"No," Lindstrom said. "Listen, I'm getting more and more uncomfortable."

Valerie hesitated for a moment. "Do you want to come over here?"

"I do," Lindstrom said in a very small voice.

"Okay. Give me your location." When he did, she said. "Just stay there. I'll have a car to you in—hold on . . . fifteen minutes. It would be sooner, but we need to make sure the area is sanitized before we come near you."

"Sanitized?"

"Swept and, if need be, cleaned of watchers," Valerie said with the patience of Job.

Lindstrom looked around wildly, as if he had been thrust into a horror film. "Now you're frightening me."

"I don't meant to, Paulus, but these are frightening times. Mobius has made it so."

The moment Valerie severed her connection with Lindstrom, she removed another mobile from the drawer of her bedside table, unlocked it with a passcode, and punched in a speed dial number. She spoke in low, urgent tones to the man who answered, giving him the particulars of where Lindstrom was and the parameters of the circumstances he had found himself in.

Then she called Preach.

"There is no reason to worry," he said in his soft Louisiana drawl.

"But he's being threatened by Luther St. Vincent, the head of NSA's Directorate N."

"Again, there's no cause for concern. I am familiar with Luther."

Valeria was used to this. Preach seemed familiar with virtually every-one; his personal network seemed endless.

"You made the right move, as always," Preach continued. "The situation will take care of itself."

"I can never understand why you're so sure everything will always go our way."

Preach laughed, and somehow, deep down in the base of her brain, she was wholly reassured.

When Preach's armed driver delivered Lindstrom to her front door, Valerie had a large hot toddy waiting for him. He loved hot toddies even on warm nights. He was always cold, he'd told her.

"Do you know why Luther St. Vincent was so insistent about Mobius?" Valerie said.

Lindstrom shook his head, miserable.

"And up until now you had no inkling of either his interest or his involvement?"

"No. Omar Hemingway had been in charge of Mobius from the get-go."

They were sitting together on her sofa. All the lights were on, another thing he liked. He was totally averse to darkness or shadows in a house.

Lindstrom was holding the mug with both hands, staring into it.

"Did you give it to him?"

Lindstrom looked up, startled. "What?"

Valerie sighed inwardly. "The update on Mobius."

"I didn't want to; he scares me. But I did."

"I think he scares everyone, Paulus."

Lindstrom's head sank down onto his shoulders, like a startled turtle withdrawing into its shell. "Even so," he said mournfully.

Clearly, St. Vincent had upset Lindstrom, frightened him, badly. If it had been anyone else, Valerie would have given him a reassuring pat on the knee, but she knew Lindstrom wouldn't appreciate that.

He looked at her from under heavy brows. "I don't want to go back to my apartment."

"I don't blame you." She smiled with the supernatural reassurance Preach had given her. "You'll stay here."

"Really?"

He was such a little child. "You can bunk right here on the sofa; there's plenty of room." She rose. "I'll get you bedclothes." She was also going to update Preach, although he might already know; he was uncanny that way. She pointed. "The bathroom's right down the hall. There's a spare toothbrush in the medicine cabinet and I'll put out a set of towels for you."

As she was about to turn away, he said, "Valerie?"

"Yes, Paulus."

"I just wanted to say . . ."

"Yes?"

He smiled up at her shyly. "I like your apartment."

They stood in moonlight, like the best of friends; many of the streetlights were out, a testament to the District's ongoing fiscal crisis. The asphalt was opalescent from the rain and the occasional oil slick. The city had grown quiet, as if the last of the rain had swept all sounds away along with the dust, grime, and grit that had been in the air. Only a distant hum, as of a colossal generator, came to them, like a rumor from some hidden underworld.

Sydney gestured to a car that had appeared out of the night, and had now pulled up to the curb, its engine idling. "Someone is waiting for you."

Julie looked at the car: it was black and it appeared armored. For an instant her heart lurched in her chest. Had Hemingway come here? At once, her eyes lowered; she felt engulfed in shame.

Sydney stood very close to her. "Don't do that, kitten. Shame is bad for your health." She tapped the side of Julie's head. "You know, here, where things get fucked up easily."

"Who's in the car?"

"A friend I phoned. All he wants is to talk."

Julie stared into Sydney's beautiful, cat-like face.

"Listen, kitten, everything is in your hands. If you don't want to get into the car you can simply walk home."

For some reason she could not explain, she trusted this woman. "I don't think I want to do that." She took a step toward the car, then turned back. "Why do you do what you do?" she asked. "Is it out of necessity?"

"You mean is it the only thing I can make money at?" Sydny laughed. "I have a degree from Georgetown. Poli-sci, the theory and practice of politics." She arched an eyebrow. "In this town, I'm making the best use of my degree." She squeezed Julie's hand. "And there's something else. Something important, vital even. I like it, kitten, and in life you have to do what you like, otherwise your life is shit. I love being onstage. I love showing off my body. I love the sheen my skin gets when I work the pole; it's the same sheen I get during sex. But most of all I like the control I have over the men watching me. I can see what's in their eyes. They fantasize about me in the dark, and after they go home. They fuck me in their minds. I can't tell you how great that feeling is. It's like, I don't know, like how I imagine having wings would be, soaring up into the clouds."

A pair of worry lines appeared between Julie's eyes. "But what about what happens, in, you know, Heaven?"

"What, the lap dances? They don't mean anything. It's acting 101, kitten, nothing more."

"But there are exceptions."

"I don't fuck everyone who asks, only the ones I like. I'm not a whore."

"Women as well as men?"

"Sometimes. Sure, why not?"

Julie chuckled softly, as with a shared secret. She stared into Sydny's glittering eyes. "I want to see you again."

"What you want is to find the power inside yourself."

"That's what I mean."

"Then of course we'll see each other again." Sydny walked her over to the car. The rear door opened. Julie's heart thudded as she ducked her head and slid into the backseat. At once, the door closed behind her and the car took off.

The driver kept his eyes fixed on the road and on his side mirrors. He did not once even glance at her. Well trained, she thought. Then she turned her attention to the figure wedged into the far corner of the seat, his face deliberately in shadow. Though she couldn't see his face, by the shape of his torso she knew he wasn't her boss. Who, then?

All at once the figure moved and in the strobing illumination from the passing streetlights, a strong, rugged face appeared.

"Good morning, Julie," Whitman said.

Julie, trying to regain her equilibrium, found events running over her like a Mack truck. "I don't know what to say."

Whitman shook his head. "You were just doing your job. I'm here now because I want you to tell me what Hemingway's idea was, because I don't have a clue. What were you doing at The Doll House?"

"She told you about me."

"Everything she knew. I intuited the rest."

Julie watched his face go from shadow to light and back again as they traveled through the dark and silent city. "Just tell me one thing. Was everything Sydney said to me an act?"

"Sydney genuinely likes you."

Julie blushed and turned away. For the moment, she could not bear to see how he was looking at her, how he might be judging her. "But I lied to her. Repeatedly."

"She thought that took guts." He paused for a moment. "She sees something in you."

Julie ducked her head. "So she said."

"I would take that at face value, if I were you. Sydney's an extraordinary woman."

"Can I tell you something?" Her eyes at last engaged with his. "When I'm with her she makes me feel . . . alive."

"Mission accomplished," Whitman said with a chuckle. "Now tell me what you were doing at The Doll House."

Julie settled herself, hands overlapping each other in her lap. "Hemingway called me into his office, said he had a line on this stripper named Sydney who worked at The Doll House, a place he knew you frequented. He knew she was your favorite dancer."

"He knows more than I thought." Whitman rubbed his chin. "What did he want you to do?"

"Talk to her, 'woman to woman' as he put it. See if I could find out what you're up to when you're off duty."

Here's what I've been doing in my off hours, besides visiting Flix, Whitman thought: finding out that Ibrahim Mansour is nothing more than a punk running a wildcat cadre he claims is affiliated with al-Qaeda, which none of my private back-channel contacts can verify. In other words, he was a soft target: an easy win for NSA, currying favor with POTUS on the defensive domestically. But he brought up none of this to her, instead saying, "What could Hemingway be suspicious of?"

"On the surface, it would seem that after the blown mission, he's looking at everyone, including you. But I'm thinking, actually, he's after Luther St. Vincent." She cocked her head. "You're St. Vincent's bête noire, so Hemingway thinks. Is that right?"

"Tie this all up for me, would you?"

Julie swallowed hard. Being between Hemingway and this man was an exceedingly uncomfortable place to be. "This is just a guess, you understand."

"I'm listening."

"Hemingway was hoping I'd scrape up some dirt on you to use as leverage. He wants to force the issue. He wants you to take out St. Vincent for him."

"Hands perfectly clean."

She nodded uncertainly. "Like I said—"

"It's a good guess," Whit said slowly as she chewed over the scenario. "My world is full of pricks."

There was a small silence, which ended when Whitman said, more gently than she could have imagined, "One thing. Why in the world would Hemingway send you?"

"I asked him that myself. He told me he thought a civilian like Sydny would respond better to someone like me, who wasn't a trained field man; that a field man might spook her."

Whitman was about to say that her boss was full of shit, when she piped up.

"But you know I kind of liked it. I mean I was a little scared, but he called me into his office."

"So you said."

"But the thing is—the odd thing—is that he asked me to close the door behind me. That's SOP for agents, but he's never, ever done that with me before. When I'm in his office the door is always open."

"What d'you make of that?"

"Well, naturally I was flattered, and thrilled when he gave me this assignment. At last, I thought, he's giving me a chance to be of use to him, instead of just being a drone pushing papers."

"What was it that changed your mind?"

"Frankly, you. Your presence here—you picking me up—has made me rethink the entire episode. It's why I asked you if Sydny was lying. I was wondering whether she belongs to Hemingway, whether this was a clandestine way of having me re-vetted."

"Put your mind at ease on that score," Whitman said. "Sydny belongs to no one. She's my friend."

Julie bit her lower lip. Something was nagging at her, and she wondered whether she could trust Whitman. A deep connection ran between him and Sydny that made her envious of Sydny. Why couldn't she have that? What was wrong with her? She intuited that Sydny held the answer, perhaps the answer to everything. If Sydny trusted Whitman then so could she. Her gut told her to go ahead, and she did: "There's something you need to know. It has to do with this Lebanon mission."

Whitman stiffened, a darkness coming into his eyes. "Explain, please."

"Hemingway told Cutler that taking another run at Seiran el-Habib is now off the table."

"Right. He's slipped the intel leash; no one can find him. Cutler told me."

"Yes, but it isn't the truth."

"What?"

"Seiran el-Habib is exactly where he has been, in that villa your team assaulted."

Whitman couldn't believe what he was hearing. "Then why would—"

"An action directive from POTUS via NSA, to bring in a major success."

"Bringing Seiran el-Habib in *would* be a major success."

"Except that the crisis in Lebanon has taken precedence."

"Is this something you have verified independently or are you just parroting what Hemingway told you?" Cutler had sold this very same line to Whitman.

Julie's silence spoke volumes.

Whitman sat back against the cushion. "Capturing and wringing Seiran el-Habib for intel would give POTUS more airtime than any target we could find in Lebanon," he said. "They're all lying. The question is why."

At that moment, the car slowed, pulled into the curb, and stopped. "You're home." Whitman opened the curbside door. "A piece of advice, Julie. Never let them see what you're thinking."

"That's so basic. Keep a poker face."

"Believe it or not," Whitman said, "there are agents—the great ones—who can read a poker face, or at least infer from it some things better left secret. No, what you want to show is emotion."

"What emotion?"

"It doesn't matter, as long as it's not the one they're expecting. It's simple misdirection—a form of sleight of hand, the illusionist's most intimate companion. You see what I mean?"

"I do, and I'm grateful."

"One more thing. Pushing papers, as you put it, has two sides. Those papers contain important information. Information is power, Julie. Give that notion a thought."

She nodded. "I will." She hesitated as she was about to clamber over his legs.

As if intuiting her thoughts, he said, "What is it?"

"I should tell you . . ." Her head swung away as she stared out the side window. It was suddenly very quiet inside the car. Her head swung back and her eyes engaged with his. "I've been sleeping with your boss."

Whitman seemed not to react at all. "You're not surprised?" she asked.

Instead of giving her a direct answer, he said, "You're Cutler's conduit?"

"You could say that."

"That sounds about right."

"What does that mean?"

"Have a good think before you decide to continue, that's all I'm saying."

She opened her mouth to say something, then decided against it.

"Okay, then." He grinned and said in his best Hollywood Western accent, "Now git along, little doggie."

As she climbed over him, he added sternly, "This never happened."

She stood on the pavement and glanced back at him. "What never happened?" She gave him a complicit smile, still digesting everything he had told her. She caught a crescent of his face in half-light, before the door slammed shut and the car, nosing out into the silent and deserted street, continued its mysterious journey through the city.

Her mind still buzzing, she crossed the pavement, went up the stairs to her building. Behind her, the eastern sky had turned the color of an oyster shell.

13

St. Vincent came for Orteño at eleven a.m. and transported him back to the Bethesda Institute of Mary Immaculate. Once again, Sister Margaret met them in reception and led them down the various corridors to the conservatory.

Lucy was sitting in the same chair but she was no longer playing cards. She held an iPod and was apparently listening to music through a pair of earbuds. As before, St. Vincent took up position by the door and Sister Margaret retreated back down the corridor. Neither of them had said a word to Orteño; it was clear to him that she did not approve of taking his niece off the meds prescribed for her by the in-house psychiatrist.

Flix sat down opposite Lucy, waited until she pulled out the earbuds, and then, smiling, he held out a small box wrapped in gaily colored paper. "I brought you a present, Lucy."

She studied him as if he were a postmodern painting, trying to make sense of the scrawls and loops. Wordlessly, she took the box, unwrapped it with steady hands, and peered inside. She took out a necklace that held a cameo.

"That comes from Marilena, your mother," Flix said hopefully. "It was given to her by your great-grandmother in San Luis Potosí, just before Mama Novia died." He pasted a smile on his face. "You know, San Luis

Potosí, where Mama Novia comes from, where she returned to die, was a very important city, Lucy. It was the capital of Mexico, not once, but twice in its history."

Lucy said nothing, stared fixedly at the cameo in the palm of her hand.

Flix felt a sudden rush of anxiety. He had to stop himself from leaning toward her; he did not want to alarm her. "It's beautiful, no? Do you like it? It comes from your mother with love." That last part was untrue. St. Vincent had enjoined Flix from telling his sister anything about her daughter other than that she was alive and well. Marilena had given the heirloom to him years ago in hopes that it would encourage him to get married.

"My mother never loved me," Lucy said without taking her eyes from the cameo.

Flix felt that sick feeling in the pit of his stomach again. His heart broke, both for his sister and for his niece.

"What has happened to you, Lucy?" The question was out of his mouth before he could stop it. He was sure he'd made a terrible mistake, that she would stand up and walk away, but he was wrong.

She looked up at him. Her coffee-colored eyes were clear as a spring brook, and there was an animation behind them, the sign of a mind at work without being dulled insensate by chemical cocktails.

"You wouldn't believe me if I told you, *Tío*."

Tío. She called him Uncle. "I want to know, *guapa*. Why don't you try me?"

This produced in her the barest hint of a smile. "I remember how you used to call me *guapa*."

"Because that's what you always were to me—what you still are—beautiful."

"Yes, well—" her eyes clouded over, the hint of a smile fleeing for its life, "nothing beautiful happened to me."

"Tell me."

"What's wrong with your right shoulder, *Tío*?"

He smiled inwardly; it was a good sign that she was noticing things outside herself. "I was shot."

"Shot?!" She was clearly shocked. "Why?"

"I was overseas, in a war zone. It's part of my job."

"To get shot?"

"Possibly, but hopefully not. This time something went wrong."

"You're okay?"

"I'm fine, *guapa*. Really. I'm at the end of rehab. I'll be deployed within a day or so."

"For how long?"

"Not long. These deployments are usually forty-eight hours or so." Short but intense, he thought. "When I get back I'll take you out of here. We'll go together to see your mother."

"No!" Lucy closed the cameo in her fist. "I don't want to see her."

"But why not?"

Lucy looked away. The fist enclosing the cameo trembled perceptibly.

"But, *guapa*, she loves you."

Lucy's head swung back, and she looked at him with eyes brimming with tears. "Did you ever ask yourself why I ran away?"

"You fell into a bad crowd, got hooked on drugs, and—"

"*¡Basta!*" she cried. Enough! "She told you that."

"Yes."

"It's a lie. The truth . . ." Lucy shook her head back and forth like an animal caught in a trap about to chew off its paw. "The truth . . ."

"Lucy—"

"The truth will kill me."

Now Flix did lean forward, took her free hand in his, noted how damp it was with cold sweat. "*Guapa*, this is me. I could never be there for you when you were young, but I'm here now. I won't let anything happen to you. This I swear with all my heart and soul. Please tell the truth now. You must see that keeping it to yourself is what's killing you."

Lucy stared at him with eyes swollen with tears and years of unknown heartbreak. "Maybe you're right, *Tío*. It's why I slipped into drugs, then fled the house." All at once, her fingers gripped his with a terrible ferocity. "It was . . ." She choked, pulled back, and then with an enormous show of courage, pressed forward. "It was my father. Mama didn't protect me against him. She knew all about it. She *knew* and did nothing to protect me."

"Wait a minute, your father abused you and my sister knew?"

Reacting to the shocked look on his face, she said, "She was terrified of him—and of you."

Flix found himself reeling. "Me?"

Lucy nodded. "She was afraid of what you'd do to him if she told you."

"Damn right. I would have—"

"And landed in the stockade? Court-martialed? Jailed for life?"

Lucy's voice sounded to him like the oracle of Tikal, her words like a chant or a prayer, as if it were coming from another plane of existence, one he could not ever have imagined until this dreadful moment. Not in *his* family. Never. "Aiii!" Flix clutched his head, which felt like it was about to explode.

"*Tío, por favor. Tío!*"

Setting aside the necklace, she pushed herself into his arms, holding him as he had wanted to hold her, comfort her, protect her. But how could you protect someone from the past? It was a task far beyond him. Still, they clung to each other like survivors of a shipwreck, which, in a very real sense, they were.

"She loved something about that shitbag, though God alone knows what it was," she whispered in his ear.

Flix knew she was right, but that knowledge only caused the pain to burrow deeper inside him, like a worm intent on feasting off him. In a whispered voice he did not recognize, he said, "What, *guapa*? What did he do?"

"We had a basement, do you remember?"

"Marilena said no one went down there. It was too damp."

"That's where he took me, most nights. He tied me up, but it wasn't what you think."

Lucy was shivering; she clung to him more tightly. Out of the corner of his eye, he noticed St. Vincent start toward them. His allotted time with Lucy was up, but he wasn't having any. He shot St. Vincent such a poisonous look that the man stopped in his tracks, retreated to his former post, but not before tapping his watch face.

Lucy was still whispering in his ear. "He had a stack of magazines he got through the mail. Japanese periodicals on Shibari, ritual rope bondage. Much later, I learned it's an art form in Japan, but my father had other uses for it in mind. He'd spend hours binding me, then he'd hang me from the ceiling, sometimes upside down, other times in a lotus position, still others with my arms and legs spread-eagled. By then, he was ready to burst." Her voice broke apart like a sheet of glass shattering. "He . . . was . . . like . . . a . . . demon—the devil himself." Each word was driven out of her as if it was her last breath.

She hung in his arms, limp and shivering. "But that wasn't the end of it. Then he started in on the photos—hundreds of them. He posted them on a Web site, where people paid to see me . . . like that. They even sent in suggestions they'd pay a premium price for. Naturally, my father liked that best."

Now St. Vincent was coming across the room, and by his grim expression and the firmness of his stride Flix knew there was nothing more he could do to hold him off.

"Time," St. Vincent said.

Lucy either didn't hear him or did not wish to hear him; she did not want to let go of her uncle.

"Listen, *guapa*, listen to me. You rest here for a while—a short while—and then I'll be back, okay?"

She wiped her eyes and nodded against his shoulder. She gathered up the necklace, gave it back to him, but she kept the box, carefully folding the wrapping. She placed it in the box, held it between her hands like a temple offering.

"I'll keep this," she said. "Okay?"

"Better than okay." He kissed her on both cheeks, then rose to his feet. A swell of great affection overcame him. He felt as if he had made a long, arduous climb with her.

She looked up at him with a tentative smile. "Come back for me, *Tío*."

"You have my word." He grinned. "*¡Hasta próxima, mi guapa!*"

"Look at him," Charlie exclaimed, paging through the surveillance photos on Whitman's mobile. "He's got the neck of a chicken!"

"Meet Ibrahim Mansour," Whitman said. "Our new target."

They were seated in Whitman's favorite diner, having breakfast. The place had the appearance of being from the 1930s, which was why Whit-man liked it.

"The only thing missing here," Charlie said, looking around as she handed him back his mobile across their plates of eggs and bacon, "is a juke playing 'Begin the Beguine.'"

He met her frank gaze. "'These Foolish Things,' more like it."

They ate in silence for a few minutes. The waitress came and refilled their coffee cups without being summoned. Whitman was a regular. The door opened, letting in the golden late-morning sunlight along with a young couple with their arms around each other.

"There but for fate go we," Charlie said.

Whitman strained and failed to read her inflection. She had always been something of an enigma to him. Just one of the things he loved about her, one of the things that had driven him away.

"We deploy in thirty-six hours," he said.

His change of direction was obvious, not to mention unsurprising. She decided to go with the flow. "To take apart a soft target."

Whitman went back to his eggs. His bacon was already gone.

"She's better, yes?" St. Vincent said as he walked with Flix out of the Bethesda Institute of Mary Immaculate.

There was no sign of Sister Margaret, or anyone else for that matter, out in the semicircular driveway. Just St. Vincent's SUV and an ambulance. Beyond, the staff parking lot was all but full.

"You'll take good care of her until I get back, no more drugs," Flix said. It wasn't a question.

"That's part of our bargain." St. Vincent stopped by the side of the SUV. "Just make sure you fulfill your end of it."

"No need to remind me," Flix said.

St. Vincent opened the passenger door and Flix ducked his head, about to climb in.

"Watch out!" St. Vincent said as he plunged the needle of a syringe into the side of Flix's neck.

St. Vincent caught Flix as he collapsed. His driver was already at his side. Together, they hauled Flix to the rear of the ambulance. St. Vincent slammed his hand against the double doors. They opened, revealing a pair of young men in nurses' uniforms. They took possession of Flix, transferring him to the collapsible gurney inside.

"He's all yours, Doc," St. Vincent said when Paulus Lindstrom's pale face appeared in the doorway.

"What did you inject him with?" Lindstrom asked.

"A synthetic form of curare concocted by our Psy-Ops division."

"What if he remembers the needle?" Lindstrom asked in a none-too-steady voice.

"If he remembers anything it'll be me shouting 'Watch out!' When he wakes up, the nurse in his room at Walter Reed will assure him that he hit his head while getting into the SUV and suffered a mild concussion. End of story."

"You'd better be right."

"Doc, I'm always right. Always." He gestured toward Flix's supine form. "You'd better get a move on. You have twenty-six hours until he's scheduled to report to Universal Security for the final team briefing prior to deployment. He needs to be mission-ready before then."

Lindstrom glanced nervously from his patient back to St. Vincent. "As I told you, we're only beginning to move on to human trials."

"And as I told you, I want one of those trials in the field."

Lindstrom winced. "It's too soon."

"We've already been through this argument. The security of Mobius may have been compromised, Doctor. It is imperative that the trials be accelerated. This is the ideal way to do that."

"There is nothing ideal about what you are ordering me to do." Lindstrom looked like he was about to have a stroke. "Remember the monkey that tore its face off."

"That was a fluke." St. Vincent's voice was calm, reassuring. "You said so yourself."

Lindstrom licked his lips. "As long as you understand the risks. I can't be held responsible."

"If not you, Doctor, who?" St. Vincent slammed the door in Lindstrom's ashen face, and the ambulance drove off to its date with destiny.

What both Lindstrom and St. Vincent failed to notice was Lucy's face, peering out of one of the front ground-floor windows. Having asked to use the toilet, she had adroitly sidestepped Sister Margaret and all the other sisters, making her way to what was quaintly called the parlor within whose thick drawn-back drapes she stood while observing what had happened to her uncle. It was impossible to hear the conversation between the two men, but she didn't need to. She knew Flix was being taken to a place he did not want to go.

PART TWO

WAR

Resolute imagination is the beginning of all magical operations.

—Paracelsus

14

The Red Rover team, thirty thousand feet over the Atlantic, was LIM.

Any other team Universal Security Associates put in the field would have been transported via either commercial flight or small cargo trans-shippers. Red Rover was special, and so they were embedded in a cadre of the 26th Marine Expeditionary Unit ground combat element.

In other words, Red Rover was LIM: Lost in the Military. There was no trace of them having left the States, nor would there be. There would be no trace of them when, in approximately twelve hours, they were on the ground in Djibouti. The Horn of Africa was one of the major staging areas for Marine ops. Its forward posts were manned by members of Marine Intelligence, who worked around the clock trying to make sense of Babel, otherwise known as Middle East chaos.

The C-17 Air Force transport was loud, uncomfortable, and shook like an old man with palsy. Its interior looked like a warehouse. Men were crowded in on either side with boxes and crates lashed down with thick netting in the center area.

Flix fell asleep almost as soon as they took off. To Whitman, his wound seemed to have taken more out of him than he would have expected, going by the chart he had purloined on his first visit to Walter Reed. The rest will do him good, he thought as he turned his attention back to Charlie.

"I find it interesting that Cutler hired me," she said, automatically adjusting the timber of her voice to compensate for the ambient noise.

"Why do you say that? You earned your way onto the team."

"Nevertheless he clearly hated my guts."

She and Whitman were sitting close together on utilitarian pull-down seats, and the upside of the clamor was that no one was going to overhear their conversation.

"That's a bit of an exaggeration," Whitman said.

"Don't bullshit a bullshitter." She cocked a thumb in Flix's direction across the fuselage from them. "Not to mention your friend Orteño there. I thought his eyes were going to bug out of his head when he saw me." She cocked her head. "Did you for some reason give him the impression I was male?"

"I may have. I don't recall."

Her laugh was mocking. "Please. You *recall* everything—the good, the bad, and the ugly." She shrugged. "Anyway, I don't think Orteño approves of your choice in armorer."

"Wait until he sees what you've brought along. And call him Flix; it'll help smooth things over."

"Aye, aye, Captain."

Again that mocking tone, which he chose to ignore. "I've got some news for you regarding our brief. I'm ripping it up."

"What? Why are you telling me this now?"

"Our last brief was compromised. The target knew we were coming and was prepared."

"A leak."

Whitman nodded. "Most likely in NSA, but I can't rule out Universal Security. Which is why I waited until we were in the air. The security on a C-17 is tighter than a duck's ass."

"Then Mansour is out."

Whitman nodded again. "You're right, Ibrahim Mansour does have a chicken neck. He's also a minor player—very minor."

"Then why have we been sent to kill him?"

"My opinion? It could have been almost anyone. Since there's a crisis brewing in Lebanon and he's in Beirut he was a logical choice. As a target, he was supposed to make sense to us."

"But it doesn't to you."

"It doesn't matter. I think the Mansour brief is misdirection."

"From what?"

"Red Rover's original target: Seiran el-Habib, a very big fish in the terrorism world. Cutler told me that NSA had lost track of el-Habib, that he was no longer at the villa in Western Pakistan we were sent to. Turns out Cutler lied. El-Habib is exactly where he was."

"Why would Cutler lie?"

"Because the NSA, who pays all our salaries, told him to."

Whitman could see that he had piqued her interest.

"Which means what?"

"That we've been caught between the cogs of a government machine that doesn't know what it wants. NSA is like a child with ADHD. Every other minute there's a potential disaster that needs attending to, so the one before is dropped by the wayside. No matter the crisis du jour, the danger posed by Seiran el-Habib is still acute, maybe more so now that time has passed. Since NSA is running around like a chicken with its head cut off I figure it's up to us to make the decision."

"Without anyone knowing. Without sanction. What will Cutler say?"

"Fuck Cutler. He's become another cog in the great machine. He's lost his sense of purpose."

"There must be another way."

"If you think of it between now and the time we land," Whitman said, "let me know."

Hemingway came out of his inner office as soon as Julie reported for work the next morning, an open file in his hands. "Lock the outer door."

When she had done so, he lifted an arm. "Sit."

Again, she complied silently. Like a dog in front of its master, she thought.

"Report, please," Hemingway said, standing over her like a university professor.

"Sydney is a dead end," she said.

Hemingway closed the file. "Nothing's a dead end until I say it is."

"Here's what Sydny knows."

"You mean Louise Kapok."

"By whatever name you wish to call her," she said. "She thinks Whitman's name is Adam. He told her he's a skip tracer. That's all she wrote."

Hemingway glared at her as if this dead end was her fault. She instinctively felt cowed, but then she remembered what Whitman had told her. She refused to be intimidated. Instead, she employed the sleight of hand he had suggested. She gave Hemingway her most seductive smile.

"Anything else on your mind, sir?"

Immediately, he recoiled. "That will be all," he said in a tone she had never heard before, and scuttled back into his office.

The sound of his door slamming behind him brought her an immense measure of satisfaction.

Trey Hartwell was a calligrapher, a cartographer, an illuminator of medieval manuscripts, as well as an antiquarian bookseller. His two main pleasures were ferreting out rare books and sharpening his cryptography. His shop, above which he lived in three-story splendor, was a well-known lair for like-minded individuals—wealthy men of impeccable breeding. It was located in a discreet town house on Dupont Circle. The town house was composed of limestone and was designed by Stanford White; it had a history all its own, which was why Hartwell had bought it twenty years ago, when such town houses could be had for something less than a Saudi prince's fortune.

Over the years Hartwell had amassed a fortune that rivaled that of any Saudi prince. His money, however, did not come from the antiquarian book business, which was not only a niche market but a variable one, as both books and their authors rose in and out of favor like a series of incoming waves. But he had no reason for concern. Other avenues of revenue had opened their arms to him. Like Aladdin in the cave of secrets, he kept finding openings, as he had ever since he had met Preach.

Hartwell had been a sickly boy—pale and weak. He was also short and overweight—the perfect prey for bullies tormented by their own inadequacies. Of course, as bullies will with uncanny accuracy, they found the perfect name for him: Humpty Dumpy. He knew them, intimately, but he could never figure out how to deal with them. Until the tall thin man with the shock of white hair and the piercing blue eyes happened along during the last of his regular street beat downs, ugly encounters that began with his tormentors surrounding him, quick-marching him to a deserted section of the railway yards. Then the taunts would start, proceed to filthy epithets, and end with a barrage of clenched fists striking him over and over. "You go to anyone, Humpty Dumpy, even your mama," he'd be reminded by Cary, the biggest and meanest, always the instigator, as he lay bruised and half-conscious, "and you're a dead fucking duck. My promise to you, dick-face." Laughter, receding across the gleaming tracks while the wind rustled the leaves in the trees on the other side of the dilapidated fence.

This particular afternoon, however, was different. High school had let out for the steamy Mississippi summer. The leaden air was filled with barrages of insects, loud as Piper Cub engines.

He was on his back, his ribs and kidneys aching, when he heard a commanding voice say, "Get up."

He looked between his tormentors' legs and saw a tall, thin man with a shock of white hair and piercing blue eyes. The man was looking right at him and addressed him directly: "Get up, you fool!"

No one else appeared to have heard him. Trey didn't think they'd let him up, but, oddly, they did, backing up a pace as he struggled to his feet. They laughed, though, as he staggered on his sore and swollen left knee.

"Now hit Cary," the man said.

Trey glanced at him, between the bodies of the boys surrounding him.

"You know you want to."

Trey did want to, but he was afraid. He knew he couldn't hurt Cary, and the beating that would result would be horrific.

"Nothing to be afraid of," the man said, as if he had climbed inside Trey's head. And when Trey still hesitated: "Son, do you want to be a victim all your life? That's the path you're on, you know."

Suddenly, Trey was filled with a violent rage. Curling his fingers into a fist, he struck Cary in the center of his face. To his astonishment, there was a spurt of blood. Cary went down and stayed down. Silence in the circle around him. The laughter died in their throats. Then they broke and ran, leaving Trey alone, standing over the fallen bully.

The man strode closer, to stand only paces away from Trey. "How did that feel?"

Trey stared down at Cary, then at his balled fist, the knuckles spattered with blood. "Good," he said. "It felt good."

"Sure it did. Now tell the boy what's on your mind."

Trey bent down. His heart was hammering against his ribs. His throat was engorged with sick emotion. "If you come near me again . . ." he stopped; he couldn't go on.

"That's all right," the man said gently. "Start over."

Trey swallowed hard, almost choked on his saliva. "If you come near me again, I'll . . . hit you."

"Try again," the man said, so gently this time it might have been the wind skating along the tracks.

Trey's cheeks puffed out. He was sweating with the effort not to vomit. "If you come near me again," he said to Cary, "I'll kill you."

Then, unable to bear the sight of his triumph another second, he turned away, only to face the man who introduced himself as Preach.

"Do you want that strength, that power," Preach said, "even when I'm not here?"

Trey nodded his head. There wasn't even a moment's hesitation.

"All it takes is time," Preach said. "Come with me."

"But what about my parents?"

Preach smiled. "They won't even know you're gone."

And, amazingly, they hadn't.

Hartwell had cause to think of his first encounter with Preach as he closed his shop promptly at six o'clock. Normally, he would spend two hours at the martial arts club, as he did five days a week, but this evening was reserved for the Alchemists. He was fit and strong now, in both mind and body—that was Preach's doing, as was so much else in his life.

He opened the locked door at the rear of his shop, trotted down the stairs. Through another door lay a square anteroom, lined with antique books, all valuable, several immensely so. As he always did, he paused, running his hand over the rough cover of one of these. It was very old, the cover made of the cured skin of an animal—mammal, amphibian, lizard, it was impossible to tell, the march of ages having worn away the specificity. It was Trey's most precious and beloved book. He knew it by heart. One could say it served him as a talisman.

Beyond the anteroom was the much larger meeting chamber, filled with a round polished wood table and seven straight-back cherrywood chairs. Ranged around the buff-colored walls were woodcut portraits of the first ten American presidents.

At precisely 6:25 his compatriots began to arrive. They did so via a rear entrance accessed by a steep flight of stairs that led down to the basement of the town house. In all, six men arrived, all within fifteen minutes of one another, which meant that by seven p.m. the full complement of Alchemists had been achieved. Punctuality was not merely a duty, but a moral imperative with each of the seven. This rectitude was but a single example of their determination to be true to the Alchemists' motto: *Uno Animo, Uno Voluntatis*—One Mind, One Will.

At the stroke of seven the men, who had been standing still and silent, their spines as erect as the chair backs, took their appointed seats in a soft rustle of expensive suit fabrics. It was a sound not unlike the susurrus of cicadas at twilight in high summer. In front of each member was a file in a black jacket. A diagonal red stripe ran across the upper right-hand corner, denoting the content as ultra-secret. These files were never taken out of the town house, and at the end of each meeting where they appeared they were put through a shredder, the shreds then incinerated.

With the flat of his hand on the tabletop, Trey Hartwell called the meeting to order. At table, all members were known by noms de guerre, as they referred to them, taken from the names of past American presidents. Hartwell was Madison. "Going forward," he said, "if we are to gain complete control of this country's military-industrial complex, we have to provide a service that is capable of winning any kind of war anywhere in the world. As we know from painful experience that's not going to come from shock and awe, missiles, carpet bombing, or any of the other mechanized modes of modern warfare. Against terrorists and insurgents they're all ineffective and outmoded. We're facing a foe that is not afraid to die. This is asymmetrical combat at its most extreme. We must reply in kind, fight fire with fire. We create our own answer—the only answer that makes sense—an answer that will win us the wars overseas: weaponized warriors that leave conventional soldiers in the dust. With extraordinary power, no sense of remorse, prepared to die each time they are deployed.

"These warriors will not be soldiers who are weak-willed and return home only to be a burden on this country and its citizens. When they return home they will be ready for another tour of duty, and another and another, without end. We have taken a page from Putin's book—rounding up criminals, sociopaths, the disaffected, disenfranchised, and the delusional—and have gone a giant step further. The Mobius Project will transform these misfits into the mighty fighting machines of tomorrow, enhanced warriors who will bring us victory wherever they are deployed, in international hot spots with missions whose objectives can adapt to the rapidly changing political environment. And when that happens we will have created an entirely new method of waging war, one that can bring us victory after victory without the humiliation of even a single defeat."

Every member of the Alchemists nodded his head in agreement. So far, this was all known to them, but they were aware that it was but prologue to the news that was to come.

"Now that Mobius has moved into human trials," Hartwell said in the deep, sonorous voice of a Southern statesman, "I believe it would behoove us to consider reopening the Well."

The bombshell dropped, his voice was quickly damped down, the soundproofing swallowing whole all murmur, no matter how minute. There would be no echoes in this room, no matter how heated the conversation became.

"Now hold on a minute," Jefferson said. He was a slim, silver-haired gentlemen with keen eyes and a Boston Brahmin's accent. He had made his fortune several times over, first in insurance, then real estate, and latterly, in venture capital. "We shut that place down for a number of very sound reasons, not the least was survival."

"Agreed," Van Buren said in his clipped Midwestern accent. "The Well became the most dangerous place on earth. It was our personal black site, where we conducted articulated renditions of foreign and domestic terrorists in order to glean knowledge for future projects."

"And it was shut down," Jefferson said, "to ensure we wouldn't get caught up in the misguided congressional witch hunt against legal torture of enemy combatants."

"Everything Congress does is misguided," Van Buren said, which brought knowing chuckles and guffaws all around.

"That was why all documentation amassed during its existence was destroyed," Adams interjected, putting an end to the levity. He was a tall, tanned, sandy-haired man from Tennessee who had founded one of D.C.'s most powerful lobbyist firms. He shuddered visibly. "Never again."

"You're far too squeamish." Washington had a narrow, angular face with thick salt-and-pepper hair that came down over the tops of his ears.

"Squeamish is one thing," Jackson, an ex-military man with a tactical bent, said. "Danger is quite another. We are engaged in a precarious situation as it is. Reopening the Well will only add to the potential peril."

"I disagree," Hartwell countered. "We embarked on Mobius with a specific goal in mind. Our handpicked emissary has spent months negotiating with the Iraqi Kurds."

"Preach!" It was like a mini-explosion coming from Luther St. Vincent, known around the table as Washington.

"There's no need to get into that at this stage," Hartwell said with a quick flicker of his eyes toward Monroe, whose expression was, as usual, entirely neutral. Trey shrugged mentally. Better this way, he supposed. He raised a hand, directed himself to St. Vincent. Best to throw him a bone here, lest he begin his Preach rant again. No one wanted that. "By all means, Washington, pick up the thread. You lit the fire."

St. Vincent settled himself, arranging his tie as a peacock will show off its tail, and Hartwell knew he had made the right decision. Preach had taught him about decisions. *These decisions,*" Preach had said, "*will lead us into a newer, better world.*"

"These men—these warriors we are creating—" St. Vincent said, "will stand by the Kurds to defend the oil fields in northern Iraq, which are in Kurdish territory. They will help the Kurds stand up to and repel the Shi'ites, and now the scourge of IS, who have already taken brave American lives."

"Islamic State," Hartwell said softly, as if prompting an ADHD student.

"IS, right. This terrorist group is an unacceptable disease that must, at all costs, be excised from the corpus of the world." St. Vincent nodded. They were in his bailiwick now. No one within the Alchemists knew as much about IS as he did. "Seven years, that's how long Mobius has been in gestation. Our aim, as I said, was to take control of the oil fields in northern Iraq. To understand completely we must go back in time to before this country's invasion of Iraq. There *were* weapons of mass destruction inside Iraq—the reports were correct, but Saddam knew nothing about them. They were brought in by our people, controlled by our people masquerading as Saddam's elite forces for the benefit of reconnaissance drone flights. The moment Cheney, Wolfowitz, and our talking head neo-cons pushed Bush into believing he had no other choice but to invade Iraq, we spirited them out of the country.

"The result you know. Our people played on the arrogance of the high-level neo-cons so that they never gave a thought to what must actually happen in the aftermath. They assumed a nice tidy pro-Western government would be set up by the grateful populace, which Democratic elections would ensure. And the enormous cost of the war would be paid for by Iraqi oil. That was a pipe dream. None of it happened, as you all know. The chaos that resulted was just what we had envisioned, just what we wanted."

St. Vincent paused to open a bottle of water and take several sips before continuing. "But, frankly, I had concerns that the chaos of tribal warfare would not reach the Kurds, would not threaten their territory. My fear was that they would not solicit our help.

"Then everything changed. My backdoor agreement with Universal Security Associates bore fruit. One of King Cutler's foreign assets told him about a newly forming group known as ISIS, Islamic State in Iraq and al-Sham, now simply known as Islamic State. This interested me greatly for two reasons: first, ISIS's stated aim was to absorb Iraq, Syria, Jordan, the Levant, Palestine, and Israel into a radical Islamic version of the ancient land known as al-Sham. Second, ISIS was too radical even for al-Qaeda. Even at that time, its leaders had distanced the organization from ISIS." St. Vincent shook his head. "Still, I had no way of knowing the steps ISIS would take in order to achieve a goal that, frankly, appeared far beyond their grasp.

"Cutler's foreign asset had captured a member of ISIS. He was going to be executed, as an example to ISIS. Instead, I had Cutler fly him back here. I myself escorted him under heavy guard to the Well. But this man was entirely different from any other terrorist we had renditioned. The interrogator will usually appeal to the prisoner's rational side—the one invested in his self-interest. In other words, saving his life. This method is successful nine out of ten times—it's simply a matter of how long the prisoner can hold out. But this man had no rational side; he seemingly had no interest in staying alive. He was, to put a fine point on it, completely emotional."

"And that's when you brought Whitman in." No one used Whitman's Alchemist's name anymore.

"Whitman was our best interrogator at the Well, this much I'll admit," St. Vincent said. "To make a long story short, he got what we needed out of this prisoner, though, at the end, the man was scarcely recognizable as a human being. We had to dump him down the *cenote* in pieces. How Whitman accomplished his task is a mystery even to me. The point is, with the intel he extracted we were able to intervene in the formation of ISIS. Through third and fourth parties, we were able to make contact with them—provide them with funding and tactical support; we were able to accelerate their timetable for becoming a force to be reckoned with in Iraq."

Trey was smiling. "A new war, with an enemy that even our dovish president dare not ignore."

"Neither can the Kurds," St. Vincent said. "They're terrified, and rightly so. ISIS is ruthless, unyielding, impossible to negotiate with. And they are cruel beyond human understanding. You've all seen the most recent videos coming from Iraq and Syria. These people cannot even be classified as human beings."

St. Vincent rubbed his hands together. "And so to the fruits of Mobius. The troops we are creating are afraid of nothing and no one; they cannot be intimidated. They will enable the Kurds to do what they have never been able to do before: carve out their own sovereign state within Iraq. In return, we send in our people to run the oil fields, and we reap the enormous windfall from those rich wells."

"This is irrefutable," Hartwell said. "Mobius was born to make money. Incalculable amounts. After all, the Alchemists are a profit center: we make money from war. And this fucking president has been making our lives miserable. No more. Our manufactured war in Iraq will have the added benefit of putting an end to his mealy-mouthed peacemaking. The profits from our holdings in military hardware, aerospace, metals mining, and high-tech industrials will balloon, and, God willing, keep on ballooning."

Washington nodded. "Wisely spoken. However, it seems to me, though not expressed verbally, that Mobius's inevitable missteps would necessitate reopening the Well, as Mr. Madison has wisely suggested."

Monroe, his expression neutral, his thin lips pressed tightly together, as usual, kept his own council. He was an enigmatic figure, to be sure: African American, charismatic, deeply conservative, and the only member to feel the use of the presidential pseudonyms at table to be childish and unnecessary. He was also possibly the smartest mind in the room, which was why he frightened Hartwell, a man not prone to fear on any level. Monroe, a behavioral scientist by training, a CEO of a large multinational company by trade, rejected all overtures at friendship. He seemed to be averse to any form of intimacy, no matter how small or sincerely offered. On the other hand, Hartwell mused, since the Well was his brainchild and since he had run it for the entire length of its first life, perhaps that was hardly surprising. Hartwell knew that Monroe harbored a resentment against the other members for shutting down his operation. He himself had stood with Monroe, but the two of them were outvoted. Hartwell kept a keen weather eye on him, wanting to see his reaction to its resurrection.

Van Buren, a raven-haired captain of the shipping industry with pale skin, nodded. "I, for one, wish to have nothing further to do with it."

Adams, along with the others, looked to Madison. "Why in God's name should we reopen it now?"

"The human trials," Washington said.

"Indeed." With a congenial nod to him, Madison said, "Gentlemen, please open the file in front of you to the first page."

The six men did, almost in unison, and almost in unison four of them gasped, for there staring up at them was a color photo of the chimpanzee who, under the influence of Mobius's implants, had torn off his own face. Neither Washington nor Monroe showed any reaction whatsoever.

"The failed test subjects must be disappeared without a trace." Hartwell waited a moment or two to allow the shock to subside, then said, "All in favor of reopening the Well under the supervision of Mr. Monroe please indicate with an 'Aye.'"

After the smallest hesitation, seven ayes were uttered. Hartwell saw the briefest flicker of a smile animate Monroe's face. Relief and fear struggled for supremacy inside him.

15

The morning sun cast long shadows across Djibouti. Deplaning with the Marine cadre, the Red Rover team crossed the tarmac and, without further ado, climbed aboard a twin-engine jet as sumptuous as the C-17 had been Spartan.

"One thing's for sure," Flix said, checking it out. "Cutler didn't order this up for us."

"Who did?" Charlie asked as they seated themselves in the wide, butter-soft leather seats.

"Friend of mine," Whitman said.

"When can I meet this mystery man?" Charlie said.

Whitman gave her a look, and there the topic stopped dead in its tracks.

A uniform from immigration came on board just before they took off, but all he was interested in was baksheesh, which he came away with in spades. When they were airborne a flight attendant in a tight-fitting jacket and short skirt took their drinks order and told them breakfast would be served in thirty minutes.

Whitman turned to Orteño, "How you doing, m'man?"

"Tolerably well." Flix looked at Charlie, then back to Whitman. "I'm a little put off by this sudden change in plan. Does Cutler know about this?"

"It was all planned," Whitman lied.

"Then why wasn't I told about it?"

"Security. Cutler doesn't want a repeat and neither do I."

Flix's eyes switched to Charlie again. "You know about this?"

Her gaze held his challenging one without even the hint of a flinch. "I found out the same time you did. I assume it was all between Whit and Cutler."

"Whit, is it?" Flix picked at his nails. "Little soon for that, no, *chica*?"

"I'm your armorer," Charlie said with more than a trace of steel. "I'm not even *chica* to my friends."

"Wrong friends," Flix muttered, but his eyes slid down to his nails.

Whitman rose, slid into the seat next to Orteño. "What's up with you, *compadre*?"

"Nothing." Flix looked out the Perspex window.

"Doesn't sound like nothing to me," Whitman said softly. "You've been kind of spooky ever since you reported for this brief."

"Huh! Really."

"Hey, man, how long we know each other? How many briefs have we been on? How many times have we saved each other's life? Something's wrong, I can feel it. I mean, are we friends or are we not friends?"

Flix said nothing. The flight attendant brought breakfast, which the three of them ate in silence. Not until they were finished and the trays had been taken away did Flix turn to Whitman.

"You're not gonna give up on this, are you?"

Whitman bared his teeth. "Nope."

Flix heaved a deep sigh. "All right, fuck it." He paused, appearing to be ordering his thoughts. "Okay, you remember me telling you about my niece Lucy? I showed you her picture?"

"Sure. The runaway."

Flix nodded. "She's been found."

"That's great news."

"No, it's not, Whit. The cops have her on felony drug possession charges."

"No problem. I'll get Cutler to—"

"She crossed state lines."

"Ah. So the FBI is involved."

Flix hung his head. "I went to see her. She hardly knew who I was. It was so bad, I haven't had the heart to tell Marilena. I mean, what's the point? She's already had her heart broken once."

Whitman's heart went out to Flix, but at the same time something nagged at the back of his mind. Why during this whole story had Flix not looked at him? He was staring between his feet as if reading from a text written on the carpet. Whitman couldn't put his finger on just what, but something was wrong, something Flix didn't want to talk about.

"*Siento mucho, compadre*," Whitman said with a pat on Flix's good shoulder. "Get some rest, okay?"

Flix nodded, but didn't lift his head.

When Whitman slipped into his seat beside Charlie, she whispered, "What's with your pal there?"

Whitman looked over to where Flix was holding his head in his hands. "Damned if I know."

"Well, you'd best find out before we hit enemy territory," she said. "A team member who doesn't have his eye on the ball is very likely to get us all killed."

"Luther St. Vincent continues to be a problem," Valerie said into her mobile, as she strolled through a park in Anacostia on her lunch break. She was far enough from Cutler's office to assure her of anonymity.

"Enlighten me," Preach said.

That was a joke. It was Preach who had taught her enlightenment when she was just a little girl. She took a bite of her hot dog, bare as a man coming out of the shower. "Luther St. Vincent is like a maddened pitbull."

Preach laughed. "Just so."

The park was a grubby place, filled with sand and grit and the detritus of human beings who took no notice of their immediate environment. They strolled amid blighted trees, passing men and women of uncertain age slumped on benches, insensate to the outside world.

"I'm imagining me here," Valerie said, "on one of these benches, sad and wasted."

"What's the point?" Preach had instructed her to call him from this park; he knew the point, he just wanted her to say it.

"A lesson in humility," Valerie said.

Preach grunted. "You should be more interested in the lesson Luther St. Vincent wants to teach you."

"Like what? When it comes to NSA policy, Luther St. Vincent is it. As head of Directorate N, he's got the ear of not only the national security adviser but POTUS as well. The two of them dote on his words—they rely on him absolutely. What Luther St. Vincent says goes, no questions asked. His intervention in Mobius puts him in direct opposition to Hemingway. And we're caught in the middle."

"Which is where we want to be," Preach said. "It was important that I know when Luther decided to make his move."

When, not *if.* The difference wasn't lost on Valerie. "St. Vincent has already done damage. Paulus was a nervous wreck when he showed up at my house."

"And he's staying there. This was anticipated. Make him comfortable. I want him where you can keep an eye on him. I want him close to you."

"I don't think that will be a problem."

"See that it isn't," Preach said in that tone of voice she had quickly learned brooked no contradiction.

DARPA was in a constant state of modified lockdown, as secure as Fort Knox. Nevertheless, even in a facility where secretive projects were as common as houseflies, there were three areas within it so restricted almost no one had access. Almost. Paulus Lindstrom was in charge of one of these. A magnetic chip embedded in the pad of his left forefinger and an iris scanner were employed to gain access.

Lindstrom entered and immediately stepped into an ultrasonic cleaning chamber. The outer door closed, a red light switched to blue and the inner door slid open. He went through, into the heart of the Mobius Project.

The laboratory was windowless, the frigid air constantly cleaned, filtered for microbes, and recirculated. It was large, high ceilinged, and compartmentalized into four discreet areas, Blue, Green, Yellow, and Red. Lindstrom had two assistants: Ben and Jerry. The jokes around the confluence of their names had long gone stale and now were never mentioned. In the early days, either Ben or Jerry would bring in ice cream, but those days were gone, too.

Maybe they had ended when the first chimp had torn off its face, for, contrary to what Lindstrom had told St. Vincent, there had been more than one simian subject to end its life in this grotesque fashion. Lindstrom had told St. Vincent what he wanted to hear and, in so doing, had descended into an entirely new level of hell, one that Dante would not recognize.

It had never occurred to him that St. Vincent would want to try out Mobius in the field at this far too early stage. Progress, as all scientists knew, was not achieved in a straight line. It was, in its way, akin to psychiatry, where it was often one step forward, two steps back, or, if you were exceedingly fortunate, two steps forward and one back. Those who stood outside the laboratory, who had no knowledge of or interest in the scientific method, could not understand. What they understood—what they wanted—were results. Nothing else interested them. This was why he had lied to St. Vincent. The idea of his funding being cut was intolerable. But now he had sent a human being into the field, his mind altered by the Mobius implants.

God have mercy on his soul, Lindstrom thought as he nodded good morning to his assistants. Ben and Jerry were already busy in Green, prepping the first official human subjects for the Mobius implants. Ben and Jerry had had nothing to do with the male subject St. Vincent had provided Lindstrom, who had remained anonymous, referred to by St. Vincent, and now thought of by Lindstrom, simply as Alpha. "For your own protection, Doctor," St. Vincent had said, though Lindstrom was disinclined to believe him. This had less to do with any sixth sense toward humans—Lindstrom's condition made it nearly impossible for him to read human emotions—than his habit of believing all people he disliked were liars. Valerie would have recognized this as another facet of Lindstrom's childish behavior, and she would have been right. However, in this instance it served him in good stead. St. Vincent had nothing positive in mind for Mobius. Such was the nature of Lindstrom's brain that it never occurred to him that nothing good could ever have come from a project like Mobius to begin with.

The idea behind Mobius was, at its root, simple enough, and had more to do with the psychology of the brain than it did with any scientific breakthrough. In fact, it had come to Lindstrom, like a bolt out of the blue, when he was reading an account of a deeply charismatic homicidal maniac who somehow persuaded a woman and her ten-year-old daughter to come home with him. Again, inexplicably, he had persuaded the mother to allow him to sexually assault the daughter. All of this, though terribly sordid, was, sadly, not so very uncommon. What struck him, however, was the fact that the maniac had stood before a full-length mirror and watched himself and his victim as he penetrated her from behind.

This set in motion a thread of thought in Lindstrom's mind. One of his college professors had posited that the human brain sees the world in two ways: real and unreal. When, for whatever reason, this dichotomy is interrupted, the brain veers off course. Fantasy becomes as real as reality. What the maniac was doing during his assault was trying to reassure himself that his actions were real and not a fantasy his mind had concocted. In other words, his connection with reality somehow had become disabled. He could no longer distinguish between cause and effect. His mind occupied a space outside that of his actions.

What would happen, Lindstrom had thought, if he could find a way to artificially induce this disconnect. He would thus create a man—or woman—without a moral center, someone who would commit any atrocity and not feel responsibility. This was the premise of Mobius and, to his credit, with triptyne Lindstrom had succeeded. But only up to a point. There were those pesky chimps for whom the disconnect was intolerable. They looked at themselves in their water bowl and did not know what they saw. Rather than live in that state, they ripped that unknown face off.

"All set, Doctor," Jerry said.

"The subjects' vitals are normal," Ben said.

"Then they're ready for Blue," Lindstrom said via an intercom.

He watched through a two-way mirror as his assistants led the subjects—one man, one woman—from Green to Blue. He had decided to use a male and a female because the success rate among female chimps was unaccountably higher than among males.

Ben and Jerry laid the two subjects facedown on operating tables set up in Blue, affixed oxygen masks so they wouldn't suffocate when sedated, then administered Propofol IV. After scrubbing his hands, wrists, and forearms, Lindstrom entered Blue to begin the procedure of implanting the triptyne into the place where the spine met the skull. The alkaloid had to be delivered in just the right way at just the right dose. From this moment on, every move, every decision was critical.

As he began work, Ben said, "A guy walks into a bar. There's nobody there except the bartender and a beautiful woman. The man says, 'I'm buying that woman a drink.' The bartender says, 'You don't want to do that. She's a lesbian.' The man says, 'I don't care.' After the woman gets the drink, she raises the glass to her benefactor. The man strolls over to her and says, 'Hi, I'm Bill Williams from Terre Haute. So how are things in Beirut?'"

Jerry almost doubled over in laughter. Not to be outdone, he said, "A boy catches his mom and dad having sex. He watches them for a moment, then asks them what they're doing. His dad replies, 'Making you a brother or sister.' The boy thinks a minute, then says, 'Do her doggy style; I want a puppy.'"

More guffawing and general hilarity ensued.

Lindstrom made a face. "I fail to see why you two feel the need to tell what I assume to be jokes while crucial matters are in progress."

"Tension," Jerry said.

Lindstrom's mind was firmly on the procedure. "What about it?"

"Sometimes it needs to be broken."

"Again, why?"

"Because it gets to be too much."

"You're in the wrong profession," Lindstrom said.

"Forget it, Jake," Ben said with a wry smile, "he's Chinatown."

Lindstrom didn't bother to ask who Jake was; he didn't care. He had other, more pressing matters to deal with, such as narrowing his focus. He did not want to think about who these subjects were, where they came from, how they were chosen, or what they had been told. As to the last, lies, he was certain. He kept his thoughts tightly concentrated as his hands went about their business. Advances in medicine would never have been possible without subjects such as these. They were part and parcel of history. As such they were no less heroic than the men and women in the Armed

Forces serving in battle zones overseas. If Mobius could shorten those battles by even a week, Lindstrom told himself, as the instruments he wielded penetrated skin and flesh, all sacrifices would be worth it.

"Doctor," Jerry said, serious at last, "are we going to give these subjects the polyprednaline tabs to take for the first ten days?"

"I don't think we have a choice." Lindstrom stanched a bit of bleeding with a sterile pad. "The polypred seemed to help in the final simian trial." Alpha had been given a ten-day supply with urgent instruction not to miss a dose.

"With all due respect, Doctor, it's too soon to tell."

Lindstrom lifted his head for a moment. "Get back to work, please, Jerry."

As Ben handed Lindstrom the syringe, Jerry switched on the music and the Beatles' "A Day in the Life" exploded through the operating theater. The volume made Lindstrom wince, but he said nothing. It was imperative to keep his assistants happy, as he had neither the time nor the inclination to train replacements. Plus which, he worried for their future if they ever did quit—a future that was sure to be determined by St. Vincent. He feared their future would be very short indeed.

16

Everyone was asleep, even the flight attendant. Charlie had fought sleep for as long as she could, then she, too, succumbed. Everyone was asleep, except for Whitman. He had noticed Flix surreptitiously swallow a pill before he sank back into his seat.

Whitman stole across the aisle and, kneeling, rummaged through Flix's pack until his fingers curled around a smooth cylinder. It was a pill container, made of brown plastic. Opening it, he shook out a couple of tablets, expecting a painkiller for Flix's headaches. They were a charcoal gray, unlike anything he'd ever seen before, but obviously a prescription medication. A typed label on the cylinder said: POLYPREDNALINE. TAKE TWO DAILY BY MOUTH, MORNING AND NIGHT, FOR TEN DAYS. What the hell was polyprednaline? Whitman wondered. According to the label the prescription had been filled by Valient Pharmacy on Connecticut Avenue. There was also a phone number.

A hand on his shoulder made him start. He turned to see Charlie standing over him.

"What the fuck are you doing?" she mouthed silently.

Whitman shoved the tabs back into the cylinder, replaced it in Flix's pack, and, rising, guided her to the rear of the plane. The galley was to their right, the toilet to their left. The flight attendant was sound asleep in her seat just in front of the closed door to the cockpit. Though they were alone, they stood very close together, speaking in whispers.

"I want to know what Flix is taking," he said. "Do you know what poly-prednaline is?"

"What do I look like, a pharmacist?"

Which gave Whitman the idea. He checked his watch, calculated where they were and backtracked the time in D.C. Just before five p.m. He pulled out his sat phone, dialed the number of Valient Pharmacy from memory. He waited patiently for someone to pick up, but got only a voice-mail message: "The pharmacy is closed at this time. Please call back during regular hours." If five in the afternoon wasn't regular hours, what was?

Utilizing the jet's Wi-Fi, he typed Valient's name and address into the Google page on his mobile's browser. Nothing. Then he brought up Google Earth, inputted the full address, watched as the globe of Earth spun until it honed in on the United States, then D.C. On Connecticut Avenue, he switched to street view, searching for the address. The program stopped in front of the storefront at the address on the medication container: it was Valient Dry Cleaners. "Special Orders Welcome," he read. Not as special as polyprednaline, he reckoned.

Charlie, witness to the search, said, "What the hell is going on?"

Whitman shook his head. "I wish I knew."

"We'd better keep an eagle eye on your *compadre* from now on."

"I'd trust Flix with my life."

"Commendable, but in this case irrelevant," Charlie said. "Is that man the Felix Orteño you knew?"

"You look like you've gained some much needed weight," St. Vincent said on his next visit to the Bethesda Institute of Mary Immaculate. "That's good."

"I'm feeling much improved." Lucy, having bribed one of the guards, had received advance notice of his visit, and had prepared herself. "Like a new woman."

"Even better." St. Vincent had not taken off his overcoat. His wrists lay on his knees, looking like weapons at rest.

They were in Lucy's room, she sitting on the edge of her bed, he on a chair he had turned around from its place by the desk. As protocol dictated, the door was open to the hallway behind.

"I imagine you'd rather be seeing your uncle," he said.

She cocked her head. "What gives you that idea?"

She could see that she had surprised him.

"Well, I don't know, he's family, after all."

"I hate his guts," Lucy said with no little venom. "I hate my mother."

Frown lines appeared on his forehead. "You can't mean that."

"If I had the chance I'd kill them both." She uttered this with a kind of chilling neutrality. "That clear enough for you?"

"No."

"My mother stood by while my father abused me over and over."

St. Vincent shook his head. "How could a father do that, Lucy?"

"You're a man. You tell me."

He sat for a moment, hands now clasped together, fingers intertwined, as if changing his aspect from inquisitional jailer to priestly confessor. "I have no answers for you. I'm not that kind of man."

His personality was that mercurial, a quality Lucy recognized and noted for future exploitation.

"I believe you, Lucy." His voice softened like butter on the dinner table. "I believe you would kill them."

An example, Lucy thought, of people believing what they want to believe. And she should know. There was a time when she was at war with those she had left behind, with those skunks and weasels around her. More significantly, she had been at war with herself. In her experience people fell into drugs because they were weak or unhappy, or both. That was why they could rarely get out of that hole: it felt too good in the place where the pain of the real world faded away.

That had not been Lucy's problem. She had had no problem. Her aim was to push herself as far as she could go, right to the edge of death, if need be. It was only in the fiercest crucible that absolute truth would emerge.

She had gone there. Now she was someone else, some other Lucy who had none of the former's hate and bitterness. She was no longer at war with herself, only with the people, like St. Vincent, bound and determined to use her for their own ends.

The state police finding her, forcing her to dry out, and here, the so-called shrinks, putting her on yet another drug cocktail to take the place of the one that had taken her apart, all that wasn't a mistake on her part. It had been time for her to return from the back of beyond. To her dismay, she had discovered that she could not do it herself. She needed help. Hence the police.

Being taken apart had revealed to her all her flaws, weaknesses, strengths, and beauty. She finally could embrace that beauty and not be afraid of it—afraid of where it might lead her, afraid of the false flattery that might force her down dark and twisted alleys. She had already visited those terrible places, and she had survived, though, it was true, in pieces. But she was whole now—better than whole, because now she could see in others her own strengths, flaws, and weaknesses. She could play off the strengths, work the flaws and weaknesses like "A Lil Mexican," as Mookey Baby rapped in such fine fashion.

She smiled at St. Vincent—the precise kind of smile she intuited he wanted from her. It was a form of restrained seduction—a come closer, but not too close, smile. He wouldn't want that; not yet, anyway. He was a man of great rectitude, a man who believed absolutely in what he did. He believed himself invulnerable to corruption, but it was clear to her that he had a great capacity for self-deception. His foundation, which he thought rock solid, was full of cracks; he was already thoroughly corrupted—his almost religious fervor had blinded him to the fact.

"It seems ages since I was taken seriously, Mr. St. Vincent," she said in her little girl voice.

"I take you seriously," St. Vincent said. "And it's fine if you call me Luther."

"You won't take offense."

He laughed. Lucy felt warm inside, like melting taffy. She had a strong suspicion that when you made a man like Luther St. Vincent laugh, you were inside his defenses.

———

Monroe should have been home with his wife and five children. Instead, he was seated in a central pew of his church, listening to the footsteps of God. The soft echoes of God's presence fell all around him like a velvet rain. It was Monroe's habit to come to church when he was distressed or overwhelmed by the minutia of life, not so much to pray, but to listen. It seemed to him that church was the only place where he was capable of listening these days.

The decision to reopen the Well weighed heavily on his mind. It was the right decision—he knew that as fact. Nevertheless, the Well was not a place one went to without trepidation. Even he, its creator, its guiding light, could not escape its dreadful spell. Now, here, in the presence of God, he needed to summon the strength required to once again crack open the doors to the underworld. Here, in church, he allowed his mind to drift.

Monroe came from a background that was as unusual as it was humble. His great-grandfather murdered first the black overseer on the plantation where he was a slave, then the white master himself. The slave was hanged from a tree, without a trial or the benefit of legal defense, but at least he got to spit in the overseer's face, for the betrayal, a much worse crime than the master's ignorance. Those were the days.

Monroe, whose real name was Albin White, a name he savored, had seen a photo of his great-grandfather's master, posed stiffly in a starched cream-colored suit and looking for all the world like a caricature of a ruthless plantation owner. Albin knew his name, Grayson Withers, and had years ago gone to find his great-grandson, Jordan, who still resided in Georgia. The plantation had long ago been trashed beyond recognition by Union troops, but the great-grandson had replicated the whitewashed manor house on a three-acre parcel of the former plantation he had carved off for himself. He was a developer, building cheaply made McMansions and selling them for exorbitant amounts to the newly wealthy. In other words, by fucking over the locals, he was approximately replicating more than just his forebear's palatial residence.

Albin White went about his business. He watched the plantation house for a week, noting the comings and goings of everyone in the household:

his target, the man's wife, his two boys, aged eleven and thirteen. At a stable several miles away, he hired a horse from a tall, thin man with a shock of white hair and piercing blue eyes. He rode at night onto the plantation grounds. The moon was full and what clouds raced overhead were thin and lacy. He rode the horse slowly until he came to the place where he imagined the lynching of his great-grandfather had taken place. A massive oak rose above his head. There was a branch, thick and gnarled as the trunk, that, as a human arm might point to something on the horizon, extended parallel to the ground. Looking up, he saw the rope being slung over that branch, the noose being slipped over his great-grandfather's head to settle around his neck, the knot drawn tight so that when his feet jerked off the ground, his neck would break.

The horse snorted and pranced nervously, as if disturbed by White's thoughts. He stayed like that, his hands on the pommel of the Western saddle, while he listened to the night birds. Grassy weeds twitched about the horse's fetlocks. The saddle creaked as he shifted slightly. The cold moonlight fell on him like an affirmation of memory.

To the east of the house was a three-car garage, the only visible modern touch. The great-grandson had a car fetish. Vehicles that cost three hundred thousand dollars should not be kept out in the open.

White was inside when, at precisely ten p.m. on the eighth night of his silent vigil, the door was remotely raised and the sleek black Lamborghini eased into its slot, beside the 1939 Bugatti Type 64 and the fire-engine-red Ferrari F40 that looked like it could take off at any moment. He was standing in the shadows, a length of stout rope wound around his left shoulder, a silenced handgun in his right hand. His plan was to waylay his target, take Jordan Withers out to the oak tree, and string him up.

But he never did. He watched, still as a sentinel, as the great-grandson of his great-grandfather's oppressor climbed out of the car. For a moment, as Jordan stood, admiring his prize and those parked just beyond, a tableau was formed that White was to remember for the rest of his life. Part of him longed to take action; another part knew that he would not. Frankly, he was afraid of the dark part of himself that longed for revenge, that would contemplate taking a life. It was repugnant, but if it was, how could he even consider it? Did he dare? He knew he had it in him, which was what frightened him the most. In the end, he crept out of the garage, through the hedges, past the trees, and to the edge of what was left of the plantation. He stopped there, panting, though he had not run. Turning back, he unfastened his belt, pulled down his pants, and, squatting, defecated on Jordan Withers's lawn. Such a poor, paltry act, but it was all he was capable of. Then he left. Like a dog, he thought, with its tail between its legs. The bitter taste of ashes was in his mouth.

On the flight back to D.C., White looked down at the passing landscape and wondered what his great-grandfather would have made of the view. Beyond the old man's ken, he imagined—as would have been the news story that arrived in his mail three days later, meticulously clipped from a local Georgia paper. It concerned the odd demise of Jordan Withers, choked to death when his unmade tie caught in the steering column of his Ferrari F40 as it sped down the local highway. "It was almost like poor Jordan was hanged," police captain Art Miller was quoted as saying, at the scene of the accident.

White had read the story three times, each time with a deeper sense of incredulity. An accident? He didn't think so. What then? He turned over the envelope, read the return address. Looking it up, he discovered it was off a rural road just north of New Orleans. He booked the next flight out.

The evening of the same day he came face to face with Preach—for the second time, it turned out. The shock of white hair and the piercing blue eyes were unmistakable, even backlit by firelight.

"Thank you," he had said. "I wish I could have done that."

"All it takes is time," Preach had replied, turning away toward the firelight. "Come with me."

Now, the echoes falling softly around him, his thoughts returned to the Well and the restocking of its personnel. Though he needed only a few, recruiting hadn't been an easy task when he had first conceived of the Well; in this day and age, when a person could obliterate secrets at an upload speed of 20 Mbps, finding the right people would be doubly difficult. Although, he could see the backs of the heads of two or three of the men who had worked under him in the Well, and he would approach them.

There was one particular thing that made his job even harder now: the one person he wanted most back at the Well was the one person he would never get to return—Gregory Whitman.

17

Being on the ground in Pakistan, as they had been two weeks before, gave Whitman an eerie feeling, as if he were experiencing this in a nightmare regurgitation of their ill-starred first encounter at Seiran el-Habib's villa, doomed by betrayal before it even began.

As they began their trek in the middle of the night, Whitman felt like he'd stuck his head into a sea of wasps, as if whatever God existed had turned His back on this blighted sector of Western Pakistan.

Flix had plowed on ahead, working his equipment without respite to seek out and disrupt any enemy communications. He was bound and determined to have this second mission succeed on every level. "Nothing less is gonna make my day," he'd told Whitman as they had exited the jet.

Whitman, night goggles on, felt Charlie come up beside him. Even through his body armor he could sense she had something on her mind.

"Not now, Charlie," he said to forestall her.

Which was when she grabbed his elbow, spun him around to face her.

"Yes, now. There are things we need to say to each other."

"We couldn't have done this on the flight over?"

"You wouldn't have paid attention."

Well, she was right on that score, he thought with no little annoyance—at himself as well as at her.

"Let's not get too far behind Flix," he said, and they continued on over the terrain illuminated in luminous green and black.

"It's this place," Charlie said.

A little chill, like a spark of electricity, flashed through him. "What about it?"

"It smells . . . It stinks of evil, of unnatural death." Something creaked, a bone perhaps, as she turned her neck. "It reminds me of . . . someplace else."

Of course, she was right again. He smelled it, too, with his sorcerer's nose. That sensation of wasps all around him had only come from one other place.

"Whit," she said all at once, "why did you take me there?"

It was no longer the accusation that had begun each of their more and more acrimonious clashes, until the moment he had walked out the door of her apartment, bleeding from ten thousand cuts, feeling flayed to the bone, aching where she had clocked him. It was simply a question; one he wasn't prepared to answer.

"To this day you can't speak its name."

"And nor should you," she said. "But that's beside the point. Answer me, Whit. I begged you not to take me, but you insisted. 'It will be our little secret,' you said. And you took me. It was a form of violation, an abduction. And now we *both* carry with us the burden of what happened there."

"That wasn't supposed to—"

"Oh, but it was, Whit. Down there your eyes were alight with a kind of demonic energy."

"Let's not get melodramatic, Charlie."

"Oh, don't even," she warned him. "I'd never seen that kind of energy in you before."

"There's only one kind of energy, Charlie."

"No, there isn't. This was a dark energy; a sorcerer's energy."

He recalled Cutler saying almost the same thing to him.

"I hope to Christ I never see it again," Charlie said.

"I have no idea what you're talking about."

"Sure you do. You just don't want to admit it, even to yourself." She shook her head. "You're so pathetic, Whit. That place had you hooked heart and soul. *That's* why you took me there. You wanted me to be a part of that . . . that horror. That secret had made its home in your belly. Like a tapeworm it was taking you piece by piece from me."

He looked away from her, toward the next rise of hills beyond which Seiran el-Habib slept in the central keep of his fortress-villa, surrounded by his well-armed cadre.

"The truly dreadful part, Whit, was that you couldn't see it, let alone admit what a hold the place had on you."

"It was called the Well," he said with more force than he had intended. "The Well."

Valerie was waiting in the parking lot across from the DARPA building when Lindstrom exited at noon. He looked agitated, shaken even, an observation that was borne out when he almost walked past her car. She slid down the window, called softly to him. He was leaning forward as if pressing into a frightful headwind, though, in fact, there was barely a breeze. He looked at her with the eyes of a deer caught in a vehicle's headlights. She called his name again, more urgently this time, and his vision cleared. He blinked heavily, then a smile broke out across his face.

"Oh, hullo."

"Get in, Paulus."

Leaning across, she opened the passenger's side door. He nodded, and like an obedient boy, trudged around the front of the car and slid in beside her.

"Close the door, Paulus." Did she have to tell him everything? This thought disturbed her. It made her realize that the rising tension of the situation was causing her to lose her patience with him. Taking a step back, she slowed her breathing, working to clear her mind and start over with him. Something was terribly wrong; she could see it written on his face as if he had printed it there.

She was about to reengage him in the manner she knew would get through to him when her gaze passed across her rearview mirror. A quick flash of reflected light came from a car three rows behind her. A figure was sitting behind the wheel, binoculars trained directly forward. Valerie was visible, as was the figure, through the windshields and rear windows of the intervening vehicles.

Lindstrom, whose antennae were always up even when he was seemingly calm, said, "What's the matter? What's going on?" He saw Valerie's eyes flick down from the rearview mirror to the mobile in her lap.

"Don't turn around, Paulus," she said.

"Is someone watching us?"

"Tell me about Lizzy," she said as she began a text to Preach. Lizzy was the boxer Lindstrom's parents had had when he was a boy. He had loved that creature more than life itself.

Lindstrom closed his eyes. "I don't want to talk about Lizzy."

"Sure you do. You love talking about Lizzy."

"Not now," he insisted weakly.

"Remember the time you taught her how to sit up and shake hands?"

Lindstrom smiled. Valerie finished her text to Preach and sent it off. Ten minutes was all the time it would take, but at the moment that seemed like a lifetime away.

"How did you do it, Paulus?"

"With treats I made especially for her. She wouldn't eat the store-bought treats my mom would buy her. She was a picky eater."

"Just like you, Paulus."

The smile that had faded on his lips arose again. "Just like me," he sighed.

His eyes were still closed. He did this when he was remembering his childhood or when he was really frightened in the present. Valerie kept one eye on the rearview mirror and the other on her mobile's screen. Having received the text, Preach had established an open line, which now consisted of a digital clock counting down the seconds.

Paulus continued with his memory of a boy and his boxer.

But now the figure in the car had put down the binoculars. Valerie could see that it was a man, but his features were indistinguishable at this distance. He turned off his engine, and her heart rose into her throat. He bent over, as if he were drawing something out of the glove box. Then he opened the door. Valerie's nerves were shrieking.

The man got out of his car and strode directly toward them. He was holding his right arm by his side. In his hand was a gun with a noise suppressor screwed to the muzzle. She could make out his features—regular, craggy, like an ex-wrestler or an ex-Marine.

He was more than halfway to where she and Lindstrom sat when, as if from out of nowhere, a gray Range Rover crept up behind him. Two of Preach's men got silently out and approached him. He must have sensed them at the last moment, but it was already too late. The man on his left slammed something hard just above his left ear, the other man caught him as he slumped over. The first man bent, scooped up the silenced gun, and together they hustled him into the back of the Range Rover, which now disgorged a third man, who got behind the wheel of the gunman's car and, following the Range Rover, drove off. None of the men looked at Valerie as their vehicles passed hers.

Lindstrom's eyes opened. Valerie sat very still in her seat.

"What was that?" Lindstrom asked.

"Just a passing car."

"And the danger?"

"Also passed."

Her mobile buzzed, and she looked down. The open line had been disconnected. In its place was a text from Preach: GET GONE. KEEP L W/U. FURTHER INSTRUCTIONS TO FOLLOW.

She fired the ignition and did what she was told, thinking, Now it's outright war, plain and simple.

18

"Fuck-damn!" Flix exclaimed as they came up to where he crouched at the crest of the hill. "Looka there, *compadre*. It sure feels good to be back."

Charlie shot Whitman a look he couldn't—or, more likely, didn't want to—decipher.

The familiar crescent glow rising up from the far side of the hilltop floodlit the villa in orange light. So far, Flix told them, he had found no other communication than the normal chatter between guards posted at intervals inside the perimeter of the villa. As they closed in on their target, Whitman discovered why there were no longer patrols outside the walls: repairs had been made to the crumbling sections. The wall was now thicker and seemed reinforced. Of course, they hadn't had the benefit of drone overflight photos to let them know in advance of these enhancements. Never mind, Whitman told himself. The trade-off of total secrecy was more than an equal trade-off. Besides, he didn't view the new features as anything more than a slight inconvenience. In fact, having all the guards inside the villa was a distinct benefit. They would not get ambushed again on their way to the extraction point, where the jet was waiting, refueled from reserve tanks onboard.

"Payback's gonna be such a fuckin' bitch for those motherfuckers, Sandy," Flix said, addressing their dead compatriot. Hunkered down low, he fiddled with his equipment, which seemed to include a lot more items than the last time. Clearly, he was taking no chances. "By the time we go in I'll have jammed every fucking piece of their comm net. They'll be deaf, dumb, and blind."

"Just the way we like 'em," Whitman said.

Charlie snorted. "You two sound like you're playing a video sim."

Flix lifted his head, glared at her. "What d'you know about it, *nene*?"

"Call me a baby again," she said, "and you'll be eating out of your throat."

"Back off, you two," Whitman said. A fight was the last thing they needed at this juncture. "You're both professionals. Make me believe."

Flix made a face, but said, "You can count on me, *compadre*."

Whitman nodded, turned to Charlie. "No more talk, got it? I want you focused on the mission."

"Don't worry about me," Charlie said. "I'm your gunslinger."

She handed Whit an assault rifle whose configuration he'd never seen before. It was as light as a feather.

"What's this thing made of?" he asked.

"Titanium, mostly." She slapped the side gently. "It uses 5.56mm ammo I made myself. The copper tips are soft enough to flower open on impact. Trust me, you don't ever want to get shot with one of those babies."

She brought out a fully automatic FN Herstal gas-powered F2000 assault rifle. It was configured with a 40mm FN EGLM grenade launcher. "This is a fucking cannon. Apart from the grenade, it's loaded with custom incendiary ammo. Anyone who gets in its way, they'll be scraping pieces of him off what's left of the wall behind him."

Whitman had been taking infrared photos through the Bluetooth connection in his night goggles. They took off, circumnavigating the compound. When they returned to the place where they had started, they looked at all the photos together.

Flix's forefinger stabbed out, pointing to a spot on one of the high-angle photos taken from their hilltop perch. The shot was grainy, due to the long lens on the night goggles, but the black rectangle was clear enough. "The generator junction is right there. They haven't moved it since the last time."

"Get me to within a hundred twenty yards of it," Charlie said, patting the side of her F2000, "and it's history."

"Right." Whitman considered a moment, shuffling the photos. "Infiltration begins here."

"At the front gate?" Flix said. "Are you nuts?"

"It's the last place they'll be expecting an assault," Whitman said. "Besides, it's the best egress within sight of the generator complex. I can take out the iron gate, giving Charlie a clear shot."

Flix eyed their weapons. "I want a cannon like . . ." He broke off, looked at her. "Like you have."

"Stick to what you know best," she said. "Your AR-15 will be more than adequate." She turned to Whitman, handed him two small black squares. "Incendiary phosphoric compound of my own design. That white fire will melt any and every metal up to titanium. Just make sure you're at least fifty yards away when you set them off with this." She held out a wireless ignition no bigger than his thumbnail. "So you're up first."

As they headed down the far side of the hill, Whitman held Charlie back for a moment. "Listen, I'm not a bad man," he said.

She stared at him, unblinking.

"I just meet bad men."

Charlie pushed past him without giving any sign that she had heard him.

Luther St. Vincent, on his way to visit Lucy at Mary Immaculate, drove his own car, even though one of his many perks was an armored government vehicle and driver of his choice. St. Vincent loved to drive; he did not like to be driven. When he was behind the wheel, he was reminded of the low, watery tracks in Louisiana, when he drove his daddy's beloved battered pickup. He started when he was ten, tall for his age, so he could see over the steering wheel, and stringy as a field dog. He was tasked with running errands for his mother—a well-known preacher woman who worked out of a waterproof muslin tent with colossal red crosses stitched to its four corners. The tent was erected and struck by his mother's crew of acolytes—her inner circle, as she called them—brawny men with flexed muscles and concrete jaws who believed in God. Luther was convinced they believed in her more. She was a striking woman with dark eyes and long hair like living flames. When she preached no one sat. Everyone was on their feet, clapping, stomping, and praising God at her command. Afterward, in the darkness of her trailer with the curtains drawn, she gave other commands to the men of her inner circle—all seven of them—in ones and twos. As insatiable as she was in her proselytizing, she was just as insatiable in her frantic fucking. You couldn't call it lovemaking—not from the glimpses the young and impressionable Luther saw.

Until he was older, he didn't know if his father knew and, if he did, couldn't understand how he allowed her this unbridled freedom. There came a time, however, when he got the grasp of economics, and realized that the products of his father's farm did not come near enough to paying the family's fare in life. His father needed his mother for her income, just as she needed him for the legitimacy of a husband and children.

It was a simple, hateful equation—one from which Luther removed himself as soon as he was of age to join the Marines. There, he prospered the moment he transferred into intelligence, rising in rank more quickly than his fellow recruits. But in time he came to realize that the Marines had too narrow a focus for his ambitions. Declining to re-up, he set sail for wider horizons and came ashore at the NSA, where the flag he raised was both recognized and greatly valued. His freedom, in turn, allowed him to pursue personal agendas with a minimum of questions and no interference.

He pulled up at Mary Immaculate in hazy sunlight, got out, and went through the main entrance. He spoke for a few moments with Sister Margaret, who updated him on Lucy's condition. Astoundingly, she had not backslid one iota. This was so astonishing for a recovering addict that he wouldn't believe Sister Margaret until she showed him the doctor's chart. The blood work confirmed the sister's report.

"We're dealing with a remarkable young lady," Sister Margaret said, struggling to keep up with him as he strode along the corridor. "She must have superlative willpower. It's a crime that she wasted years on drugs and sinful degradation." Just before they stopped in front of Lucy's door, she said, "What will happen to her now? There's really no earthly reason for her to remain here; the doctor's given her a clean bill of health."

"That will be up to her, I imagine," St. Vincent said. "She'll need to find a line of work."

"Which you could help her with, yes?"

He smiled thinly. "I try to follow your suggestions at all times, Sister."

The nun made the sign of the cross. "Bless you, my son."

St. Vincent rapped on Lucy's door, then stepped into the room, as usual leaving the door open.

"Hello, Lucy," he said amiably. "How are we feeling today?"

"I don't know about you, Luther, but I'm feeling fine." She shrugged. "But I imagine Sister Margaret told you as much."

"I'd prefer to hear from you."

"*De boca del propio interesado.*"

He laughed. "Yes, from the horse's mouth."

She liked to make him laugh, knowing it was not an easy thing to do, that not everyone could manage it. Today she was dressed in jeans and a red-and-white-checked cotton shirt. Very patriotic. It seemed to her that he liked her outfit, especially the way she had left open the top three buttons of her shirt, allowing her cleavage to peek through. She was justifiably proud of her breasts, high and firm. The nipples were sensitive and so almost always erect. She wore no bra, not needing one.

"Shall we sit?"

He lifted an arm. "It's such a beautiful day, why don't we go for a walk?" Sister Margaret wouldn't like that, but today it was necessary to speak with the girl in absolute privacy, and St. Vincent knew that in his world there was hardly a wall that didn't have electronic ears.

She grabbed a light jacket and they went out the back, down the wide lawn toward the copse of murmuring pines where once the pond had beckoned the most deeply ill of the patients into its depths. Lucy had much to think about on that short stroll. When St. Vincent had lifted his arm, she had caught a glimpse of the tattoo on the inside of his wrist, and now she was more interested in him than ever.

"You've been given the all clear, Lucy," he said as they paused to gaze at the swaying tops of the trees. "You can leave whenever you want."

"Hella good. I don't want to wait till my uncle gets back." Lucy took a step closer to him.

St. Vincent was suddenly lost in contemplation of the past. He was recalling a time when he had stood next to his mother. She had just come off

Christ's stage, as she called the platform from which she addressed her congregants and took their money. Her arms and neck glistened with sweat,
and she gave off a smell like a mare in heat that caused Luther's nostrils to
flare wide. She was a charismatic woman, but this hardly said anything about
her, since all successful preachers were, by definition, charismatic. Her
charisma was bound up in her sexuality, which emanated from her in waves
so heady it could take your breath away. For the first time, Luther understood how utterly she drew the inner circle to her, engendering absolute
loyalty in them. She put her arm around him, enveloping him in her scent,
the side of one thrusting breast against his shoulder, and Luther grew so
hard his phallus ached.

"You don't worry about your uncle?" St. Vincent said, pulling himself
back into the present.

She turned her face up to him. "Why should I? I don't give a fuck
whether he lives or dies." This was all part of her plan to make him feel that
she had only him, Luther, to rely on.

"Then I may have something for you." She was standing so close to him
their arms brushed. Tendrils of her hair, tossed by the breeze, caressed his
cheek. "Would you want to work for me?"

"Fuck, yeah!"

His nostrils flared as he took in her scent.

The first explosions turned night to a comic-book day and took out the
gates. Charlie was reminded of *A Clockwork Orange.* A bit of the old ultra-
violence that kicked the living shit out of the occupants of the house called,
appropriately enough, HOME.

Then, scuttling forward, she fired the grenade. It destroyed the entire
generator complex and from white, black returned, deeper than ever. Someone brushed past her. She thought it was Whit, but it was, in fact, Flix who,
having disrupted all communication within the compound, leapt over the
ruined gate, his AR-15 firing.

Charlie raced after him, Whit at her side. "What the hell?!" she shouted.

Rather than spraying the compound with fire, Flix was targeting enemy
combatants with frightening speed and accuracy. Three were already down

by the time she and Whitman began targeting their own enemies. But Flix was already ahead of them. Three more went down under his withering bursts. His advance was so on the money, he was killing them even before they had a chance to fire back. There seemed to be little for her and Whit to do but to head for the villa's front door.

As Flix dealt with the compound guards, Charlie applied the working end of her F2000 to the door, which burst apart in flaming shards. Shouldering past her, Whit was the first to enter. The interior was completely dark; no one had had the time to light even a single candle. His goggles guided him from room to room.

"Seiran," he whispered as he progressed. "Seiran, death has found you, my friend."

To Charlie, now right beside him, he said, "These villas are all the same. The target's always in the central living area, the most heavily protected place against drone attacks in the compound."

Through the kitchen, which was a bit of a mess, through two small bedrooms, each with rumpled sheets, past two modern baths, down another corridor, then into the central room, larger than all the others put together. Charlie lunged, caught a girl, cowering in a corner, by the biceps, and pulled her to her bare feet. She was Asian and could not be more than fifteen.

"What is this, Whit, white slave trade?"

"Later," Whitman said. "Talk to her."

"Seiran el-Habib," she shoveled into the shivering girl's ear, "where is he?"

The girl opened her mouth, but a brief chattering of automatic gunfire from behind them caused her to jump, her lips clamped shut. Whit turned, weapon at the ready, but it was only Flix.

"One more down," he said. "That's the end of the guards, so far as I can tell."

Even through her goggles, Charlie noticed a weird light in his eyes, as if he was not quite there, as if his body had been possessed by something else, something of which she had no knowledge. Suppressing a shiver, she turned back to the teen and repeated her question.

The girl looked at her, said, "I'm not paid enough for this shit." She pointed to a closet on the other side of the room.

Flix went for the door, but Whitman stopped him with a hand across his chest. "You've got our backs, *compadre*."

Whitman waited for Flix to nod and return to the entrance to the room, to stand vigil. Then he approached the door.

Wait, Charlie signed to him. *I have a better idea.* They had learned to sign together, thinking it would be a fun way to have sexual adventures in public without anyone being the wiser.

Okay. Let's have it, Whit signed.

Charlie pointed to the girl, and after a brief hesitation, he nodded and stood back.

"Go," Charlie whispered to the girl. "Announce yourself. Open the door, then get the fuck out of the way. Understand?"

The girl nodded, and Charlie let her go. She picked her way to the closet door, knocked on it. "It's Beth," she said, her lips close to the door. "I'm coming in."

Her hand went to the knob, turned it, and she slowly opened the door. Before she had a chance to dance away, two shots blew her off her feet.

"Shit!" Charlie said as she and Whit turned on their portable spotlights, effectively blinding whoever was in there. She held her position while Whit dragged out two figures: another girl, also Asian, this one surely not more than eleven or twelve, and a male, aged around thirty-five. He had dark skin, a full beard, and was wearing what appeared to be a caftan. He was also wearing a pair of Tod's loafers.

Whitman grabbed the gun from him—a vintage Walther PPK, as if this guy had been reading too many James Bond novels. It could kill someone just as easily as a modern-day handgun, witness Beth, who lay in a pool of blood with two holes in her chest—one through a lung, the other through her heart, judging by their placement. Whitman frisked him carefully, but he was clean. Charlie had hold of the preteen, peering at her in the beam of her light.

Now that he was disarmed, Seiran el-Habib himself was offering no resistance whatsoever.

"There's been a terrible mistake," he said over and over.

"You don't know how lucky you are, shitbird," Whitman said. "I've got some surprises for you back home in America."

They were about to move out when Charlie said, "Whit, there's something wrong here."

"You bet there's something wrong," Seiran el-Habib said.

Ignoring him, Whitman dragged him closer to where Charlie stood. "What is it?"

She was shaking her head back and forth. "This girl . . . Whit, this girl's American."

"What?"

"It's what I've been trying to tell you," Seiran el-Habib said. "Beth was American, too."

Flix, abandoning his post by the door, rushed at el-Habib. Only Whitman's intervention stopped him from running full-tilt into the Saudi.

"Why the hell should we trust him?" Flix said from around Whitman's shoulder. "All these motherfuckers know how to do is lie—lie and kill."

Charlie pushed her goggles up on her forehead. "Whit."

Whitman could see the terrified look in her eyes. He couldn't blame her.

"Take them," he said, consigning Seiran el-Habib and the girl to Flix. Not the smartest move, he suspected, but right this moment he had no choice. Then they all retreated from the room, moved through the maze of rooms and corridors until they reached the first of the interior guards Flix had shot to death.

Aiming his light onto the subject, Whit knelt down beside the corpse. He was dressed as an Arab, but there was something wrong, though he couldn't immediately put his finger on it.

"Whit," Charlie said, "check out his boots."

Whit bent closer, changing his angle so he could see the boots beneath the robe. They were U.S. Army issue.

"Christ," he whispered.

"It could mean nothing," Flix said, suddenly as nervous as a ceiling-fan storeowner with a comb-over.

"Idiot," Seiran el-Habib said, "it means everything."

Flix slammed the butt of his rifle into el-Habib's side. "Nobody asked you, motherfucker."

With added urgency, Whitman searched beneath the guard's robe.

Fishing around, his fingers felt something hard sewn into the lining. He ripped the cloth down the seam, and a dog tag fell into his hands.

"Jesus," he breathed. "Jesus Christ Almighty." All the air seemed to go out of him.

"Whit, what is it?" Charlie asked.

The tone of her voice told him precisely what she was thinking.

"Flix, you just killed Marine sergeant Alexander Stephen Moran."

"All the others," el-Habib said, "the same."

Whitman looked from Orteño to Charlie, then he rose to face the Saudi.

Seiran el-Habib's upper lip curled with disdain. "That's right, you fools," he said, "I was being guarded by the American military."

19

"I have a routine," Paulus Lindstrom said. "At eight o'clock I play baseball with my lab assistants for precisely one hour. By nine-oh-five, I've entered the lab. Ten minutes for a bowel movement, then wash up, change clothes. I'm working by nine-twenty-five. Forty minutes for lunch." He looked around nervously at Valerie's living room. "I leave work at six precisely. Not twelve-thirty. Here's an entire afternoon drifting in front of my eyes."

"Aimlessness doesn't suit you. I understand perfectly," Valerie said. "But unusual times sometimes call for a break in routine." She did not want to alarm him any more than he already was. An agitated Lindstrom was not a pretty sight. She was still waiting for Preach's further instructions.

His hands were working themselves into knots. "But I have my subjects to . . ."

"What subjects?"

Lindstrom turned away.

"Paulus?"

He went into the kitchen. Valerie followed him, arms crossed over her breasts, watching as he drew water for himself from the sink. His Adam's apple bobbed wildly; he drank like a man who had been out in the desert for days.

"Paulus," she said softly, but she knew better than to approach him in his distraught state. "Paulus, please talk to me." And then, because she knew what he needed at this moment, "I'm worried about you." A pang of remorse flew through her like an errant arrow. In one way or another, she had been manipulating people all her life, but Paulus was different. He was as vulnerable as a newborn once you got to know him. She did not love him, but she liked him, whereas most people pitied him. Their mistake.

He stood facing the sink, his back to her. His pale, long-fingered hands gripped the edge of the sink as if for dear life. He stared out the window at the garden she had created out of the postage-stamp-sized patch of ground.

"Do you grow vegetables as well as flowers?" he asked.

"Tomatoes and cukes," she said.

"Did you ever try beans?"

"No."

"You need poles for beans. They grow vertically, so you don't need much room. You should try growing beans."

"Okay. Would you help me?"

He turned suddenly, his face pale and stricken. "I'm the one who needs help."

"Then let me help you."

He blinked, as if slowly and carefully digesting her words. "I want to stay here."

She smiled, nodding. "All right." Sounding too eager would be a mistake. She sensed they were on a knife-edge. He could come toward her or bolt like a rabbit for his metaphorical warren, and then she would lose him. Trust was the only thing that mattered to a man whose life revolved around routine.

"You won't mind?"

She ventured a smile. "I haven't so far."

That made him laugh, and she knew they had stepped off the knife-edge onto what he felt to be solid ground. He let go of the sink at last, crossed back into the living room, and sat on the sofa that was also his bed. She could see how much comfort it gave him. He always sat in the same spot— the corner where he could rest his left arm along the sofa's arm.

She sat on a chair facing him, not wanting to insert herself into what she knew was his private space. "Paulus, I think it might be time to tell me what's troubling you." She paused for a moment. She was running purely on instinct. "Is it your subjects? Are you worried about them?"

"I am."

His voice was so soft she had to lean forward to hear him. "Are they in danger?" She matched the volume and tone of his voice.

He stared down at his hands, which hung between his knees, the fingers twining and untwining as they had in the kitchen. "I don't know." Twining and untwining. "I'm terribly afraid he might be."

A bolt of electricity shot through Valerie. Words could sometimes do that to her; they could have a visceral effect on her being. "Paulus," she said softly, gently, "you said 'he,' not 'they.'"

"Did I?"

There was no point in answering, she suspected. He knew very well what he'd said. This was a man who used language as carefully and precisely as he moved through life itself.

"There's a particular subject you're worried about." She was making a statement, not asking a question.

He nodded. Then he raised his head. His eyes were enlarged, liquid with unshed tears. "I was forced to take a step that was . . ."

"Was what, Paulus?"

"Unscientific. Unsound."

"Someone made you do this?"

He nodded. "Luther St. Vincent."

Something hard and unyielding contracted in the pit of her stomach, and now she was angry. "Why didn't you tell me this before?"

He visibly shrank from her. "I was afraid. What he had me do is unethical, at the least. At worst, it could cause a man his life. What would you think of me if I confessed?"

"The only way I would think less of you is if you lied to me."

"I don't lie, Valerie."

She smiled. "I know, Paulus. But you did withhold this information."

"But not for too long." His answering smile was water-weak. "I'm sorry."

Her smile brightened. Now was the time to make him into a hero. "What's past is past. We go on from here, and now you're the only person who can help this subject who you say may be in mortal danger." She lowered her voice to reinforce the urgency of her question. "Who, Paulus? Who is the subject?"

"Orteño."

Preach was listening carefully to every word Valerie said, though he had no reason to. Crow had already told him.

"Felix Orteño," she said. "St. Vincent tried to keep the subject's real identity secret, but Paulus, already becoming worried about Luther's objectives, found out."

"A field trial, is it?" Preach barked a laugh. "My, but Luther is racing toward his own death."

"Aren't we all?"

"Some more quickly than others," he said quoting Crow, though, of course, Valerie didn't know that. Silence for a beat. "This news has to make its way to Gregory Whitman, and at once. Who would be best suited to do that?"

"Cutler," she told him. "I know just how to feed it to him, too: as caff scuttlebutt."

"Go forth," Preach said, proud of her, "and multiply."

Severing the connection, he opened the screen door, went out on the porch, where the rocking chair he had made himself a lifetime ago awaited him. He sat, his knees creaking, an odd thing, to be sure. He waited for Crow to come to him; it always did, in its own time and in its own way.

The late-afternoon sunlight lay heavy on his lids, the bayous were still, as if warn down by the day's heat. Surrounded by his home, he began to drowse, the past rising up like a specter, crowding his drifting mind.

When he was eleven years old Preach awoke to find that he was unable to move his limbs. He had set up camp at his usual spot in the densest part of the bayou, on the edge of the Chitimacha village, having temporarily lost his desire to sleep at home, a craving that came over him now and again when his father, paralyzed from the waist down after being shot with an arrow through the base of his spine, started raving. People believed he spoke in tongues, that he was a kind of shaman, connected to the Old Ones—creatures out of nightmares who, it was said, had roamed the bayous long before the Chitimacha came into existence. The boy Preach was having none of it, a practical bent having been forced on him in order to keep food on the table and a roof over their heads, leaky and patchwork as it was.

His father had hunted the Chitimacha with a passion beyond Preach's comprehension—as if they were encroaching on his territory rather than the opposite. Preach did not resent them shooting his father; he'd killed six of their people. They had to stop him. In fact, Preach, inquisitive to a fault, sought them out. To his surprise, they befriended him, even, in their way, adopted him. He did chores for them and they paid him, both in food for his family's table and in wisdom old as time. Their elders taught him how to identify, observe, and learn from the wildlife that, in those days, teemed through the bayous.

It was early morning, and he sensed that he was hovering somewhere between sleep and wakefulness. He thought of his father, unable to walk. But in the next moment he was distracted by a different sensation, that of being in a place that was neither sleep nor wakefulness, nor anything in between. A new place; an unknown place. Nothing looked right—or the same. The butterfly hovering over his chest, the ant toiling across the back of his hand, the leaves on the trees, the lacy pattern of the thin twisted branches. In fact, he could see through the leaves, the branches, the treetops. Through the mountains beyond, through even the sky. He found himself staring at his own face. And yet it was one he didn't quite recognize. Inside him a glowing coal began to burn—no, no, not a coal—a second heart, that beat to a rhythm so complex it made him dizzy even though he was lying on his back.

He blinked, sucked in the dank, heavy air of the bayous, and was once again able to move his fingers and toes, his arms and legs. And that's when he saw the crow. It was sitting on a branch of a nearby tree, which was dead, split down the middle by a lightning strike.

The crow regarded him with its beady black eyes, cocked its head, and, damn, if it didn't look like it was smiling at him.

Later on, the crow spoke to him, a voice in his mind. Later still, the crow suggested he kill it. But it was far more than a suggestion. *I'll be more valuable to you dead than alive*, it whispered. *How can that be?* he asked. And the crow had answered, *You'll see.*

I don't want to kill you.

I know, the crow said. *Trust me.*

With a heavy heart, he slit its throat with one quick slice of his pocketknife. And then, to his utter astonishment, he did see. He saw everything.

20

"You are well and truly fucked." Seiran el-Habib was grinning from ear to ear. "You can't take me back to America, can you? No, no, no. And you've been here so long I'm thinking your transport out of here is gone. Am I right? And as for those surprises you promised me, I'm thinking they just dried up and blew away."

"*Now* can I kill him?" Flix said.

"Not until we find out what's going on," Whitman said.

"But where are we going to go?" Charlie said. "He's right. We can't bring him back to the States."

"And after what happened here," el-Habib said, "you three are outlaws—fugitives from your own government. You are in no-man's-land with nowhere to hide."

Flix slammed him in the side again, and Whitman didn't object. "Charlie, take the girl into the kitchen."

Charlie raised one eyebrow. "And?"

"You know what and."

He turned to Flix. "I want you to take a reading of the compound. Make sure we're alone. See what happened to the dogs we ran into last time out. And Flix—for the love of God try to find someone who's still alive and bring him back here. We need answers."

Flix nodded and, with a last venomous look at the Saudi, vanished down a corridor. That left Whitman alone with Seiran el-Habib.

The Saudi, seeing the look on Whitman's face, held up his hands, palms outward. "Don't expect me to help you, pal. You fucked up my situation royally."

Whitman pushed el-Habib into a chair, used phone wire to tie his ankles to the legs, his wrists behind his back. He grinned. "Well, now we have a start; you have a situation."

Seiran el-Habib grimaced. "That's the beginning and the end of it."

Whitman cocked his head. "Are you even a Saudi?"

El-Habib's mouth remained closed.

"Uh huh." Whitman stepped forward, flicked open a plastic lighter, and set fire to el-Habib's beard.

The reaction was almost instantaneous. After a split second of shock, the Saudi tried to raise his hands to bat away the flames. Whitman watched as the Saudi squirmed and twisted, screaming and cursing while the flames turned his beard to charcoal wisps, and then began to eat at the skin of his face.

El-Habib kept screaming, his eyes opened wide and staring, the whites showing all around. "Stop it!" he panted. "Stop it!"

"I can't," Whitman said, "you won't let me."

"What . . . what are you talking about?"

"You won't talk to me, el-Habib, or whatever the fuck your name is. And as soon as the fire eats its way through your jaw, you won't be able to talk to anyone."

"All right! All right!" Tears were rolling down the Saudi's cheeks, sizzling as they met the flames. "I'm dying here!"

"Not yet you aren't."

Whitman used his forearms to snuff out the flames, but the lower half of el-Habib's face was black, red, wet, and raw. He was hysterical, cycling between screaming out his pain and sobbing.

"Sit still." Whitman crouched down in front of el-Habib. "Fear not," he said, his voice gentle now as he snapped open his first-aid kit. "I'll take care of you."

———

No sooner had St. Vincent returned with Lucy Orteño to his office, than he received an urgent message for him to come down to IESAC—Integrated Electronic Surveillance and Command. Parking the girl with Jonah Dickerson, his SIC, his second in command, he hauled ass down the stairs three levels, used the fingerprint scanner to gain access.

IESAC was as large as an airplane hangar. It existed belowground, and was far larger than the footprint of the building above it. Thirty monitoring stations, manned round the clock, ranged along the right side of the space. To the left was the semicircular bank where five analysts worked collating the high-priority signals and assigning operatives to deal with them.

St. Vincent was not encouraged to see his boss, General Lewis Serling, standing with his hands locked behind his back, staring at one of five screens arrayed like a cross.

"We've lost the signal, Luther," he said as St. Vincent came up.

Not wanting to show his ignorance, St. Vincent chose an agnostic reply. "I have a lot of signals out, Director."

"This is the only one that concerns me," General Serling said in his trademark rasp, caused by forty years of smoking three packs a day.

His lungs might be black as night, St. Vincent thought, but he was as healthy as a college athlete. Some humans were just built that way. He stared at the general's forest of ear hair before saying, "And why does it bring you down to IESAC?"

"Because," Serling said slowly and carefully, "it belongs to Bluto."

A little shiver of premonition eeled its way through St. Vincent. Bluto was the field name for Martin Price, the agent he had following Paulus Lindstrom.

"I understand," the general went on in the overprecise tone drunks used when they didn't want anyone to know they were drunk, "that Bluto lost Dr. Lindstrom once or twice already." General Serling wasn't drunk; he was very, very angry. "That for the past several nights Dr. Lindstrom has not gone home." He turned to face St. Vincent, his gaze piercing, implacable. "Where was Lindstrom? What was he doing?"

When St. Vincent did not answer, the general said, "There are weapons that are simply voiced thoughts. Prejudices can kill and suspicion can destroy. Do you understand me?"

"I do, but—"

"But nothing." General Serling launched his final arrow. "Bluto is missing, Luther. He is nowhere to be found. His car was discovered about twenty minutes ago in Rock Creek Park, abandoned. Also, wiped clean, which would leave one to believe that Bluto is no longer among the living."

Serling's expression darkened. "Bluto. A death on your watch."

"Are you questioning my actions, Director?"

"I'm questioning the impulse behind your actions." When St. Vincent remained mute, Serling moved so that he was between St. Vincent and the monitors. "Up until now you've led a charmed life, Luther. But your protection has given you a sense of entitlement that is unwarranted and unwise. Good as you are at your job, there is still a line you have to toe just like anyone else."

The general's eyes were like dark pits; he looked as if he had forgotten how to smile. "Some people possess talent, others are possessed by it. When that happens a talent becomes a curse." He held up a warning finger as St. Vincent was about to interrupt him. "I'm not the only one who thinks so. This—let's call it an intervention—comes straight from the national security adviser himself." He paused for a moment. "Imagine, Luther, if POTUS ever got wind of this death."

"Is that a threat?"

"Don't kid yourself, bucko. He loves his image—he loves it a shitload. He may love you now, but believe me, like any politician, he'll throw you under the bus as soon as look at you if the need arises. Bedrock self-preservation is his business—his only business. I urge you to keep that in mind as you move forward.

"And move forward you shall, because you need to redeem yourself in my eyes and those of the national security adviser. Bluto's death has sent serious reverberations throughout NSA. It's up to you to deliver the counterblow." He bared his teeth like a lion confronted with raw meat. "Who sent us this message, Luther? Find out, will you, son? Because as sure as God made little green apples we are under attack on our home turf."

———

"Are you going to hurt me?" the little girl said.

"No," Charlie answered. "I'm going to make us tea." The girl was as thin as a wasp, her breasts just budding. "Why don't you light some candles?"

Looking at her more closely as the light turned from harsh to soft, Charlie was reminded of *Lolita*—not the film versions, but the transgressive novel wherein Nabokov's prose describes Delores, Lolita, Lo, the object of Humbert Humbert's ardent desire, as being prepubescent.

Charlie checked the stove to make sure it ran on gas, then turned on a burner. She had found loose tea in a canister, alongside a wooden rack of knives, to the left of the stovetop. Sticking her nose into it, she inhaled the rich aroma. Somewhat surprised that it wasn't the usual Pakistani or Afghani varieties, she took a pinch between thumb and forefinger, kneading it, then smelling the released oils. Jasmine, she thought. But not just any jasmine—this tea had an ineffable essence that spoke of extremely high quality. Moving the canister into light thrown by a candle, she saw lines of Mandarin, below which, in smaller type was the English: Zhangyiyuan Tea Shop, 22 Dashilan Street, Xicheng, Beijing. Charlie had heard of Zhangyiyuan. It was one of the finest tea purveyors in the Mainland, with nearly two hundred teashops in Beijing. In fact, she had read somewhere that its jasmine tea-scenting technique had been elevated to one of the state-level intangible cultural heritages. What in the world would this tea be doing in a villa housing a Saudi terrorist, guarded by U.S. soldiers in the middle of Western Pakistan? It made no sense. Still pondering the possible meanings, she spooned the tea into a pot.

"The secret is to keep the water from boiling," the girl said. "Boiling water spoils the flavor."

Charlie turned, studied the girl, who sat like a schoolgirl, back straight, hands one atop the other on the table.

"Thank you," she said, though she already knew this cardinal rule of tea brewing.

The girl started as she heard el-Habib's cries.

"What's going on in there?"

"Why don't we concentrate on us?" Charlie poured the tea into two glasses and brought them over to the table where the girl sat on the edge of her chair. Her teeth were all but chattering. Sitting at right angles to the girl, Charlie set the tea in front of her.

She waited some moments before saying, "We'll have less difficulty talking if we know each other's name. Mine's Charlie. I'm from Indiana."

"I saw what happened to Beth. Is the same thing going to happen to me?"

Charlie drank some tea. "Seiran el-Habib shot Beth," she pointed out.

The woman and the child looked at each other in a moment of distrust/ trust that only comes in an extreme situation like this one. The silence was punctuated once more by el-Habib's cries. This time, the girl didn't flinch.

"Alice," she said at last. "My name is Alice. I'm from Washington, the state."

"Sip your tea," Charlie said.

Alice did so, clearly grateful. "I was paid good money to come here."

"Who?" Charlie said. "Who paid you?"

Alice shrugged. "Some suit."

Charlie counted to ten to keep her blood pressure at normal. "Did he give you his name? Can you describe him?"

"His name was Dante."

Dante. *The Inferno*, Charlie thought. Very good.

Alice took another sip of tea. "He was bald, but you know the way men shave their heads, cuz he wasn't old or anything. He smiled all the time. He was nice to me. And he was handsome."

"Any distinguishing features?"

"His eyes were kind of a milky blue."

"That's good. Any visible scars or tats?"

Alice shook her head.

Charlie turned her glass around and around between her fingertips. She was no longer interested in the tea. "Help me with something, Alice. How were you and Beth recruited?"

Alice's eyes slid away to a corner of the kitchen where the candlelight could not penetrate. "We were sold."

I was right, Charlie thought with a lurch in her heart. Slave trade. "Tell me."

"Beth and I were taken off the streets."

"Were you related?"

She shook her head. "We said we were cousins, but, you know, we be-came family on the streets. She took me in, kept me safe, until . . ."

Her voice died out into the shadows that surrounded them. Charlie wished she felt more for this little girl, but she had a job to do and she knew she could not allow emotion to get in the way of thinking clearly and making the right decisions going forward. "Beth's dead, and you didn't even shed a tear."

"What's the point?" Alice cried. "Will crying bring her back?"

"No, but mourning might help you feel better."

Alice laughed harshly, and raised her arms. "Look around us. You see anything that's ever going to make me feel better? My life is shit. It always was shit, it always will be shit."

Charlie sat back. Words failed her. The chasm between her life and Alice's was simply too vast to bridge. No matter how much she tried she would never be able to imagine what the girl's life might be like.

"Tell me," she said, because there was no other way to go with this child. There would be no relevant information without a semblance of rapport.

"The shit?" Alice snorted. "It began when my father stroked out. My mother, already one of those tiger moms, seemed bent on driving me in-sane. I was now the only thing in her life, and she wouldn't let me alone. I ran away, yeah? A couple of real fucked-up things later, I ran into Beth, and for a time things weren't so bad. We foraged when we could, stole when there was nothing for us in the garbage cans and Dumpsters, went to bars, had guys buy us drinks, in exchange for a suck or a fuck. Sometimes we even got a dinner out of it." She laughed, a naked, awful sound. "Those were the golden days, yeah?"

She gestured. "Then blue eyes showed up, waving money around. He was offering us a better life in a faraway place. Six months, then we'd be free with a shitload of money to take us flying anywhere we wanted to go. Anywhere but the States."

Charlie's antennae came to full alert. "Wait a minute. He actually said that. 'Anywhere but the States'?"

"Word for word." Alice drained her tea, set the glass down. "What did we care? The last place either of us wanted to be was back in the States. So we said yes. And found ourselves here with"—she pointed to the doorway—"that piece of shit." She shook her head. "At first, Beth rebelled, said no to the things he wanted her to do. Then came the beatings, the starving out, the lack of light and tactile sensation. He nearly drove her crazy. He broke her. She was no problem after that."

"And you?"

Alice held her head defiantly. "I was paid money. I was promised more. I did everything he said."

Now that she had been softened up, Charlie finally got down to the nitty-gritty. "How long have you been here, Alice?"

"It'll be six months three days from now."

Charlie's heart started to thump against her ribs. "And what is supposed to happen in three days?"

"Blue eyes said he would come."

"And you believed him?"

"I have no reason not to. The prick in there gets bored with his girls after five or six months. Like a stud bull, he requires fresh bodies or his thingy doesn't rise to the occasion."

Charlie threw her head back and laughed. It was something she never thought she would do in a slaughterhouse.

21

There were three life lessons Joe Kinkaid's father taught him when he was growing into manhood: never back-talk your boss, never be led astray by a woman, and never get in over your head. The problem facing Kinkaid now was that he was very much afraid he was in over his head.

This thought was uppermost in his mind as he strode down the corridor in the subbasement of the building built and occupied by the FBI. He was on his way to his second interview with Martin Price, field name Bluto.

Going toe to toe with NSA was a sure way to have his career cut short, as his father's had been. Nevertheless, the incidents of today had led him in that direction. But maybe, no, it was his involvement with Preach that had led him down this path, which might be good or bad because he hated Luther St. Vincent with a passion.

As he stood in front of the cell where Bluto was currently cooling his outraged heels, Kinkaid had reason to think of his father again. Regal Kinkaid was a big man. When Kinkaid was growing up, he seemed as huge as Paul Bunyan, and just as heroic. That all came crashing down when Regal Kinkaid was hauled off to prison the week after the energy company he ran went bankrupt. The company's ambitious expansion into new forms of energy was revealed to be nothing more than a Ponzi scheme, using investors' money to construct a house of cards without value. There weren't any new forms of energy the company was pursuing, only Regal Kinkaid's golden tongue. And how was he brought down? Through the NSA's domestic spying program. And who was the head of that spying program? Luther St. Vincent. And because of that success and others, St. Vincent was given his own fiefdom, Directorate N, where he directed God alone knew what evil mischief.

People lost their lifesavings; several committed suicide. Regal Kinkaid was convicted, began serving what was supposed to be a twenty-five-year sentence. But somehow he and his lawyers cut a deal with the feds, and he was out in three years.

"I got in over my head, son," he said to Kinkaid the day he was released. Then he winked. "But I had a life preserver. You got to have a good one if you're unfortunate enough to get in over your head."

So there were, in fact, four life lessons, Kinkaid thought, as he unlocked the cell door. Which is why he had sought out his own life preserver: Preach.

Orteño made his methodical, almost mechanical, circuit of the villa and compound looking for life, and finding none. As he progressed, he policed his brass—that is, he picked up his spent shell casings, as any good professional would do. Leaving no trace of their presence was essential. He had learned to police his brass at an early age. It was so ingrained in him that he hardly thought about it—it had become automatic, which was just as well because his mind was elsewhere.

Ever since he had woken up in the hospital after his concussion, he had felt different. The report sent to Cutler from Bethesda, though entirely routine, had almost derailed his getting back in the saddle. Cutler was wary of concussions in his people—far more than he was of bullet wounds or broken wrists or ankles. "Concussions can fuck with your sensory input," Cutler was fond of saying, "not to mention your judgment." Flix had Whitman to thank for his continuing on with Red Rover. His *compadre* had gone to bat for him with Cutler, vouching for his health, saying he was indispensable, and that if Cutler wanted the brief to be completed successfully Flix had to be part of the team.

Flix, never one for expressing his emotions, hadn't known what to say or how to thank Whitman, so he'd simply nodded and kept his own council. Again, that was just as well, as he didn't know how to convey to anyone else how the world had changed for him. BC, before the concussion, it had been dull and gray. Now it was bright, clear, almost radiant.

Rip currents of color registered not only in his brain but throughout his entire body; he *felt* the colors as well as saw them: the deathly pallor of the faces of the dead, the smell of death, like a freshly opened casket. With the sight of each of the guards lying in unnatural positions memories flashed through him of how easy they were to spot, how easy it was to target them, pull the trigger, keep going, pulling the trigger again. It was as if his mind, his body had melded with the AR-15, or, conversely, as if it had come alive in his hands, as if it was telling him what to do and when. He had not missed with even one shot, and each one was a killing shot, even though that seemed improbable to him. And yet, he was seeing the proof with his AC—after concussion—vision. There simply was no denying it.

Something deep inside him contracted with each of these memories, as if quailing at the implications. He went in search of the dogs in order to shift his thoughts in a different direction, but he saw no sign of them anywhere. Seven dead, not including one of the girls being held by el-Habib. He had killed seven Americans. He should have felt sadness, remorse, self-revulsion even, but he felt none of these emotions. In fact, he felt nothing at all. It was as if he had scored 100 on his target at the USA firing range. What the hell, man?

Taking one last look around the compound to make sure nothing was moving, no one was coming down the dirt track over the hill, he turned and went back into the villa. Somewhere deep inside him, that thing that had contracted whispered that he should tell Whitman of the inner changes. But then a battering pain quashed the thought, and by the time he rejoined Whitman he had forgotten all about the growing dichotomy inside him.

"I'm not telling you anything," Bluto said, sitting on his hands in one corner of the steel bench. "I'm not an enemy combatant; we're not in-country. I've got rights. This is America, buddy."

"I'm not your buddy," Kinkaid said.

"You can't do this," Bluto said. "You touch a hair on my head and you're toast, fucker."

That was when Kinkaid took out the noise-suppressed handgun Bluto had been wielding when he'd been taken into custody. With one hand he compressed Bluto's nostrils, then, when he opened his mouth to breathe he jammed the end of the noise suppressor between his teeth.

"You came after one of my people with this." By "my people" Kincaid meant one of Preach's people, but he was happy to let Bluto believe he meant FBI. "You were all set to put a bullet in her temple, so don't you fucking tell me you're not an enemy combatant, that we're not in-country. Don't you dare claim this is America. You have no rights here. You've broken the law. NSA is forbidden to issue briefs on American soil. That's strictly for the FBI."

"I didn't fire that," Bluto mumbled around the metal. "You've got nothing on me."

"Nothing, you say?" Bending over, Kinkaid shoved most of the barrel into Bluto's mouth, making him gag. "Here, in my world, where you are, intent is nine-tenths of the law. When you got out of your car, drew this gun, and approached my people, you made your intent perfectly clear."

Kinkaid shrugged. "So now you know the situation you find yourself in." Inch by inch, he withdrew the gun from Bluto's mouth. He unscrewed the noise suppressor, put away the two pieces of weaponry. "But, now I come to think of it, I wonder . . ."

Grabbing a chair, he spun it around, straddled it, folding his arms across the back. He sat, staring into Bluto's face. "You may not know this, but my father was once in jail." He spoke in a normal conversational tone, as if they were two friends exchanging war stories over drinks. "He was an embezzler—a mighty one, too. He had some powerful mojo going for him, even when he was in prison. Somehow—don't ask me how—he got his sentence reduced to barely more than a tenth of what it had been. Can you beat that?"

He lifted a hand, waved it back and forth before allowing it to settle back on top of the other. "Anyway, when he was released, you'd think he would have been a changed man. Not a bit of it. He was the same unrepentant sonuvabitch I'd known all my life. I mean, he was always good to me, but in business, Jesus, he didn't care who he cut off at the knees."

Kinkaid's gaze wandered off Bluto's face for a moment, as if lost in memories. All at once, his gaze snapped back sharper than before. "Where was I? Oh, yeah. When my father got out of prison he had me meet him somewhere out in a vacant lot in some godforsaken part of the city, never mind which one. At three in the morning, can you imagine? Huh!" Kinkaid sounded as if even at this late date he had trouble believing it himself. "'Son,' he said to me, 'I have money stashed. A boatload of it. Some I'm gonna use to make a new start for myself in another part of the country or maybe overseas, who knows? But the bulk of it is yours.' When I told him I didn't want it, he looked more surprised than when the feds came for him three years before. 'But you gotta take it. It's my legacy, to make sure you'll be okay, no matter what should befall you.' So I told him again because I thought maybe he hadn't heard me the first time. 'But why?' he said. 'I don't get it.' 'That money isn't yours to give me,' I told him. 'You stole it from people—' 'Stupid people,' he interrupted. Typical of someone who knew—*knew*—he was always right. 'People who should have known better if only they'd done their due diligence,' he said. 'Son, don't you get it, it's like finding a pot of money at the end of the rainbow.'

"I asked him how he could break the law, keep on breaking it until people he didn't know, people he'd never even met, died, and d'you what he said, Bluto? He said, 'The law doesn't apply to me.' Then he laughed. 'I keep getting away with murder, son. It's a beautiful fucking world, isn't it?'

"See, it was he who didn't get it. He didn't see what he'd done wrong. You know why? He was a psychopath: he drew people to him, spoke so convincingly they put their faith in him, just like one of those televangelists. He fleeced them like sheep. And now I'm wondering whether you've deluded yourself into believing that following the orders of a psychopath is good and right, that gunning a woman down in the middle of the nation's capital is how you see your life going forward. Because, you know, the moment you pulled that trigger there would be no going back. You'd belong to Luther St. Vincent—you see, I know it was St. Vincent who ordered the termination—body and soul. From that moment on there wouldn't be anything he would ask of you that you wouldn't do, because sure as you're sitting here he'd disavow any knowledge of the murder, which would leave you under the federal truck speeding right at you."

Kinkaid stood up. Time to let Bluto contemplate his next step. Would he see the error of his ways? Who knew? Well, he bet Preach knew—he'd make book on it. Clever Preach. Kinkaid knew he'd done his best, and that was all he could ask of anyone, including himself.

"It would have been easy for me to pull the trigger, but I'm not that kind of guy. You'll realize that soon enough." At the door to the cell, he turned back. "You thirsty, Marty?" It was crucial now to switch from Price's field name to his real one. It would underscore for him the potential for change in their relationship. "Christ, I could use a nice frosty Coke. Sound good to you?"

22

Jonah Dickerson took one look at Lucy Orteño and felt his heart tumble out of bed. The pulse beating a tattoo in the hollow of his throat made it all but impossible for him to swallow comfortably. He felt in desperate need of a belt of Irish whiskey, preferably a double.

Instead, he cleared his throat and said, "Are you hungry? We can go down to the canteen."

Lucy shrugged. "Sure." But she kept her eyes on Dickerson, a tall, wide-shouldered man with light hair and eyes.

He knew he wasn't handsome, at least not by traditional American standards, but there was something about him, as if he were missing some essential element, that seemed to intrigue women. Lucy Orteño appeared to be no exception.

The commissary was three floors down. He led her to the elevator, the car came, and they descended.

"When will Luther be back?" she asked.

"No idea."

They stepped out into another corridor, this one bustling with men and women whose tunnel vision attested to their busy workaday lives. The commissary, a large, bright space, was at the far end. It was an off-hour, so the place was sparsely populated—just a couple of people at the vending machines, buying snacks to take back to their offices, desks, or workstations.

He ordered them both hamburgers, fries, and Cokes, then chose a table in a quiet corner. He liked the way she ate, baring her teeth, taking small bites, chewing for a long time before swallowing. Nothing put him off more than a woman who bolted her food like an animal.

When she was halfway through her burger, she put it down, wiped her hands on a paper napkin, and said, "Do you have any idea what kind of a job Luther has in mind for me?"

Dickerson registered surprise. "Up until you said it I had no idea he'd offered you a job."

Lucy looked at him soberly. "I have nowhere to sleep, either."

"I'm sure Luther's considered that."

There was a silence between them. He was starting to feel a bit disconcerted when she said, "Have you ever killed someone?"

Now he looked startled. "God, no. Why d'you ask?"

She shrugged, peered into her Coke as if wanting to lose herself there.

He almost choked on the next question. "Did you?"

"Almost." She glanced up, met his gaze. "Not quite." She breathed. "But close."

"What happened?"

She sighed, sat back in her chair, which, intentionally or not, gave him a better view of her thrust-out breasts. "I ran away from home. Don't ask for details." She ran a hand through her thick hair, which brought one breast into further prominence. "Anyway, people I was with were doing H—mainlining. One of them was a guy who had been giving me a lot of shit. I hated his guts. This one night, he slipped down, further down than he had been before, I guess. He was on his back when he started to vomit. His mouth filled up and it started to dribble down his cheek."

Dickerson felt his stomach clench, and he pushed his plate away, his appetite suppressed by incipient nausea.

She took a breath, maybe to distract him, which it did. "So there he was, on his way out of the veil of tears. In a couple of seconds he started to choke, then suffocate. I stood there watching. No one else was conscious, let alone in a position to help him. Only me. I wanted to just stand there and watch—watch the man who had tormented me over and over die. But I couldn't. I turned him on his side, smacked the back of his head, and he was okay."

She looked at Dickerson with her huge coffee-colored eyes. "To this day I don't know whether I did the right thing."

"Why d'you say that? Of course you did the right thing—the only thing. You did God's work."

"Yeah? Well, two weeks later he stabbed a girl to death. The cops caught him, put him away, but so what? Is that any consolation to the girl he killed? I was her only consolation, and I failed her."

Dickerson shook his head. "But, come on, how could you have known?"

"I knew him," Lucy said. "I knew what he was capable of. He was a rageful, violent, sadistic piece of shit."

He wondered why she was telling him this, what she was trying to work out. "Sounds to me you were in a no-win situation. No matter what decision you made that night, you were always going to look back." He put his hands flat on the table. "I think you need to confess."

She looked up, alarmed. "What?"

"I mean, you're Mexican, yes? Roman Catholic. So it should . . ." He paused, thinking of how best to proceed. "It's clear you've strayed, Lucy. Your distance from God has obviously hurt you. My parish church is nearby. I know when I'm troubled it's the place to go to find peace . . . and to get answers."

"God speaks to you?"

He laughed softly. "Not in the way you mean. But when I open my heart to God, answers always come." He nodded. "Come, we'll go together."

Lucy shook her head. "Sorry, no. I have nothing to say to God."

Charlie was foraging in the dead refrigerator with her light for something for her and Alice to eat, when her vision blurred for an instant. Seeing the sudden pallor of her arms and hands, she dug into her pocket for the vial of Imuran, popped two pills, and swallowed.

Even through this precursor to another attack of Takayasu's, she was aware that Alice had risen from her seat at the table. On little mink's feet she crossed to the counter where the knives were housed in their wooden rack. Charlie waited until she felt Alice coming at her, knife pointed at her back, before turning.

Grasping Alice's extended forearm, she jerked her toward her, twisted the arm so hard the girl cried out. Charlie took the knife, dragged Alice to the counter, and forced Alice's hand down, fingers splayed.

"What are you going to do?" Alice said in a shaky voice.

"Teach you a lesson in humility. When someone is nice to you, you don't try to stab them in the back." Wielding the knife, she said, "Which finger do you need the least?"

"What?"

Alice almost fainted. Charlie had to use her hip to keep her on her feet. "Choose, Alice. Or I'll choose for you."

"Don't!" Alice cried, trying and failing to work her hand free. "Please don't! I'm sorry!"

"Okay," Charlie said. "My choice."

She lifted the blade above Alice's hand and brought it down hard and fast. The girl screamed. The knife blade buried itself in the counter so close between Alice's first and second fingers it drew blood from the vee of the webbing.

"Oh, my god!" Alice sobbed. "Oh, my god!"

Charlie let her go, and she slid to the floor in a spent jumble of limbs. Crouching down beside her, Charlie showed her the knife, the very tip crimson with her own blood.

"Alice," she said softly, "if I were to give you this knife now what would you do with it?"

The girl looked up at her out of red-rimmed eyes. A nerve in her cheek was spasming uncontrollably. "Nothing," Alice said in a voice as tiny as one of Zhangyiyuan's magnificent tea leaves. "Nothing."

The Federalist Club occupied a handsome Florentine Renaissance building on the corner of I Street and 15th Street, NW. It was designed around the turn of the nineteenth century by the same firm that had designed St. Matthew's Cathedral several blocks away near Connecticut Avenue.

Luther St. Vincent, addressed as Mr. Washington by his fellow Alchemists, was already seated in the clubby library when Albin White walked in. Groupings of high-backed chairs were scattered across the carpets at discreet distances from each other. A fire roared in the stone fireplace, as it almost always did, except during the insufferable summer months. An oval table at St. Vincent's right hand held an old-fashioned glass of Scotch and a small jug of branch water.

"Good evening, Albin," he said as White took a chair catty-corner to him.

"And to you, Luther." White did not have to signal; a waiter made his presence known. White ordered a lager, and the waiter retired, after informing the gentlemen their table was ready any time they chose to move to the dining room.

The two men chatted amiably until the beer arrived, along with a bowl of mixed nuts. White looked around at the few occupied seatings. "When did they start letting women into the club?" he said, sipping his lager.

"That's very funny, coming from you."

White frowned. "I didn't mean it to be funny." He drank some more beer. "Did you ever wonder why there are no females in the Alchemists?"

"Frankly, Albin, I never thought about it."

"What could we possibly get, Luther? A beast, who'd try to impose her will on us, or a looker who'd surely be as lily-livered as Adams and Jackson are proving to be."

"I admit the looker might be distracting."

White grunted. "Especially to someone like you."

St. Vincent eyed the other for a moment. "A man like you, with your—what shall we say?—unorthodox tastes, has no business chiding me."

White finished off his lager, licked his lips. "Well, this is going well, isn't it?"

As if by an unspoken agreement, the two men rose and made the short walk to the dining room. The wainscoted corridor was adorned with portraits of great patriots and conservatives from America's past. The dining room, though elegant, was a tad fusty for White's taste. He could still imagine the uniformed Negroes bowing and scraping to the white members as they lived to serve, just like plantation slaves.

They were shown to a table for four, in the far corner, close to the leaded windows looking out onto the rose garden. Menus were set before them, further drink orders were taken, and they were left alone.

"I called earlier," St. Vincent said, picking up the menu. "I had them make fried chicken as a special."

"I hate fried chicken," White said, determined not to be baited.

"No, you don't. You love fried chicken, and the version they make here is spectacular." He put down the menu. "That's what I'm going to have."

"Suit yourself."

St. Vincent smiled as their drinks were delivered. "We're not ready yet," he told the venerable waiter, who all but clicked his heels before he withdrew. He took a sip of his Scotch.

"I'll be having the chef's salad."

"You poor bastard, Albin. Spiteful in everything you do, even toward yourself."

White reached for a roll and, in doing so, knocked his drink off the table. The glass fell to the parquet floor, shattering with a sound to lift every head in the room, even the one or two ancients, dozing over their Dover soles.

"Oops," White said, staring at St. Vincent.

Not one but two waiters hurried over to clean up the mess.

"I hope that made you feel better," St. Vincent said when they had ordered and were alone again.

"Better than a blunt stick in the eye," White observed.

St. Vincent settled himself more comfortably in his overstuffed chair. "Look, Albin, no one appreciates more than I everything you've done for us—especially when it comes to the Well, where, as you know, we're on the same page. But some days—and today's one of them—it seems a pity that I dislike you so as a human being."

"Frankly, I don't think about you at all, Luther, not even when I'm with you."

"You know what your problem is? You despise everyone who isn't black, conservative, and rich. Who isn't you, in other words. Worse, you enjoy punishing them for those supposed sins. You remind me of those plantation blacks who served their master in his mansion, turning against their own in the fields. They were often crueler than the owners ever were."

White was on the verge of rising and walking out, but their dinner was served.

St. Vincent grinned without an iota of warmth. "Timed that just right, didn't I?"

White picked up his fork and knife in a manner vaguely menacing.

"Go ahead," St. Vincent said, "if that's what you want."

White put down the cutlery. "What is it you want, Luther?"

"I want to know that the resurrected Well will be better than its predecessor."

"And you think baiting me with your racist shit is going to do the trick?"

"Hmm. Remember what you said when you first walked into the library?"

"What? About the women? That was a joke."

"And what came after?" St. Vincent shook his head. "We both know that's a lie, Albin. You're as sexist as they come."

"What if I am?"

"You've got to curb that instinct."

"Why?"

"Because I have a recruit for you. Young, strong-willed, vicious, even by your standards."

"Sounds perfect."

"Truly. Her name is Lucy."

23

"To answer your first question, yes, I am Saudi." Seiran el-Habib's voice was garbled, as if he was speaking around a mouthful of stones. "I am one of those not of the royal family who resents the terrible grip it has on Arabia."

"Like Osama," Whitman said.

"The easy rejoinder, to be sure."

Dawn had arrived in Western Pakistan. Light, thick and filthy, seeped through the villa's windows like lava flowing downhill. The chill of the night was slowly abating.

"But it wouldn't be the correct one." El-Habib regarded Whitman out of eyes sunken deep in their sockets. He was sitting opposite Whitman, a damp towel wrapped around his face, as if he were about to have an old-fashioned shave with a straight razor. The razor would have been kinder to him than the fire. Islets of blood oozed from his cheeks and chin, staining the towel. "I have no dog in the religious hunt. You see? Trained in America. I know the idioms well enough to make a hash of them." He grinned, then grimaced. "Ow, ow, ow!"

Whitman lifted a bottle. "I found liquor in that cabinet over there."

"For the girls."

"You like them drunk, then."

El-Habib's expression turned sour, and his eyes darkened, as if they were all pupil.

"But we're not here to discuss your deplorable sexual proclivities." Whitman offered the bottle. "It will ease the pain."

"I relish the pain," the Saudi said. He was on his third bottle of water. "It's a constant reminder of what you did to me."

"Stop your crying," Whitman snapped. "Whatever happens to you now is the consequence of your own actions." He set the bottle down between them. It was a boundary as well as a symbol of who ate above the salt and who did not. "You made some bad decisions, Seiran. And here you are."

"I am protected."

"Correction. You *were* protected." Whitman sat back, regarding his prisoner for a moment. "Two questions, Seiran. Answer them and we're done here. Who is protecting you? And why?"

"You will die for this transgression, you know that."

"Do I look frightened?"

"You and your people."

At that moment, Flix entered the room. "Not a creature was stirring, not even a mouse," he said, in a weirdly jovial tone of voice. He stopped, momentarily taken aback by the state of the Saudi's face. "What the hell happened to him?"

"He and my lighter had a disagreement."

Flix whistled a snatch of a tune, cut off abruptly when he saw that Whitman was annoyed at the interruption. He sobered up immediately. "Seven down, *compadre*."

"And you whistling away. Christ on a crutch."

Whitman was about to add to this malediction when Flix held up a finger, tapped his encrypted sat phone. He toggled on the phone, listened for a moment, then held it out. "For you," he said, then mouthed "*The King*."

"Tell him I'm busy," Whitman said.

"I won't." Flix came toward Whitman. "And, trust me, you shouldn't either."

Reluctantly, Whitman rose. Pointing to el-Habib, he said, "Keep an eye," as he took the phone and went out into the corridor where he could not be overheard.

"Gregory, where the hell are you?" King Cutler's voice buzzed in his ear like a trapped bluebottle.

"Where d'you think we are?"

"Why haven't you checked in with your designated local contacts? No one has had a hint that you're in Beirut."

"All due respect, those locals are NSA's people."

"And?"

"I only sail on a leaky ship once."

There was a pause while Cutler seemed to digest this. "How d'you propose—"

"I have my own contacts."

Silence on the line. Then, "So. Are you making progress?"

"Slowly but surely. You can't believe what a mess Beirut is."

"Worse than expected?"

"Much worse."

"Mansour?"

"We'll get to him. It's a delicate balance, and the situation is more complicated than we were led to believe. The approach has to be finessed."

"We need this brief to be a success; future contracts depend on it. I'm counting on you, Gregory."

"Don't worry."

"That seems to be all I'm doing these days."

He could hear Cutler sigh as if he were standing right next to him.

"Meanwhile, we have a more immediate problem."

"I already have enough problems on the ground. I don't need another one from fifty-eight hundred miles away."

"The problem is closer than that," Cutler said. "It concerns Orteño."

"You're not going to start with the concussion business again. We put that to bed yesterday."

"Yeah, well, something's come up. It turns out Flix didn't have a concussion."

Whitman stood stock still, and yet his heart was racing. "What did he have then?"

"According to what I've heard, an operation." Cutler's voice sounded strained, as if it were being beamed in from another dimension. "An unauthorized operation."

"What?" Whitman moved so that he could look back at Flix, who was standing over el-Habib. "I don't understand."

Then Cutler told him about St. Vincent, Paulus Lindstrom, and Mobius.

Julie was supposed to meet King Cutler for dinner, but instead she was standing outside the side door to The Doll House, waiting for Sydney to emerge. Cutler had called at the last minute to cancel, which was fine by her as she'd been contemplating canceling herself. The tension in his voice was palpable. Something was amiss at Universal Security. She felt the urge to ask him about it, but bit her tongue, knowing he'd just snap at her and hang up abruptly. His certain rejection of her—and her new suspicion that she couldn't trust him, or anyone but Whitman, for that matter—was something she could not countenance on this night when the streets felt strange and she was surrounded by strangers.

It was at times like this that she hated herself for remaining married to Gary. What a coward she was! She could tell herself all she wanted that she was doing it for his career, but the truth was she no longer cared about him or his career. Why should she? And, dammit, here came the tears! She rid herself of them with angry swipes, fought to get a grip on herself. She scolded herself: Enough with the self-pity, Julie!

That was why she had decided to come here. Seeing Sydney again would be a reward for the terrible pressure of her miserable life. And, she finally had to admit, the powerful magnetism between them could not be denied. It wasn't simply sexual—she was still having a hard time reconciling that idea—it was perhaps even more about the power that radiated from Sydney's core. Julie wanted to be like that.

The night was unseasonably warm, and because she was as nervous as a virgin entering her boyfriend's bedroom for the first time, she extracted a joint from a secret stash in the lining of her handbag, and lit up. She drew the earthy-sweet smoke deep into her lungs, held it there as long as she could before letting it out in a hiss. By the third toke, she was completely relaxed. And so her thoughts turned wholly and completely to Sydny, a creature she admired, envied, and who, frankly, scared her stiff.

Sydny had told her that she would often come out between sets to catch a breath of fresh air. This was particularly true during good weather. Julie had been smoking for only a couple of minutes when Sydny emerged through the steel-clad door. She smiled when she saw Julie; she didn't seem in the least surprised.

Without saying a word, she lifted the half-smoked joint from between Julie's fingers and took a long drag, raising her chin and exposing her neck. Even smoking she looked sexual. Julie wondered how a woman could look vulnerable and fearless at the same time. She realized that more than anything this was a quality she wanted to engender in herself.

"You aren't surprised to see me."

Sydny handed back the joint. When she spoke it was with that peculiar sound people made when they were holding smoke deep in their lungs. "Why should I be? Your story is incomplete." With a hiss like escaping steam, the sweet smoke broke from between her half-open lips, enveloping them both. "And because I still have things to learn from you."

Julie was stunned. "*You* have things to learn from *me*?"

Sydny stood with one hip cocked. To Julie she looked like a superhero.

"Sure." Sydny wrapped a coil of Julie's hair around her forefinger. "The moment we stop learning," she said, "we die." She smiled, almost dreamily as she watched Julie finish off the joint. "Had to screw up your courage, didn't you. What were you afraid of, that I'd reject you?"

"No," Julie said softly. "I was afraid of what's happening right now."

"Why?"

"Because all my life I've wanted things, desperately, and when I got them I discovered they were meaningless."

"And you kept going on."

"Yes."

"To the next thing that disappointed you."

"Yes."

Cars passed in the street, their headlights picking out details in the storefronts that The Doll House's livid neon couldn't touch. A dog skittered into the street, ran barking after the vanished taillights. It lost interest quickly, returning to the shadowed sidewalk, where it sat sadly observing the night-time world passing it by.

Sydny dropped her hand. "You know, when I see you now, you remind me of that dog—a lost little thing, looking for someone to play with, looking for something new, looking for someone to take you to that new place that doesn't turn to shit."

Julie thought she should be angry, but there was nothing cutting in Sydny's tone. On the contrary, it was warm, intimate even. And, in any case, she's right, Julie thought. I *am* looking for that new thing, something that will change me forever.

She saw Sydny looking at her with a particular intensity that made her ears burn and the skin of her throat turn pink. "What?" she whispered.

"Let's go back to my place."

A fizzy sensation took up residence in Julie's chest, reminding her of the moment she had stepped aboard her first roller coaster. Ecstasy and terror combined. "Aren't you due another turn?"

"Gregory isn't here. It's a slow night." Sydny's smile was like a cat stretching. "Besides, I have something better in mind than climbing a pole."

24

When Charlie returned to the room where Seiran el-Habib sat, tied to his chair and guarded by a fierce-looking Orteño, Whitman was still in the hallway listening with growing concern to what Cutler was telling him.

She went right to el-Habib, and, taking out a knife, cut his bonds. "A man like you, guarded by American soldiers, shouldn't be tied up."

"At last." El-Habib glared at Flix. "Someone who's come to her senses." He worked his wrists to return circulation to them.

Flix, for his part, goggled at both of them as if they had grown second heads. "What the fuck d'you think you're doing?" he said to Charlie.

Charlie came around in front of the Saudi. "Stand up, please."

Flix swung his AR-15 into firing position. "*Chica*, I won't ask you again: What are you doing?"

Charlie ignored him. "Stand up, let's get your legs working."

"I don't think this is a good idea," Flix said, ricocheting between nervousness and anger. "Better to wait for Whit."

Charlie, continuing to ignore him, smiled sweetly at el-Habib. She reached forward, gave him a hand up. "Now, how does that feel?"

"Better," he said as he tested the strength of his legs.

She stared him straight in the eye as she slammed her knee into his groin. "How about now?"

El-Habib's mouth formed a shocked *O*. As he tried to double over, Charlie grabbed him by the armpits, kept him more or less erect as his body spasmed in agony.

"What's going on here?" Whitman said, striding in.

"I tried to stop her, *compadre*," Flix said. "She's a loose cannon. Don't say I didn't warn you."

Whitman handed the sat phone back. "Charlie, what's going on?"

"The Chinese are going on," she said. Her face was so close to el-Habib's she could smell the stink of fear and pain coming out of his mouth. "You're in bed with the Chinese. Isn't that right, fucker?"

El-Habib stared at her, shaking.

"*Compadre*, how long are you going to let her—"

He broke off at the sight of Whitman's raised hand. "Seiran," he said softly, almost gently, "I'd like to intervene, really I would. But this woman is a force of nature. Once she starts down a path even God can't stop her, so I'm going to take a step back and give you two the space she needs."

"*Dios mío*, Whit, she's out of control."

Whitman whipped around. "Shut the fuck up, Flix. Go back to what you do best, monitoring comms. Make sure no one's trying to reach the compound. And take it outside, will you?"

Shooting a dagger of a look Charlie's way, Flix made his exit, muttering a string of filthy Spanish imprecations. For her part, Charlie had reached down and grabbed el-Habib's balls, squeezing hard. Tears flew out of his eyes and a dribble of saliva appeared at one corner of his mouth. He said something unintelligible.

Whitman stepped forward. "I can't hear you, Seiran."

"Make . . . make her stop."

Charlie bared her teeth. "Only you can do that, fucker."

"H-how?" he said through teeth clenched in pain.

"Tell me about the Chinese."

"I . . . I don't know what you're talking about."

"I saw the tin, fucker. The tea tin. That didn't come from Mecca or Kabul or Islamabad. It came from Beijing, courtesy of your friends there."

"*Khara*," el-Habib said. "*Khara, merde*, shit."

She turned to Whit. "You wondered why the NSA first targeted this prick? Now you know. He's in bed with the Chinese."

"Doing what?" Whitman inserted his face next to Charlie's. "What are you doing with the Chinese, Seiran?"

"I–I'll tell you, but get her to let go of my private parts."

Whitman shook his head. "No can do. Her interrogation, her rules."

For a long moment, el-Habib's eyes beseeched Whitman's. Then, finding no solace there, he closed his eyes.

"Please," he whispered, to Charlie, Whitman, or Allah.

"I'll let go when you're done," Charlie said. "Not a moment before."

The Saudi nodded. "I'm a kind of middleman."

Charlie tightened her grip. "Either you're a middleman, fucker, or you aren't."

More tears leaked out of el-Habib's eyes, squeezed shut against the grinding agony. "Okay, okay, I am a middleman."

"Between who and who?"

"You know."

"I want to hear you say it, fucker."

His teeth ground together. "The Chinese and the Americans."

Charlie gave Whit a meaningful glance, then she said, "The American government."

"No. A private group." Then he let out a scream as she increased the pressure on him.

"Liar. You were guarded by members of the U.S. military."

His eyes flew open. The capillaries in the whites were bloodshot. "I'm telling you the truth, I swear."

"Evidence says otherwise."

"I can't help that. The person who comes every six months—"

"He brings you new girls because you get bored with the old ones."

His eyes opened wide. "Who told you that?" he whispered.

"Alice."

"She's a born liar." He looked around. "Where is she, anyway?"

"In the kitchen, fast asleep." Charlie's hand pulled him back to her vector. "A man with milky blue eyes will be here in three days," she said. "Is that a lie, too?"

El-Habib quailed beneath her withering gaze. "N . . . no. He . . . he'll be here."

"With a new pair of girls."

When the Saudi did not respond, Charlie said, "Answer me or it won't matter how many girls he brings."

"Please. Have mercy. Yes, he'll be bringing the girls."

"His name is Dante?"

"The girls know—knew—him by that name."

"And by what name d'you know him?"

"The same."

"And Dante works for what private group?"

Seiran el-Habib hung his head. He was done; Charlie had wrung him nearly dry. "It calls itself the Alchemists."

"I want to lean on your shoulder."

Sydny's cat's eyes watched Julie in the apartment's semi-darkness.

"On every level imaginable."

Sydny smiled. "That's why you're here."

"That's the new thing you're leading me toward."

"One of the new things, but only one. Anyway, as you'll soon learn, they're all interconnected."

Sydny's one-bedroom apartment was unnaturally large, as if she had bought two apartments and made her one-bedroom out of them. The walls and ceiling were enameled black, the high gloss giving the optical illusion that the rooms were even larger than they actually were.

The bedroom surprised Julie. Though the room was super-sized, the bed was only a double; the rest of the room was furnished in High Spartan fashion: a carved armoire, a high-backed leather chair, a dressing table and stool before a theatrical makeup mirror. Nothing else. The wood floor was bare, as were the glossy aubergine walls. And not a speck of dirt to be seen anywhere.

"Where in the world do you keep your clothes?" Julie asked.

Striding ahead of her, Sydny touched a button and part of the rear wall slid back, revealing a walk-in closet the size of a Manhattan studio apartment. Julie stepped in and a light went on: racks of clothes, racks of shoes and boots. She stood stock-still as Sydny came up behind her.

"You like?"

Julie nodded, dumbstruck.

"Let's have you try something on," Sydny whispered in her ear. "What do you say?"

Julie's eyes closed as she felt Sydny's breath on her bare neck. "Pick an outfit for me," she whispered in return.

"Isn't that why I'm here?" Sydny said with a laugh.

Julie turned around to face her. "Don't laugh at me."

Sydny placed her palms against Julie's cheeks. "Poor lamb, not knowing who you are."

Their eyes locked.

"There's nothing inside me, Sydny. Nothing at all."

"You know that's not true."

"No? Then where is it? I can't feel it."

"Remember what you felt when I kissed you the other night?"

Yes, Julie mouthed, as if she were afraid to give voice to that feeling.

"Why are you so afraid of it?"

"It's not me," Julie said automatically.

"Kitten, do you hear yourself? You're a walking oxymoron. Everything you say, everything you want cancels itself out. And what are you left with?"

"A vacuum."

"But nature abhors a vacuum, so we're going to fill the vacuum."

"With what?"

Sydny took down a shimmering black bustier and tap pants set. "With everything you think is wrong."

Flix, monitoring the ether in the compound's near courtyard, felt as if his brain was about to explode. There was a pulsing behind his eyes that turned brown to black, green to blue, red to gray. His breath came in hot spurts, as if being ejected from the end of a pistol. His pulse fluttered like a terrified bird, and a nerve twitched in his upper eyelid.

As he listened to a bandwidth of static, he watched a tremor start up in his hands, as if he were looking at an image on a movie screen: it was both larger than life and removed from himself. For a terrifying moment, he thought he was screening *Zero Dark Thirty*, then he pulled himself back from the brink and knew who he was and what he was supposed to be doing.

But in almost the same moment, the pain behind his eyes began again. Who was he, what had he become? It was as if someone—some*thing*—else had taken up residence in his brain and body, some malevolent force that was out to bury him, incinerate him, obliterate whatever it was that made him Felix Orteño. It had no use for Felix Orteño. He had to stop it before it finished him.

His hands went to his face, fingers curled, turning into claws. He felt his own nails digging into the flesh of his temples, and experienced a sudden flash of insight: the only way to stop it was to tear off his face.

25

"... *person of interest who works there. Pole dancer, occasional lap dancer. She goes by the name of Sydney.*" That was Hemingway's voice. "*Real name—*" The sound of paper shuffling "*—Louise Kapok. . . . She's working tonight. Starts at ten, but I want you to be there earlier to get the lay of the land, as it were.*"

St. Vincent cringed at the sound of Omar Hemingway's fatuous chuckle. After his unpleasant dinner with the bigot Monroe, he had returned to the office. He'd been so preoccupied with the disappearance and probable murder of Bluto that he'd fallen behind in listening to the daily tapes of conversation in Hemingway's office.

"*Let me get this straight.*" St. Vincent identified Julie Regan's voice. "*You want me to stake out The Doll House?*"

"*That's right.*"

He'd had Omar's office bugged for months, which was how he had found out that Hemingway had targeted Seiran el-Habib. Lucky for St. Vincent; he'd spiked that Universal Security brief and then had mustered all his political force into getting the NSA to move on to other targets.

" *. . . but I don't want a field man,*" Omar the Idiot was saying now. "*I want you to talk to Sydney woman to woman.*"

In addition, and against any other off-the-books incursions, St. Vincent had ordered a cadre of seven soldiers to guard el-Habib. He was most concerned with Gregory Whitman, who he knew from the man's time in the Alchemists. It fact it had been St. Vincent himself who had recruited Whitman, at Preach's suggestion—though, really, when he thought about it Preach never made suggestions. St. Vincent recalled going to see Whitman. He was a profiler in the FBI's Washington field office at 601 4th Street NW. He was one of the FBI's prized possessions, having been instrumental in the capture of half a dozen serial murderers in his four years on the job.

St. Vincent recalled the intensity with which Whitman listened to his recruitment pitch, but it was the mention of Preach's name that intrigued him the most and, unless his memory was playing tricks on him, caused him to agree to join the Alchemists. And yet no one wanted him at the heart of the matter; no one wanted him to know the Alchemists' true goal of furthering their own power and wealth. Monroe was convinced that Whitman was an altruist. He did what he did for the good of the many, not of the few. And so essential secrets were withheld from him. What he told Whitman: they were fighting terrorism in ways the government could not.

For a while, St. Vincent and Whitman had been friends—close, even, principally because of their connection to Preach, though from what little St. Vincent gleaned from Whitman, their experiences with Preach were altogether different. It seemed to St. Vincent that Whitman had no fear of Preach at all, and this knowledge gradually turned envy into hate.

And then came the incident at the Well that, for the two men, changed everything.

At the Well, St. Vincent had been witness to much of Whitman's extraordinary work. Whitman possessed an extraordinary talent for extracting the deepest, most closely held secrets of their terrorist prisoners. It was as if, after he had opened them up, so to speak, they could not resist him.

The other interrogators at the Well opened the terrorists up the way people open a can of peas—cutting through layers with puncture and blade. They were rough, unrelenting, and, most times, successful, though later it was discovered that the victims had simply parroted back what their interrogators wanted to hear, rendering the cruel and bloody process useless.

Not so Whitman's subjects. He invariably got out of them the most secretive truths that were a boon to the Alchemists' plans. Possibly it was this same uncanny talent that caused Whitman to become a cause célèbre among his brethren at the FBI. And gradually it dawned on St. Vincent that there were aspects of this talent that reminded him uncomfortably of Preach.

Nevertheless, Whitman's work at the Well was so successful Monroe had no choice but to use him more and more. Then came the day when Whitman overheard St. Vincent and Monroe talking over the intel Whitman had extracted from an Iraqi member of ISIS regarding the terrorist organization's plans to take over Iraq, Syria, Jordan, and Palestine and resurrect the ancient area known as al-Sham. It was blockbuster intel that played right into the Alchemists' plans to aid the Kurds in northern Iraq. And so on that day Whitman learned how his rendition had played a key role in the Alchemists' furthering the ISIS cause for their own ends. At first, when he confronted them, he threatened to expose them, but St. Vincent rightly pointed out that exposure would only destroy Whitman's career, reputation, and, most likely, his life. Even then, Whitman remained adamant. He was outraged at what he termed "their hideous plan." The idiot said his life was nothing compared to the death and suffering ISIS was going to unleash with the Alchemists' help.

That was when Preach showed up as he always did, without warning but, uncannily, at a crucial moment. He took Whitman aside. "Whatever you're thinking of doing, don't. If you open your mouth about this you can be sure no one will believe you. You'll be branded a madman; you'll become an object of derision. Your credibility will be shattered. Your life in this country—anywhere, for that matter—will be over."

Whitman abandoned the Alchemists, kept his mouth shut, but from that moment on, despite Preach's assurances concerning the coming newer, better world, St. Vincent felt compelled to keep an eye on Whitman, lest he do something really stupid. "*You betrayed me,*" Whitman, the weak fucker, had said. "*You used our friendship. That's something I'll never forgive or forget.*" Monroe had been right about him after all—Whitman was altruistic, a contemptible trait that would not be tolerated by any true Alchemist.

To keep an eye on Whitman, he had contacted King Cutler, advised him to make Whitman an offer he couldn't refuse, and ordered him to keep Whitman busy out of the country, and in line.

And, fuck me, St. Vincent thought now, the sonuvabitch found a way to insinuate himself back into my business.

From what he'd gleaned there had been fallout from the aborted brief to take el-Habib into custody. Just the thought of that sent him into a paroxysm of rage. Seiran el-Habib's contacts inside Mainland China were key to the Alchemists' continuing plans. Any disruption of the content those contacts were supplying could not be tolerated. If there was a continuing danger to el-Habib it would surely be from the man whose demonic persistence in the Well St. Vincent had observed firsthand. Which was why he had messengered over the brief on Ibrahim Mansour to Hemingway's office, marked "Eyes Only from the Office of the President of the United States." St. Vincent had deemed keeping Whitman occupied by sending him and his team off to Beirut the best option to ensure el-Habib's continued safety.

". . . *this has to stay between the two of us,*" Omar the Idiot was saying now. "*It's not an official op, which, as you know, we are forbidden by law to conduct on U.S. soil . . . Also I don't want her spooked.*"

"*Why in the world would she be spooked?*"

"*Because one of her best clients is Greg Whitman.*"

That, of course, caused St. Vincent to come to full alert.

"A word," Whitman said.

Charlie nodded, followed him out, down the hall, into one of the rumpled bedrooms.

How was it, Whitman wondered, that the Alchemists kept coming back into his life, ever darker, evil, bent on wholesale destruction? It was as if the hand of Fate was pulling him back into their orbit—St. Vincent's orbit—in order to put a stop to them. None of this was in his expression when he said to Charlie, "What the hell was that back there?"

"You know perfectly well what it was."

"Alice was your responsibility. El-Habib was my interrogation."

She looked him hard in the face. "No, you made Alice my responsibility."

"There's only one head to this monster. Me."

"Well, I've seen that monster, Whit. The real monster. Down in the

Well that was you. So, really, what I was doing was saving you from yourself."

"I don't remember that being part of your job description."

"And I don't remember saving me as being part of yours."

They stood toe to toe, so close their noses all but touched. Only once before had the tension between them reached this pitch—the night she had hit him, the night he had walked out.

His side ached where she had struck him; he hated that, hated them both for the damage they had inflicted on each other, but he could see no way for either of them to stop. You might as well ask the sun and moon to join hands, he thought.

"We are who we are," she whispered.

"It is what it is," he said.

"And never the twain shall meet."

Afterward, neither of them could remember who said that last line, and perhaps it no longer mattered. Their Mexican standoff was shattered by the sound of a chair crashing. At once, both turned and, as one, raced back down the hall into the room where they had been interrogating Seiran el-Habib, but nothing was amiss there. He still sat on his chair, a mass of misery with no thought of standing, let alone running away. Still, protocol had to be observed, and Whitman called to Flix to come back and watch over their prisoner.

"The kitchen!" Charlie said, suddenly breathless.

She arrived an instant before Whitman. When she'd left, Alice had been asleep in the chair, her head resting peacefully on her arms on the tabletop. Now the chair was on its side, as was Alice, who lay in a spreading pool of blood so dark it looked like oil. One of the kitchen knives, its blade bloodied, lay near one of her hands. She had slit her wrists the correct way, with longitudinal cuts along the veins, rather than across them.

Charlie ran to her, knelt in her blood to take her pulse, but it was too late, there was none. She sat back on her haunches. "Ah, hell." Her voice was a harsh whisper. "I thought she was stronger than this. But she was just a little girl, lost and terrified."

Whitman stood over her, staring at the back of her neck. "She was your responsibility, Charlie."

"I know that."

"You left her to make a name for yourself in Red Rover by interrogating el-Habib."

"No."

"A first step in taking over."

"Oh, my god, you're crazy. This is like our last night together. I can't talk to you when you get like this."

"Like what?" Whitman crouched down beside her. "And this isn't anything like that night. I'm your boss, Charlie. This is strictly professional."

"Nothing is ever strictly professional with you, Whit. You weren't aware of it, but you made that perfectly clear down in the Well."

Whitman waved aside her words. "You left your charge and she killed herself. How much intel was still left inside her that we should have gotten?" He put his head close to hers, but there was nothing intimate in his demeanor. "You were negligent. You let her get away, you let the mission get away."

"Fuck you!" Charlie stood up and strode out without a backward glance.

It was very late, but St. Vincent had no desire to go home. Instead, he pressed a button on his desk and a wall slid back, revealing a monk-like cell, with a narrow bed consisting of a metal frame, a thin mattress, a set of undyed muslin sheets, and a walnut-hull pillow that would put a crimp in anyone's neck but his.

When St. Vincent went in, he was sealed off from the world, save for a small slit of a window left over from the time the space had been an executive toilet. Now, to use the facilities, St. Vincent was obliged to pad down the hall.

He shrugged off his suit jacket, stripped off his shirt and tie. Bare to the waist, he sat on the edge of the Spartan bed and stared at his hands, wrists placed on knees. Then his gaze drifted along the blue lines of his veins to the small tattoo on the inside of his left wrist: a triangle with a looped tail—the alchemical symbol for sulfur, one of the most important elements in the *arcana*, the secret of all life, according to Paracelsus, a sixteenth-century Swiss-born physician, birth name Theophrastus Philippus Aureolus Bombastus von Hohenheim, who viewed medicine as being chemical in nature and believed that the key to human life, therefore, was alchemical.

St. Vincent's thumb rubbed back and forth over the symbol, as if to release some of its latent power. His stomach was growling but he would not eat; he was a man used to deprivation—savored it, even, as his mother had before him. He switched on the old black-metal gooseneck lamp he'd had since he was a kid, his bed then a bunk in the Streamline trailer parked behind the revival tent with its huge crosses, shining as if to impress themselves onto the sky.

He remembered sitting on the edge of his bunk, time after time, listening to the finale of his mother's sermons—her voice lifted to the very crosses painted on the tent top, worked to a fervent crescendo. In the eerie silence that would follow, the natural sounds of crickets and birds seemed soft, muffled, as if his mother's words had cowed them as well as her congregants.

In his mind's eye, he could see the tent slowly emptying, the people filing past his mother who had stepped down from the platform to shake hands, accept both praise and prayer, while her acolytes, who flanked her on either side, raked in the money. Then they, too, melted away and his mother, still covered in holy sweat, a fragrant dampness under her arms, between her thighs, mounted the steps of the Streamline, and entered the world made up of two inhabitants.

Her cheeks were flushed, her eyes still sparking the holy scripture as she sat down beside him and said, "How's my little man?" She put a hand on his thigh. "It's late. You're not asleep yet?"

"I was listening to you, Mother."

This brought a smile to her face. It was a Pavlovian response; he hadn't even heard of Pavlov back then, but later he would come to understand the dynamic between them, though never completely, and never at its deepest level. He was too close to her, the experiences too subjective for rational dissection. And, of course, there was a part of him that refused to look at what would happen next.

"Luther," she whispered, "what have you done?"

She knew! But then she always knew. "There was someone in the crowd," he said. "A lost woman coming to you to help her find God. I snuck out and watched her."

"She was a wanton woman."

"Yes."

"The sight of her drew you."

"Yes."

His mother's eye were upon him. "She was evil, and you were evil, Luther."

"She was, Mother. And I was."

His mother's dark eyes seemed to grow in size, to become luminous, like the moon gleaming in the sun's reflected light. "You need to be punished, Luther."

"Yes, Mother. I do."

26

"What is this?" Julie picked up a black latex hood. It came down over the face. Two small holes had been punched for the nostrils; above and below were zippers where the eyes and mouth would be. Up high on the forehead were two protrusions that Julie took to be horns.

"The hood?"

Julie nodded. "That, and what was underneath it."

"The SIG Sauer. I have a permit. In my line of work you can't be too careful. The cops didn't disagree."

"I hate guns." Julie shuddered. "Any guns."

"Then don't go near it, and for god's sake don't touch it."

"Don't worry, I won't."

"Good girl." Sydny nodded. "Now back to the mask." She was still holding the bustier and tap pants. "Do you find it interesting?"

"I find it frightening. What are these horns for?"

"Those are for another evening. You're only a beginner here."

Julie shook her head. "It's nightmarish."

Sydny smiled a secret smile, so that Julie felt compelled to say, "What?"

Sydny stepped out of the closet, drew the drapes over the windows, effectively sealing them off from the outside world. "Do you know *Story of O*?"

"Should I?"

"It's a novel—a great one, a groundbreaking story—written by Pauline Réage, a writer who up until the novel's publication no one had heard of. In fact, for many years it was assumed by critics and intellectuals—mostly men—that Pauline Réage was a pseudonym for a man, because only a man could write about such sexual debauchery. Of course, they were proven wrong. The writer was a woman named Anne Cécile Desclos."

Sydny circled back to where Julie stood in the entrance to the closet. "The heroine's name—O—is the shortest possible, though her name is Odile. She is rarely called that. So. O could also stand for object or orifice."

Julie stared at Sydny wide-eyed. "What happened to O?"

"Adventures." Sydny's eyes sparkled in the warm lamplight. "The preface was titled 'Happiness in Slavery.'"

"How is that possible?"

Sydny shrugged. "It's a way of life, of stripping away the layers of civilization that bind all adults, layer by painful layer. It's a way of arriving at the nature of things."

"I don't understand."

"You will." Sydny put a hand on Julie shoulder. "Most people are under the impression that sex is pleasure."

"It seems to me it is. Or should be."

"Then why are you so afraid of allowing yourself an orgasm?"

"I . . . I don't know. It's complicated."

"No, it's the opposite of complicated. Having an orgasm means letting go—everything you cling to: guilt, fear, shame, the terror of doing something unforgivable."

"I equate sex with love, with happiness."

"No, you don't." Sydny shook her head. "You equate sex with humiliation, ineptitude, manipulation, and—what am I leaving out? Oh, yes, lies." Sydny was as unflinching in her gaze as she was in what she was saying. "Happiness is an ideal, something you've been told you need to work hard toward, when, in fact, happiness is nothing more than exercising an illusion."

"You're saying it's not real. That I can't be happy?"

"Not at all. But it can't be reached until you understand that sex is power.

Happiness lies in understanding the true nature of things. Otherwise, what are you? A slave to the illusions you create for yourself."

"Sydny, you're scaring me."

"Only because that new thing you crave is not yet understandable to you. It's alien, frightening. But think. The so-called laws you grew up with were all meant to inhibit your passions, to drive them underground so they would seem filthy, immoral. But I will tell you this: the only true way to a woman's heart is along the path of torment."

Sydny took the hood from Julie's hand. "You don't believe me."

"I don't see any reason I should."

"Look. I told you that sex is power. You don't believe me? How many women have you seen lose touch with themselves, simply disappear when they attach themselves to a man?" Her lips curved upward. "You're smart. When you go to political dinners or cocktail parties what do the women look like to you? Ornaments, icing, *objects*. Isn't that right." It wasn't a question.

Julie continued to look at her, but seemed incapable of forming an answer.

"That abdication of power is pathetic, don't you think?" Sydny cocked her head. "Do you want to leave?" She gestured toward the door out to the living room. "You're not a prisoner. If you don't want to be here, please leave."

Julie, both frightened and fascinated, stood rooted to the spot.

Looking as stern as a military commandant, Sydny said, "You need to voice it, Julie."

"I want to stay." Her answer was immediate. Her voice seemed to come from a place inside her she did not recognize.

Sydny nodded. "Give me your handbag." Julie handed it over without protest, watching as Sydny opened one of the doors to the armoire, tossed the bag into a space behind a line of boots with heels so high just looking at them gave Julie a nosebleed.

"You have on too many clothes," Sydny observed. "Get rid of your jacket. Just drop it on the floor." Julie complied. "Now come sit over here." She indicated the high-backed leather chair. Julie sat, her bare knees primly together. She smoothed her pleated skirt over her thighs.

"Now take off your panties. That's right, slide them down your legs. When you sit back down, lift the back of your skirt up so there's nothing between you and the leather."

Holding up her skirt, Julie sat back down. Gooseflesh sprang out on her thighs and arms as her private parts made contact with the cool leather. She watched Sydny duck into the closet. She emerged holding a pair of velvet-soft gloves.

"Put these on."

They ran all the way up to Julie's elbows.

Approaching her, Sydny said, "Lean slightly forward." When Julie did so, she unbuttoned the first two buttons of Julie's silk blouse. "Don't move." She found the straps of Julie's bra and cut them with a small, opal-handled penknife, then snipped the front. The bra's cups came away from Julie breasts. Reaching in, she lifted the bra out and away.

Sydny eyed her. "I can see the outline of your breasts through your blouse. Your nipples are hard. Are you excited?"

Julie could scarcely breathe. Her voice failed her.

Sydny approached her, slid her hand under Julie's skirt, felt the dampness between her thighs. "You are." She smiled in the way a mother smiles at her daughter, a connection, a certain intimacy that cannot ever be repeated with anyone else. "Are you ready to surrender." Again, it wasn't a question.

She handed Julie the hood.

27

Even in the most desolate climate there was always beauty. Whitman, however, was in no condition to ferret it out. Even though he stood in the compound with his back to the villa, even though the sunlight brushed his cheek, the breeze ruffled his hair, he was somewhere far, far away.

Around him rose walls of iron and steel, down one of which a sheet of water dropped like a curtain in a mortuary viewing room. At the bottom of this particular wall was a rectangular trough, constructed of hand-hewn stones, into which the water spilled. Stories inside the Well told of this trough being bottomless, like the myth of the sacred *cenote* at Chichen Itza, a thousand years old. So many blood sacrifices had been made at that *cenote*, the bodies of so many of the Mayan enemies had plunged into its depths, that it had come to be known as The Well of Souls.

The stench of the Well filled his nostrils, clogging them with the fetor of terror, human excrement, blood, and flesh stripped from its rightful place on the body. In this Charlie was right, he had made a fatal error in taking her there. Why had he? No, so many years later, he could not say. He had told himself that he'd wanted to share everything with her, but truth could be a terrible thing, especially when it came to the Well.

He knew he couldn't long survive this kind of introspection; he was not the suicidal type. He also knew memories of the Well had been triggered by Alice's terrible death. For someone so young to die was agony enough, but that it should come from her own hand spoke of a despair beyond comprehension. But that was another lie he was feeding to himself. Of course he could comprehend her despair; he'd seen it every night he had worked down in the Well.

Fumbling in his backpack, he found his iPod and earbuds, plugged them in, and listened to the original 1927 recording of Hoagy Carmichael playing "Star Dust," which in the years following the addition of lyrics, became known as "Stardust." Back in the day, he and Charlie would get dressed up, sneak into wedding receptions in order to foxtrot to the hired bands, the last of the venues where these bands could find work. But these happy memories only impressed upon him how his relationship with Charlie had deteriorated. A final blowup, then atrophy. And here they were, in the bleakness of the enemy's stronghold, at each other's throats.

How could his life get any worse?

It came as a revelation to Preach that death could be a good thing—a wanted thing—a powerful thing. This had never occurred to him, and why should it? He had never died. Unlike Crow.

And Crow came to him while he was in his great circular marble bath, which was situated in the center of his ramshackle house deep in the bayous. It was the house he had lived in for many, many years, the place from which he had battled the evangelical preachers so drunk on their own power they relished lording it over their sheep-like followers. He had spent decades fighting their invidious lies, couched in half-truths. He had felt like a lone voice in the wilderness, which, in fact, he was. Not altogether by his own choice.

The three female acolytes swam around him like Homer's sirens, their long, fiery hair darkened by water to the color of fresh blood. Their sheer gowns were plastered to their lithe bodies, more erotic than if they had been nude. Their beautiful milky-skinned faces, one lightly misted by freckles, were all turned to him as flowers turned to the sun. Their hands were on his flesh, moving—always moving. They were happy—he was happy.

A commotion turned his attention to the bath's door. A young man in a policeman's uniform strode in, unbidden, unannounced, but not unanticipated. His name was Kneckne. He was new. He didn't know the score.

His hand was on the butt of his service revolver. "You the man they call Preach?"

"I am," said Preach.

Officer Kneckne approached the tub. "There've been complaints about this place, about you."

"What sort of complaints, son?"

Kneckne frowned, his eyes taking in the three sirens. "Lewd and lascivious acts; profane acts against God and Nature. Evil things."

Preach smiled. "I don't see anything evil around here. Do you, son?"

"Why, sir, yes, I do." He stood at the edge of the tub, unsnapped his holster. There was a film of sweat on his upper lip and a dangle of snot in one nostril. "You're going to have to come with me."

"Oh, I don't think so."

"Sir, I see you're an ignorant man. You don't understand the laws of the land. You don't have a choice in the matter."

Knechne didn't know the score, and now he never would.

Preach uttered a single word under his breath and the three acolytes rose up, as one, grabbed Knechne while he was still gawping at their near-nakedness, and pulled him under the water. He thrashed, his arms and legs beating a tattoo, sending waves lapping over the sides of the tub, but his head never reappeared.

The acolytes weren't sirens; they were death-dealers. Preach had taught them how to kill; they performed their task by instinct, unhindered by thought or choice.

When he stopped thrashing, they hauled the corpse out of the tub. Two of them took him outside to the woodshed, where, later, he would be fed into the chipper. As usual, they would bicker over who would have the honor; Preach would let them. A bit of spirited competitiveness was healthy.

When they returned, they slid back into the water as if it was their natural element. Preach smiled at them and they smiled back. Their long, strong fingers recommended their caressing of his nipples, scrotum, and phallus.

Preach closed his eyes and sighed deeply, his thoughts running his long life backwards. He had many talents, but making money wasn't one of them; he lacked the patience to work for other people; he lacked the temperament to start at the bottom and work his way up a corporate ladder. He was a ferocious autodidact, unschooled in any traditional manner. His worldview was diametrically opposite of those in the world's corporate suites. He had learned this early on in life, so he used other people to make money for him. He was good at influencing people—better than good, actually. Nobody did it better.

His parents were dirt-poor. They had nothing; they wanted nothing. Unlike them, Preach wanted everything—everything except fame. He shied away from fame, the limelight, being known. He lived in the shadows at the edge of the world, and he was smart enough to understand that that was where he belonged. He was out of his element walking among the hordes of men and women who teemed across the continents.

But he could select a precious few, draw them to him, indoctrinate them, work through them while deluding them into believing they were making decisions of their own free will. Life was filled with forks in the road, decisions to be made that led to one future or another. His will was done by taking away certain forks. Editing their lives. As a pack of baying hounds will cut off the fox's myriad escape routes until it had only one way to go, with the foreknowledge that Crow gave him, Preach manipulated people into moving inexorably toward a future he had devised like a sculptor exploring a block of marble, seeing, as only he can, the end result.

He had created the Alchemists. They massed money, more than he might ever need, and power. Their tentacles had spread to virtually every corner of the globe. Of course he had a vast network, in law enforcement, politics, economics, merchant banking, but those people were passive: messengers of intel, nothing more. The Alchemists were an active group. Its members did what he directed them to do, when he directed them to do it. All save Greg Whitman. Much to Preach's chagrin, life was not a block of marble. The future of which he was given glimpses was not a block of marble. Whitman, he had discovered, had a way of mucking up even his most meticulously laid plans. But then Whitman was special. He knew that the instant he pressed his fingertip to Whitman's father's breastbone. Moments later, the man died of a cerebral aneurism. Preach had had a moment of regret—one of the very few in his long, long life—but it was fleeting, and left no imprint on him. The death was necessary to remove the fork in the young Whitman's life that would have led him away from Preach. He could not have that. Whitman was like Preach, he could have a familiar—like Crow—if he wished it. He might divine the future, as Preach did. He had mastered the resurrection technique almost as if he'd known it in his bones. And he might know more—he might—but he would have to unlock those secrets himself. Whitman was like a son to Preach, someone who might one day surpass even his own accomplishments. Like all of the people Preach brought into his orbit, Whitman had a streak of cruelty in him. It was others' penchant for cruelty that Preach exploited, that bound his people to him. But Whitman's cruelty was a reptilian thing, glimpsed in light, vanishing in shadow, one moment there, the next not, so that Preach could never be sure of it, never be certain of his hold over Whitman, even despite his pounding into Whitman the glory of the newer, better world to come. For there was a part of Whitman, Preach suspected, that rejected his own cruelty, was repulsed by it, while the others savored theirs like vintage wine.

It was in this reflective mood that Crow found him. The acolytes could not, of course, see Crow, but they felt his shade move across their bare shoulders like a sudden icefall, and they shuddered, pulling back to the far side of the tub, eyes glassy and, for the moment, fearful.

Crow brought him up to date on all the people in the net he had cast far and wide years ago. But as of this moment everyone was performing as planned—even, this time, Whitman. The future was still as Crow had envisioned it.

28

At any given moment of the day or night, St. Vincent had at his disposal a virtual battalion of people: not only a driver, bodyguards, security detail, but also, should he required them, a chef, masseuse, even a psychiatrist. But there were times when circumstances dictated that he be alone. This was one of them.

A sliver of moon seemed to beckon him onward. He drove carefully, keeping to the various speed limits. As with anything that had to do with Gregory Whitman he struggled to keep his emotions in check, but there was so much history, so many memories he wished to annihilate that it was tough sledding. His mind kept going back into the Well, to his time there with Whitman.

He slid the car to the curb in front of The Doll House. Fifty bucks got him inside without the usual scrutiny, and a hundred more to the manager on duty bought him key information: that Sydny had left for the night, the name of the nearby café she frequented, and her home address. Neither place was far away.

A brisk walk brought him to the café. He went in, ordered a Scotch, which was some cheap crap he scarcely touched. As he paid for it he asked the bartender if Sydny was there.

"Haven't seen her all night," he said.

"Brings all her johns here, does she?"

"Go fuck yourself," the bartender said before he went off to fill the order of a pair of regulars at the other end of the bar.

Back in the car, St. Vincent shook out a cigarette and lit up. He hadn't smoked since the Well closed. But it was open again, and that meant Whitman would be involved again whether or not anyone liked it. He most certainly did not, though he knew Monroe would welcome it. St. Vincent was certain that of all the Alchemists Monroe alone would be happy to see Whitman again. Perhaps happy wasn't the right word. Relieved? Grateful? St. Vincent could see why, but only by straining his brain to its limits. Whitman was far too dangerous to be allowed anywhere near the reopened Well. Hadn't Monroe learned anything from the first time?

He sat and smoked until the car's interior was as smog-bound as a Beijing street. He closed his eyes. Maybe he was getting too old for this. Wasn't it true that in every gunslinger's life there came a time when a younger one was faster, smarter, stronger?

But not yet. Not today, or even tomorrow.

St. Vincent turned the ignition on, eased the car out into the street. Eight minutes later he was parked across from Sydny's apartment. He lit another cigarette, opened the window, stared at the façade of her building. He let his mind wander, allowed his imagination to take root, until visions of what Sydny might be doing and in what stage of undress flashed across the scrim of his mind. He tried to imagine the depths of such a lewd woman's sins. Then he tried harder, so hard an ache began behind his eyes, the same kind of ache he'd get when he slid into bed after one of his mother's visit, as if he were inside a storm of wasps.

He smoked the cigarette down to the nub, flicked it into the road. He was about to get out of the car when his mobile buzzed. Dickerson.

"How are you and Lucy getting along?"

"Fine," Dickerson said in his ear. "But I—"

"Where have you put her up?"

"My place for the time being, but boss—"

"I'm busy, Jonah. You have thirty seconds."

"We have a situation, boss. Sergeant Moran has failed to check in."

"Maybe he's taking a crap." St. Vincent stared up at the light coming through the living room windows of Sydny's apartment. The bedroom was dark.

"We can't raise anyone in the cadre," Dickerson said. "It's as if the comm at the villa doesn't exist."

Now he had St. Vincent's full attention. A thought entered St. Vincent's mind—a terrible thought. "Jonah, where is Whitman and the Red Rover team?"

"They're supposed to be in Beirut."

"I know where they're *supposed* to be, shithead." St. Vincent was truly irritated now. Irritated and more than a little alarmed. "Find out where they *actually* are. You have thirty minutes. If, by then, you can't give me a definitive answer, pack your possessions. You'll be cleaning toilets in the congressional bathrooms."

Enough! Whitman shouted silently. He was team leader; he had to remain unshaken by everything no matter what. He had to heal someone.

"*Compadre!*" he called. "*¡Ven aquí, por favor!*"

Flix appeared a moment later. Whitman was shocked at how much he had changed in just a matter of a half hour. His cheeks were sunken, his eyes looked like black holes in a skull. Worst of all, bloody vertical tracks scored down either side of his face, like war paint or ritual incisions. Crescents of crusted blood were visible under his nails.

There were still other changes: he moved as if on ball bearings, his boots scarcely touching the ground. He made as much noise as an owl on the hunt, which was to say, none. His eyes seemed focused on both Whitman and on the immediate environment, which, so far as Whitman knew, was impossible.

But then again maybe not. Years ago, he had been sent down to the swamps of southern Louisiana as part of his training for the Well. He'd spent six months in that hellhole, which was literal as well as figurative. While there, he met a young boy, not more than twelve or thirteen, riding a bike. The kid looked no different from the other kids Whitman had seen in his time down there amid the mishmash of religions, superstitions, and ethnicities. The kid could have been Creole, but he also could have been mestizo, or a mix of anything, which was pretty much the norm in the noxious bayous south of New Orleans, where voodoo and Santería spawned their love children.

He'd come across the kid in the red glare of early morning, when the Spanish moss didn't seem so malignant and the stench of oil wasn't so pervasive. Whitman was taking a run when he saw the kid, sitting astride his bike, eating his breakfast. What made Whitman stop was the faux license plate on the bike. Instead of a series of numbers and letters it was imprinted with the phrase: CTHULHU IS COMING.

Whitman had read Lovecraft. He'd found *The Call of Cthulhu* in his mother's night table and, stealing it, had read it by flashlight under the nighttime bedcovers, far after he should have been asleep. Cthulhu was one of what Lovecraft called the Old Ones, demonic, God-like beasts worshipped by people of a certain, half-mad stripe. Cthulhu was described as a colossal cephalopod with many tentacles and bat wings. Truly the stuff of nightmares.

As it turned out, Cthulhu wasn't the only bizarre thing the kid was into. As Whitman engaged him, the kid generously shared his breakfast and started talking a blue streak. Turned out he knew a man named Preach, a big kahuna in the swamplands, according to the kid, for many, many years. People came to him for potions, curses, voodoo, and Santería spells of every shape and variety. According to the kid, Preach had been at the forefront of the struggle against the demonization of non-Christian religions, directed by the area's fire-breathing evangelical preachers, of which there was no shortage.

The kid claimed he had witnessed a zombification ritual that had been performed by Preach in order to ease the pain of a friend diagnosed with a fatal disease.

"The idea of zombification's simple," the kid had said. "Course all those comics an' movies an' junk would have you think otherwise. Zombification's a purifying ritual—at least Preach's was. It cuts off what goes on in the head from what goes on in the body, so you feel no pain no matter how much hurt is put on you." The kid had shook his head. "All that undead stuff, I dunno. Preach told me he once met Papa Legba—midnight in our local cemetery. Rolled some dice, had a drink, a couple of laughs, that was it."

"And you believed him," Whitman had said.

The boy had peered at him queerly. "You would, too, if you'd'a seen that zombie. Grateful as shit, that zombie was. Gave Preach all his money, he did, for takin' away his sufferin'."

Even after all these years, Whitman could still hear the kid's laughter echoing through the dead trees, as the air thickened to okra stew with the rising of the vicious sun.

So now, here in Western Pak, Whitman could not help but feel that he had come face to face with a modern-day zombie. Because it was clear enough that Flix was no longer himself.

Whitman reached out. "Flix, come on over here and sit down."

He pulled Orteño into the shadow of the roof's overhang, sat facing him. "Tell me what's going on."

Flix held his head in his hands. "I would if I could," he said, "but I don't even know who I am. I can't recognize . . ." He dropped a pile of dog tags in the dirt between them. "Whit, I can't believe I killed these soldiers. How did I do it? I have no fucking memory of it. One minute I'm jumping into the compound, the next you're sending me out to check on all these dead men I shot." His head turned back and his feverish eyes clocked on Whit's. "I mean, what the fuck, man? What. The. Fuck!"

"Calm down, Flix."

Whitman squeezed Orteño's shoulder. The gesture caused Flix to rear back, his eyes open wide and staring, his hands up, ready to defend himself.

"Flix, for Christ's sake, it's me, Whit."

Orteño continued to stare at him as if he were the enemy.

"Flix, something happened to you back in the States."

"What?" Orteño blinked several times, his pupils contracting. "Oh, yeah, I know. The concussion. Could be that's what's—"

"You didn't have a concussion, Flix. They did something to you while you were unconscious."

"'They'? Who's 'they'?"

"One step at a time," Whit said. "What's the last thing you remember before waking up in the hospital?"

"I . . ." Flix frowned. "Who the fuck remembers?" He passed a hand across his eyes. "Wait, I had gone to see Lucy, my niece. She's been at the Bethesda Institute of Mary Immaculate, recovering from drugs."

"Who put her there, Flix?"

Orteño's face went vacant again, and Whit thought, zombified.

"St. Vincent," Flix said, at length. He seemed like two separate people.

"Luther St. Vincent?"

"Uh huh."

"From NSA?"

Flix nodded.

"Was he there on your last visit?"

"He's always there. He supervises the visits."

"Why? What's Luther St. Vincent have to do with Lucy?"

Orteño looked away. His face was pale and sweating, as if the two people inside his brain were fighting a dreadful war.

Whit suppressed an urge to lean forward. "*Compadre*, what is it?" He didn't want to trigger another aggressive response.

"She . . ." Flix licked his lips, his head dropping down. "She was in trouble with the law. State police, he said. And the FBI. Cuz she got caught crossing state lines with drugs."

Now it all became clear to Whitman. "So he got Lucy out of hock—if she ever really was in trouble with the feds."

Flix's head came up. "What d'you mean?"

"The whole thing could have been staged by St. Vincent." Whitman peered into his friend's face. "Flix, d'you understand? The cocksucker is using your niece as leverage." Whitman struggled to hold Flix's gaze with his own. He couldn't afford the eyes going out of focus, his consciousness beaten back again at this crucial moment. "Why, *compadre*? What's St. Vincent using Lucy for?"

"Jesus, Whit." Orteño looked and sounded miserable. "Jesus, don't be pissed. He wants me to spy on you. To report back whatever you do. He said it was because of the leak."

"And you believed him?"

"Honestly?" Flix blinked back a budding wetness in his eyes. "Honestly, I was thinking of Lucy, and my sister Marilena." Then he groaned. "Christ, Whit, what the hell's happening to me?"

"Let's get back to that last trip to see Lucy. You saw her and then what?"

Flix closed his eyes. "It's all one big kaleidoscope, *compadre*. My brain feels like a piñata that's been hit over and over."

"I know, Flix. But *think*. Try to concentrate. You left Lucy and . . . ?"

"And nothing, *nada* . . ." His expression was horrible to see—twisted, seeming to morph from one aspect to another, gripped by interior shadows. Then he gasped, surfacing again. "No, wait a minute. I remember St. Vincent walking me out. There was a car, an ambulance, then he said, 'Watch your head!' as I was getting into . . ."

He shook his head. "Nothing, Whit. Nothing, except waking up in the hospital." Unconsciously, he put a hand to the side of his neck.

"What is it?"

"Nothing. I . . . don't know."

Whitman leaned in, turned him a bit. He peered at the spot Orteño had touched. "It's a needle mark, Flix. St. Vincent injected you, knocked you out. You were abducted."

It was then that the convulsions started and, fingers curled to animal claws, Orteño tried to rip his face off.

29

"You've waited long enough," St. Vincent's mother had said to him. "It's time you saw the face of the enemy."

St. Vincent, sitting in his car, another cigarette dangling between lips, checked his wristwatch. Twenty minutes to go. At the end of that time, whether or not Jonah had called, it would be time to confront Sydny.

He inhaled the smoke deep into his lungs and, as the nicotine hit, his memory flowered open to meet his present self. He remembered the evening, unnaturally clear as a bell, with a full moon riding the corner of an animal-shaped cloud.

Sitting next to his mother in the rattling Woody station wagon, he watched the swamps, the hunched trees, freighted with Spanish moss. The stench of sulfur and oil combined to coat the inside of his mouth. After what seemed a long time, they turned off the paved road onto a dirt track, bumping along for a mile or so.

Abruptly, his mother stopped the car and they got out. Thick tendrils of fog curled about their ankles, though all the time they were driving the night had been perfectly clear. He looked up, but could no longer find the moon.

Because his mother needed no light to guide her, he deduced that she had been here before, possibly many times. Turning sharply to their left, he saw pale lights burning through the windows of a house. Not even that; he saw as they came closer that it was more like a shack that was long past its sell-by date.

Inside they were met by a young boy with the disturbing ebon eyes of a crow. Behind him sat a man with prematurely white hair and a horrifying smile. Behind the man, spread across the rear wall more as a fetish than a trophy, hung a great wolf's head and skin, the teeth and claws painted in primary colors: red, yellow, blue.

The white-haired man had been studying something in his hands, which were folded in his lap. He looked up as they entered. St. Vincent was shocked. He'd been expecting eyes old and rheumy as the flesh around them, but these were the vivid color of a bluebird, alight with the vigor of youth.

"Ruth," Preach's voice rumbled like thunder, "you have been expected. Be seated."

"I prefer to stand."

Again, St. Vincent was shocked. He felt his mother's fear like a clap of thunder rolling across the bayous. He smelled it like the aftermath of a lightning strike, as if the atmosphere inside the hovel had suddenly filled up with ozone. The tip of his nose wrinkled; he felt like sneezing, as if to expel the fear he had absorbed.

"Desmortiers," she said. "This is my son, Luther."

"Preach, Ruth. Everyone calls me Preach."

"You think I give a shit what others call you, Desmortiers?"

The creature turned his blindingly blue eyes on St. Vincent. "I know your father, boy."

"No you don't," his mother said quickly. "You couldn't possibly."

"Why?" Preach said. "Because you don't?"

His cackle sent shivers down St. Vincent's spine. "Why do you do it, Ruth? Strive to save people's souls through the spirit of Christ. When will you learn that there is no God."

"No," Ruth said with a sneer, "there is only you, Desmortiers."

"Me?" That cackle again. "I do not exist, Ruth. That, too, you refuse to believe."

The two of them eyed each other, mortal enemies on either side of a blasted battlefield.

"And yet," Desmortiers went on, "you continue to come here, you continue to seek me out."

"You need food. Even if you do not exist, that boy has to eat."

"You know nothing about the boy," Preach said. "In any event, my parishioners care for us."

Ruth glanced around the hovel. "So I see." She smiled. "The truth is, I feel compelled to do you favors every once in a while. Without you my tent would not be filled to the outer stakes, I would not have had to spread increasingly larger tents over the past five years. Your presence fuels my works like no one else."

"It's good to have an enemy, in other words."

"Yes."

"Because someone like me validates your existence." A crack appeared in that awful face as the smile that terrified her appeared again. "And now you bring your son to me. Why? So I can tell him who his father is?"

"Don't you dare!"

"You told me you didn't know, Ruth. You've lied to me."

"It isn't the first time."

"Knowing you as I do, I would hardly think so." His head moved, as if with great difficulty. "Still, he has a right to know."

"Luther's all mine!"

"On every level, how you deceive yourself. The truth surrounds you. Just because you deny its existence does not change its legitimacy. Tell him, Ruth, or I will."

St. Vincent became aware that he had come under the young boy's scrutiny. He was more or less the same age as St. Vincent and in all ways unremarkable. And yet the look he gave St. Vincent was pregnant with meaning, as if he knew something about St. Vincent, something even Ruth didn't know.

And then there were two explosions that threatened to fracture St. Vincent's head. He leapt backward, stumbling. When he had righted himself he saw his mother holding the largest handgun he had ever seen, and in his time he'd seen plenty. Preach Desmortiers and the young boy were both sprawled on the floor.

"Now d'you understand why I brought my son?" Ruth said.

Outside the shack, striding along behind his mother, St. Vincent saw a bicycle, probably the kid's. As he took it, he glanced at what looked like a license plate, except it read: CTHULHU IS COMING.

Ruth did not look back, but her son did. A scream stifled in his throat as he saw an enormous crow fly out of the open door, and behind it, the shadow of the creature his mother was certain she had killed.

Preach Desmortiers's lips curved into a smile, and then he winked at Ruth's son.

St. Vincent, having absently sucked on his cigarette until it was finished, was jolted from the past by the sound of his mobile. This had better be Dickerson, he thought. It was a text, not a call. Opening the text, he discovered a still frame from a CCTV camera. Underneath the photo was the time and date stamp, along with the log line: "JIB."

St. Vincent knew what that stood for: Djibouti-Ambouli International Airport. He squinted at the photo, used a hand gesture to zoom in, just to make sure. Dickerson had come through. Once again, he glanced up at the lights from Sydney's apartment. The uneasy truce is over, he thought. This is war.

30

"I can't see," Julie said.

"That's the point." Sydny's voice seemed to float in the air in front of her. "You're here to feel."

Julie, sitting on the chair in Sydny's blacked-out bedroom, felt her thighs tremble. The dampness seeping out onto the leather was warm as blood. Squirming a little made the leather slick as her latex hood.

"Now come," Sydny said, "slide off the chair . . . No, don't try to stand. Kneel. Kneel with your legs spread."

"I don't like this," Julie said. Her body was stiff and unyielding with incipient terror.

"Of course you don't like it. You're still clinging to your past, to the things you think shaped you, without any idea that you can free yourself, shed your past like a snake sheds its old skin."

She could sense Sydny standing over her, heat radiated from her like a sun.

"I seem to have heard that argument before," Julie said.

"Don't be confused. This isn't some kind of break-you-down-to-build-you-back-up bullshit. That's the province of cult leaders. That's brainwashing, pure and simple."

Sydny's voice was abruptly closer, almost beside her right ear. "Kitten, there is a time, a place—with a *someone*—to let go, to submit, to give yourself wholly to that other person—to do what they say, to respond when they command you, and then to *feel*. Once you do that, once you fight through your fear, what you gain is incalculable."

"What?" Julie's voice could not have been smaller if she were a mouse. "What do I gain?"

"A strength you never knew you had. A power no one can ever take away from you." Sydny ran her fingers through Julie's hair. "A new life is waiting for you, kitten." She took her hand away, leaving Julie alone. "You have only to reach out and take it."

And yet not alone. Julie submitted, slipping off the chair to kneel with her legs spread as Sydny had commanded.

"Bend over until your forehead touches the floor."

She bent over until her forehead touched the floor. Fear grabbed her; she had never felt so vulnerable.

For some moments thereafter nothing happened. Then Julie felt something slick and smooth penetrate her from behind. "What is that?"

"No questions. Just feel. Feel."

The thing—possibly a dildo—moved in and out of Julie. At first she resisted. She wondered whether this was what it felt like to be raped. Then she realized that she was holding on to fears engendered by notions, misconceptions, outright lies that were part of her past. She trusted Sydny, though she could not say why. Maybe it was because Gregory Whitman trusted her, but she suspected that, even more, it was because she was sick until death of her gray past. She wanted to be rid of it, burn it on the pyre of the unknown future.

"*You can free yourself,*" Sydny had said, "*shed your past like a snake sheds its old skin.*"

She wanted that, oh, yes, she did, she discovered, with every fiber of her being.

She began to relax, to, as Sydny kept reminding her, feel. But a new fear began to creep in to replace the old, engendered not by the penetration but by the realization of having no control. To cede control as an adult in the modern world was a terrifying experience.

As if she were reading Julie's mind, Sydny said, "But you see, we have no control over what happens to us. We may think we do, but we're just fooling ourselves. Life is random. Life is chaos. The pretense of control is what keeps most people sane. But here, with me, you don't have to keep up the pretense. Here you confront life as it really is—raw, primitive, unfamiliar. Here you will find out the truth about yourself."

With her complete and utter submission her fear faded, and with the banishment of her fear, the pain was transformed into—what? In perceptible increments into pleasure, which rose and rose like a shining tower before her until it blotted out the sky, the sun, the moon, everything. She groaned from deep in her belly and, for the first time in her life, she came. Wave after wave of pleasure washed over her, until she was inundated, until she dropped below the surface, immersing herself without any fear of drowning. In fact, the opposite was true. As her orgasm raged on, she sensed the power in it—a power beyond her imagining.

And then it subsided, slowly, languorously, leaving her on a shoreline, without breath and with a pounding heart. She wanted nothing more than to look back at the eternal waves, to crawl back into that tide of pleasure.

But there was a distant sound, as of a bell tolling. From behind and above her, she felt the cool draft of Sydny moving away from her, her footsteps exiting the bedroom, heels clicking down the hallway and across the parquet floor of the living room—how clearly these small sounds came to her in her new private world, as if they were whispered intimately into her ear!

She heard Sydny's voice call out "Who is it?" as if it were a shout.

And then the roar of gunshots ripped through the apartment, shattering every perfect note that had come before. The fragile shell of her brave new unvarnished world cracked open.

So I've kicked Whit out twice, Charlie thought as she exited the toilet. Our history has a way of repeating itself, as if both of us are bound to a wheel that raises us up and then almost drowns us. Maybe, she thought, as she rose to her feet, drowning would be a blessing compared to the wreckage we're left with.

She looked through the rooms of the villa. The blood, the sheer human waste. Her mind had had time now to count the pileup of the dead, the modern process of death so clinical the mind couldn't properly register it as it was happening. I am part of this, she said to herself. A willing participant in the death of Americans, no matter how misguided their motives.

Dimly, she became aware of a rhythmic beeping. Turning, she sidestepped the body at her feet on the hallway floor, went into the room where Seiran el-Habib was still a prisoner, tied again to his chair. He cringed visibly as she strode toward him, but she went past him, picked up the sat phone that Flix must have dropped or left behind. Where was he, anyway? And where was Whit. She shouldn't have cared, but she did. Very much so.

Toggling on the phone, she said, "Hello?"

"Who's this?" said a male voice that sounded both staticky and very far away.

"Charlie. Who's this?"

"Your boss," King Cutler said. "You know what I'm looking at, Daou?"

"How could I possibly—"

"Stick it! At this very moment, I'm looking at a surveillance photo of you, Flix, and Whitman getting on a private plane in Djibouti. I know you're nowhere near Beirut. And, furthermore, I can guess where you are."

"We have el-Habib," Charlie began.

"You what?!? Never mind, I should've known. Whitman's like a dog with a bone—he'll worry it to death until he gets at the marrow." He sighed heavily. "Did you at least find out why el-Habib was being protected?"

"He's part of a pipeline that runs from Beijing to Washington."

Cutler felt a tiny shiver of fear run down his spine. "Christ, don't tell me it's political." For USA to get involved in a high-level political maneuvering would mean a death sentence for the company.

"He mentioned a group called the Alchemists."

True fear took hold of Cutler. "Alchemists." St. Vincent's group, Christ. The shit that fucker wasn't telling him. "Who are the Alchemists?"

"No idea, at this point."

"Are you still interrogating him?"

Silence. Static. Silence.

"Daou." And what will Gregory do now that he's found out he's up against his former employers? "Daou! What the hell's happened to our connection?"

Silence. Over the next twenty minutes he tried to raise Red Rover six times. The connection was dead and could not be resurrected.

Sydny's cry was like a knife shoved between Julie's ribs. She felt completely frozen in terror. Then Sydny screamed, and, in a flash Julie got to her feet. She tried to rip off the hood, but sweat made it stick to her like a second skin. Fumbling, she pulled on the upper zipper tabs and, blinking like an owl in sunlight, could see again.

Sydny was whimpering. Then came a man's voice raised like a cudgel over hers. Julie, heart racing, was in a panic. What can I do? she thought. The intruder has a gun. Surely, he'll check the other rooms and then he'll find me. There's nowhere to hide. I'm helpless.

And then she remembered the handgun. She lunged for the closet, felt along the shelf until her fingers closed around the grips of the weapon. She recalled the way Olivia Benson held her gun and almost laughed at the thought of imitating a character on a TV show beloved by her.

She held it as Olivia would, left hand supporting the butt while the forefinger of her right hand extended just above the trigger guard, ready to move into firing position. Her pulse filled up her throat as she advanced across the bedroom to the doorway into the hall. Beyond, the lights of the living room rose with a feral glow, like a forest fire.

On bare feet she went silently down the hall, through shadows and light, striped like a stalking tiger, invisible in the tall grass. She could hear Sydny mewling like a cat, and felt her gorge rise. She swallowed hard to keep from retching.

Faster now, compelled by the desperate urgency in the noises coming from the middle of Sydny's chest. To save her meant everything, so she ran, as desperate now as Sydny, clinging to the last bloody threads of life.

She burst out of the hallway and into the spotlights of the living room, and the moment she did so she knew she was a dead woman because the man standing over Sydny was Luther St. Vincent, head of NSA Directorate N, and his head came up, he saw her, and Julie knew it was the end. He knew how to use a handgun; he was trained. What did she have except scenes of Olivia Benson flying through her head like clouds ahead of an oncoming storm?

31

"You were once Whitman's property, his fuck-mama," St. Vincent said as he stood over the female body. "Now you're nothing but a bloody piece of meat. Think he'll like what he sees?"

Between his spread legs, Sydney, curled on her side in a fetal position, moaned.

"Still trying to talk?" He bent over her. "But you can't. You're a thing, and things can't talk. They can only spread their legs, suck cock, immerse themselves in the basest perversions." He bent lower. "You disgust me. People like you belong in the gutter to waste away. I'm here to accelerate the process."

He was about to grab her ankle, when movement at the periphery of his vision caused him to stand up straight. Someone else in the apartment? But the bedroom had been dark, giving him the impression that Sydney was alone.

And then whatever it was appeared framed by the doorway to the hall. He was in the process of lifting his arm to shoot first, ask questions never, when he caught sight of the head, appearing out of the deep shadows. Except that it seemed to keep the shadows with it. Lamplight spun off the shiny black skin, the horns. The metallic glint of the three zippers completed the picture of a monster, not a human being. Into his mind shot a memory of Desmortiers's hovel, of his mother's palpable fear, of the wolf spread across the shack's rear wall like the bat wings of Cthulhu.

And so, with the handgun halfway lifted toward the fetish image come to life, he froze. He could not believe his eyes, he was unnerved, and because of that the fetish had just enough time to shoot him.

He spun around, clutching his right shoulder. He tried to lift his right arm to shoot it, but couldn't. As he was clumsily trying to transfer the weapon to his bloody left hand, the fetish fired again, this time wildly.

It didn't matter; he was undone. In shock and pain, he ran out of the apartment, along the hallway, down the fire stairs. Away from the fetish; away from what he had done; away from what was happening in that hellhole of an apartment.

Julie, her courage unwinding with the flow of adrenaline in her system, ran to the front door, slammed it shut, and double-locked it, because the doorknob and latch were shattered. Then she ran back, knelt beside Sydny, pulled her head into her lap. With a supreme effort she pulled the hood off her head, threw it under the sofa

"Sydny," she crooned as she wiped her sweat-streaked face with her forearm. "Sydny, what did he do to you?"

Sydny's lips moved, but she was unable to speak. Julie brought out her mobile, called 911, gave their address, then she turned back to her friend.

"What? What is it?" She saw the mass of blood on one side of Sydny's abdomen, another in her chest, and she began to weep. "Oh, dear god." Shucking off her top, she pressed it against the abdominal wound, keeping one hand there.

Through her tears she saw Sydny making a supreme effort to speak. Julie bent over her, ear to Sydny's lips.

"Kitten, did . . . Did you see?"

"See what?" Julie said without changing her position.

"Man . . ."

"I saw his face, I know who he is. I'll hunt him down, Sydny."

"No! Tell Whit. He'll—"

"Whitman isn't here. I don't know where he is. I'll take—" Julie pulled back as she felt Sydny's body heave against her. "Don't move! For the love of god, stay still!"

Her mind was racing. She had to tell someone, but who? Not the capital cops. God, no. This had to be kept strictly internal. She wished Whitman were in D.C. Who could she turn to but her boss? The trouble was she didn't trust Hemingway, not completely anyway.

"Oh, Sydny, I'm so . . ." But her words trailed off.

"Kitten . . ." Sydny's eyes were looking at her but they weren't seeing her. The pupils were fixed and staring. Her breathing had ceased.

"So sorry."

She rocked Sydny back and forth in her lap, then threw her head back and, inconsolable, screamed. It was the howl of a wolf in torment.

PART THREE

THE WELL

[Alchemy] is like unto death, which separates the eternal from the mortal, so that it should properly be known as the death of things.

—Paracelsus

32

The Well had been built in the shape of an inverted bell. It was sunk deep into the earth like a mine shaft. It was both sacred and profane: a place of blood sacrifices and the home of unknown gods, terrifying in their different guises. The gods were Monroe, St. Vincent, and his handpicked cadre of behavioral scientists, forensic psychiatrists, as well as experts in the art of persuasion. The blood sacrifices were the ones who never made it out of the Well, the terrorists captured, renditioned in blood-soaked fury, then disappeared. Interrogators were gods. Though their dominion was tiny, they were, in their way, very real masters of life and death.

None of this history Monroe told to Lucy as he guided her from room to room. Actually, "room" did not come close to describing the spaces inside the Well, which were designed to instill in the "visitor" a violent dislocation, disorientation, and, finally, vertigo, destroying the "visitor's" equilibrium. The impossibly high metal walls leaned in or out, or both, with no logic or adherence to the tenets of architectural integrity. The curved spaces abruptly gave way to walls angled sometimes less than ninety degrees, sometimes more, never squared off. It was not only their vertiginous dimensions, but also the distinctive fug of the spaces, comprised of paranoia, despair, and terror. Though these viciously elicited emotions did not have scents per se, Lucy was well enough acquainted with all three to detect their presence in every square inch of the Well. Monroe led her like a docent at a museum, through spaces long and narrow, elliptical and triangular, all with floors that tilted one way or another. Their footsteps fell like hammers on an anvil, with dull, metallic echoes.

At last, they came to the waterfall, and stood before it. Lucy was silent, looking at the glittery glyph carved into the stone wall, visible now and again through the cascade of water.

"This is the Well," Monroe said.

"Or as the Maya called it, a *cenote*. It's where they disposed of the bodies of their sacrificial victims. The one at Chichen Itza is known as the Well of Souls." Lucy glanced down. "You built this?"

"No, it was here, it's natural. We built the Well around it."

"Limestone. Probably been here for ages." She craned her neck. "Like all *cenotes* this one seems very deep."

"I understand you have a facility for killing." Monroe said this as if he were pointing out a favorite sculpture of his.

Lucy looked up, glanced at him speculatively. "Is killing what's required of me?"

Monroe nodded. "It may be. On occasion." He eyed her. "Will that be a problem?"

"Hardly," she said. "I've been aching to get my hands wet."

"Grudges to settle."

"Exactly."

Monroe grinned. "A woman after my own heart. What do you drink?"

"Tequila, mezcal. Period."

"Beautiful." He put a hand lightly at the small of her back. "I know just the place."

"It had better be authentic."

"Huh," Monroe said, leading her out through the maze of spaces. "I think they grow their own worms."

Flix was lost. He felt himself tossed in a bloated bag of water, blood, and bone. He was everywhere and nowhere. He was falling, flailing, failing even to remember who he was or had been.

Dimly, he was aware of Whitman crouched beside him, Charlie flitting in and out, there, not there, back again, like the shadow of death he had often dreamed about when he was a boy. That shadow was now more real to him than the human figures around him, his memory of it more real than the fog of the present. Time seemed as elusive as water, moving forward, then flowing backward, repeating patterns that should have had meaning for him, but were as inscrutable as starshine.

Only the shadow, eyes in a hidden face staring at him as if they could see straight through to the core of him, as if the shadow wanted to feed off his brain, as if it wanted nothing but him. And as if the shadow was some terrible harbinger, his chaotic mind was suddenly filled with the child Lucy, the nights when his sister must have tucked her into bed, when she had looked up at Marilena with those huge coffee-colored eyes, asking for something Marilena could not give her. His shame took the form of the shadow, silently laughing, as if it wanted to tell the world his secret longing. And then his shame was crowded out by the monsters of *The Odyssey*: Medusa, the Cyclops, the Sirens, Scylla and Charybdis, the Chimera, and, finally, the Lotus Eaters, where, he imaged, Lucy had run off to find—what exactly? Lost. She had been lost to him, and who knew what horrors she had been witness to during her long exile?

A wallop like a bolt of lightning rent the skies of his memory-clogged mind. He felt something palpating the back of his skull, the nape of his neck. Then everything lit up as if he were on the Vegas strip when, at day's death, all the neon signs pop on at once, obliterating night by creating a blinding, unnatural day.

"I hadn't meant to go there," Lucy said. "In fact, it was almost the last place on earth I'd intended to end up in."

"The bayous of Louisiana can be a dangerous place."

Monroe sat back as their mezcal was served, along with the fiery Mexican food Lucy had ordered. They were sitting at a wooden table painted with scenes from typical Mexican peasant life, at Cantina No Sé, heavy on the dark wood and the primitive painting, but 100 percent authentic.

"How did you wind up there?" Monroe asked.

"To be honest, I have no idea. I fell in with a group of meth heads. They had a van. One night I woke up in the bayous." She downed her mezcal in one gulp, then looked at Monroe. "That carving in the wall behind the waterfall—the triangle with the tail."

"That's an alchemical symbol for sulfur. Why do you ask?"

Lucy shrugged. "No reason. I thought I'd seen something like that before."

"Unless you were studying alchemy, that's highly unlikely."

She picked up a wedge of lime, squeezed the juice onto her food, then popped it into her mouth, chewed reflectively for a moment. Spitting out what was left of the lime, she said, "The image I saw was voodoo—at least that's what the locals claimed. I saw it first carved into a tree, then, later, painted on the side of a church that had been deserted by its flock. Others had moved in. At midnight it was lit up by flares and torches. I didn't see the inside, at least not then, but I watched the people as they filtered through the brush to get to it. Ugly folk, sick-looking."

"You mean the halt and the lame. A preacher inside claimed to be a faith healer."

Lucy shook her head. "I mean sick inside—like they saw the world differently than you or me."

"How in the world could you know that?"

"The people I shared a van with. They had that same look. Sick as rats been fed poison."

Monroe looked disconcerted. "You must be wrong about the sigil. I don't see how it would show up in the Louisiana bayous."

Lucy fell silent for so long Monroe called for more mezcal, watched her down it in one gulp all over again, and asked for the bottle to stay with them. This time, he leaned over, refilled her glass himself. Then he took a sip. Their food was growing cold.

"Lucy," he said softly, "something's clearly on your mind."

Her eyes rose to the level of his. For a moment they were out of focus. Her thoughts seemed to be locked in an incident in the past. "I was lost for some time."

He nodded. "Luther told me a bit of that. As much as he knew, I suppose, which wasn't much."

"No one knows," Lucy whispered. "No one knows."

Monroe waited, then decided to take another tack. "I'm known as Monroe, but you can call me—"

"Mr. Tibbs."

He threw his head back and laughed. "You do have a wicked sense of humor, my dear. But, no. My name is Albin White. I'd be pleased if you called me Albin."

She cocked her head. "Albin. I like that."

"Lucy," he said softly, "tell me what happened to you."

"Why should I?" She said this not defiantly, not defensively, but out of genuine curiosity.

"Because," White said, "I suspect the moral of that particular story will explain why you're so eager to kill."

Lucy appeared to think about this for some time, then she nodded, as if to herself. "A week or so after I arrived in the bayous, a man found me down the road from one of the bars I was hanging out in at night. He had so much hair on his face I could barely see his features. I wasn't interested in him, and I told him so. He only grinned like a moron—grinned because at that moment two of his friends came up behind me and grabbed my arms. When I struggled, the hairy man punched me in the jaw. I stopped after that. I was crying so hard I had no strength left, anyway."

She paused, staring down at her drink, as if trying to find her reflection there. "They carried me, as if I were a sack of grain. I had a flash of the church, the triangle with its curled little pig's tail painted on the side. Inside someone had made it into a living thing, a sculpture in rusted iron. In front of it was—well, a kind of altar, I guess. They stripped me to the bare skin, and raped me."

She coughed, and for a moment White felt certain she was going to be violently ill, but then she caught hold of herself, or perhaps he was wrong altogether.

In any event, she went on, but seemingly in a different vein: "Albin, do you know what a chimera is?"

He nodded. "Nowadays, the word is used to define a terrible vision, but I believe it's a mythological beast of some sort."

"When I was little, my uncle Felix used to read to me from Homer. *The*

Odyssey, can you imagine?" She gave a little snort. "He started with *The Iliad*, but I couldn't bear it—all that blood shed for the stupidest of reasons." She sipped her mezcal, seeming to have calmed a bit. "So *The Odyssey*. Man, I loved those strange creatures and people, you know? So, anyway, it was Homer who first described the chimera and, if you can believe it, I remember the passage. Let me think now, oh yes, 'a thing of immortal make, not human, lion-fronted and snake behind, a goat in the middle, and snorting out the breath of the terrible flame of bright fire.'"

She looked up from her mezcal, and White was startled to see that her eyes were enlarged with tears. "They raped me, Albin, one at a time. Then they poured liquor all over me, and all three took me together, like a three-headed monster, like chimera: snake, lion, goat."

In the silence that ensued, the small, everyday sounds of the cantina came rushing in: the clatter of plates, the call of orders, the ring of the cook's bell, the murmur of small talk, an occasional burst of laughter that to White felt absurdly out of place.

He cleared his throat. "What happened then, Lucy?"

"What happened then?" She blinked. "They left me there, smeared with my own blood, their sweat, and their semen. But what did it matter? The deed had been done. To them, I was nothing more than a lump of clay. I had no warmth, no heartbeat, no breath. I was dead to them, as I always had been."

"I'm sorry," White said, surprising himself that he actually meant it.

"Why should you be sorry? You're not a woman."

And in just those few words she had put him in his place, had defined the unfathomable space between them, had made him see that whatever he thought he knew about women and life, he didn't. He should have felt resentful, angry even. He imagined he would have with anyone else. But Lucy Orteño had a quality he could not describe, let alone understand. However, there was one thing he knew for a fact: he would never let anything bad happen to her again.

33

The spinal cord is made up of nerve fiber bundles that deliver messages from the brain to the body. These bundles, protected from trauma by the bones of the spine, run down from the base of the brain through a canal in the center of those bones. This is the network that carries messages back and forth from brain to body and vice versa.

This simple anatomy lesson had been explained to Whitman not by a doctor, nurse, or neurosurgeon, but by a man apparently of middle years with no formal medical training. He didn't call himself a doctor, or anything of the sort. Yet people came from all over the bayou to seek his counsel and, in some cases, feel his hands upon them.

The man had extraordinary hands—long and slender of finger, their movements both supple and subtle, as if they had not aged past twenty years or so. The man's name was Preach—at least that's what the locals called him, though Whitman finally discovered his family name was Desmortiers. The boy on the bike Whitman had met that morning in southern Louisiana was in some way attached to Preach, though later he discovered they were not related. Preach was not married—never had been—and he had no children. But there was something odd about that kid that had stuck in Whitman's mind. Maybe it was the fact that he had the black shiny eyes of a crow.

Preach was a man with prematurely white hair, long on top, so short on the sides his skull was visible. His eyes were the palest blue Whitman had ever seen. His long, crooked nose and thin lips gave him a cruel countenance, but he welcomed Whitman cordially enough. He was bare to the waist, sweat pouring off him in thick rivulets. Whitman couldn't help but notice the deep crater in the right side of his back, lacquered with skin so shiny it almost glowed.

"I was shot with an arrow," Preach said, clearly noting the direction of Whitman's gaze. "When I was just about that boy's age. Left for dead."

"I'm sorry," Whitman said.

"Why? You didn't do it." He turned to face Whitman, revealing another, smaller pucker in the flesh of his chest. "Plus which, I've survived worse—a gunshot, for one."

After that, Whitman got down to business. He told Preach that he had been sent to the bayous to learn.

"Learn our crooked ways," Preach said with a glint in his eyes. "And I don't mean corrupt, fraudulent, or faithless." He looked Whitman over. "I dunno. Can't learn nuthin' here lest you have the gift. D'you have the gift, Mr. Whitman?"

"I'm not sure."

Preach grinned, his teeth as yellow and snaggled as a dragon's. "Well, then, let's you an' me find out."

Preach worked him all that afternoon and late into the night. An hour or two after midnight—time in Preach's presence was as malleable as it was uncertain—he sat back from the fire he'd made and said, "Okay, then. Ask your questions."

Whitman did just that.

"This is how we create zombies," Preach said near the end of their time together. "And this is how we return them to a normal state."

All the skills Preach had taught him Whitman now brought to bear on Flix, for he suspected that the poppy-based alkaloid drug administered to his friend was having much the same effect as Preach's zombification ritual.

"You've got that look on your face," Charlie said, squatting beside him. "That look you had when you came from the Well."

Whitman, concentrating on what he needed to do, said nothing.

Charlie licked her lips nervously as she watched Flix. "Will this work?"

"Hold his hand, if he becomes agitated."

"You mean restrain him."

"No, I mean precisely what I said," Whitman said as slowly as if he were speaking to a child. "Flix doesn't need to be restrained; he needs to be grounded by a human touch."

"Right. Got it." Charlie nodded. "Okay."

But her question, *Will this work?* still hovered in the air between them.

Of course, if he was wrong, Flix was doomed, but Whitman chose not to dwell on that possibility. It was Preach who had said, "In negative thoughts lie your destruction."

Palpating the base of Flix's skull, he found the channel where the main nerve bundles resided. Tracing the line down, he came to the nape of Flix's neck, and found it abnormally stiff, as if it were a slab of steel instead of flesh, blood, meningeal fluid, and articulated bone. This partial paralysis was not unfamiliar to him. Preach had made him run his fingertips up and down the neck of a member of his "parish" who he had zombified to keep him alive after a horrendous accident. Whitman should have been reassured that he was on the right track, but Flix's paralysis was much worse.

Well, there was no help for it but to press on.

With his fingertips at the base of Flix's skull, he said very softly to Charlie, "Take his hand. Now."

Charlie did as he asked, and he began. There were twelve cranial nerves. The one Whitman needed to get to was the trigeminal. As its name implied, it was divided into three branches. The problem, again, was the paralytic that was a part of the injection given to Flix, in effect making the nape of his neck armor-plated. The only recourse was to try and access the vagus nerve, which affected the esophagus, chest, and heart. Interrupting the vagus signals would cause brief unconsciousness and thus a lessening of the paralysis. The problem was if Whitman wasn't careful, if he couldn't get the vagus functioning in time, Flix would die.

But what choice did he have? With Charlie holding his friend's hand, he found the vagus, which was far easier to get to, and, as Preach had taught him, interrupted its signals. Immediately, Flix's eyes rolled up in his head and he slumped, unconscious, into Whitman's arms.

"What's happening?" Charlie cried, alarmed.

"Don't worry," Whitman assured her. "Keep hold of his hand. And get those dog tags out of the way."

With her free hand, Charlie scooped up the pile of dog tags Flix had dropped on the ground.

Whitman's fingertips searched for Flix's trigeminal nerve. Seconds ticked by, but he forced himself to slow down, to calmly find his way through the loosened paralysis to the right spot. Flix's heart had stopped. His breath was stilled. And Whitman's fingertips were up against what felt like a bar of steel, the last, most powerful defense the poppy alkaloid serum had created to protect itself from being interfered with.

In short, Flix was dying, and Whitman didn't think there was a damn thing he could do about it.

"Did you kill them?"

Lucy put down her fork. "What?"

"It's a simple enough question," White said. "Did you kill the men who raped you?"

"I never saw them again."

Lucy went back to eating. She seemed oblivious to the fact that the tacos had grown cold, the lard in the refried beans was congealing. To White, the food was slops, fit only for dogs. But then he hadn't been where she had been, hadn't suffered as she had suffered. Watching her now shovel the food into her mouth with a single-minded concentration, he caught an inkling of just what a privileged life he had led. Despite his innate hatred of Caucasians, despite being hyper-aware of his origins, the indignities that had been visited on his great-grandfather, he was an inauthentic African American. He'd been born with a silver spoon in his mouth, had never suffered even a fraction of what his forebears had. He was far too wealthy and powerful for any white man to insult him, even in jest.

In contrast, what did Lucy Orteño have? Nothing. He wondered now whether she was telling the truth. If it had been him he would have moved heaven and earth to find those men and punish them. She looked to be the kind of person who would do that—who had, in fact, done it, but short of coaxing a confession from her he would never know the truth.

He wondered whether, in the end, it mattered. She was ripe for dealing death. He recognized the flinty spark in her eyes, in the fierceness of her demeanor. She had descended into the depths of hell and had emerged still alive, if not unscathed.

At that moment, she picked her head up, wiped her lips with the back of her hand. "I want to ask you a question."

"Anything," White said, once again surprising himself because he meant it.

"Was that carving there when you built the Well?"

"No, it was carved by one of our members." He paused, his expression turning thoughtful. "One of our ex-members, I should say."

"Can you tell me which one?"

"I shouldn't."

"You said I could ask you anything."

She was right, he had, and he was nothing if not a man of his word. "Well, okay. You might even know him since he's a friend of your uncle Felix. Gregory Whitman finished carving that alchemical symbol a day before the waterfall began to churn the surface of the *cenote*."

"He's dying," Charlie said.

"Tell me something I don't know." Whitman could tell Flix was on the verge of death, and in a minute or so, even if he managed to revive his friend, he'd be worse than dead, his brain deprived of oxygen for too long.

Whitman closed his eyes, imagined Preach's delicate-boned hands, felt Preach's presence mixing with his own gift—as Preach had called it—still a mystery to him. And there it was! All three branches of the trigeminal beneath his fingertips. He sensed the blockages the alkaloid cocktail had set up, interfering with the nerve messages between Flix's brain and his body.

Quickly now, he manipulated the nerves as he had been taught, playing them like the strings of a violin. He wasn't yet quite done, but he couldn't wait any longer. With his free hand, he stimulated the vagus nerve. At once, Flix sucked in a lungful of air, his heart beat strongly, and, as his eyelids fluttered open, Whitman completed reestablishing the brain-body connection through the trigeminal.

Flix's eyes were clouded, out of focus. Whitman slapped him hard across one cheek, then the next, much as an ob-gyn will slap a newborn's behind to wake him to the new world.

Flix gasped, his eyes focused, staring up at Whitman.

"*Compadre*," he said through a thickened tongue, "I sure could use a shot of tequila right about now."

Whitman laughed, and Flix, clearly feeling his old self come flooding back to him, turned his head to look at Charlie.

"You're holding my hand."

"I can drop it, if you'd rather."

"Thanks," Flix said. "Thanks for that."

Charlie's gaze drifted over his head to lock onto Whitman's face for a moment. "Anytime," she said. "We're all in this together." Then she broke contact with him and rose. "There's no tequila here, but water will be better for you anyway."

"Flix," Whitman said, as Charlie went back into the villa. "Tell me how you feel."

Flix ran his tongue around his parched lips. "Once, when I was a kid, I was real sick. I don't recall what it was, but my temperature spiked to 104, 105. Two days later, it broke. I feel now like I felt then. Like I'd come out the other side of a hallucination or a nightmare." He shook his head. "To be honest, Whit, I don't remember much of what happened since we've been here." His expression turned troubled. "Except . . . something . . . I don't know . . ."

He was interrupted by Charlie returning with a large glass of iced water. He drank it greedily, over Whitman's admonition to take it slow. When he had drained the glass he put it down beside him. That's when he saw the clutch of dog tags dangling from Charlie's fingers.

"Oh, God, oh, Jesus. It's true then, it wasn't a nightmare. I killed all those American Marines."

"Well, that's the thing." Charlie crouched down beside the two men. She spoke to them both as she held up the dog tags, jangling them one against the other. "I've been looking at these tags and I can tell you there's something horribly wrong."

34

As a child, Julie had never been alone. Her sister, Bridget, had been her constant companion. But as an adult, Julie was alone. She had no friends, she and her husband barely spoke, and her occasional nights with Cutler were a complete sham. She and her sister hadn't spoken in five years, the result of a terrible misunderstanding that, to this day, Julie could not recall clearly. But even in her extreme distress there was no way she could see herself knocking on Bridget's door, even if she had still been living where she had been five years ago—with Bridget no sure thing.

But there was Orrin, Bridget's ex-husband, who had cried on her shoulder for weeks—no, make that months, she thought—after the very messy breakup. He had trafficked in the knowledge that she and Bridget didn't get along; he had no girlfriend, no female friends at all, so far as Julie could tell. So she had come at his summons, had dinner with him, sat on his sofa, held his hand while he poured out his anguish. Evening after evening after evening.

Orrin worked for the attorney general's office, one of those jobs for life, therefore his whereabouts were as predictable and unchanging as the rock of Gibraltar. That simile accurately described Orrin's personality. Bridget had apparently found him boring. Julie wondered why she had married him in the first place, but even before their estrangement her adult relationship with Bridget was never intimate enough for Julie to ask the question. For Julie, Orrin was something of a landmark in the turbulent sea of conspiracy and secrets in which she often felt herself drowning.

So, leaving Sydny's bloody apartment, it was to Orrin's she went to seek shelter from her own private storm. It was near to daybreak when she rang his bell, but even at that ungodly hour she knew he wouldn't be asleep. Instead, he'd be working out on his rowing machine. She just hoped he wasn't already in the shower, unable to hear the bell. But a moment later, her anxiety was alleviated when she heard his voice, metallic and thin, asking who it was.

"Julie," she said, her mouth up against the microphone grill.

"What the fuck are you doing here at this hour?"

Not *Are you all right?* "Can I come up?"

There was a moment's silence when her heart threatened to pry apart her ribs and leap out of her chest. She kept looking behind her like an idiot. She could swear she smelled gunpowder and Sydny's blood on her clothes, though she had washed herself thoroughly before wiping her prints off everything she remembered touching. That meant retrieving the latex hood from under the sofa where she had thrown it. By that time, she'd heard the sirens of approaching police cars. In Sydny's neighborhood, where a gunshot was never heard, the neighbors would have likely mistaken the shots for a car or truck backfiring. Julie was safely out the basement back door when they swarmed the building's entryway.

"Orrin?"

She expelled a shuddering breath when the front door buzzed and she pushed through into the lobby. She took the elevator up to the sixth floor, went down the deserted and silent hallway. The door to his apartment stood open, and she stepped inside.

Orrin lived in Foggy Bottom, that odd area of D.C. that lay in the down low between George Washington University and Georgetown. It was inhabited almost exclusively by federal civil servants; he fit right in with all his neighbors, which must please him no end, Julie thought as she closed the door behind her.

Orrin padded out of the kitchen. He was in a thin robe, his feet bare. His face glistened with sweat; he must have just finished his turn on the rowing machine. He held a mug of hot tea, which he handed her. He did not comment on what she felt sure was her bedraggled state.

"Okay," he said, after she had taken her first sip, "you come knocking on my door at six in the morning. What the hell's up with you?"

She perched on a stool at the open-plan kitchen counter, curled her hands around the hot mug. Orrin looked no different from the last time they had had dinner. He was a sandy-haired man with a soft face, kind eyes, and a mild manner. Inoffensive was how she would sum him up.

But now that she was here, now that he had asked her the hundred-million-dollar question, she had no idea what to say. Gee, Orrin, I just shot a man—a high-level NSA agent, at that—after being introduced to bondage, discipline, sadomasochism by a new friend—a pole-dancer. The story would have seemed incredible to her if she hadn't just lived through it. But she had to tell him something, didn't she?

"A friend of mine was shot to death last night." It was the truth, though hardly the whole truth, and certainly not the reason she had come to him at this hour instead of going home.

"Gee, that's too bad, Jules." He ruffled the top of her head as if she were a little girl. "Tough luck, huh?" He picked up his mobile, his fingers moving over the screen. "What was your friend's name?"

She felt a clutch in her stomach. "She . . . It's not important."

"It might help me find . . ." He looked up. "I mean, there's no police record of a female being shot to death in the last twenty-four hours." He turned the mobile so she could see the screen. "Jules, are you sure this happened?"

"What?"

"I mean that you didn't—you know—imagine it."

"What? You think I'm a two-year-old with night terrors?"

He shrugged, waggled the mobile in front of her. "I'm just saying."

She looked at him as if seeing him for the first time. He'd been happy to cry on her shoulder every night, but now, when she needed him, he was treating her like a child, anxious for no good reason. "It happened, Orrin, and now nowhere feels safe anymore."

"Well, come on now, kiddo, don't be silly." He held up a finger. "Hold that thought. Gotta answer this text." When he had finished he looked up. "Now where were we? Oh, yeah." He waved a hand at her. "Your apartment is as safe as Fort Knox. Nothing's changed, I promise." Now he sounded annoyed by rather than disinterested in the interruption of his morning routine.

She shivered. "I can't warm up."

"Of course. No, I understand completely." But he was already glancing at his watch; already, no doubt, toting up his schedule for the day.

The old Julie would have shrunk back, made her apologies, and left with her tail between her legs, feeling kicked to the curb, sick at heart. Heading straight on toward a majorly depressing day. But this was the new Julie, the one who had donned the latex hood, the one who had lived through a scene from *The Story of O*, whom Sydny had taught a thing or three about the nature of sex and power.

This new Julie said, "Listen, Orrin, I need a place to stay for a while."

"What?" His head came up from answering another text, and he frowned deeply. "Well, I dunno, Jules. I mean this is my busy time at the AG's—important cases pending, lots on my mind . . ."

"I'll be no trouble, cross my heart."

"I'm sure." He didn't sound sure at all. "But, no, sorry. Jesus, if Bridget ever found out . . ." He allowed his voice to trail off, *the shit*, as if confident that she would supply the words he didn't have the courage to say.

She didn't. She wouldn't.

Instead, she rose off the stool, padded to where he stood, so close to him she could smell the sweat drying on his skin. She took the mobile from his hand, toggled it off.

"What? Jules, what are you doing?"

She put her face up to his. Her lips parted. "What does it look like?" she whispered.

He took a step back, encountered the wall. She came after him, silent as a wraith. Then she reached out, her fingers slipping between the sides of his robe, finding him naked underneath.

"What does it *feel* like?"

"Jules, I—"

But her lips sought his mouth; his semi-hard penis throbbed like a second heart beneath her fingers. She felt rather than heard his deep groan of sur-render, and something inside of her lit up like a flame. For an electrifying instant, she felt Sydney inside her; and then came the seawater wash of real-ization: it wasn't Sydney she felt deep inside her, it was herself—her own true self, liberated at last.

Slipping to her knees, she parted his robe, took him into her mouth. His eyes closed, his head went back so hard it cracked against the wall. Above her, she heard him breathing out her name, which changed to "Jesus" and back again, until the two names merged into one strange, sex-sound that meant something only to him.

She brought him to the brink of satisfaction, then withdrew her lips, tongue, throat.

"What-what are you doing?" he said in that thick, sex-charged voice men get when their primitive reptile brains have taken charge.

Reaching up with clawed fingers, she drew him down to her, placed him so that he was supine on the floor. She undressed slowly, sensually, showing him bit by bit what was in store for him. Then, straddling him, she moved up his body until she was over his face. Engaging her powerful thigh mus-cles, she lowered herself until she was just above his mouth. Her lips curved in a smile of incipient delight as she quoted from Lewis Carroll, changing only the gender: "'He opened it, and found in it a very small cake, on which the words "EAT ME" were beautifully marked in currants.'"

She dug her fingers into Orrin's damp hair, lifted his head to her. Soon after, her eyes closed in ecstasy, and it was only after she had ridden him through three orgasms that she let go of his head. She heard him gasping, making little sobs, imploring her to give him what he wanted.

So she did.

Afterward, he wanted her to lie in his arms, but she rose, stood over him like an Amazon, and said, "Orrin, I have a service to ask of you."

"Anything, Jules," he said, staring up at her in wonder and stupefaction, his eyes still half-glazed with lust. "Anything you want."

35

The orthopedic surgeon had assured St. Vincent that he would have no dreams while he was under the anesthetic, but either the sonuvabitch had lied or some unusual aspect of St. Vincent's brain ruled out sweet oblivion.

He lay in the surgery of the NSA safe house in Virginia. The trouble was he felt anything but safe here.

While the surgeon was removing the bullet from his shoulder and picking out bone fragments with a Jansen forceps, St. Vincent was visited by the figure in the black latex hood, its horns distended, the eye-zippers glittering. The figure itself moved so fast it was merely a blue-white blur, sexless and ageless. It was the hood, and what lay beneath the hood—a bull's head? a crow's?—that he was fixated on. That unknown face frightened him as nothing had since his boyhood amid the Louisiana bayous, the tortuous trees, the gray nooses of Spanish moss, the things that roamed by the cold light of the moon and the stars.

It exacerbated the sense in him that he had never outrun his childhood, never outrun the intimate sessions with his mother, or his mother's murderous intent, when she took him with her, made him an accessory to a murder she believed she'd willfully and happily committed. He could not escape the feeling that by bringing him to witness the shooting, his mother had made him as culpable as she, had bound him to her with a spiderweb from which he was incapable of breaking free. All of this memory-sense had been triggered by the sight of the figure in the black latex hood—as if it were an avenging demon sent by Preach to destroy him. And the figure exposed something else, buried even deeper inside him: his guilty fear of divine punishment for his time alone with his mother . . .

When he awoke, hours later, it was to the sight of King Cutler standing by his bedside. Cutler, seeing him awake, poured some iced water, hit the pedal on the bed to elevate St. Vincent to a sitting position, and handed him the plastic cup.

St. Vincent drank gratefully, ignoring the pain in his heavily bandaged shoulder.

"We need to talk," Cutler said, placing the empty cup beside the water pitcher on the swing table. "You up for it?"

St. Vincent narrowed his eyes in distaste. "What d'you think?" He wanted nothing more than to spit out the caustic taste of bile his nightmares had left in the back of his throat.

Cutler peered at him. "I'd assumed you'd be sedated."

"I don't do sedation," St. Vincent snapped. "Clouds the mind for days I can't afford to miss." He gestured with his head. "Bring me up to date."

"The apartment has been sterilized. The woman's body has been disposed of. It's like it never happened."

"The Metro Police?"

"As far as they're concerned the 911 call never happened."

"And the neighbors?"

"Calmed and placated. So far as they're concerned the girl went out of town to be with her ill mother."

"And the gunshots?"

"What gunshots?" Cutler said. "Oh, you must mean the truck backfiring outside the building."

St. Vincent could not hold back a grin. "Excellent job," he said.

Cutler, keeping his expression neutral, thought, I am sick to death of cleaning up after him. The messes he leaves behind are extraordinary. "What were you doing at that woman's apartment anyway?"

"The less you know," St. Vincent said.

"Indulge me, this one time."

"Teaching Whitman a lesson."

Cutler frowned, shaking his head. "That was a mistake."

"Opinions are like assholes: everyone has one." St. Vincent's eyes lit up. "She was one of his sexual partners—one he valued quite highly."

"Whitman's my man. If he needs to be taught a lesson I'll be the one to do it."

St. Vincent stared at Cutler, thinking, You don't have the balls to punish Whitman; you're dead afraid of him, but he revealed none of this; Cutler was still of use to him on matters such as this, when he could not allow his NSA people to be involved. "Someone else was in the apartment—the person who shot me. Did you find any trace—"

"Have you lost your mind, man? Taking a risk like that just to satisfy some sense of—what?"

"Justice," St. Vincent said with a menace Cutler could not mistake.

"Your beef with Whitman is personal. I don't know what he did to you, but there is no justice in this world, Luther. You, of all people, ought to know that."

St. Vincent's eyes glittered with the pain. "Are you trying to teach *me* a lesson, King?"

Cutler shook his head. "No, I just—"

"Don't make me regret hiring USA. These sideline assignments you're given are part of the deal. Your words of wisdom are not."

Cutler, wanting to slam St. Vincent in the face, watched him resettle himself against the pillows like some potentate. Just wait, he thought. Your time is coming. I have Lindstrom, and you won't get him back until I'm repaid for all the humiliation you've dumped on me.

"You didn't answer my question," St. Vincent said. "What about the person who shot me?"

"What about him?"

"No sign?"

"Give me a description."

Someone in a black latex hood? St. Vincent thought not. "I can't. Only a couple of lamps were on. I was concentrating on the whore. It all happened too fast."

"Vengeance leads to tunnel vision," Cutler said with obvious contempt. "Some cop you'd make."

Keep going, St. Vincent thought. I'm taking note of every insult you throw my way. "What about Lindstrom? He's disappeared."

"Didn't you tell me you had a tail put on him?"

"The tail's missing, too," St. Vincent said sourly. "Find them both."

"I'll do my best, as always."

"What about my boss?"

"General Serling is being run ragged by the clowns on Capitol Hill. About you he's still clueless. And as for the report your surgeon was required to file, he sent it off to Serling's office, but somehow during the journey from here to there it disappeared. No one's the wiser about you being shot."

"I'm impressed." St. Vincent nodded. "You've taken care of everything."

"That's right," Cutler said with an ill-concealed smirk. "Every fucking thing."

Preach, on his sat phone, was listening to one of his Iraqi Kurdish contacts—a tribal leader with both schooling and savvy. The separate Islamic caliphate within Iraq and Syria that IS had declared last year was making faster headway than even the Alchemists had anticipated, carving its way through the chaos of both countries with horrific cunning and cruelty. This was a branch of the future Crow had not seen, one that must be dealt with in the most robust and expeditious manner. The delicate balance Preach was aiming for—to keep both sides fighting and killing each other in a bitter war of attrition—was being threatened. He needed the human fighting machines in the field faster than he had expected.

"The timetable will be accelerated," Preach said, speaking perfect Sorani, the dialect of the Iraqi Kurds. "You have my word. And my word is law."

Disconnecting, Preach took up his mobile and dialed a number in Washington, D.C. For several moments, he spoke to the man on the other end in low tones.

It was time for him to insert himself more directly in the Affairs of the Alchemists.

———

The moment Cutler left, St. Vincent picked up his mobile. His forefinger stabbed out, pressing the speed dial numeral.

"Tell me," Jonah Dickerson, his SIC, said in his ear.

"How do you give a priest a vasectomy?"

"I beg your pardon?"

"You heard me. How do you give a priest a vasectomy?"

"No idea," Dickerson said in a voice that seemed to have shrunk in on itself.

"Kick a choirboy in the ass."

St. Vincent laughed, but he was the only one doing so. No wonder; it was a cruel laugh, filled with venom.

"What we know: we've lost comm with the villa, and Whitman and his team are not in Lebanon. They are at the villa and we need to make sure they stay there—permanently."

"Why don't you ask Cutler to send in another team? Whitman's his guy."

"Because I do the fucking thinking around here!" St. Vincent passed a hand across his eyes. He was still smarting from his conversation with that shit, Cutler. "Our immediate concern is Dante. It's too late to notify him to abort. He's too close to Seiran's compound. He's maintaining our strict radio silence protocol."

"If Whitman gets his hands on Dante—"

"I know. Dante is bringing us the shipment of *Papaver laciniatum*. We can't allow that shipment to be intercepted. The team needs to burn the villa and everyone in or around it."

"It will be taken care of," Dickerson said.

"It had better be."

"Trust me, boss. You'll have it within thirty-six hours, guaranteed."

"That means Whitman needs to be neutralized."

"Believe me," Dickerson said, "he's the first thing I'll take care of."

36

"What about the dog tags?" Whitman said.

"They're phonies," Charlie answered, her eyes alight.

Flix sat up straighter. "How d'you know that?"

"This one here." Charlie laid one out in her palm. "It belongs to Sergeant Jeffrey Grant."

Flix's forehead creased. "So?"

"So I knew Jeff Grant." Her eyes flicked over Whitman's face for a moment. "I went out with him for a couple of weeks last year before he shipped out on his last assignment."

"Last?" Whitman said.

Charlie nodded. "He was killed in Afghanistan nine months ago." She let the other dog tags drop into her palm. "I'm willing to bet that all of these tags are from deceased soldiers. The men you killed, Flix, they aren't Marines. In fact, they may not even be Americans."

"Hey, wait," Flix said, "that's gotta be a stretch."

Charlie shook her head. "Not at all. I checked the mouths of two of the corpses. You can be sure their cavities weren't filled in America." A small smile played across her lips. "I know shit Russian dental work when I see it."

"Damn, this changes everything, right, *compadre*?"

"Mercs," Whitman said. Meaning mercenaries. "Probably recruited from all over."

"Where does that leave us?" Flix asked. His relief was enormous; it was written all over his face.

"With Seiran," Whitman said, "and the information he's given us."

"There's at least one more piece to the puzzle." Charlie gestured. "Let's get inside. It'll be dark soon."

They found Seiran el-Habib where they had left him. He'd soiled himself, several times.

"At least, let me take a shower," he said. "I feel like an old man."

Ignoring him, Whitman turned to Charlie. "You were saying? What piece of the puzzle?"

"Blue eyes," Charlie said. "The recruiter Alice and Beth knew as Dante. Supposedly, he'll be here tomorrow morning." She turned to face their prisoner. "Isn't that right, Saudi?"

"I have a name," el-Habib said, clearly offended.

"Not to me, you don't," she said. "So how about it? Were you and Alice telling the truth? Will Dante be here tomorrow?"

"Did I say that?"

"You did."

He looked up at them. "Then it must be true."

"That's not an answer." Charlie grabbed the back of his chair, tilted it, and started to drag him down the hall toward the kitchen, where Alice's body still lay.

Flix bared his teeth. "And you want a shower." He spat onto el-Habib's chest. "How about that?"

He followed Charlie and el-Habib into the kitchen, the rear chair legs making a screeching sound like that of an animal in pain. Charlie set the chair down in front of Alice's bloody corpse. The smell made el-Habib recoil.

"Too much for your sensitive nose, Saudi?" Charlie said. "Look how you've ruined two girls' lives. You shot Beth and you left Alice with only despair."

"I didn't do this," el-Habib said. "Is it my fault the girl was weak of will? I tell you now that Dante is coming with replacements. He was to take them back—"

"To what?" Charlie bent over him. "Where was Alice going to go? Who would take care of her?"

El-Habib looked straight ahead, his gaze firmly fixed on the far wall until Charlie grabbed a handful of his hair, pushed his head down so that he had no choice but to stare at the body.

When Whitman stepped into the room, el-Habib said, "Won't you do something to stop her?"

"I told you, she's a force of nature." Whitman crossed to stand behind el-Habib. "On the other hand, someone here has to regain their senses. Let him go, Charlie."

She glared at him, but he nodded, and she reluctantly let go. He began to slice through the cords binding the Saudi to the chair.

"You really think this is a good idea?" she said.

"I think it's a great idea."

El-Habib turned his head sideways, shot Charlie a wicked grin of triumph.

When the Saudi was free, Whitman ordered him to stand up. As soon as el-Habib complied, he said, "Now pick Alice up."

The grin vanished from el-Habib's face. "What?"

Whitman showed him the shovel he had found. "You're going to dig graves, el-Habib, and then you're going to place Alice and Beth in their final resting places. We will say prayers for the dead in which you will take part. You will ask Allah for mercy." He shoved el-Habib forward. "And all the while you're going to wonder which one of the graves is for you."

37

The NSA is involved. This dreadful sentence kept repeating in Julie's head as she stood by the kitchen sink after Orrin had left for work. She knew she had to call Hemingway to tell him she was ill and wouldn't be coming in today, but she sure as hell wasn't going to do it from her mobile. Like many people these days, Orrin had no landline, not that she would have used it either. The NSA could very well be listening in on Hemingway's lines; after the events of last night, she couldn't take the chance that they weren't. Even if she purchased a burner phone, they'd be able to connect with it the moment she called in. Luther St. Vincent, the head of Directorate N, the shadowy department within the already shadowy NSA, knew Sydny, wanted her dead, and had carried out the termination himself. This terrified Julie. If Sydny was under NSA surveillance, then it stood to reason that anyone who came in contact with her had also been drawn into their electronic net. She shivered. Why would St. Vincent have put Sydny, a pole dancer, under surveillance? She shook her head. It didn't make sense. And then her mind calmed, cleared and she remembered Greg Whitman, to whom Sydny had handed her over after their first meeting. St. Vincent was after Whitman. But, still, why murder Sydny? Because they were friends—lovers? That might explain why St. Vincent did the wet work himself. It was personal between him and Whitman. Another, deeper shiver ran through her.

She showered, dressed in her soiled clothes, and went out to buy herself a new outfit. Before she did, though, she went into a drugstore, picked her way to the rear, and found the pharmacist.

Stitching her most seductive smile onto her face, she said, "Can I please make a local call? I've left my mobile at home. It's something of an emergency and it'll only take a minute, I promise."

She called Hemingway's private line, told him she was ill and would be out for a couple of days. When he asked if she needed anything, she said *Yes* silently, but told him "No." She thanked the pharmacist and returned to the street. If NSA was listening in on Hemingway's calls the trail to her would lead to this dead end.

It was all Orrin could do not to dance around the attorney general's office. He had, in fact, danced for a moment as the subway slid into the station, as he waited for the doors to open. Everyone around him was too busy thinking their own morning thoughts to notice or care.

He'd fucked his sister-in-law—okay, his *ex*-sister-in-law—but who cared? She was hotter than hot. He'd always had a crush on Julie, but until this morning he'd kept it locked tightly away, even after his divorce. Now, though, she had come on to him—she had . . . Christ, his thighs grew tight just thinking about what she had done to him, what they had done together.

He sat down in his office chair, staring at nothing, remembering everything about her, which is how he came to remember her request. Not that it was so out of the ordinary. The AG's office was opening investigations left, right, and center every day of the workweek. For on weekends, we play golf, he thought wryly, recalling the words of his former boss, his tone deeply biblical. However, it wasn't every day he was asked to open an investigation on someone from the NSA—and especially not on Luther St. Vincent, head of Directorate N, whatever the hell that was. Not that the idea wasn't floated around the office once every couple of months, but it was always shot down by one of the attorney general's cadre of Very

Important Mandarins. Though a slowly rising star, Orrin was, sadly, not yet one of them.

Still, he knew how to open an investigation using back-channel methodology. This was to be an informal investigation, not to mention a clandestine one. There was some danger in it for him, but on the other side of the ledger he now had Julie living with him. Though she had said it was only for a day or two, he had some ideas as to how to get her to agree to stay longer. And then from that step to permanence he was fairly certain would be a snap. Wouldn't that be a kick to the head, as far as his ex was concerned.

Turning to his computer terminal, he began to type in the long log-in code from the readout on the RSA encryption tag he kept with him at all times. The electronic tag changed the log-in code every twenty minutes, ensuring the highest level of security.

Once in, he started an investigative folder. Typing in St. Vincent's name brought up line after line of information pulled from all of the federal data banks, including the NSA's. Then, he settled in and started reading. He wasn't sure what Julie was looking for, but he would note any red flags and pass them on to her, just as she had asked.

For the second time since she had been taking care of him, Valerie drove Lindstrom to Big Planet Comics on U Street, NW. As it happened, Lindstrom was an avid reader of Hulk comics. Not too surprising, when you thought about it, Valerie told herself as she stared at the garishly colored covers of comics filling the layered racks. The Hulk was Dr. Bruce Banner, a shy physicist who, when he got angry, turned into a huge green monster who wreaked havoc wherever he went. That was the beginning. These days, however, in the manner of comics' new universes, there were many Hulks, confusing her no end.

That Paulus Lindstrom loved The Hulk said quite a lot about forces hidden deep in his psyche. While Lindstrom picked up the latest issues, she leafed through a comic called "Gang War." The cover depicted a human eyeball pierced by the tip of a switchblade. Good god, Valerie thought, shoving the comic back onto its rack.

She went over to Lindstrom. "Paulus, are you ready to go?"

"As soon as I pick out a Hulk T-shirt."

At length, she shuffled him over to the register, where she paid for his haul with cash.

Back in the car, they buckled up, and she headed home.

Lindstrom had taken his comics out of their plastic bag and was staring at them as if he could not believe his good fortune. Valerie, her caution verging on paranoia after the incident in the DARPA parking lot, kept an eye on the side mirror, but saw nothing out of the ordinary.

"Do you like the shirt I picked out?" Lindstrom asked, holding it up.

"Why does it say 'The Incredible Hulk'?" she asked.

Lindstrom smiled, as if at a faraway memory. "That was the title of the comic when it first came out. Everything was either Incredible or Amazing at Marvel in those days."

She maneuvered her way through the traffic and passed a corner packed with a group of teenagers horsing around, bringing up all sorts of memories, good and bad. "Why is he green?"

Lindstrom laughed. "That's the way Stan Lee conceived of him."

"Who's Stan L—?"

A truck, running the light, slammed into her side of the car, drove them sideways into an SUV. Her car collapsed in on itself like an accordion, the vicious force crushing Valerie and Lindstrom together like doomed lovers.

38

Flix, hunkered down beside Whitman as sunlight gained ground on nighttime shadows, said, "*Compadre*, I gotta know. You gotta tell me."

"Tell you what?" Whitman was studying Charlie's face in profile as she scanned the hilly horizon with field glasses. A hundred different memories went off in his mind like fireworks.

"What did you do to me?" Flix persisted.

"I saved your life," Whitman said.

"Yeah, well, okay. But, I mean, *how* the fuck?"

"If I told you, you wouldn't believe me."

"Whit . . ."

Whitman turned, put a hand on his friend's shoulder. "Listen to me, Flix. What's done is done. You're here, alive, back from the dead. Isn't that what's important?"

"Okay." Flix nodded. "I get it."

No, Whitman thought, because if you did, you'd be about a mile from here, never looking back. Charlie knew something of what he was—but not all, god no. The only ones who did were the Alchemists, and the less he thought about them and what they had made him do the better.

But the bayous of Louisiana blazed in his memory, like an unnatural fire that burns too hot and for too long, and never goes out.

"Hereabouts, they call me Preach," the man of indeterminate age said. "You may think you know my name, but you don't. I'm Preach, even when my women cry out my name when they're in la petite mort.*"*

Preach pursed his lips, considering, and his eyes became slitted. "I can see into your mind; I can see clear through you."

"I can't say I like the sound of that," Whitman said.

Preach cawed. "I mean t'tell you! No one likes the sound of what they can't understand." He nodded. "We'll soon remedy that."

"Why?"

Preach put a hand on Whitman's shoulder, transmitting a fearsome strength without tightening his grip. "You're one of us. That's what I see. You're one of us, yes, you are. And you're going to be instrumental in building the newer, better world to come."

When you're out here, Charlie thought as she peered through the field glasses, it's like nothing else exists. No supermarkets, shoe stores, restaurants of the moment. Everyone has a gun, everyone is out to kill you, and that's what happens here—death, destruction. No one gets out alive, or at least unscathed. How had Whit managed it, all these years? she wondered. This kind of life would eventually drive her mad, she was sure of it. She was also sure that when this mission was over she was going to take up something supremely banal, knitting, maybe. Then she laughed silently. Fat chance. But, in any event, she'd be quits with this job. Besides anything else, working with Whit was like sticking her head in a beehive— unpleasant and perilous in and of itself. She could even learn to hate him—really hate him, not the little-girl spite of their fiery breakup, but true hate with a passion she had not known she possessed. On the other hand, would that be so bad? she wondered. But her thoughts didn't dwell there for long.

Movement. A column of dust, like a djinn materializing out of the fire of the desert.

"Whit," Charlie called softly. "Company."

He and Flix joined her. Blue Eyes, the man known only as Dante, could finally be seen beneath the inferno of the blinding white West Pakistan sky. The thin cloud cover seemed to have spread light over the entire bowl of the sky, so that it appeared as if the sun had expanded to ten times its size.

Dante was driving a dust-coated half-track truck. He was alone, Charlie saw through her powerful field glasses: where were the two girls, the replacements for Alice and Beth? Hidden in back? Charlie was willing to bet not. The promise of release from bondage another lie they had had to swallow.

She frowned. Did Dante know the mercs were no longer in control of the compound? Did he know he was driving into an ambush? If so, he gave no sign of it. He continued down the dusty track that wound through the foothills, and which, at length, arrived at the outer walls of Seiran el-Habib's hideout.

"Places," Whitman said softly, and they all deployed.

They were ready for this moment, every move meticulously designed—they all had their parts to play. Charlie was pleased with the plan. She had to give Whit credit; out in the field he knew what he was doing. She could imagine no one better, and this assurance provided a sense of security she would not otherwise have had.

"Wait," Whitman said. "Wait."

And then, just as the truck was within range, they heard the signature *whup-whup-whup!* of rotors, and the gunship appeared over the top of the highest hill, heading straight toward them.

Strange days have found me, Julie thought as she walked through Foggy Bottom's rain-soaked streets. Faces come out of the rain—and they're strange. She jumped at every horn blare, flinched if any passerby came too near her. She walked and walked, crossing the bridge into Georgetown, turning right off M Street past the sturdy brick façade of the Four Seasons, walking uphill past neat town houses with gardens, trim and tiny out front.

It was the hour when, on a clear day with the sun low in the western sky, shadows would stretch out like cats yawning. She entered the gardens of Dumbarton Oaks, her favorite place in Georgetown, perhaps in all of D.C. The weather had turned it into a ghost town. The laden branches dipped and wept beneath the downpour, petals spilled on the ground.

Sadness gripped her, whereas before, on the streets, it was fear. At least she felt safe here, standing beneath the stone portico, gazing out at her beloved garden with its double oval of American hornbeams, a delicious bower in summer's heat.

Even in this weather she could not resist them. Stepping out from beneath the portico, she went across to the oval. The rain had simmered down to a light drizzle. She felt it on her face. It netted her hair like a bride's veil. She would get married here, of course she would—if she ever divorced her gay husband and married for real, which seemed more improbable with each passing day.

Her tears mixed with the tiny raindrops, and she shook herself, growing angry at her self-pity. Stop it! She admonished herself. Just stop it!

She lifted her head, wiped away her last tear, and that's when she saw the shadowy figure, lurking beneath the portico where, moments before, she herself had stood. When he saw that she had seen him, he stepped out from the shadows and came very quickly toward her.

Whup-whup-whup!

"Flix!" Whitman called. "The truck!"

Whup-whup-whup!

He turned. "Charlie! Take cover!"

Charlie leapt out of the way as the Hellfire missile came shrieking at them. She scrabbled through her pack. Before they had left, she had loaded it with compact, ultra-lightweight weapons of every new design she had come up with in the past eighteen months, even the unproven prototypes. Unfortunately, to deal with a missile-spitting gunship she was going to have to employ one of those. All or nothing at all, she said to herself with a half-smile, knowing Foxtrot-loving Whit would appreciate the allusion to the 1939 Sinatra song.

She brought out what looked like a blunt instrument, fitted it into the muzzle of a twelve-inch shoulder cannon she had created that used compressed carbon dioxide as a propellant. The blunt instrument contained a highly volatile payload; a normal propellant wouldn't do.

The gunship was swinging around, machine guns chattering, sending up sprays of gritty soil as it prepared to release another Hellfire. She settled the cannon onto her right shoulder, sighted through the scope. She was about to pull the trigger when she felt Whitman beside her.

"Can you do this?" he whispered in her ear.

Something tightened in the pit of her stomach. "Watch," she said, "and learn."

The entire tail assembly was in her crosshairs. She had only a split instant before the gunship was in position to fire the missile. She took a deep breath, let it out, and squeezed the trigger. There was almost no sound from the CO_2 propellant. The blunt instrument shot upward. When it struck the tail of the gunship the explosion, a blinding blue white, burned so hot it literally melted the aluminum and steel frame. The rear end of the gunship vanished as if it had never existed. What was left of the vessel canted over to one side and plummeted down in a drunken line.

The edges of the rotors began to plow up the ground, acting like a kind of paddle wheel, impelling the ruined helo forward, directly toward where Charlie and Whitman lay.

"Jesus Christ!" Whitman grabbed her elbow as they both scrambled up and began to run. The weird, wrecked mechanism continued to follow them as if it were alive, the rotors whirling closer and closer until their sound was all they could hear, and its oily breath overtook them.

Julie's first instinct was to turn and flee, but then she recognized the London Fog raincoat with the bit of tar on its flapping hem, the Tilley hat, battered and creased by years of wear, and she waited, heart pounding, as he crossed to where she stood.

"Julie," Omar Hemingway said gently, "it's time you came in from the cold."

She stared at him. "How did you find me?"

"I like to think I haven't lost my tradecraft." He smiled, gesturing. "Why don't we get out of the rain?"

She glanced over his shoulder, then at the far corners of the garden. "I'm as far out of the rain as I care to get."

"Hmm. Well, as to that, being out in a quiet place like this is one of the least secure spots, as far as the NSA is concerned." Seeing her wince, he added. "NSA's expertise is with electronic, not human surveillance."

"Even Directorate N?"

Hemingway's eyes narrowed. "Now you've begun to worry me. How does Directorate N figure into the mess you've gotten yourself into?"

"Not Directorate N, per se," she said. "Luther St. Vincent."

Hemingway studied her for a moment. The drizzle gathered at the low point of his hat brim, coalesced, and plopped down into the space between them. "I have heard," he said slowly and deliberately, "that St. Vincent is nursing a broken shoulder." He peered at her. "D'you know anything about that?"

"I know everything about that," Julie said softly.

39

Flix, having scrambled out of the line of sight of the Hellfire missile, set his weapon's sights on the truck driven by Dante. He knew he needed to be exceptionally careful. He could have shot Dante through the vehicle's windshield, but that would have served no purpose and would rob them of whatever intel Dante might possess. How to tackle the situation? But when he saw Dante throw the truck into reverse, his mind was made up for him.

He still could not get his head around everything that had happened to him in the last several days—being drugged, becoming some kind of experiment for the NSA, and, most mysterious of all, having Whitman reverse the effects. Nothing made sense to him, but then, in war, nothing ever did. Time to put one foot in front of the other and not look back.

He sighted, blew the right front tire. Pain shot through his rehabbing shoulder, and he gritted his teeth. Funny. It hadn't bothered him at all until Whitman's ministrations had brought him back down to earth.

The truck groaned like a mortally wounded beast, sinking down into the soft ground. Flix was up and running as Dante began to climb out of the vehicle. Then the sky seemed to split open in a blinding, deafening flash, and whatever had been airborne was careening wildly downward to the earth.

———

"I shot him."

"You should have killed the fucker," Hemingway said.

Julie stared at him as if he had grown a second head. "Excuse me?"

"I told you that St. Vincent has been a pain in my ass for years now. I haven't had the leverage to shoehorn him out of NSA. It seems no one does—or no one has had the guts to try, including me." Hemingway shook his head. "What does Directorate N do, anyway? No one knows, and that's just the way St. Vincent likes it, hiding in the shadows like a fucking vampire."

"He must wield some fabulous ju-ju."

"He does, my dear. But I very much doubt it stems from the usual suspects."

Julie and her boss sat in a brown leatherette booth in a sleazy roadhouse bar off Route 270, northwest of the Beltway, past the periphery of D.C.'s action. A glorious juke burping colored lights was playing Sinatra and Fitzgerald while antediluvian barflies clung to their old-fashioneds or gin and tonics as if they were life preservers. A bartender with a pate as smooth and shiny as glass read a dog-eared copy of *The Odyssey*, never even bothering to lift his head when required to refill one of his customers' glasses.

"No," Hemingway went on, "I'm certain Mr. St. Vincent's ju-ju, as you call it, comes from a nongovernmental source entirely."

She had told him as much as she had dared about what had happened the night before. Leaving out any of the sexual context, which was no one's business but her own. He didn't question any of it, and why should he? She had done precisely what he had asked her to do: find out more about Sydny.

"It interests me that both St. Vincent and Whitman had a relationship with this woman," Hemingway said now, paralleling her train of thought.

"Oh, I don't think St. Vincent knew her at all," Julie said. "I heard him. He killed her because she and Whitman had a relationship that was a bit more than all-business."

Hemingway sat back, his fingers drumming the table as he contemplated this news. "So her death was an object lesson."

Something quailed inside Julie. But she had been there, and she knew. "That's a horrid way to look at it."

"You don't know Luther St. Vincent." Hemingway rose, crossed to the bar, and returned with a dirty martini for her, a bourbon and water for himself. When he had taken a first sip, watching her do the same, a tiny smile plucked at the corners of his lips. "So St. Vincent is finally moving against Whitman. I do believe that he's made a fatal mistake. Perhaps all I have to do now is to sit back and watch events unfold. This is good, Julie. Very good." It was then he noticed her expression. "What? Is there something you aren't telling me?"

"I think it's the other way around."

His eyes narrowed. "What d'you mean?"

She thought of Sydney, and of what Whit had taught her. Drawing herself up, she said, "I think you've lied to me from the beginning of this assignment."

Under the guise of taking another hit of bourbon, Hemingway studied her. "You're different," he said now. "Something's changed in you."

"That's not an answer."

"No, it's an observation. A mighty surprising one, I might add." He sat his glass down, rolled it back and forth between fingers and thumb.

"You won't answer me, will you?"

"Not at your pay grade." That scrutiny started up again. "You see, this is what I mean about how you've changed."

"My eyes have been opened."

"By whom?" Hemingway moved his drink out of the way, laced his fingers as he leaned forward. "Who opened your eyes, as you call it?"

Julie's smile was as enigmatic as the sphinx. "There isn't a pay grade in the world high enough for me to tell you."

Whitman and Charlie lurched sideways, ducking their heads, then sprawling belly first onto the ground. They rolled away from the splintering rotors, and kept rolling to steer clear of the bulging fuselage that was being ripped asunder.

They fetched up against a boulder whose nearside had been split down a seam by the titanic explosion. What was left of the gunship was virtually unrecognizable, as was the ground behind it, furrowed as if by a colossal knife.

No one left alive, Charlie thought. The twin onslaughts of life and death had met head on, annihilating each other. There are no words to describe this, Charlie thought, and if there were I wouldn't want to know them. Years from now, if they made it out of this hellhole alive, she would be reliving the destruction over and over, trying vainly to figure out how she could have saved lives instead of taking them. Life wasn't fair, she knew that, of course she did, but the extent of its indifference was a cruelty beyond comprehension.

Suddenly her body went icy cold. Isn't that what the Time Out Of Mind—the time leading up to juvie—was about: cruelty beyond comprehension? Willfully, she would not remember; and yet, despite her best efforts, she would always remember.

A psychotic older sister who, in her break with reality, seduced their father, became pregnant, and flaunted that obscene pregnancy within the family, until their mother, driven to the edge of madness, took a carving knife and slit open her daughter's belly, killing both offending parties. Her father turned on his wife and would have strangled her had Charlie not intervened, bringing the bottom of a heavy iron skillet down on the crown of his head again and again, until it was as flat as the skillet itself. By that time, her mother was barely breathing. Charlie, a minor, entered the juvie system. While she was incarcerated, her mother died, whether by her own hand or not was never made clear to Charlie. No closure for her; none at all, just the swirl of dreadful memories that she had finally, painstakingly collected, locked away in a shadowed corner of her mind. All well and good until the times, such as this, when the lock popped open and the memories flew out like a jack-in-the-box in a horror film, reminding her that Time Out Of Mind still existed.

"What the fuck was in that thing?" Whitman was asking now. "It melted half the goddamn helo."

"A dicyanoacetylene compound I formulated." Charlie shook herself to keep her head on straight and her thoughts flowing coherently. The lockbox was back in its shadowed corner of her mind. "Essentially, it's acetylene in which I replaced a pair of hydrogen atoms with two separate cyanide groups. Burns hot like a sonuvabitch."

They turned their attention to Flix, who had Dante by the collar of his shirt and was frog-marching him over to them.

"Too bad your cavalry sprung a leak," Flix said with a dark glint in his eye. "Now you're never gonna be saved."

"Lookee here," Whitman said as he went through the papers Dante was carrying. He held up an open passport. "Check this out." He showed the passport to Charlie.

"Edmond Dantès," she said with a laugh. "Really?"

"The Count of Monte fucking Christo," Whitman said. "In person."

"I thought you were dead a long time gone." Flix struck the back of Dante's head. "What I want to know is if you're not bringing new girls to el-Habib, just what the fuck are you doing here?"

40

"Ding dong, the witch is dead!" Trey Hartwell crowed the moment he entered the inner sanctum of the Well.

Albin White, who had been training Lucy, shot her a sideways look, and she silently vanished from the chamber. Then he turned on his fellow Alchemist. "What the hell d'you mean coming in here and blurting out—"

"Lindstrom is out of our lives for good."

White, hands on hips, said, "Explain yourself."

Hartwell told him about the car crash in which Lindstrom and Valerie had been killed.

White looked skeptical. "An accident?" He was all too aware of the schism inside the Alchemists over who would run Mobius and, specifically, Paulus Lindstrom. St. Vincent, always jealous, always fixated on power, had wanted to run it from inside Directorate N, but a cohort led by Hartwell felt that would cause eyebrows to be raised on Capitol Hill, where the House Appropriations Committee was continually sticking their collective noses into DARPA's business. The Alchemists could not afford that kind of scrutiny. Therefore, Hartwell and his cohort had recommended Omar Hemingway, who, though not under their direct control, was easily manipulated. Outwardly, White had stubbornly remained neutral, but privately he had agreed with Hartwell, which was why he had secretly plumped for

Hemingway to be put in charge. It was essential that he keep up the appearance of being Switzerland in order to maintain everyone's trust, especially St. Vincent's. Ever since the girl, Lucy Orteño, had arrived, St. Vincent's decision-making had seemed to swing from erratic to inexplicable. This was a deep concern to every one of the Alchemists, but White more than the others.

"Yes," Hartwell was saying now, "so far as anyone knows it was an accident." Then he reared back. "Albin, you don't think—"

"Calm yourself," White said. "I know you don't have the heart for wet work."

Hartwell began to fidget. "Listen, Luther doesn't know. He's been out of circulation for a day."

"Is he ill?"

Hartwell shrugged. "With Luther, who knows?" His fidgeting became more intense. "But I do know he's on his way here so when he arrives—"

"I'll break it to him, Trey." He squeezed the other man's shoulder. "Now get on back to your shop. Your books must be missing you."

Hartwell, missing the humor, nodded, and scuttled out of the Well.

Lucy stared into the waterfall, at the noxious carving in the rock face Albin believed to be the alchemical symbol for sulfur. She knew better. Down in the bayous it was the sigil for the chimera: snake, lion, goat. In the bayous, they believed in the chimera; some had even claimed to see it on the longest night of the year, when it would emerge from the netherworld where it crouched and schemed all year, to take its fill of human blood and flesh.

With a sick feeling at the core of her, she forced her gaze away from the triangle with its horrific curled tail, down into the *cenote*, black, ageless, bottomless. She inhaled deeply of the scents rising from its depths: blood, fear, and death.

With a shudder, she turned away, wandered out of the high chamber and along one of the narrow curving hallways, its ceiling so high it was obscured by shadows dense as storm clouds.

It wasn't long before she heard voices—male voices. She recognized Luther's, then Albin's raised in answer. She slid along the wall, pressing her body against it, making herself all but invisible. She inched her way to the edge of the open doorway. She could see only a narrow slice of the chamber. Neither man was visible, but she heard their voices as clearly as if she were standing beside them.

She had never been given any reason to believe a word Luther had said to her, and seeing how he had bundled her uncle into an ambulance outside the Bethesda Institute of Mary Immaculate had given her every reason to distrust him. She had been curious about his interest in her, about what he was in to. He was NSA, he'd shown her his ID, but this facility wasn't NSA. After being given the tour, she was sure it wasn't anything the feds knew of, let alone had built. And then there was the sign of the chimera she had glimpsed tattooed on the inside of his left wrist. No, Luther was into something so far underground even the NSA was unaware of it, just as they were unaware of the sigil, of the chimera. That was one reason this place was safe from prying eyes and inquisitive noses. Luther and the rest of them could do whatever they wanted here without fear of rebuke or reprisal.

". . . Lindstrom gone," Luther was saying, "the entire project falls apart."

"You know that's not true," Albin said in a resonant baritone. "As Hartwell has pointed out numerous times there's another direction to go in."

"Events have overrun us," Luther said. "We lack the time to—"

"What events? What aren't you telling us? And what the hell happened to you?"

"A bullet jumped up and bit me," Luther snapped.

"As events overran you?"

The silence buzzed like a defective light fixture.

Albin cleared his throat. "Here's the bottom line, Luther. We're not shutting down Mobius just because your pet researcher is dead."

"As I told you, we have no choice." Luther's voice continued on its knife-edge. "At this late date, we're not going to go searching in the private sector for—"

"I agree, but there's another road we can take."

"I don't follow you," Luther said.

"I have summoned Preach."

Within the terrible silence that now enveloped not only the chamber in which the two men stood, but the corridor outside, Lucy felt her legs begin to tremble, turn weak, and betray her. She felt herself kneeling on the stone, her mouth half-open, her eyes glazed over in inescapable memory.

She had lied to Albin about her trauma in Louisiana: though she had been in the church, she had never been raped by three men. No, she had been given drugs by the tall thin man with the shock of prematurely white hair and piercing blue eyes, the man known as Preach. Then he had taken her into his bed. She had gone willingly. Perhaps that willingness had been a factor of the drugs; she had no way of knowing. Initially she had not been raped; their first coupling had been transcendent. But then it had continued for eighteen straight hours. Although she was still unsure what precisely "it" was. Because at some point during those eighteen hours there had been what she had come to call "the Other Thing," when she could bear to remember it at all, because there was no word in her experience to describe it. While his penis had plumbed her to her deepest depths, Preach had somehow reached down inside her, pried open her mind, and had read what was there as easily and intently as if he were reading a book. In fact, he called it "Bible studies," when she had asked him what he was doing. She had lain on her back, naked, spread like a sea star, while he straddled her, his forehead, hot as flame, almost touching hers. She remembered the scratch of his beard against the skin of her chin and throat as he whispered what might have been prayers or curses, in a language unknown to her, possibly to anyone else.

It was rape, no doubt—of her mind as well as her body, which was far worse. The body held no secrets, but the mind was composed of secrets and intimacies humiliating for a lover to know, let alone a stranger.

And there was another thing—a memory that Lucy could scarcely force herself to touch. During this process she was certain she felt another presence, a shadow crouched beside Preach, perhaps part of him, perhaps not, because it was an animal thing, certainly not human, its breath hot with the stench of an abattoir. First she thought she glimpsed the vertical pupils of a goat, then the bared teeth of a lion, then the sinuous coils of a huge snake, sliding over her flesh like an icy wind.

"I will not have that—*thing*—here."

Luther's voice drew her back from the brink of her bayou memories.

"Too late. He'll be here in seven or eight hours."

Oh, yes. Oh, yes, Lucy chanted silently. There was a fire in her eyes now, and in her mind a sense of fate drawing her and Preach together again, for the last time.

"You've got to stop this," Luther said.

"Can't. You know his rules."

"*His* rules! Why are we under his thumb?"

"He made us, Luther. He created the Alchemists."

"You know firsthand what Preach is capable of; you're one of the few people who've seen it and lived to tell about it," St. Vincent pressed on. "Imagine what he could do if we gave him access to the triptyne."

"I am imagining it. It's something Hartwell proposed some time ago."

"Hartwell," Luther scoffed. "He has no firsthand knowledge . . . Giving Preach access to triptyne is too dangerous."

"That's your assessment," Albin said. "It's time to come clean, Luther. We both knew Lindstrom wasn't going to cut it—no pure scientist could. We're off the map here, in a place where it takes more than theory, equations, and patient titration. Mobius was in Preach's territory from the get-go. Now, at last, we'll get what we want."

"You mean what *he* wants."

"Same thing."

"Is it? What if the outcome isn't what we imagined it to be?"

"No one can predict the future, Luther. We can only summon it."

There ensued a very long silence, while out in the corridor Lucy continued her private prayer.

"This is madness," Luther said at last. "Once you let the genie out of the bottle there's no stuffing him back in."

"Your fear of Preach is elemental, Luther. It isn't rational; it's personal. And it isn't really about Preach at all. It's about Gregory Whitman." Albin grunted. "You and Whitman have a score to settle. This confrontation has been a long time coming.

"Now that Preach has been summoned, the end, as they say, is nigh. One of you—you or Gregory—is going to make his last stand."

41

Julie sat beside Hemingway as he drove along the interstate.

"I'll drive you home," he said.

"No. When we get back to D.C. I'll give you directions to where I want to go and you can drop me off."

He shot her a glance. "You sure?" Then, seeing the determination in her face, he shrugged. "Suit yourself. Just don't disappear off the grid, okay?"

She nodded, but there was a desire inside her to stay on the road all the way to Santa Monica or Portland. She felt as if nothing could reach her if only she kept on the move, following the now tarnished American dream that led west, always west. As far from D.C. as she could get without boarding a plane or a ship.

"As for St. Vincent," Julie said, just for the hell of it, and because she was coming to like taking control of her conversations with Hemingway, "I've had an unofficial investigation opened on him at the attorney general's office."

This pronouncement almost caused Hemingway to drive off the road. "You did what?" A squeal of protesting rubber, a blaring bouquet of horns brought the car back in lane. He risked a sideways glance. "How could you possibly?"

She told him about Orrin.

"Dear god," he breathed. "I don't even know who you are anymore."

"You never did," Julie said.

A sober, almost depressed silence ensued, during which Hemingway continued to drive at such an accelerated pace that Julie blurted out, "Slow down, for heaven's sake. I'd like to live long enough to have a kid someday."

Hemingway contrived to ignore her, probably out of spite, Julie thought. After what seemed a long time, his speed decreased slowly to an acceptable level.

"So this is what it's like to grow old," he muttered.

He didn't seem to be kidding so she didn't laugh. She tried to summon up some feeling for him, without success. She had worked for him for more than five years without making any sort of meaningful connection. She realized that if she decided to quit, just walk away today, it would be with absolutely no regrets. Hemingway might be feeling what it's like to grow old, but she felt as if she were waking from a medically induced coma.

Hemingway glanced her way again. "How d'you imagine St. Vincent knew about the connection between Whitman and Sydny?"

Julie shrugged. "There could be any number of ways."

"But in light of what you told me, his interest must only have been very recently piqued."

Julie instantly picked up on his meaningful look. "Our briefings."

Hemingway pounded the steering wheel with his fist. "Oh, the stones on him. The fucker's had my office bugged."

"Eddy. Do you mind if I call you Eddy?" Without waiting for an answer, Whitman took Dante by the elbow, steered him past the wrecked helo, still smoking, its half-melted, contorted metal fuselage creaking like an old man's bones as it cooled.

"Before you talk to us, there's something I'd like you to see."

At the site of the three graves he stopped, positioning Dante at the foot of the one grave still uncovered. Down at the bottom lay Seiran el-Habib, bound hand and foot, his mouth stuffed with a filthy cloth. He stared up at the two men with deadened eyes.

"Looks like he's had a bad time of it, doesn't it?" Whitman said.

"That's because he has," Flix said. He bumped into Dante, causing him to stagger forward, teeter on the edge while Whitman held him tight by the back of his collar. "Not a pretty sight, is he?"

Charlie came up beside him. "And there but for the grace of God go you."

"She's right." Whitman dragged Dante back from the brink, let go of his collar. "Now you have some serious talking to do."

"You've got the wrong person," Dante said.

"That's the bullshit el-Habib tried to feed us," Flix said. "Now look at the poor fucker, lying in his own grave." He bumped Dante again. "That what you want?"

"No, of course not. Listen, I'm just a middleman. The poppies get shipped here from China. I pick them up and send them on."

Felix leaned in. "Poppies?"

Behind Dante's back, Whitman placed his forefinger across his lips. Then he said, "Send them on where?"

"To the States."

"Where, exactly?"

Dante gave them an address in rural Virginia. Whitman indicated to Flix that he keep an eye on their new guest, while he and Charlie stepped away. The stink of heated metal mingled with the greasy animal stench of roasted flesh. They had to move upwind of the helo's carcass in order not to gag.

"That address sound familiar?" Whitman said in a low voice. When Charlie shook her head, he told her. "It's the manor house of the old Mirabelle Hunt Club. Not a thousand yards away is the entrance to the Well."

"So Seiran told us the truth."

Whitman nodded. "This has nothing to do with Dr. Lindstrom and everything to do with the Alchemists. That's why St. Vincent engaged with Flix; he wanted him for a guinea pig in the field."

"But poppies? What the fuck?"

"Excellent question," he said. "Let's ask Edmond Dantès, shall we?"

Within minutes, he'd told them all he knew about *Papaver laciniatum*, which, admittedly, wasn't much. But it was enough for Whitman to make some basic assumptions, helped along by what he had observed and experienced in Flix.

"An alkaloid—or alkaloids," he said, "distilled from this particular poppy."

"What about them?" Charlie asked.

They all had crowded around; even Dante appeared interested.

"That's what they injected into you, *compadre*." He looked into his friend's face. "You remember how you felt by the time you got here?"

"Don't remind me," Flix said.

"But that's just what I'm doing. You need to remember everything, and tell us, Flix. It's vital."

Flix closed his eyes for a moment, trying hard to block out the memories, but there were too many, they were too powerful. They crowded out everything else. He told them how he had felt detached from himself. The first sign was that his shoulder had ceased to ache. The next thing he knew he was mowing down everyone who stood in his way, just as if he had each one on a line. "I couldn't miss," he said on an indrawn breath, "even if I'd wanted to." But that was the thing: he hadn't wanted to. On the contrary, the bloodlust was running so high inside him he could think of nothing but dealing death and more death. Nothing else in the world existed. The more people he killed the better he felt. He was connected to his weapon as if it were an extension of his arms, body, mind, and heart. "I felt no hesitation, no pity, no remorse, nothing," he said.

"That's why they're importing the poppies," Whitman said. "For an alkaloid with which they're trying to make the perfect killing machine."

"If not for you, *compadre*, they would have succeeded."

"Maybe not," Whitman said. "Remember when I got to you, you were about to rip your face off."

"About those poppies you're supposed to pick up," Charlie said to Dante. "Where are they?"

Dante stared down at el-Habib. "Didn't he tell you?"

"Not a word," Charlie said. She was fed up with the Saudi's fabrications and lies of omission. She jumped down into the grave, grabbed el-Habib, hauled him roughly to his feet. He bounced off the soft wall in a shower of sandy soil as she shook him like a plaything. Then she pulled the rag out of his mouth.

"How about it, Saudi?"

He glared at her, his face a mask of naked hatred. "In the kitchen. Under the floorboards."

"Flix," Charlie said.

Flix bent over, hoisted el-Habib out of the grave. Charlie climbed out without help from anyone.

They trooped inside. The kitchen floorboards were stained with Alice's blood, dried to a shiny mahogany. El-Habib, on his knees, found the hidden latch, and the trapdoor opened onto a shallow space dug out of the ground. He pushed aside the plastic flaps of a container. At once, the sickly sweet scent of opium poppies filled the room.

"Christ," Flix said.

"What's the next step?" Whitman said to Dante.

"I make contact with the States, tell them the package is ready for shipment."

"And then?"

"I drive back to the airstrip, where a refueled plane is waiting."

"Make the call, just as if you never met us."

"My sat phone is back in the truck."

Charlie and Whitman exchanged a look. Each knew precisely what the other was thinking.

"Saudi, you and Dante bring the poppies."

Dante worked with el-Habib to maneuver the payload out of its lair. The plastic container made their work easy. It was like carrying a coffin, only lighter. Flix backed away as the poppies passed him. Charlie couldn't blame him; she was sure she would have done the same had she been injected with their alkaloid.

Back outside, Charlie directed them to shove the payload into the rear of the truck. Then Whitman monitored Dante as he placed the call. Afterward, he destroyed the sat phone.

"None of this will do you any good. You think you're escaping, but you're not. There is no escape." A peculiar calm had come over Dante, as if he had entered a kind of meditative state.

The short hairs on the nape of Whitman's neck stirred and there was a ball of ice forming in his belly. He'd seen that kind of meditative state before, had even, for a time, entered into it himself.

He shook Dante like a ragdoll. "Explain yourself, shitbird."

Dante's eyes rolled toward him, but they were slightly out of focus. "It's so simple. You don't understand. You've misunderstood everything. This isn't about running poppies from China to the States, it's not about the movement of capital from one place to another. It's about the manipulation of everyone and everything."

The ball of ice in Whitman's stomach was spinning, growing, threatening to move up into his lungs, block the inhalation of oxygen. "It's about the creation of a newer, better world."

Dante's eyes snapped into focus. "Yes! That's it exactly!"

Whitman felt the ball of ice uncurl, enter his bones, chilling him to the core. Preach. Those were Preach's words. Dante was one of Preach's acolytes.

Dante threw his arms out wide. "This is about the entire world. A shift of monumental proportions never seen before. The fall of one superpower, the rise of another, creating conflict, war, chaos. America falling, China rising. Why? Because then we'll take Iraq's oil fields with our enhanced soldiers, we'll take them away from China, and China will have no choice. They're energy-hungry. They can't afford to lose a source of oil. And out of that conflagration will come the creation of a newer, better world."

"With Preach at its head."

Dante's lips pulled back from his teeth and he laughed like a hyena over a dead body until Flix came up behind him and swung the butt of his rifle into his head, and he collapsed, his head canted at an unnatural angle.

"Leave him," Whitman said, frightened and disgusted in equal measure.

The blown-out tire was changed for the spare, and then it was time to go. Almost. Charlie, standing beside the truck, took out her shoulder launcher, loaded it up.

"No!" el-Habib screamed. "That's my home!"

"I hate this fucking place!" She pulled the trigger and, with an ear-splitting noise, the villa exploded into an immense fireball. El-Habib broke away from Flix, ran with a staggered gait toward the conflagration. None of them stopped him. No one watched as he vanished into the flames.

PART FOUR

THE SUMMONING

You see, a secret is not something untold. It's something which can't be told.

—Terence McKenna

42

Lindstrom was dead. Another pathway cut off, and that was as it should be, Preach thought as he barreled up the interstate in the dead of night. The Alchemists had had no choice but to summon him. Lindstrom had served his purpose. He had created the serum that would speed up the zombification process. Crow had informed him of the serum's deleterious side effects. No use creating soldiers who ripped their face off. But Preach was altogether certain that using the serum in conjunction with his own process would eliminate the problem while accelerating the creation of the soldiers.

Preach hummed to himself a creaky old Creole tune as the miles flew by, beating time on the steering wheel with the heel of his hand. The warm wind whistled and gnats slammed into his windshield as he cut through the night. Life—even one as long as his—was often a bowl of fucking cherries.

At two-thirty in the morning, he pulled off the interstate into the deserted blacktop parking lot of an all-night diner. It was clad in formed aluminum and looked like an Airstream recreational vehicle. Five flagstone steps led up to the front door. Preach parked and got out.

Inside, the place was as devoid of life as the parking lot. To his right and left, along the windows, was a series of booths. In front of him was the counter, fronted by a line of chromium and vinyl stools that swiveled back and forth. A blowsy blonde stood behind the counter placing pies in a glass carousel. No one was at the register. A shadowy figure inhabited the booth at the far end of the diner, where the lights had gone dark. The figure, hooded and difficult to make out clearly, was hunched over a cup of coffee that looked as if it hadn't been touched, although it might have already gone cold.

Preach bellied up to the counter and sat. The blonde turned from her pie placement and gave him a weary smile.

"What'll it be?"

"Eggs up; bacon, crisp; grits with extra cheese; coffee, black, no sugar."

"We got cornbread," she said hopefully, "fresh-baked."

"Sounds too good to pass up," Preach said.

She nodded, appearing happy as a child at Disneyland, gave his order to the kitchen, then turned back to him, poured his coffee.

"Come far?" she said.

"Going far."

"I hear ya." She nodded. "You're from the bayous, yeah?"

He heard a vehicle turn into the parking lot. It was big, probably one of those new-style SUVs. "Yes, ma'am, that I am."

"I knew it. My grandpappy was from down yonder."

He sipped his coffee, which tasted of eggshells and bitter grounds. "Ain't we all related there."

The two of them shared a laugh at that one.

The front door opened behind him, someone strode in, sat on a stool nearby: a man with a weathered face, leathery skin, big as a bear and, from the look of him, just as mean. In the corner, the shadowy figure seemed to ripple, as if with a tremor of foreboding. Preach felt it like a hand on the nape of his neck, a gentle dispatch from the other side.

"Eggs, plenty of 'em, bacon and sausage, plenty of it. And make it snappy."

"Would you like coffee, sir?"

"Did I order coffee? And why are you standing around gawping. I said make it snappy. Are you deaf as well as stupid?"

The blonde recoiled, turned, and gave in his order. She stayed that way, her back to the newcomer, until Preach's food was delivered via the high pass-through. She set the plates in front of Preach and, smiling, said, "Can I get you anything else?"

Before he had a chance to answer, the bear-man said, "Hey, what the hell're you doing. That's my food."

"No, sir, it isn't," the blonde said with a quaver of fear in her voice. "I just gave in your order."

"Are you fucking telling me that's not my breakfast right there?"

"Sir, there's no call to use that kind of language."

"I'll use whatever fucking language I fucking want." He climbed off the stool. "I want to know why you're giving my breakfast to this piece of trash here." He glanced at Preach. "I know low-country shit when I see it. Old people don't have need of food, am I right?"

"Sir, please sit back down and be patient," the blonde said. Preach could feel her terror coming off her in waves. "Otherwise, I'll have to call the police."

"Okay, okay. Relax, Blondie." Smiling, the bear-man reached into his pocket, shook out a cigarette.

The blonde's eyes grew big around and she pointed to a sign taped over the pass-through to the kitchen. "I'm sorry, sir, but there's no smoking on the premises."

"That right?" The bear-man shrugged. "Well, we don't want to break any of this shithole's rules, do we?" Holding the cigarette like a pointing finger, he jammed it down into one of Preach's egg yolks, then swirled it around until it broke open, the bits of tobacco flecked through the running yellow streams.

"Now I *will* call the police," Blondie said.

The bear-man's hand snaked out, pinned her wrist to the counter. "You ain't going nowhere, Blondie."

"Please! You're hurting me."

He grinned at her, baring his nicotine-stained teeth.

In the far corner, the shadow stirred at precisely the same instant Preach's lips moved as if in prayer. Preach's eyes slid shut, and a shimmery dimness overtook the interior, though the blonde was dead certain the lights were burning as bright as ever.

"Oh, Lordy," she breathed.

A moment later, the bear-man's SUV burst into flame.

"What the fuck?" he said, as he whirled around. Then he let go of the blonde's wrist and, striding to the front door, hauled it open. "What the fucking *fuck!*"

He raced down the steps, but somehow his feet got tangled up, his ankles turned to Jell-O, and he fell hard face-first against the bare concrete. There was a crack like lightning. He lay where he fell, unmoving. A dark stain spread out from his head, dripping from the concrete to the blacktop, where it glimmered in the diner's fluorescent lights.

The blonde blinked as the shimmery dimness lifted. "He dead, d'you think?"

"Any minute now," Preach said.

The blonde clucked her tongue. "That's a shame." She reached for his plate of ruined eggs. "I'll have Hector quick-fry you up a fresh breakfast."

"Don't bother."

"On the house."

"The eggs served their purpose."

She regarded him with curiosity, shrugged, "Just as well, I suppose. I'm gonna have to call the cops."

Preach rose, digging out his wallet, but the blonde shook her head. "Like I said, your money's no good here. I never charge family."

Preach nodded. "Much obliged."

"Careful on your way out," she called. "Bound to be slippery out there."

"Always am, ma'am."

When he was gone, the blonde gathered her courage to peer into the far corner. The shadowy figure had vanished. As she sighed her relief, the light above the booth snapped on. She turned away and, shuddering, picked up the phone to call the police.

43

The casualties from the Mobius Project arrived at the Well around noon. Albin White supervised their entry and subsequent incarceration. It was as well that he was busy; it kept his mind from dwelling on the imminent arrival of Preach.

Summoning Preach was a calculated risk; he knew that from the get-go, but he also knew that Preach's involvement was a necessary evil—just as the Well was a necessary evil—for Mobius to be successful. Lindstrom had been a brilliant researcher—they never could have gotten anywhere without his breakthrough with *Papaver laciniatum*. For that alone White would be forever grateful to the scientist, but now that he was dead, only Preach would be able break down the complex alkaloid to rid it of its pernicious side effects.

Down the darkly gleaming corridors he went, emerging into one of the vertiginous chambers. Three of the casualties were on their knees, wrists tied behind their backs, gas masks with the eyeholes blacked out over their faces. They were all bleeding from beneath the ears and the chin, depending on how badly they had clawed at their faces before they were sedated. All had bloody crescents beneath their fingernails, some of which were ragged and torn. Their chests beat in the threadbare pulse of the panicked and the despairing.

Lucy was already in the chamber, which was adjacent to the waterfall with its ages-old *cenote*.

"Well," White said, regarding her with both care and precision, "will you have difficulty killing them?"

Lucy pointed. "Look at them. Would you want to live like they're living?"

"Not a second more."

He handed her a Heckler & Koch P30L handgun, saw with interest that she checked the magazine. She recalled with perfect clarity how Preach had taught her how to handle an old Mauser, how to load it, fire it, clean it, take it apart and put it back together in pitch darkness. How he had kissed her in the moonless night as a reward. Before tying her back up and laying her down with a tenderness she had heretofore never experienced, before he had taken her from behind, grunting and rutting like a sweat-slicked animal. Afterward, as he pressed down on her in the heat of a night with not even a whisper of a breeze to cool her off, she had burned with the humiliation his repeated violation of her body caused her. And still the violation of her body was the least of it. Each time he took her she could feel him inside her mind, worming his way through her thoughts, emotions, and memories. This was the thing that terrified her down to the marrow of her bones, the thing that caused her to steal the Mauser while on a nighttime bathroom run, shoot the man who was guarding her, and tear off through the bayous surrounding the church like a series of circular picket fences.

She ran and ran, fully expecting Preach—or a posse of his acolytes—to come after her, but either that didn't happen or she managed to elude them. Near dawn, she jump-started a jeep outside someone's house, and drove all day, until the tank ran dry. Then she hitched rides on semis, sometimes giving her body as payment, sometimes just talking with the lonely drivers. Heading north, always north, snorting lines of coke in an increasingly desperate attempt to forget what had happened to her in the Louisiana bayous, until somewhere in North Carolina the state police and the FBI had caught up with her in the forecourt of a sad motel.

Now, without hesitation, she stepped behind the first casualty, placed the H&K at the base of his skull and pulled the trigger. In a burst of blood and bone, he lurched away from her, sprawled over on his side. She held the second one down as she shot him. The third one gave no resistance at all—he was too far gone to know whether he was dead or alive, or to care.

As she handed the H&K back to White, two men wearing plastic overcoats entered the chamber and began to carry the dead men out.

Lucy looked at White. "You have the stones?"

"As you asked," he said. "But I'm still unclear as to why you need them."

Instead of answering him, she followed the two men with the last of the corpses. As soon as they had cleared the chamber, high-powered jets of water sluiced the blood and bits of bone down a large central drain.

The bodies were waiting for her at the waterfall. They had been stripped of their gas masks. The two men in slickers waited, patient as Roman sentinels. On the lip of the *cenote* was a small pyramid of stones about the size of her fist.

"Bring the first one," Lucy said.

The two men lifted the first corpse, laid him on his back against the lip. Lucy opened his jaws and one by one stuffed the stones into his mouth until it was filled. Then she closed the jaws and nodded to the men, who lifted the weighted corpse over the side of the *cenote* and dropped the body headfirst. It plunged into the dark turbulent water, vanishing within moments.

When the same procedure had been performed on all three, she turned to White and said, "Is that all for today?"

When he told her it was, she discovered that she was disappointed. She had to content herself with the knowledge that Preach had been summoned, that very soon he and she would be reunited, just not in the way he had foreseen.

"Someone's gunning for you," Jonah Dickerson said into his mobile.

St. Vincent, sitting in Ben's Chili Bowl on U Street, NW, had just taken a painkiller for his shoulder so he could enjoy the pair of chili dogs, fried onion rings, and jumbo Coke he'd ordered, and was in no mood for bad news. "What the fuck d'you mean?"

"Our contact in the AG's office tells me an investigation jacket has been opened on you."

St. Vincent sat up straight, the deep throbbing in his shoulder all but forgotten. "That's impossible. I'm invulnerable. He must be mistaken."

"It's an unofficial investigation," Dickerson said, "and he's not mistaken. I'm looking at an electronic copy of the information they've pulled on you. I have to say it's pretty damn impressive."

"You don't have to say anything," St. Vincent snapped. "Recall you don't have an opinion."

Silence on the line. St. Vincent didn't care. The pain in his shoulder was nothing compared to the roiling in his heart. From the moment that shit-for-brains White had told him Lindstrom had been killed an icy fist had gripped his intestines, causing an existential pain indescribable to anyone else. There were three things in life he despised above all others: losing, being wrong, and Preach. Of course, White was aware of his fear of Preach, which was why St. Vincent was sure he had reveled in their conversation. He might pretend to be the neutral bulwark in the Alchemists, but in the matter of Mobius and Preach, St. Vincent knew precisely where White stood. He did not relish the thought of he and White being adversaries, but shit happened, didn't it? He'd have to adjust to the changed landscape, figure out a way around White—or through him.

"Sir?"

Dickerson's voice in his ear was like a woodpecker attached to the side of his head. "Who?" he said. "Who initiated the jacket on me?"

"Someone named Orrin Jameson."

St. Vincent took up a dog, bit into it, and chewed. "Who is he?" he said around the food.

"A drone, so far as our contact knows. Odd thing, that. According to our contact Jameson is about the last person to initiate an unofficial jacket on anyone."

St. Vincent washed the dog down with a large swig of Coke. "Someone must have given him orders."

"It would seem so."

"Who, Dickerson?" St. Vincent took another bite of dog, but he'd bit off more than he could chew, and he almost choked. He coughed, let his anger at himself shift to his assistant. "For fuck's sake, don't drag this out."

"Our contact swears it's no one within the AG's office."

"Well, that makes no sense. The AG's people are immune to outside influence. Unless . . ."

"Unless what, boss?"

"What do we know about Orrin Jameson, other than he's a drone in the AG's office?"

"Hold on a minute."

There was a pause. St. Vincent pondered taking another painkiller, then decided against it. He took another bite of the chili dog, savoring the river of flavors.

"Okay, here we go," Dickerson said. "Well, sorry, boss, there's not much. This guy's something of a boy scout. In fact, he *was* a Boy Scout." Dickerson chuckled, but when he heard no answering sound at the other end of the line he sobered up. "Guy's divorced some time now. I mean, that's it. He's so squeaky clean it's downright disgusting."

And yet there must be something. St. Vincent closed his eyes. What was he missing? "Who was he married to?" It was a shot in the dark, but he had nowhere else to go. Plus, it paid to be thorough.

"A woman by the name of Bridget. Bridget Regan."

St. Vincent's eyes popped open. "Spell Regan."

"R-e-g-a-n. Why?"

"Bridget have a sister, by any chance?"

"As a matter of fact, she does."

"Her name Julie?"

"Jesus, boss," Dickerson said, "sometimes you just amaze the shit out of me."

44

Home, Charlie thought, as she sat in the Alchemists' jet, thirty-five thousand feet above the ocean. What does home really mean to me? Fire and ice, and everything nasty. Betrayal, rage, death. And blood everywhere, a skating rink of blood.

Charlie looked over to where Whitman sat across the aisle from her. His eyes were closed, his head against the seat rest. She got up and moved next to him.

"Charlie," he said softly without opening his eyes.

"What will happen when we land?"

"That's up to the Alchemists."

"You mean you'll let them get the upper hand?"

His eyes opened, his head turned, and his eyes engaged with hers. "What do you think?"

"Mysterious as ever."

"It's what you love most about me, isn't it?"

She barked a soft laugh, then grew silent for some time.

At length, he said, "That night."

"What night?"

"The night you struck me. The night of the severing."

"Is that how you think of it—a severing?"

"I do now."

"Whit, when I hit you . . . It was pure instinct."

"That's what made it so terrible."

She watched him out of the corner of her eye, as if she were unsure whether to face him fully. "Everything we did then was driven by instinct."

"We were children—at least with each other."

She took her time digesting this idea. "We didn't know any better." Now she turned to him. "Do we now?"

"I think you know the answer to that question."

"It would be refreshing to hear you say it."

A small silence settled over them, like a blanket.

After a time, she stirred. She might have shrugged or the tiny movement might have been something else altogether. Either way, she drew infinitesimally closer to him. "I'm tired, Whit," she said quietly. "I'm tired of hiding, of running. Most especially, I'm tired of . . . The hate I've held on to has curdled my heart."

He searched her face. "It was as if you were afraid to let go, afraid you'd lose the hatred."

"That's because . . ." she swallowed hard. "Because, you know, I think it came to define me. Because after I was . . . without you, it's all I had left of you and me."

He reached out. "I'm sorry . . . about everything." His hand covered hers. "Especially roping you into Red Rover."

Her dark laugh was infused with infinite sadness. "Red Rover's been the least of it." She looked down at their hands, one atop the other. "Whit, there's something I want . . . something I need to tell you. It's about what happened to me a long time ago."

"You don't have to, Charlie."

"Don't," she said. "Don't keep protecting me. Just let me talk."

Afterward, she counted the silence in heartbeats rather than seconds. She had not told the story of her Time Out Of Mind since she had confessed it to the Elf Lord. That was years ago, when she was right out of juvie prison and the wounds were still raw and bleeding. But now she went a step further.

"I learned to fight in juvie," she said now, almost in a whisper. "'Fight or die' was the watch-phrase in that place. It was supposed to be humane in there because we were, you know, kids, but actually it was a hellhole. The population was divided into tribes. That's SOP in prison, but the two most powerful leaders were sworn enemies. They would've torn each other apart if the guards had let them, but that wouldn't have been any fun. So we had endless running battles, full-scale guerrilla warfare."

"And you were caught up in it."

Charlie looked him full in the face. "I was one of the two leaders." Reacting to his look, she produced a wan smile. "I told you it was 'fight or die.' I was rageful beyond words. Looking back, I suppose I wanted to kill myself as much as I wanted to kill everyone around me."

"What happened?" Whitman said.

"Time passed. I grew up."

"And the power struggle?"

"Power in prison is like sand running through your fingers. It's as fleeting as fame—in other words, useless. That's the second lesson I learned inside."

Whitman considered a moment. "I wish you had told me sooner."

"Why?"

"I could have—"

"You couldn't have done anything, Whit, believe me. And the last thing I needed was your pity."

"I wouldn't have pitied you."

"Are you sure?"

"I don't pity you now, Charlie. I just know you better."

A shadow of a smile passed across her lips. "A good deal better now than I know you."

He regarded her levelly. "Are you sure you want to go down that road?"

Slipping her hand from under his, she took his arm, turned it so the tattoo of the dragon was visible. "The dragon," she said. "What's in its mouth?"

"It's the alchemical sigil for sulfur."

"Why is it in the dragon's mouth?"

"That," he said, "is a long story."

She glanced at her watch. "We still have over seven hours flying time. Is that long enough?"

"I think I have what you want," Orrin said, his face flushed with triumph as he came through the apartment door.

Julie looked up from the chopping board where she was dicing tomatoes and mincing cilantro. She had gone food shopping, needing to ground herself in some form of normalcy before she lost her mind. Making a meal was the best way for her to feel as if she was in control of her life. The tomato stains on her blouse were testament to her immersion in the activity.

"That's great news." She wiped her hands on a paper towel and picked up the file he laid down on the kitchen counter. Opening the folder, she scanned the pages inside. "You didn't have any trouble finding this information?"

"Some." He grinned. "But nothing I couldn't handle."

She glanced up. "No one knows about your digging around?"

"No one at all." He took off his jacket, loosened his tie. "Don't worry. I was careful with every search I made. I left no ISP fingerprints. The AG's office has its ways."

"So does NSA," she said.

"And I'm aware of all of NSA's ungodly methods. That's how I make my living, remember?"

She put the file down for the moment. "Make yourself a drink. I'm going to change my shirt."

She went into Orrin's bedroom closet, where she had tossed the shopping bags of clothes she had bought earlier in the day. She pulled out a cap-sleeve shirt and started to pull it on. As she did so, one of her arms brushed against a line of his shirts and trousers all hung up neatly, arrayed like soldiers. That's when she saw the niche behind his clothes. Pushing them aside, she found herself looking at a line of homemade DVDs in clear plastic cases. She slipped one out. "HEIDI" she read, along with a date. Her heart rate abruptly elevated, she checked out others. Each one was labeled with a female name and a date. At least half of them predated Orrin's di-vorce from Bridget. A sickness rose in her gorge.

She took one of the DVDs from its case, slipped it into the DVD player. Turning on the TV, she navigated to the correct input. Thirty seconds of watching Orrin thrashing around naked with "NOREEN" was enough to assure her that she had been dead wrong to take Orrin's side in the divorce. The intense sibling rivalry she and Bridget had endured all their lives had blinded her to the truth. How could she have been so wrong about Orrin? The shmoo had turned into a weasel right before her eyes.

"Julie?"

She started at the sound of his voice, rose quickly from the edge of the bed, extracted the DVD, slid it back into its case, and replaced it in the closet. She switched the input back to TV seconds before Orrin came into the bedroom, a stemmed glass of red wine in one hand.

"What were you doing in here so long?"

"Just checking the news for, you know . . ."

"You've got to stop obsessing over the incident."

That's what Orrin had taken to calling Sydney's murder. It so trivialized her death it made Julie want to slap him. And now that she knew who and what he really was, she had far more incentive to.

Instead, she smiled at him, switched off the TV. "You're right," she said. "Of course you're right." She almost retched, pecking him on the cheek as she passed him.

He was right behind her as she went down the hallway and into the living room, where a man was standing, legs slightly spread, muscles tense as a pulled bow-string. He was dressed in black, unshaven, with the coarse features of a thug.

"Who the hell are you?" Orrin said. He seemed rooted to a spot behind and just to the left of Julie. "How did you get in here?" He turned on Julie. "Did you forget to lock the door?"

"You came home after me, Orrin." Julie did not take her eyes off the intruder. There could only be one reason he was here. But how on earth had Luther St. Vincent found out about Orrin's electronic investigation? *I'm aware of all of NSA's ungodly methods,* he had said. Clearly not.

Orrin had his hands up. "I don't know what you want, but take anything. Just leave us in peace."

The intruder went over to the kitchen countertop, briefly paged through the file on Luther St. Vincent.

"Oh, god." Now Orrin got it. His gaze was fixed on the file, which, Julie now realized, he never should have taken out of the office. It would mean his job, his career. He'd be finished in the public sector—doubtless the private one, as well.

But Julie was looking where she should be looking—in the intruder's eyes—and she saw the twitching of his face when it should have been still, the rolling of his eyes when they should have been focused on either the file or on Orrin. She moved just before he did, and was on him as he drew his weapon, a snub-nose Glock revolver. He pushed her roughly aside, against the kitchen counter, but she came back at him as he leveled his gun at Orrin, who turned and ran down the hallway. The intruder grabbed her throat, squeezing with unholy strength.

Julie gasped, brought her knee up hard into his groin, then, as he grunted, pitching his torso slightly forward in reflex, she clawed at his face. This caused an astonishing chain of events that happened so quickly they seemed to occur all at once. The intruder let her go, dropped his revolver, and fell to his knees. Now his facial muscles seemed to be spasming wildly, his eyes opened so wide they showed the whites all around. He began to claw at his face, just as she had done, but more deeply. His nails dug beneath the skin, ripping into the fascia and muscle beneath. His eyes found hers; they seemed to cry out to her for help or for solace, she could not tell which.

Blood welled up, streaking his face. His chest was heaving violently, his mouth working. But only a series of grunts issued from it; he looked to be in agony beyond imagining. Then, with what seemed an extraordinary effort, his gaze went from her to the Glock lying on the floor between them. His gaze rose again. He was as grave as a judge about to pronounce sentence, and she knew what he was asking of her.

"I can't." She tried to back away, but the kitchen counter was in her way. She tried to brush past him, but he clutched her leg with one hand. "I can't."

But his nails dug into her as they had his own flesh, making her cry out, pulling her downward until she was on her knees in front of him. She stared into his agonized face. She picked up the revolver. At once, his mouth ceased its twitching. It hung open, a dark cave, waiting. His hand left her leg, guided her hand until the short barrel was where he wanted it.

"I can't," she said, and pulled the trigger.

45

"You might think the dragon tattoo a symbol of initiation," Whitman said, "but it isn't." He looked past Charlie's shoulder to make certain no one else was listening or even in earshot. Flix was sound asleep, snoring softly, and the putative Edmond Dantès was eating a meal up front. Whitman had given him plenty of incentive not to converse with any of the crew.

"What is it, then?" Charlie said, prompting him.

"A graduation present." Whitman rubbed the head of the dragon, as if reacquainting himself with the beast. "From a man I hope never to meet again."

Charlie opened her mouth, but before she could speak, all the color drained from her face.

"Charlie . . ."

"It's okay."

She fumbled in her backpack, shook out two Imuran tabs. Whitman called the flight attendant for water, but Charlie swallowed them dry. Cold sweat had broken out at her hairline, and her face looked wan and drawn. The water arrived and Whitman made her drink some. Then she laid her head against the seat back and closed her eyes.

"It's okay, Whit," she whispered. "I'll be fine."

"You haven't been taking the Imuran regularly."

"In that fucking hellhole? Who had the time?"

"You've got to make the time," he said. "You've got to take the Takayasu's more seriously."

"What did I ever do without you, Whit?" she said with a bite in her voice.

"The color's coming back to your face."

"I'm feeling more myself." She nodded. "Now, about that man . . ."

"Relentless doesn't even begin to cover it."

She opened her eyes and smiled at him. "That's why you love me."

He grunted. "He called himself Preach, and for him we have to go back a long way."

Whitman was nineteen when his mother and younger sister vanished. He had already been overseas twice in Special Forces, having lied about his age and altered documents that proved he was older. His father was already dead of a cerebral aneurism incurred while building a corral. He returned from Iraq to find their apartment empty, dirty dishes in the sink, tea and cakes set out on the kitchen table. No clothes were missing. It was as if they had been plucked from the apartment in the space of a heartbeat. How was that possible?

The authorities were of no use, so Whitman set out to find them. He spent the next eighteen months in monomaniacal pursuit, after which he had to admit to himself that he was no closer to finding out where they had gone or what had happened to them. It was as if they had fallen off the face of the earth.

He was of no further use to Special Forces, so when his tour of duty ended he left. "I joined the FBI, became a profiler, as you know. What I never told you was that I had met a man named Preach. It was Preach who told me he could find my mother and sister. Little did I know then that the reason he could find them was because they were dead."

"It's safe now. You can come out."

Julie waited for Orrin to appear, but when he did not, she went down the hallway and into the bedroom. He was standing, his back to one of the two windows. Outside, the muffled sounds of passing vehicles; across the street a building loomed with floors filled with empty eyes. There was a baseball bat in his hands. She wanted to laugh, but he quailed away from her, and she looked down.

Orrin stared from her face to the revolver she still held and back again. "What . . . what happened out there?"

"He's dead. Suicide. We're safe."

"I'm afraid not."

She whirled to see Luther St. Vincent. He was aiming a silenced handgun in his good hand at a space equidistant between the two of them.

"Drop the Glock, Ms. Regan." The muzzle of his gun moved toward her. "Really. I mean it."

She allowed the revolver to slip from her icy fingers. This is the end, she thought. No one here gets out alive.

The handgun swung back slightly. "And now you, Mr. Jameson."

Orrin let go of the bat. What was he going to do with it anyway?

"How did you find out?" Julie said. She found that, at the end, she was intensely curious about every detail that had led to this moment.

"We have a contact inside the AG's office." His gaze swiveled toward Orrin. "You were careful, Mr. Jameson, just not careful enough. This is the NSA you're dealing with, Directorate N you're trying to fuck with." He shook his head. "That won't do. Not at all."

"What . . . what are you going to do?" Orrin said, his voice breathy, as if he'd been running a marathon.

"What do you think I'm going to do, Mr. Jameson?"

"He's going to kill us, Orrin," Julie said. "He's going to shoot us dead."

St. Vincent turned to her. "You're smart for a woman. Maybe too smart for your own good."

"Smart enough for you to recruit me into Directorate N?"

This raised St. Vincent's eyebrows. He seemed genuinely startled. "Is that a joke?"

"Not at all. There's so much I could tell you about Omar Hemingway's shop."

"Like what?"

"Like he hates your guts."

"I already know that," St. Vincent said dismissively.

"No, he *really* hates your guts. So much so that he's actively working to publicly humiliate you."

St. Vincent laughed. "He wouldn't; he hasn't got the balls. He couldn't; he doesn't have the juice."

Julie wisely held her tongue, but her gaze remained steadily on St. Vincent's face, until he was forced to ask, "How? How the fuck does he think he's going to do it?"

"That's a question for after my recruitment."

St. Vincent's eyes narrowed. "I don't believe a word of this. You're just delaying the inevitable. But your little playlet bought you a bit of time." The gun moved back to Orrin. "Him first, then you."

His finger tightened on the trigger. The smell of hot urine invaded the bedroom as Orrin lost control. They both heard the shot at once. The window glass shattered, St. Vincent arched backward as the hollowpoint bullet tore through his chest cavity, disintegrating like a pipe bomb.

As if by a giant fist, he was hurled across the room, against the inner wall, where he bounced, collapsed, and fell dead, bleeding out onto the carpet.

Julie ran to the ruined window, looked to the armored sniper framed in the open window of the building across from them. Seeing her, he gave a half salute.

Moments later, Omar Hemingway was in the room, looking from one occupant to another. He smiled at Julie. "I trust the contact mic wasn't too uncomfortable."

"I didn't feel it at all."

"Good. We've got it all on tape." His smile broadened. "You're one brave field operative. I'm goddamned proud of you."

For a moment, Julie thought he was going to embrace her. Instead, he held out his hand. She didn't even glance at it, let alone take it. "This was your plan all along, wasn't it?"

Hemingway's face darkened. "I don't know what—"

"Oh, don't give me that shit. From the moment you dropped Sydney's name into my lap as an extracurricular assignment your hope was that it would end like this." She pointed to St. Vincent's corpse. "You knew he had bugged your office—you knew all along, and you fed him the bits of disinformation that he wanted." She shook her head. "No, no, that he *needed*."

"That's some imagination you've developed, Julie."

"Too bad for you, Omar. You couldn't get to St. Vincent via normal channels—you said so yourself that day in your office. So you recruited me. Why? Because you knew I'd be too proud to question the assignment. Because any one of your field personnel would have smelled the rat that I missed. This was a personal vendetta—don't even bother to deny it. I've seen it all the way through and I know. You set Sydny up as bait—you didn't care if she lived or died."

"Her death was an unfortunate—" He sighed. "She was collateral damage."

"Oh, please." Julie shot him a poisonous look before she left the room.

"Wait," Hemingway said. "Where are you going?"

There was no response. He did not go after her, nor did he call out again. Instead, he turned back to Orrin. "Jesus, what a mess," he said. "But not to worry. I've called for our cleaning service. God knows the apartment needs it."

46

"I'm so sorry, Whit," Charlie said. "I had no idea. You never even mentioned your family."

"Now you know why."

She nodded. "So it was this man Preach who gave you the tattoo?"

Whitman nodded. "I stayed with him far longer than Luther St. Vincent, a member of the Alchemists, would have wanted me to. Preach saw in me a kindred spirit. Even more, he realized that I possessed something he had thought only he had."

"What was that?"

"A doorway to . . . somewhere else."

Charlie frowned. "I don't understand."

"Yeah," he said. "Join the club."

"Wait a minute. Are you talking about what you did to Flix? How you saved him?"

Whitman nodded. "That's part of it, but only a part."

Charlie swallowed. "Now you're scaring me."

"That's precisely why I never told you." He leaned over, kissed her cheek. "I knew I had already frightened you enough."

"I don't frighten easily." She have him a tentative smile. "Only by things I see that defy explanation."

"You don't ever want to meet Preach then." Whitman's gaze turned inward, as memories continued to come to the fore. "Everyone was frightened of Preach. He never said much, but then he didn't have to. People came to him for help, and he gave it."

"What kind of help?"

"Cures, spells, the advice of angels and demons." Whitman nodded. "I knew that would make you smile." He put his head against the seatback. "Then there was the kind of help I asked him for. He can see across the divide, from life to death, or, as he refers to it, from this life to the next." His head bobbed. "Yeah, I don't think I believed it either, although I have to admit that from the moment I met him some part of me knew he wasn't full of shit. That was the part he recognized, the part that came to connect us, the part he chose to nurture, teach, allow to grow in strength and knowledge."

"I imagine the other Alchemists were frightened of your power. Did they kick you out?"

"No. I left them."

"Why?"

When no answer was forthcoming, Charlie changed direction. "Did Preach tell you what happened to your mother and sister?"

"They told him, he said, from the other side."

"And you believed him?"

He could read the skepticism on her face. "The people I had been targeting in Iraq were very powerful. They had ties all across the globe, more than I or anyone in Special Forces knew. But Preach knew because my family told him. Sympathizers here in the States, acting on orders from Iraq, abducted my mother and sister, took them into the countryside, and slit their throats."

"Retribution."

"That. And a warning."

"What did you do after you found out?"

"Before I could do anything I got a call from King Cutler. I joined Universal Security Associates, assembled Red Rover, and took the team to Iraq."

"USA is a military contractor. Cutler allowed you to do that on your own?"

"It was part of our initial negotiation. I wouldn't have come aboard without that assurance."

"And what happened over there?"

"We stayed there for six weeks. In that time, we killed twenty-seven members of the cadre that had ordered my family slaughtered. The twenty-eighth—the leader—I saved for myself."

The plane had started its descent, and they both buckled up. They were almost home.

"You used your dark arts on him," Charlie said.

Whitman's eyes cleared as he looked at her, but there was no point in him answering her; she knew.

Charlie leaned in toward him. "The Well," she whispered, "why in God's name did you take me there? Why did you expose me to that horror? The blood, broken bodies, the *stench*. Christ, Whit, it almost killed me. It's why I hit you that night, afterward. I couldn't believe . . ." Her eyes searched his; she needed an answer. "Why did you want me to see what you were capable of? What were you thinking when you exposed me to that . . . living hell? Was it forgiveness you were looking for? Did you think I'd absolve you of your sins? Or were you just trying to drive me away, kill my love for you?"

Love. It was the first time she had intimated in any way that she had loved him. Did she love him still? Like her, he needed an answer. "It was none of those things. Charlie. Charlie." His voice was as dry as a reed at summer's death. "I wanted you to know everything there was about me, I wanted to let you in—the only person I would ever trust in that way. You made me feel . . . different. Better. You made me realize that I didn't want to be alone anymore."

Silence between them. The wind rushing by outside and their ears clogging and clicking open as the plane slid down the flight path of its final approach. His hand sought hers, their fingers twining.

By dawn's early light, Preach saw the rolling hills of Virginia, wreathed in pearly mist, insubstantial as ghosts. That was fine by him; ghosts were as familiar to him as old friends at the dinner table.

Crow flew ahead of him, showing him seconds, minutes, an hour into the future, for in that state of being time had no meaning. Past, present, and future melded into one and ceased to have the meaning put on them by human beings in a vain attempt to draw order and structure out of chaos.

More blood, more death, this is what Crow saw. That was fine, too. In his long, long lifetime Preach had waded through blood and death more times than he could count. The transition was what interested him. Through Crow he had experienced what others called death, what he knew to be the metamorphosis from one state of being to another. Crow had assured him of this; through Crow's eyes he had peered into the world beyond, and found it worthy.

The countryside began to be populated, first by a house here and there, then by groups of houses, cheek by jowl, all looking like clones of one another. A blight upon the landscape is how Preach thought of these increasingly large communities sprawled like great spiders casting their evil webs, tearing down forests, leveling hills, building up valleys, making everything uniform for their drone dwellings. Preach was sickened unto his soul, and still he kept going, knowing, through Crow, he would make another stop before he came in sight of the place where Albin White stood, waiting patiently for him.

He did not dislike White; though he knew Whitman best, he knew White longer. But it was Whitman, his brother in fact if not in blood, he missed. He knew where Whitman was; he always knew where he was. They were connected as deeply as if they were twins, as if their heads had been fused at birth. The divine force that had caused this was beyond even Preach's ken, but that was to be expected. He was connected to so much more than human beings, but this only made him aware of how much more existed that he could not reach. It was his fervent hope that one day Whitman could attain what he had not. He was generous that way, with Whitman, at least, if not anyone else. His life in the bayous had taught him to withhold most of himself, to be an enigma, and therefore to engender fear in those who came in contact with him. They all feared him—all except Whitman, who knew better. Who understood the Nature of Things.

And so while looking forward to the highway patrolman waiting for him, he also looked backward, and saw Luther St. Vincent's death. He felt neither elation nor pity. St. Vincent's death at that precise moment was ordained the instant he came into Preach's orbit.

On the other hand, the highway patrolman had yet to make his appearance. Preach was driving the speed limit. Not that it would matter to the patrolman, whose job it was to flag down out-of-state motorists and give them tickets. Sometimes, Preach thought, a scam is just a scam.

Over a rise he jounced and there, on the far end of the downslope, was the highway patrol cruiser. It allowed him to pass, then turned on its flashing light and siren, took off after him. Preach didn't need to look at the oncoming image in his rearview mirror. He slowed and pulled over onto the verge of the highway, sat still as a statue, concentrated on his breath. He could feel Crow circling back toward him from somewhere in this world's future. He expected nothing less.

After some time, the patrolman emerged from his cruiser. He came toward Preach, one hand on the butt of his holstered pistol. The grim look on his face made Preach want to laugh.

"You know why I pulled you over, old timer?" the patrolman said.

"I do not, sir."

"You were speeding."

"All due respect, sir, but I was doing the limit. I checked my speedometer."

"Why would you check it if you weren't speeding?"

Preach chose to say nothing.

The patrolman opened his book, started writing. "Guess you didn't know the fine for speeding in this area is two hundred dollars."

"I don't have two hundred dollars, sir."

"Too bad for you, old timer. I'll have to take you in." The patrolman stopped writing, looked up. "You got a hundred on you?"

"That I do," Preach said.

The patrolman showed his teeth. "Tell you what, then. Give me the hundred and I'll rip up this ticket."

Preach nodded. "Sounds fair to me."

"It's more than fair, old man. It's a fucking gift, is what it is."

Preach dug out his wallet. The patrolman snatched the two fifties greedily.

"Okay then," the patrolman said. "We're done here."

"Not quite." Preach leaned out the window. Crow was close, very close. He felt the shimmer, as if the air itself trembled. "You're looking a bit pale, if I may say. Do you have a headache, perchance?"

"What?" The patrolman put fingertips to his temple. "Now that you mention it . . ." He winced, one eye closing.

"Sir, I do believe you're having a cerebral aneurism."

"A what?" But the patrolman was already slurring his words. "Hey," he said. His eyes opened wide, then rolled up in his head as he collapsed onto the tarmac.

Preach got out of the truck cab, took the two fifties out of the patrolman's clutches, and a moment later was on his way to the summoning.

47

"This is going to be the last act," Trey Hartwell said as he joined Albin White.

White nodded. "Down and dirty."

The Colonial-style porch of the property's original hunting lodge, across from the entrance to the Well, was where they sat in side-by-side rocking chairs, like old friends chewing the fat. All that was missing were corncob pipes and a packet of loose Virginia tobacco.

"There was no other way," White said.

"None," Hartwell affirmed, "according to the *Peranomicon*." He placed the book that he had tucked beneath his arm onto the top railing. It was small, no larger than Trey's hand with his fingers spread. It was the book he touched before every meeting of the Alchemists.

It was very old. It had come into his possession from one of his sources in Turkey, who had discovered it in a dusty antiques shop in Tevfikiye, a crumbling stone village near the site of the ruins of Ilium—Homer's Troy. But its true origins lay in ancient Persia. It was written in the Old Persian cuneiform of the Achaemenid dynasty, dating it to around 500 BC, long before the Muslim armies conquered the empire. The cuneiform also positioned the composition of the *Peranomicon* somewhere in Persis, in the southwest of the country, which was known for its magus's pursuit of the more arcane aspects of the Zoroastrian religion. Possibly the *Peranomicon* was a part of a vastly powerful magus's private library; it did not appear in any compendium of the Avesta, the Zoroastrian collection of sacred texts, that Hartwell had studied.

"It was this book that told us who and what Preach is," White said, "though part of me still doesn't believe it."

"And yet it was through the *Peranomicon* that I was able to summon him." Hartwell drummed his delicate fingertips in the complex rhythm prescribed in the text. For an instant, a shadow flickered midway between them and the kitchens building, then was gone.

"Crow," Hartwell said. "We must be mindful of the bird's shade at all times. It's a good part of Preach's power to divine the future, what he and the *Peranomicon* called *Haxāmaniš*, 'to see a friend's mind.'" Trey threw a sideways glance at White. He was intimately familiar with *Haxāmaniš*, if not in the actuality of Preach's power, then in the theory, which he had put to good use ever since reading about it in researching the *Peranomicon*. "To see a friend's mind," though *friend* could mean many things, as the text had revealed to him. That was a revelation he had not shared with White, nor any other member of the Alchemists, for that matter. The theory had led him to a conversation with White in which he had maneuvered White into asking to make the summons himself. Trey had had a good laugh at that one. He had had no intention of summoning Preach himself—that would have placed him squarely in Preach's crosshairs. Preach could not touch him, nor any of the Alchemists—passages in the *Peranomicon* had ensured that, making them invulnerable to retaliation for the ways in which they used Preach. The book ensured that he was in their power— enslaved, in the same way the genie was bound inside his brass lamp. However, Preach had a long memory. He was fiendishly clever, and Trey had no doubt that there surely would come a time of reckoning. He intended to be on the sidelines when that future was conjured out of thin air and shadows.

As soon as the plane had taxied to a stop, Whitman grabbed Edmond Dantès and Flix, and they offloaded the poppies into the back of a waiting jeep. There was no driver; that was part of Dantès's job. But Whitman didn't need him; he knew the way to the Well.

Back inside the plane, he saw that Charlie had already breached the cockpit, brought the pilot and navigator back to the passenger section, sat them down with the flight attendant so there was no chance they could use the plane's radio. She had taken possession of their mobile phones long enough to remove the batteries before handing them back to their respective owners.

Whitman took Flix aside. "*Compadre*, you're going to stay here with the crew and Dantès."

"But—"

"No buts. Someone has to keep them incommunicado for the time being. Besides, after what you've been through I don't want to—"

"I'm fine, *compadre*. Have the girl babysit."

Charlie advanced on him. "*¿No qué no, eh?*" Really? "After everything?"

Immediately Flix looked abashed. "Sure, sure. *Lo siento.*" Sorry. "It's just . . . I wanted to be in on the last act."

"And you are."

"You don't trust me now, because of—" He tapped the side of his head. "You saw what I did back there."

"I saw what happened to you," Whitman said, "and I took care of it. I trust you like I've always trusted you." He squeezed Flix's shoulder. "Red Rover's a trio. It always was; it always will be. Okay?" He smiled at Flix, who nodded, smiling back.

"*Orale pues.*" Okay then. "*Todo se vale, guei.*"

"That's right," Whitman said, signaling to Charlie. "It's all good, dude."

"See you on the other side, Charlie," Flix said as they exited the plane.

Albin White was waiting for Preach when his rattletrap truck pulled up outside the complex of buildings in rural Virginia. The beginning of the summoning was a ritual in and of itself, and Hartwell played no part in it. White had a bottle of White Lightnin' corn likker in one hand, two shot glasses in the other.

The moment Preach climbed down from the truck's cab, White poured the drinks, handed one of the glasses to Preach, and they drank.

"I trust your journey north was without incident," White said, as they headed toward the Well.

"Why have you summoned me?" But of course he knew. He had created the knowing. Acceleration was the name of the game now. Lindstrom had to die in order for Trey Hartwell to use his book, the *Peranomicon*, to "summon" Preach. That was a joke in and of itself. Preach had created the book. What fun it had been to write it with a Persian scholar of a contact's acquaintance! He had discovered that ancient shamanism around the world was remarkably similar, so much so that he now believed the underlying principles must have originated in one place, with one people. Not the Old Ones, of course, but perhaps folk like them.

After they had finished, he had a talented forger in his employ create the cuneiform pages as an ancient tome. He had shipped it overseas. He had made painstakingly sure Hartwell believed in the book's ethos, rites, and rituals. It served his purpose to have the Alchemists believe that he was under their control instead of the other way around. It made manipulating them so much easier.

"The Mobius Project."

"Do tell." Preach made a face. Sometimes knowing everything could be a bore. "You have a—what do you call him—a *scientific researcher* working on that."

"He's dead."

"My condolences." Preach shrugged. "But life must continue."

"The man discovered an alkaloid distilled from *Papaver laciniatum*. Now he's dead, we want you to take over creating the soldiers."

Preach threw a sideways glance in White's direction. "I'm at your service, Albin, always have been."

White pushed open the door to the Well, and they went through into the dim, noxious interior. "We're in a bind. The serum works, but has . . . undesirable side effects." He led Preach around another of a seemingly endless number of corners. "Ah, here we are."

He unlocked an iron door, and they stepped into one of the Well's vertiginous rooms, the curving walls seeming about to cave in from the top.

"You really do have a fucked-up sense of humor, Albin."

"What sense of humor I once had was burned out of me long ago." White pointed to a man kneeling on the floor. He was hooded and his wrists were bound at the small of his back. "We kept this one for you. He's already been injected with Lindstrom's serum, but it's too early for any side effects to be presenting."

"I wouldn't worry about side effects now." Preach crossed to where the man knelt, took out a switchblade, and cut through the plastic that bound his wrists. Then he helped the man to his feet, drew off his hood. The man blinked, trembling from hours in the same agonizing position.

"Hello, my friend. My name is Preach. What's yours?"

"Billy."

Preach smiled somewhat sadly. "What did this sorry excuse for a human being do to you, Billy?"

"Some of them," White said, "have tried to claw their faces off."

"I told you not to worry," Preach said. "Now keep still, I'm talking to Billy." His smile widened. "Now, Billy, tell me what's happened to you."

"I . . ." Billy glanced fearfully at White. His tongue ran around his dry and peeling lips. "I was taken off the streets. Things were done to me, but I don't . . . I don't remember. I don't know."

"Well, we'll soon fix that." Preach put one hand on the back of Billy's head, the other at the small of his back. "Just relax," he said in a soothing singsong. "Nothing bad will happen to you now. My promise to you."

As Whitman had done with Flix, he felt for the trigeminal beneath his fingertips. He sensed the blockages the alkaloid had caused, scrambling the nerve messages between this man's brain and his body. He sensed what the alkaloid was meant to do, and how it had partially failed. What science didn't know contaminated the universe with its distortions, delusions, and outright ignorance, he thought with bitter contempt as he ran his delicate fingertips up the man's spinal cord to the nape of his neck. In that sense it was no better than religion. There, he thought. There!

Billy gave a galvanic start beneath his hands. His eyes cleared and his breathing became deep and even, as if in a resting state or deep in a kind of powerful meditation.

Preach turned to White. "You have what you wished for." No, it was what he wished for. "Now I need another stiff drink."

"My journey," Preach said, as if nothing had occurred between the time White had asked the question and his answer, "was like all journeys. Though, as in all physical matters, it depends on your point of view."

They were sitting on the porch of the old hunting lodge in the same rocking chairs that White and Hartwell had occupied an hour before.

"Never two the same." White nodded, pouring them a second helping of the moonshine. "I understand."

Preach sucked down his drink, smacked his lips as he thought, You don't understand a damn thing, as many years as you know me. We met when you were, what?, a teenager full of rage. Only your rage never abated. I could feel that and I fanned it every time it threatened to subside. You had a role to play, but you were just a man—ordinary, but fated to accomplish extraordinary things—with my help, always with my help. Not that you ever knew or even suspected. No, you'll die an ignorant man, and I won't be sorry. The Alchemists have outlived their usefulness.

Too much bickering and internecine warfare had eroded his confidence in the solidarity, the oneness, of the group. He had the electronic keys to their accounts. Those and the alkaloid serum were all he required of them now. Time to move on to another set of people whose cruelty and greed could be used against them. Not that he was going to destroy the Alchemists himself. There was no need.

At that moment, Lucy emerged from the entrance to the Well, crossed to the building housing the kitchens. Preach put his shot glass on the wooden railing, stood up, hands jammed into the back pockets of his dusty jeans.

"Huh," he said.

White rose to stand beside him. "Something troubling you?"

Preach smiled. "Just admiring Lucy Orteño."

"You know her? Luther recruited her."

"Well, whataya know." Preach gave a hoot so close to that of a screech owl it was startling. "Life is just chock-full of ironies."

White leaned closer. "Come again?"

Preach watched Lucy enter the building across the sloping expanse of lawn. "St. Vincent's dead."

"What?"

Preach turned to White. "You haven't heard? Well, that's unsurprising, I suppose. Hemingway was involved."

"What happened?"

"Shot to death. That's all Crow showed me. That's all I needed to know. You, too, I imagine."

"Unless Hemingway is coming after us."

"Hemingway knows nothing about either the Alchemists or the Well. Rest easy on that score."

"Well, that's reassuring," White said. "Now tell me how you know Lucy Orteño."

"She was a guest of mine some time ago."

White knew all about Preach's "guests." He said, "How was it that you let her leave?"

"An oversight," Preach said with his eyes half-closed, "that can now be rectified."

48

Lucy was eating a hot fudge sundae with peanut brittle crumbled on top, which the chef had whipped up especially for her, when Preach entered the commissary. He slid into the chair next to her, folded his arms on the table perilously close to her.

"How you doing, Lucy?"

"How d'you think I'm doing?" She took a spoonful of the sundae, savoring the melding of sweet flavors.

"Looks to me like you're doing all right for yourself, but I gotta tell you your patron, Luther St. Vincent, is dead."

"Fuck him." Lucy continued eating, never missing a beat. "You want to talk, Preach?"

"I do. You know I do."

"Then put Crow away."

He paused. "Okay, he's gone."

"Bullshit. I can still feel the shadow he casts." Her eyes met his. "How d'you think I got away from you?"

He nodded. "Fair enough."

His eyes rolled up for a moment, and Lucy felt the shadow lift off her. She breathed deeply. "Chef makes great sundaes here. Want one?"

"I don't eat sugar."

"You don't eat anything, so far as I remember."

He smiled faintly. "That isn't quite correct."

"Close enough." She attacked the hot fudge as if it were Crow. "Mmm. You don't know what you're missing."

"You surprise me, Lucy."

"Oh, I doubt that."

"You're curiously unmoved by your mentor's death."

That was just like him, Lucy thought. Anyone else would say, You *seem* curiously unmoved, for how could they really know? Preach did know.

"He's wasn't my mentor—jailor, more like it."

"Tell me."

"He put me in his debt; he used me to get to my uncle Felix."

"Why would he do that?" Preach seemed genuinely interested.

"He wanted to use Felix—for something, I don't know what. I saw him inject something into Felix's neck, then bundle him into an ambulance."

Preach considered a moment. "He was using your uncle as a guinea pig in the wild."

"I don't understand."

"The test subjects that have come here—that you've been . . . processing."

"What about them?" Lucy didn't bother to ask how he knew these things because she knew: Crow.

"They were in the same program your uncle is in."

Lucy's heart thumped painfully in her chest. "You mean he's dead?"

Preach shook his head. "He's not dead. In fact, he's close by."

"Why did St. Vincent—"

"Luther was running ahead of everyone else," Preach said. "As usual."

"Is Felix safe?"

"As safe as anyone can be in this life."

She nodded, seeming to liquefy with relief. She could tell he wasn't lying.

He studied her for a moment, leaned in. "Tell me something. Why did you run?"

Lucy just managed to stop a spit-take. "Make a guess."

"Didn't I treat you well?"

"Is that a joke?" She put her spoon down, her hands balled into fists. "In what universe does raping me repeatedly fall into the category of treating me well?"

"I never raped you, Lucy."

"What was it then—" she snorted, "consensual sex?"

"I believe it was, yes."

"Wow, I can't believe what I'm hearing. Go peddle that shit to your zonked-out followers, not here. I know what you did to me. It was my body you violated, over and over."

"But you liked it."

She reared back. "What the fuck?"

"I know you liked it, Lucy. Your body told me. I'm attuned to such things."

"You're attuned to getting what you want." She did not bother to keep the disgust out of her voice.

"That's neither here nor there," he said. "You wanted what I gave you."

"Now I know for sure you're nuts."

"You wanted power where you had none. You could feel it flowing into you with every thrust. You could feel the power over life and death spurt into you."

"Completely bat-shit crazy."

"You love the power I gave you—a power you never could have had, the power you longed for. It was why you ran away from home."

"I ran away because I was abused."

"It's why you sought me out."

She laughed. "I didn't seek you out. Our meeting was pure happenstance."

"I wonder." He cocked his head. "How long will you need to feed yourself these falsehoods before you recognize the truth that's right in front of you?"

Her expression turned incredulous, her tone mocking. "What? You're telling me you set it all in motion—the abuse I suffered, the group of kids I met heading south, the days and nights of drugs, everything?"

Preach smiled at her benignly, as a grandfather smiles at his beloved granddaughter. "I want you back, Lucy."

"Well, gee, that's just too fucking bad for you."

"You have the gift."

She shook her head. "What gift?"

"You're a death-dealer."

She shook her head. "Stone-cold insane."

"Don't look so alarmed. I won't force you; I won't have to. You'll come back of your own accord."

"When the temperature rises in heaven."

"We'll see." He grinned as he stood up. "Enjoy your sundae while you can. No sugar allowed at home."

Lucy stared down at her half-eaten dessert. The ice cream she had consumed seemed to have congealed in her stomach. She had thought about this reunion for a long time; the conversation hadn't gone anything like what she had imagined. That fucker had something nasty up his sleeve, she could feel it in her bones. Before he unleashed it she would have to find a way to protect herself. Then she'd destroy him.

Deliberately, she took up her spoon and resumed digging in. Even though her stomach was clenched tight, she was determined to finish the sundae, even if in the next minute she might vomit it all up.

Preach stood just inside the door to the kitchens building, his eyes closed to slits, in intimate communion with Crow. Trey emerged from the house onto the porch, settled into the rocker next to Albin. As Preach had expected, Trey had with him the *Peranomicon*, which he foolishly believed would protect him from what was to come.

The future was like an ancient tree: it had many branches, most alive, but some dead, awaiting the bite of the lumberjack's axe. The branches were a maze, so thickly tangled not even Crow, whose perspective was more far-reaching than his, could see them all. Preach liked things to be as neat, clean, geometric as a chessboard, and while the tree was no chessboard, he had done his level best to fashion it into his playing field. Moves had been planned out, not over days or weeks, but years. Salvation was coming in the form of the son he had never had, the son he had trained, guided, manipulated all toward the tip of this particular branch, which

Crow had seen in his aerie of no-time. He had spent more than a decade climbing this tree with great care and deliberation so that he would arrive here, now, with all the required elements in play.

The future had arrived at last. It would be a surprise to everyone but him.

49

"You're prepared," Whitman said, as they drove away from the landing strip for the short, jouncing ride to the Well.

Charlie fingered the backpack, feeling the familiar contours of its contents through the leather and canvas as if she were sight-impaired. "I am."

"I'm counting on you."

"And I'm counting on you."

They glanced at each other, then away: Whitman at the road ahead, Charlie at the blurred greenery passing by.

"The Elf Lord warned me against consorting with you again," she said at length.

"Huh! Consorting. That's a word the Elf Lord would use," he retorted.

"She didn't," Charlie said, "but I did."

Whitman gave her another sideways look. "Is that what we're doing? Consorting?"

"Would you prefer 'pal around with'?"

He laughed. "Yeah, that's just what we've been doing."

There was silence between them for a beat or two.

"Whit," she said, "what are we in for?"

He considered for a moment. "You recall 'mind-no mind.'"

She nodded. "From my martial arts training, sure."

"What did you learn?"

"Come on, Whit. What does this—"

"Indulge me."

"In mind-no mind you let go of all thought, all anticipation, all expectation."

"This is the place where we're headed."

"React in the moment, *at* the point of attack and nowhere else."

"And?"

"Attack with absolute commitment."

The double meaning of the word *commitment* hung in the air between them, a bridge of sorts, visible only to the two of them.

Whitman made a sharp turn to the left, and structures appeared piecemeal beyond the dense web of tree branches, as if seen through a kaleidoscope.

"This is what is required of us now."

Lucy sat over the remains of her sundae, the sick feeling in the pit of her stomach pinwheeling as if she were on a roller coaster. Preach had crawled right into her mind. As always. But, she thought, what if Preach was telling the truth? What if he had arranged everything so that she would be taken to his church of fire and sex? Was it even possible? And even if it were, why would he do such a thing? Who was she that he wanted her so badly?

She heard his voice, as clearly as if he were still beside her: *"You're a death-dealer."* What could he mean by . . . ?

And then of course she saw herself, as if from an odd angle, above and almost beyond, killing the failed clinical trial patients, the victims, whatever you chose to call them, one after another, boom! boom! boom! all in a row. Then filling their mouths with stones, watching them slide into the *cenote* headfirst without a care or an iota of remorse.

Preach was right about her. She was a death-dealer. Then it stood to reason he was telling the truth about everything. Ev-ry-thing. Including her coming back to him of her own free will.

With a sudden, violent motion, she swept the bowl and utensils off the table, felt a kind of satisfaction hearing the pottery shatter. And then she wept. It was such a tiny victory—and so terribly petty, meaningless even.

Free will. What a joke! As if she had had free will, manipulated every step of the way by Preach until she lay beneath his thrusting hips, feeling his sperm gush into her depths, burning her insides, turning them black as night, black as death.

Christ, no, she thought, as she pushed herself back from the table and rose. Christ, no. Never. Even hell had to be better than being his creature.

50

"While you two have been jawing," Preach called out, "your nemesis is on his way."

Hartwell snatched the *Peranomicon* off the porch railing, stashed it away on his person. "What's he talking about?" he said to White.

"I'm talking about Whitman." Preach strode toward them. "He's on his way here with a load of poppies."

Hartwell and White exchanged concerned looks.

"How on earth did Whitman, of all people, get his hands on our Przemko poppies?" Trey whispered.

"Obviously St. Vincent's measures failed to deter him," White said.

"Are either of you really surprised?"

"Is that why Whitman is here?" Hartwell asked. "Because of a bouquet of fucking poppies?"

Preach laughed.

"He's here," White said, ignoring Preach as best he could, "because Luther abducted one of his people and had Dr. Lindstrom administer the Mobius serum to him."

Hartwell's eyes widened and his nose twitched like a rabbit scenting its own death. "So he knows everything."

"Presumably," White said.

"Definitely," Preach said.

Preach was watching them from the lawn. He seemed disinclined to join them on the porch, which White took to be an ominous sign. He felt his heart rate skyrocket.

"Seems you'd best prepare yourselves," Preach said.

"Don't worry," Hartwell told him. "We've an extensive array of bleeding-edge deterrents at every point around the perimeter. Whitman won't have a chance of getting near us."

Preach grinned up at him. "I can't help but be fascinated by your stupidity."

"He's right," White said. "Whitman's been here before, don't forget. He got to el-Habib and neutralized his protection detail. He escaped an entire gunship and made off with our latest shipment. That means he has Dante and the jet. The entire trade route is compromised." He headed inside, beckoning Hartwell to follow him. "But I know how to handle him, in the event he gets inside our perimeter."

"That's the spirit!" Preach called after them, snickering. "Gird your loins for battle! It's Ragnarök, boys! Twilight of the Alchemists!"

For Charlie, the past ceased to exist, or, rather, it was stowed away behind a thick sheet of glass, to be looked at now and again, perhaps as a curiosity, but never again to be touched. The hurt was gone, as was the anguish it had engendered. Sometimes the end—or was it the future?—had a cauterizing effect on what had come before. This, come what may—even if she should die—was such a time.

"You see it?" Whitman said softly in her ear.

"I do."

"Just to the left of the gate. It looks like a farmer's wooden stile along the stone wall."

"But it's not," Charlie said.

"It houses an infrared beam that runs just above the top of the wall. There's a separate beam that crosses the gate, should anyone try to crash through it. Dante gave me the code to open the gate, but he thought he was clever in not telling me about the infrared beam. Break the beam—"

"And an alarm sounds."

"Break the beam," Whitman said, "and a hail of bullets shreds you. Nasty."

"Not a bit of it," Charlie said opening her backpack, "because I'm gonna take it out."

They were sitting in the jeep. The sky was low with sullen clouds. The late afternoon smelled of rain, but the clammy air was as still as the skin of a summer pond. Inside the jeep, the cloying scent of the poppies had become overpowering.

"Open the gate," she said.

Whitman leaned out the open window, punched in the code Dante had given him. The high iron gates yawned soundlessly open. Charlie removed from her backpack a weapon that looked like nothing more than a light-weight plastic toy, the barrel blunt and wide. She attached an oval container to its underside, using a pair of thick gloves.

"Ultra-cold atoms," she said, "using both lasers and a magnetic trap." She aimed the weapon at the stile. "Watch what happens."

She squeezed the trigger and a controlled spray of translucent liquid, gray as a battleship's hide, enveloped the stile. Moments later, it cracked in two, its delicate electronic insides frozen solid.

"Let's roll," Charlie said, as Whitman crashed the gears.

"He's in," Preach said. "He's breached your vaunted defenses."

Hartwell moaned, but White was watching Preach, gauging his expression and the tenor of his words, his mind calculating—always calculating. Preach seemed bubbly, almost elated that Whitman was coming. White tried and failed to understand the source of these emotions.

"Oh, Christ," Hartwell murmured, almost unconsciously.

"The power of Christ won't save you," Preach said. "Not here, not now, not ever."

Flix felt Edmond Dantès's intent before he made a move. How he was able to do this he did not know, nor did he question it. He was up out of his seat and moving as Dantès lunged toward the jet's galley. There was a return of the absolute focus on the enemy Flix had felt in el-Habib's villa, only without the terrible, ripping horror that had held him prisoner in his own head. He was himself, and yet more than himself. He moved with absolute resoluteness, without hesitation or conflict: he had become a weapon.

As Dantès reached for the paring knife on the galley counter, Flix grabbed him from behind. Dantès jammed an elbow hard into his ribs, but Flix barely felt it. Reaching around Dantès's jaw, he grabbed it with one hand, slid his free arm across Dantès's throat, and gave a violent twist. The crack of his victim's cervical vertebrae snapping resounded through the interior, causing the flight attendant to jump.

Flix released the corpse, and it collapsed onto the deck. He turned to the other three: the pilot, navigator, and the attendant, impaling them one by one with his steady gaze.

"Who's next?" he said.

51

Lucy stood in the doorway, in shadow. She watched the weather roll in, felt the dampness on her face, the backs of her hands. The fine hairs on her forearms lifted. Her fingers twitched, the thumbs cocked, as if they were grasping Preach's throat. She was aware of White, a mousy-seeming man at his side, and, of course, Preach, but she saw them all as though through a scrim, indistinct and muzzy. It was as if she had finally arrived at a far-off place, a shingle of beach that abutted a vast ocean across which was a promontory inhabited by the others, a bit of land she had once been to, but was now a distant memory. The stir of breeze, fitful before dying, the thick layers of clouds, the coming storm were all more real to her, companions that sang in her ear, speaking in tongues, while the three men babbled on to no effect, as if they were apes failing at human speech.

And then, turning, she became aware of what she should have seen sooner: Preach wasn't among the babbling apes; he was part of the land-scape, along with the wind and the clouds and the incoming rain. He inhabited the same place she did, an outside place, where neither shadows nor light could survive. They were beached together.

At the precise moment of her revelation, he turned to face her. His grin was terrifying, though she had promised herself that he would never terrify her again. He began to walk toward her, and she felt her skin scrawl. She wanted to back up, to run, but she was rooted to the spot.

"Ready or not," he said, "here I come."

Whitman turned the wheel hard over, just missing the first land mine, but his altered course led him right into the second, and the detonation brought the jeep to its knees. The windshield blew inward. Bleeding from a number of cuts, none of them deep, he and Charlie leapt out of the jeep, ran on foot across the inner perimeter. Inside the circle of land mines, they crouched down, moving crabwise among the trees, using the trunks as cover.

"You okay?" Charlie whispered.

He nodded. "You?"

She grinned at him.

"They'll have more surprises to throw at us."

Her grin widened as she slapped the side of her backpack. "I have everything in here except a fire-breathing dragon."

"No, that man over there's got one of those." Whitman indicated Albin White standing on the porch with a shotgun cradled in his arms. "That shotgun is loaded with incendiary iron pellets, one of which will cause your clothes to burst into flame."

Charlie knelt. "We've got to get him before he fires that thing." From her backpack she removed the weapon she had used on the stile, but this time, she dropped a wasp-like missile down its throat. She settled it in her grip, peered through the scope, and squeezed the trigger. The missile hissed through a narrow gap in the trees, struck the porch's underpinning, blew the entire structure to smithereens.

White was thrown off his feet, tumbling through the air. He fell against the shattered balustrade of what had once been the stairs. Preach turned, watching the action unfolding in front of him. For the moment, Lucy was forgotten.

White, clearly stunned, shook his head as if to clear it. Then he rose, trained his altered shotgun at the trees where Whitman and Charlie were hiding.

"Incoming!" Whitman said, just before the blast set the trees around them aflame.

They withdrew, moving quickly to the right of the area of burning trees. White was striding toward them, blood streaming down one side of his face, his clothes blackened and singed. He was about to fire the second barrel into the trees when Billy, the lone Mobius Project subject left alive, emerged from the Well. With hollowed-out eyes, he looked first to Preach, and it was clear, at least to Whitman, that Preach was controlling him. The man nodded, then sprinted toward White with alarming speed.

White became aware of him just in time. He whirled on his heel, fired the second barrel directly into the human missile's chest. The man's torso burst into flame. He took a step backward, then staggered forward, kept coming even while he was burning alive. Reversing the shotgun, White began to club him over the head, again and again, until Whitman, breaking cover, shot White dead.

Billy turned his dead eyes on Whitman. He appeared totally unconcerned that his body was being consumed by flames. Kneeling, Whitman shot him in the throat. The upward trajectory of the bullet shattered the spinal column at the base of the man's neck, instantly severing the preternatural connection Preach had created. The man's eyes turned white as he collapsed. Instants later, the flames consumed him completely.

Whitman turned his attention to Preach then. Behind him, much to Whitman's surprise and consternation, stood a beautiful young woman whose large, dark eyes and aggressive nose he recognized from the photo Flix had shown him in the hospital: Lucy Orteño. Briefly, he wondered what the hell she was doing here at the Well. He was about to voice his confusion to Charlie, but she was off and running toward a small man who had avoided injury in the blast by his proximity to the doorway. It was Trey Hartwell, an adder among the serpents, and Whitman shouted to warn her. Hartwell appeared harmless, but he was probably the most dangerous of the Alchemists. He was certainly the most brilliantly devious.

Without knowing whether Charlie had heard him, he left the trees behind, took off across the severely manicured lawn, toward the spot where Preach stalked Lucy.

––––––––––

Charlie realized that the man she was after had the advantage of knowing the layout of the house whereas she did not. Therefore she paused in the two-story entryway, assessing her immediate surroundings. To her right was a salon, complete with an enormous stone fireplace, flanked by a pair of well-worn oversize leather sofas. She could smell the faint whiff of embedded cigar smoke wafting in the air. To her left was a hallway. She could see the first room off of it, its paneled sliding doors open: a library. Dead ahead was a marble and brass staircase winding up to the second floor.

As soon as she attuned herself to the miniscule noises every house makes, she heard the small scuffle and creak of shoe soles against old wooden floorboards, and, shrugging off her backpack, stowing it in a deeply shadowed nook, she moved off in that direction, down the wood-paneled hall. Past the library, with its dry, almost spicy scent of old books, past a closed door, then into the third room. Every inch of its four walls, even the back of the door, was completely covered with mirrors. Charlie saw her image reflected back on herself from every conceivable angle. She turned, for a moment disoriented and slightly dizzy. Whether it was the mirrors or a reoccurrence of her Takayasu's was impossible to determine, but it was foolish to take chances. She dug in her pocket for the vial of Imuran, but at that moment she spied a moving shadow out of the corner of her eye, and in turning toward it, she lost control of the vial. It bounced off the floorboards, rolling toward a far corner. And as she scrambled after it, Trey Hartwell barreled into her.

52

"My son, my son!" Preach cried. "At last we meet in the future that's occupied my mind for decades."

No one but Preach and Whitman should have known what he was talking about, but Lucy found that she did. The branches Preach mentioned were his manipulations—the chess moves he made so far in advance no one understood what he was doing, let alone had a clue as to what his objective was. But she knew—suddenly she knew.

She stared at Whitman, her expression tense. "Who are you?"

"Whitman, Lucy. Flix's—"

"Preach has talked about you," she said. "And now the situation's making more sense. Preach brought us both here for a reason."

"What are you talking about? How do you know—"

"Listen to me, Whitman. Everything that's happened to us has been for a reason—*his* reason."

He frowned. "How do you know that?"

"Because," she said, "I've been where you've been."

His frown deepened. "With *him?*"

"Again and again and again." She switched her gaze to Preach. "You understand what I mean, don't you, Whitman?"

Unfortunately, he did.

———

Charlie felt this creature, this homunculus, drive his knuckles agonizingly into one of her kidneys. She groaned, arching her back, and he slammed his other fist into her left breast. He was grinning as he straddled her, slapping her head back and forth as she squirmed beneath him, her exertions taking them closer and closer to one of the walls of mirrors.

He was small, but terribly quick, and he clearly knew jiujitsu, the American form of hand-to-hand combat, as well as some other crap she couldn't identify. In any event, she was taking a pounding. The homunculus clamped his knobby knees down on her wrists, pinioning her. His own hands were free, and she knew she had only moments left in which to counter him.

Drawing one leg back, she slammed the heel of her heavy boot against the mirror. It trembled, but did not break. The homunculus's thumbs were pressing into her windpipe, aiming to rupture her cricoid cartilage. She changed her angle and kicked out as hard as she could. The mirror shivered and broke apart.

Startled, he reared back, taking his hands from her throat to instinctively shield his face from the silvered glass raining over his head. Charlie wormed her right hand out from under his knee, grasped at a shard of mirror. She felt the bite of the edge cut into her, felt the hot blood running. Then she whipped the shard up and, in a perfect horizontal strike, severed his throat from one side to the other. She rolled away from the blood gushing like a cataract, rose onto her knees, watching the homunculus writhe and claw. His shoe soles beat a crazy tattoo against the floor. Then, with a last thick gush of blood, he died.

"What's this about you wanting us here, Preach? Is she right?"

"I told her as much about herself," Preach said. "Yes."

"And me?"

"You." Preach laughed. "You, my son, are the chosen one."

"That means nothing to me," Whitman said.

"And that's so part of your charm. You have no ego about it. You don't know and, furthermore, you don't care. That all ends here, now. That's why I brought Lucy here. She's all ego, while you have none. You're sun and moon, brother and sister; husband and wife, if you choose." He shrugged. "That part is up to you. Both of you are perfect. Any way you slice it, you were made for each other."

He beckoned. "Come here, Lucy. I want to show you something you alone will appreciate."

"Stay where you are," Whitman advised.

"Of course, he's going to say that, Lucy. I know him better than you do, but that will all change when you both come with me. Advanced studies beckon." He gestured again. "Now come."

She took a step toward him.

"Lucy!"

"Shut up. I know what I'm doing, Whitman."

Preach smiled benignly. "Of course she does." He held out his hand. The instant she took it, he jerked hard, pulling her to him, against him. Whitman saw the knife emerge from her fist, but Preach did, too, and he tried to wrench it out of her hand. "What are you doing, you little fool?"

Off to their left, the hunting lodge that had been smoldering from the missile strike now flamed up and began to burn in earnest.

"Charlie!" Whitman shouted. "Charlie! Where are you? Get out of there, the whole house is going up!"

Smoke was billowing, but Preach and Lucy, oblivious, continued to struggle. Then, all at once, she ceded control of the knife to him, lifted her arms, and began to press her thumbs into his eyes.

Preach's lips moved silently, a shadow fanned across the spot where they stood, and Lucy cried out, then stood paralyzed, as if she had been turned to stone.

"I schooled you, trained you, gave you the power you wanted most, and still you betray me." He made a gesture, and the shadow deepened and spread over Lucy, turning her skin white as milk. "Why would you betray me? I was your mentor, the font of your power. Without me you were nothing. Less than nothing." With every beat of her heart, her life's blood seemed to be evaporating inside her.

"Stop it!" Whitman cried. "Preach, leave her be. You're turning her into—"

"I know what I'm turning her into," Preach said.

In the extreme periphery of his vision Whit saw Charlie emerge from the house, holding her partly singed backpack by one of its straps, and his heart lifted. She was coughing, her eyes streaming. She leaped off what was left of the ruined porch, stumbled, and regained her footing. Behind her, the house was in flames, steaming like an engine, the rain not yet strong enough to slow the fire.

Preach spun in her direction, but his eyes did not focus on her. "Who is this?" The shadow left Lucy and moved toward Charlie. As it did, the rain came, spattering Lucy's upturned face. Her lids trembled.

The shadow crossed over Whitman, and he shivered.

"Who are you?" Preach yelled out to Charlie. "You don't belong in this future."

"It's no longer the future," Whitman said. He tried to move closer to Preach, but the air had turned glutinous. Each step felt like wading in water with the tide going out. He kept getting sucked back in the direction from which he'd come.

"God." Lucy blinked. She murmured, as if to herself, "Jesus help me."

"Charlie," Whitman called, "stay away. You don't know—"

"He doesn't see me, Whit." She continued coming on toward Preach. "Even now, he doesn't know who I am."

The shadow reached out for her, and instantly disappeared. Preach cried out. "Crow, where are you?"

Whitman lunged forward and grabbed Preach by the front of his shirt.

Preach lifted up his head. "Crow, why hast thou forsaken me?"

"In your darkest hour." Whitman struck Preach a blow of such proportions that he collapsed onto his knees.

"The joke's on you." Preach's head was swiveling from side to side. "I used you. You killed Albin and Trey for me. Lucy is right. I killed your father. That started the train of events that brought you here, now. I thought I had bound you to me. But you have crossed the line. This was one possible future, one I never believed would come to pass. Now that it has . . ." His grin was the rictus of a soul in eternal torment. "I have taken Lucy in your stead. Fair warning. There's still time to turn back. Otherwise, I will command her. If you're still determined to embrace death—a real and lasting death—she will do my bidding. She will kill you."

He threw her the knife he had taken from her. Lucy's face was still lifted to the rain, the drops hitting her open eyes without her blinking or flinching. Now she caught the knife deftly, without even looking at it. Her head lowered, her marble eyes fixed on Whitman, the blade leveled at his heart as she stepped toward him. Her skin was even paler than before. It had taken on a waxy texture, the rain rolling off her as if she had been made impervious to earthly elements. As if she were no longer human.

"She's a death-dealer, my son," Preach said from his position on his knees. "You'll have to kill her before she kills you."

"No," Whitman said, "I won't." And shot Preach between the eyes.

Preach's head snapped back from the percussion, then righted itself on his neck. "Not enough," he said. "Not nearly enough." The bullet had made a black hole, but no blood seeped out.

Whitman saw her coming out of the corner of his eye. "Charlie . . ."

"Take care of the girl," she said, as she flew past him. She put her forehead against Preach's, and he screamed. She backed up as the blood pumped out of his wound.

"No," he whispered. "It's impossible. I don't even see you. You're no one. You're nothing."

"On the contrary," Charlie said, "I'm everything you're not."

Whitman scarcely had time to register shock. He had come to grips with Lucy. Her dead, staring eyes confirmed what he already knew. She was no longer the Lucy Flix had known, no longer simply Flix's niece. She was wholly Preach's creature now. Preach had started the process when he had called her to him years ago; today he had completed it. There was nothing left inside her—no blood, no beating heart. She was hollow, and that emptiness, that lack of life, the death that was no death, that imprisonment, cruel beyond measure, engendered a rage she could not control.

She struck him a blow with her entire body; he wasn't certain she even remembered that she held a knife. In any event, it was of no interest to her. Preach had turned her entire being into a weapon, an arrow aimed at his supposed son and heir's heart and soul. Her jaws gaped open and she snapped them together. He saw how her teeth had changed, become elongated and pointed. They had a silvery sheen, as if coated with toxic saliva.

Her arms, hands, and feet beat an infernal tattoo, striking, slashing, battering at his body and legs, while her jaws snapped at his face, threatening to bite through his nose, lips, and cheeks. The blows he landed had no effect whatsoever, and just as he was about to be plowed under by this nonhuman pile driver, he placed his palm between her breasts, finding the vagus nerve, the tenth cranial nerve, as it was sometimes called, and slapped it very hard, once, twice. The third time he struck it, she collapsed—or rather her body did. Her eyes kept their unwavering predator's stare at him, her jaws kept working, her teeth clashing together like a sword striking armor.

Whitman struggled her down to the ground, then called out to Charlie: "I need two strips of material. Use Preach's shirt."

She did as he asked, brought them to him. He wadded up one strip, but Lucy's clashing jaws, the movement of her head from side to side, defeated his purpose. Divining it, Charlie knelt on the grass behind Lucy's head. She grabbed Lucy's jaw, clamped her thumbs against the hinges on either side. The moment Lucy's mouth opened, Whitman stuffed the ball of fabric into it. Quickly now, he used the second strip over Lucy's mouth, pulling it tight and tying it behind her head.

"Whit," Charlie said, "what the hell is this? What did Preach do to her? Was it the same thing you did to Flix?"

"You know it isn't," Whitman said, "but, unfortunately, it's related." He glanced over at Preach's body. "He's dead."

She nodded.

"How did you manage it?"

"I had a mild attack of Takayasu's inside the house. By the way, I slit that little shit's throat. Anyway, in the fight I lost my Imuran and then with the house on fire I had to scramble out. I saw that shadow, I saw that Preach didn't know I had come with you. He didn't know who I was."

"That's right, he couldn't see you," Whitman said. "And neither could Crow." At her puzzled look, he added: "The spirit of Preach's familiar. The shadow you saw. Crow helped Preach see the future."

"Not *this* future, surely."

"No. In the end, Crow failed him."

"As did everything else."

Whitman nodded. "The Takayasu's disease—go on."

"Right. You saw the way the shadow—Crow—vanished when it got to me. It struck me then that something in my brain was affecting Preach. It was the only logical explanation. It also made sense that the closer I came to him the stronger my effect would be on him."

"The change in your brain chemistry the Takayasu's caused somehow negated Preach's power."

"I took a chance and I was right. The moment I touched my forehead to his, the bullet acted as any bullet would. It penetrated his brain and killed him."

Whitman looked at her with different eyes. She was as altered as he was, only in different ways. "How are you feeling now?"

"I'm okay, for the moment, at least. I'll need my medication, but for the first time I feel better the way I am." She looked down. "What about Lucy? We should get her to the jet. We can fly her to an airport, get an ambulance to Walter Reed."

Whitman scooped his arms under Lucy's hips, indicated to Charlie that she should do the same with Lucy's shoulder blades, and they lifted her up. He led the way across the lawn.

"What are you doing?" Charlie said. "The plane's the other way."

"We aren't taking her to the plane," Whitman said. "We're taking her into the Well."

53

King Cutler, driving as fast as he felt safe, had crossed out of D.C. and was in Virginia proper. He had received the text from Whitman telling him to come to the Well as quickly as he could over an hour ago, but he had been so focused on trying to get a handle on his future business with NSA that he hadn't noticed it. Omar Hemingway wasn't returning his calls, and with St. Vincent dead there was no one else to contact.

Cutler had already determined there could be no good news coming from that quarter when he saw his mobile blinking and, snatching it up, read Whitman's text with mounting dread. Whitman had never been in Beirut, he wasn't in Western Pak anymore, he was right here in Virginia. What the fuck? Whitman had always been a loose cannon, but up until now he had kept his boss in the loop. This time, however, he had traveled completely off the map. Daou had said el-Habib was working for the Alchemists. The trouble with working sub rosa for St. Vincent was that he was told only so much and no more. He hated the fucking Chinese. He wanted no part in any back-channel machinations with Beijing.

But underneath the dread, he was gripped by an all too familiar sense of resentment. From bits and pieces gleaned from both Whitman and St. Vincent, he surmised that the Alchemists were a fractured fraternity, broken up into the Ins and the Outs, putting the lie to their motto: *Uno*

Animo, Uno Voluntatis—One Mind, One Will. He knew, for instance, that St. Vincent, Albin White, and Trey Hartwell were the Ins. What to make of St. Vincent's death then? Had he been ordered shot by outside enemies or by Hartwell and White for some unknown infraction? He had no idea, but he knew that it must bode ill for him. The vast bulk of his business was funneled through NSA via Hemingway. But Hemingway was an unwitting channel for the Alchemists. Furthermore, the highly lucrative work he did on the side for Directorate N and St. Vincent personally was vital to his own bank account. St. Vincent's death was going to severely impact USA's business, as well as his own private fortune. His plan to use Lindstrom as a bargaining chip to regain the power St. Vincent had taken from him was as dead as the two principals. On the other hand, St. Vincent's death left a power vacuum at NSA. It also left him vulnerable to scrutiny. He might have resented, even hated, St. Vincent—subjected as he was to that sadist's contempt—but there could be no doubt that the man protected him from Hemingway's scrutiny.

Now that protection was gone and he was faced with Gregory Whitman's continual disregard for rules and regs. He had given Whitman his head and how had he been repaid? By open defiance and contempt for his boss. It was Whitman—the ex-Alchemist who was always three steps ahead of everyone—treating Cutler with the same contempt as St. Vincent. They were cut from the same cloth, those two. But his road to greater power had to be spotless, which meant ridding himself of the quagmires Whitman had dragged him into, past and present. He had to be dealt with quickly and completely. It had to be as if this current off-the-grid hornet's nest had never happened. Only then could he move forward with confidence.

Yes, the more he thought about it, the more solid the plan seemed.

His journey continued. Small towns and tony residential enclaves blurred by him, until he came out the other side into the pastoral hills of rural Virginia. And yet, all the while, another part of his mind was laughing evilly: where there's a sadist, it's said, there must be a masochist. He slammed the wheel with his fist. Then he pulled over, popped the trunk, went around to peer inside. He pushed aside the two assault rifles and extra ammo to reveal what lay underneath.

———

"This is crazy," Charlie said, as they hustled Lucy into the dim, echoing interior.

"Really?" Whitman hurried them down one corridor after another. "You're going to say that now?"

Charlie grunted. "Well, shit, you have a point." She looked up apprehensively at the iron walls. "Are these going to collapse in on us?"

"The architecture is supposed to make it seem that way."

"Mission fucking accomplished."

They emerged at last into the section of the Well that Whitman knew as "Home." It was the waterfall, whose splashing water fed the ancient *cenote* where, unbeknownst to him, Lucy had filled the mouths of three corpses, just as her own mouth was now filled, and then watched as they were tipped over to be lost forever in the unknown depths.

Now it was her turn.

Whitman lifted her up onto the ledge of the *cenote*. "Charlie, listen to me. We have to drop her over."

"What? Whit, she'll drown."

He nodded. "That's the idea."

"But—"

"No buts." He looked at her. "Do you trust me?"

"Yes. Of course, yes."

"Then let her go." His voice hardened. "Charlie, let her go."

The moment Charlie did as he asked, he slid Lucy's head into the black roiling water. He kept hold of her, hands on her shoulders, then the sides of her neck, settling at the nape. He cradled the base of her skull. Then he slipped the rest of her over the lip until all of her was under the surface. She hung there as he held her, all ripples, ghostly pale in the surrounding darkness. No air bubbled up out of her nostrils; her chest was perfectly still, as if she had lost the instinct to breathe. Her hair streamed out on either side of her head in Medusa-like coils, as if each one were a serpent eager to wrap themselves around his wrists, puncture skin and flesh to tear out the cluster of veins on the insides. Inhuman eyes stared up at him, magnified by the water. They were fury-filled and, as if independent entities of their own, they rolled, trembled, and shook violently in their sockets.

To the extent he was able, Whitman ignored the horror of what Preach had made of her—a cross between a Frankenstein's monster and a flesh-eating succubus. He kept a steady pressure on the nerves at the base of her skull, playing a silent melody only he could hear, and gradually the rage leached out of her eyes. Her chest gave a great heave, her body began to move again, as any human body would, and she blinked. Her arms rose until her fingers wrapped around his wrists. There was no malice in the gesture. But it was not until a clear and present terror suffused her expression, until he could hear her calling to him in his mind, *Save me!*, that Whitman hauled her out of the water, gasping and choking.

Together, he and Charlie unwound the soaking cloth from her mouth. He removed the cloth gag. Her belly heaved in and out like an accordion. She retched, but nothing came out of her mouth. She tried to speak, and retched again, gasping like a fish out of water.

"Now we take her to the plane," Whitman said as he lifted her off the edge of the *cenote*.

"Is she okay?" Charlie asked.

"She will be," Whitman said, "when she sees Flix."

King Cutler was inside the jet with Flix and the crew when Whitman and Charlie brought Lucy up the steep stairs. He had assessed the situation, getting a detailed description of what had happened, why Edmond Dantès was dead and by whose hand.

Charlie had discovered Trey's Navigator and had driven it, with Whitman in the rear with Lucy's head on his lap, back to the landing strip.

"What the hell happened to you two?" Cutler said when they brought Lucy aboard.

"Later," Whitman said as they got Lucy into a seat.

"It's a long story," Charlie said.

They all looked on as Flix, crying out his niece's name, rushed toward her and, on bended knee, looked up into her still anguished face.

"Lucy, are you all right?"

She nodded wordlessly as he took her hand, squeezed it.

"Lucy?"

"You came back, Uncle Felix."

Her voice was so thin and reedy he scarcely recognized it.

"I promised I would, didn't I?"

"I was so frightened. They took you away in an ambulance."

"You saw that?"

She nodded again. "I was watching from the window." Her hand tightened in his. "I saw what they did to you, injecting you in the neck."

Flix gave Whitman a quick, meaningful glance.

Lucy's eyes were dark with anxiety. "I want to know you're okay, Uncle Felix."

"I'm fine." Flix smiled up into her face. "We're both fine now we're together."

As Whitman had surmised, being reunited with her uncle had brought her out of herself, began to ease the effects of the dreadful trial she had been through. The less she focused on that now, the better. He and Charlie watched the reunion, each thinking the private thoughts that dwelled at the heart of their own complicated relationship.

"The flight crew can be released," Whitman said. "There's no need to quarantine them now."

"They can't fly the plane," Flix pointed out, "with the radio out of commission."

"I'm going to call my cleanup detail to deal with the situation here," Cutler said. "I'll give orders for these three to be released after they've been debriefed." He turned to Whitman. "Okay? This is your op."

"Fine by me," Whitman replied. He nodded to Charlie who handed them back the phone batteries.

Cutler guided the crew out of the plane to his vehicle to await the appearance of his cleanup detail. "Well, fun as this has been," he said when he returned moments later, "it's time we got the girl to a hospital for a workup." He clapped his hands like a cheerleader. "Let's get going, gang." He seemed almost jovial. "The girl looks like she'll pass out at any moment."

Whitman did not care for the idea of doctors poking and probing Lucy's mind and body, but he felt it more politic to keep his concerns to himself, at least for the moment. When they got away from here, he would tell Cutler that Lucy needed time with Flix, not doctors.

They got Lucy out of the plane. Charlie climbed into the SUV first, then Whitman and Flix bundled Lucy into the Navigator's capacious backseat next to Charlie. Flix slid in on the other side of his niece. Whitman got the shotgun up front, while Cutler fit himself behind the wheel. He took out his mobile, but frowned.

"For some reason, I'm not getting a signal here." He got out of the SUV, began walking away, checking his mobile's screen all the while.

Flix felt something flutter behind his eyelids. An electrical spark seemed to fly from Cutler directly into the center of his brain.

"*Jesús Cristo!*" he cried as he slammed out of the vehicle, made a bee line toward Cutler.

"What the hell?" Charlie said.

Flix ran so fast he looked like a cheetah. He smashed into Cutler just before Cutler pressed the "5" button on his mobile. He grabbed the phone out of Cutler's grasp, threw it away. Cutler punched him in the solar plexus. Flix barely felt it. He struck Cutler a blow to his jaw that nearly spun Cutler's head around. Cutler retaliated with the edge of his hand, bringing it down on Flix's shoulder, but again Flix was all but oblivious.

By that time, Whitman was a pace away. "Flix, no!"

But it was too late, or Flix had no desire to keep himself in check. He drove his straightened fingers into Cutler's throat, tearing through skin and cartilage. He curled his fingers, ripping out his windpipe.

Whitman, down on his knees, put his hand on Flix's back. Flix whirled, his eyes wide, his expression wild. He bared his teeth at Whitman. Then, all at once, the feral glow in his eyes was gone, the snarl in his throat quelled. Whitman could feel his muscles relaxing beneath his hand.

"Flix—"

"Look under the Navigator," Flix said. He rose, retrieved the phone, while Whitman, a deep scowl on his face, returned to the SUV.

"What's happened?" Charlie asked as she slipped out of the Navigator. "Dear god," she whispered once she was down on her knees, peering under the vehicle with Whitman at the small packet of C-4 explosive. "How in the hell did Flix know about this?"

"No idea," Flix said as he joined them. He had taken the battery out of Cutler's mobile, rendering it inert. "Something just told me he was going to use this to detonate the explosive."

Charlie slid under the SUV on her back, began the process of dismantling the bomb. "The same something that allowed you to run like the devil?"

"Did I do that?" Flix said. "I dunno. Maybe."

"Got it." Charlie, the packet of C-4 cradled in one hand, turned her attention to Whitman.

He stood, dusting off his hands. "Come on. Let's go home."

Charlie and Flix followed suit, Flix climbing back beside Lucy.

"I'm guessing your 'cure' didn't entirely work," Charlie said from the opposite side of the Navigator.

Whitman grinned at her. "Who said I wanted it to?"

ONE WEEK LATER

Midnight outside The Doll House. Julie pushed open the door, stood on the rain-soaked street for a moment, hands jammed deep in the pockets of her raincoat. She took a deep breath of air, then let it out slowly. But no matter how she tried to clear her lungs, Sydny's scent continued to haunt her. She missed Sydny, deeply. At first, she was perplexed by this anomaly in her life. Then she was troubled. How on earth could she miss someone so profoundly whom she had known for such a short time? Then, the first night she had returned here to The Doll House, having walked to it without conscious thought, as if she were a sleepwalker, a memory surfaced.

She was sitting at one of the small tables, a watered-down drink in front of her, watching the sleek, half-naked girls manipulate their bodies around the glistening metal poles, and thinking how none of them could hold a candle to Sydny's electrifying act. All at once, as the music changed, as the lights went from blue to red, she recalled how Hemingway had told her that friendships forged during wartime, compressed time, engendered an intimacy that lasted a lifetime. So it had been with her and Sydny—two women who had shared a slice of compressed time that had affected Julie to her very core.

Now, as she stood on the sidewalk, a limousine, still glistening with beads of rain, pulled up to the curb beside her. She was about to walk away when some instinct told her to hold her ground. The rear door opened and as she bent down, Whitman leaned across the seat, smiled at her.

"Hello, Julie. Please get in."

She climbed in, the door closed, and the limo pulled away from the curb and down the darkened street. She saw *The Washington Post*, folded over to the story detailing the FBI arrests of the surviving Alchemists, the "discovery" of the Well. She'd read the story this morning. No mention of Omar Hemingway, who had delivered the Alchemists' names to the FBI, or of Whitman, who had tipped off Hemingway. But, as she well knew, that's the way the world worked inside the clandestine services. The oddest thing, however, buried deep in the story, was the fact that the accounts—bank, bond, stocks—of the principles had been drained simultaneously. The FBI and Interpol had been frantically trying to find a money trail, but without success.

Whitman smiled. "I thought I might find you here."

"Knowing you," she said, "I don't think it was anything but a sure thing." She ducked her head. "I've been coming here almost every night since . . ." Her voice trailed off, heading for a sob.

"Why here," he said, "rather than her place?"

"I couldn't bear to be there." She wiped away a solitary tear. "Not after what happened."

"Thank you," he said, startling her, "for coming to her defense."

Her head turned toward him. "How did you know?"

He smiled, both at her and past her. "She was a very special person."

"I miss her terribly." A tentative smile broke out around the corners of her mouth. "Like during wartime."

He nodded. "I understand."

With anyone else, Julie would have assumed bullshit, but not with Whitman. She was certain he knew, just as she was certain he might be the only person alive that she could trust absolutely. "Knowing her changed me."

"Sydny had a knack for that."

"I'll be forever in her debt."

Whitman considered a moment, as outside the nighttime world slid silently by them. Then he said, "If she were here, she would be angry with you for saying that."

Again, he had startled her. "Really? Why?"

"She'd want you to celebrate the change, not feel any obligation for it. A gift, she believed, is as much a pleasure for the presenter as it is for the receiver."

Julie wiped away another tear. "Dammit!" she said crossly. "Why don't I see any tears in your eyes?"

"I do my mourning in private."

"Men," Julie said, turning away to stare out the window, but it was clear by her tone that she was far from displeased. "Will you drop me off at home?"

"Later," he said. "If you wish it."

She turned back to him. "You mean I may not?" Her tone was now light, flirty, but not sexual.

He smiled.

"You should do that more," she said.

"What?"

"A smile becomes you."

"This building," Julie said, as they pulled up in front of Charlie's place, "it looks like something out of a Hitchcock film."

"*Vertigo*," Whitman said.

"Of course!" She seemed as delighted as a child, staring at it as they climbed out of the car and went up the front walk.

Upstairs, the door to Charlie's apartment stood open. Charlie, Flix, and Lucy were waiting for them amid a celebratory atmosphere. There were drinks and platters of snacks to eat, even a balloon or two bumping up against the ceiling. And from the stereo speakers Hoagy Carmichael was playing "Star Dust."

"Is it someone's birthday?" Julie said, as Whitman introduced her around.

"Sort of," Flix said.

"Kind of," Charlie said.

"But not really," Whitman added.

Charlie laughed at Julie's expression of bewilderment, and fixed her a gin and tonic, after asking her for her choice.

"You're here," Whitman said, when they had all gathered in a loose circle, "to bear witness."

"Like me," Lucy said.

"To what?" Julie looked from one to another.

"A naming ceremony," Charlie said. "We have decided—"

"*You* decided," Whitman said. He and Charlie were standing so close together their shoulders touched. For the first time in a long, long while he felt at ease. He was here while others took credit for bringing the treasonous Alchemists to justice. That was the way he wanted it. He shied away from fame, the limelight, being known. He lived in the shadows at the edge of the world, and he was smart enough to understand that was where he belonged.

Charlie laughed. "Okay, okay, *I* decided to give our team a new name. Whit is Foxtrot because"—she indicated the speakers—"what other dance could you choose that would please both Hoagy and Whit?

"I"—she lifted up her old-fashioned glass of brown liquid—"am Whiskey.

"And Flix here is Tango."

"Yeah," he said in mock horror, "but the Tango is the national dance of Argentina."

With a look of surprise, he accepted the envelope Charlie handed him.

"It's a voucher," she said, "for a dozen lessons at Tango Mercurio."

"Wow, okay." Flix shook his head. "Sure. Why not?" He looked at her gravely. "*Gracias, guapa.*"

"*De nada, compadre.*"

Flix gave her a nod so formal it was almost a bow.

"Anyway," Charlie said, "did you want us to call you Mexican Hat Dance?"

Flix threw his head back and laughed. "Then we wouldn't be Whiskey, Tango, Foxtrot."

"Because," Charlie said, lifting her glass to meet those of the others, "*what the fuck* surely defines us!"

And they drank as one, while the gorgeous melody of "Star Dust" swelled and swelled, for that moment filling their entire world.

A moment later, there came a pounding on one wall. "Hey," a voice from the adjoining apartment yelled, "normal people are trying to sleep! Shut it down!"

"Later!" Julie called giddily.

"Never!" Lucy added.

"I'll call the freaking authorities!" the disembodied voice screamed.

"We *are* the freaking authorities!" Whitman, Charlie, and Flix cried in unison.